EXPECTATIONS

Melanie M. Jeschke

HARVEST HOUSE PUBLISHERS

EUGENE, OREGON

Scripture quotations are taken from the Revised Standard Version of the Bible, copyright © 1946, 1952, 1971 by the Division of Christian Education and the National Council of the Churches of Christ in the USA. Used by permission. All rights reserved; and from the King James version of the Bible.

This is a work of fiction. Names, characters, places, and incidents are products of the author's imagination or are used fictitiously.

The poem "This Little Flower" (for Hannah Melanie White) © 1995 by Derrell E. Emmerson. Used by permission.

Cover by Left Coast Design, Portland, Oregon

Cover images © Digital Vision/Getty Images; Max Dannenbaum/The Image Bank/Getty Images

Page 15: map of Oxford by Andrew White

EXPECTATIONS
Copyright © 2005 by Melanie Jeschke
Published by Harvest House Publishers
Eugene, Oregon 97402
www.harvesthousepublishers.com

Library of Congress Cataloging-in-Publication Data

Jeschke, Melanie M.
  Expectations / Melanie M. Jeschke.
    p. cm. — (The Oxford chronicles ; bk. 2)
  ISBN 0-7369-1437-4 (pbk.)
  1. Americans—England—Fiction. 2. College teachers—Fiction. 3. Oxford (England)—Fiction. 4. Pregnant women—Fiction. 5. Married people—Fiction 6. Friendship—Fiction. I. Title. II. Series.
  PS3610.E83E96 2005

                                                                                    2004021731

Printed in the United States of America

05 06 07 08 09 10 11 12 13 / BC-MS / 10 9 8 7 6 5 4 3 2 1

What readers are saying about Melanie Jeschke's *Inklings*

"Melanie Jeschke skillfully takes her readers into the inspiring world of Oxford in her first novel, *Inklings*. Any fan of C.S. Lewis or J.R.R. Tolkien will find themselves enthralled with this marvelous, romantic book."

—Dr. Patrick Kavanaugh, executive director,
The Christian Performing Artists' Fellowship and
author of the book *The Spiritual Lives of the Great Composers*

"Harvest House's new edition of Melanie Jeschke's *Inklings*, which includes Jeschke's sequel novel, *Intentions*, is a pleasure to read for numerous reasons. Jeschke brings the reader fully into the world of 1960s Oxford, with its churches and pubs, its quads and punts, its ivy and stone, even its student robes and miniskirts. But one of the most enjoyable aspects of both books is the tension created through a lack of candor between the characters. Jeschke pulls off this effect well, despite the novel's contemporary time frame, because of the story's proper, old-world setting."

—Trish Perry, editor of *The Ink and the Spirit*

"Melanie Jeschke has a writing career sure to last a long time if her debut novel is any indication. *Inklings* is a romance with so much more than just fluff; it also educates its reader on the lives of classic literary giants such as C.S. Lewis and J.R.R. Tolkien. Set in 1964 shortly after C.S. Lewis's death, it combines fact and fiction so well, the reader will truly believe the hero actually did know Lewis in real life. Come take a tour of Cambridge and Oxford with Kate and David as your tour guides and sit in on some meetings of the *Inklings*; it is truly an amazing adventure!"

—*RomanceJunkies.com*

"First-time author Melanie M. Jeschke has written a beautifully readable book filled with literary allusions and the essence of spirituality. *Inklings* is clearly the start of what will be a luminous writing career for Melanie Jeschke."

—*The Romance Readers Connection*

"For romance lovers out there, this is the book for you."

—*Teens4Jesus Library*

"I really believe this book should be a requirement of all teenagers approaching the dating age. It gives them a good perspective and guidelines of how a serious relationship should be handled. I ANXIOUSLY await the sequel."

—*Heavenly Sunshine Newsletter*

"What a wonderful gift Melanie Jeschke has given to the Christian community in her book *Inklings*! She has crafted a story which makes personal holiness and the glory of God vivid without being preachy. At the same time the romantic tension between the characters makes you cry: 'Yikes! This is so real!' *Inklings* qualifies both as great entertainment and as a ministry tool to introduce Christians and non-Christians alike to the joys of following God's ways in human relationships. Bravo!"

—David Bruce Linn, pastor–teacher

With love and gratitude to my husband, Bill,
and to all our children:
Katherine Ryan and Christopher Craddock
Christen Marie and Jared Young
Cheryl Anne, William Brett,
Richard Aaron, Mark Devereux,
David Scott, Brendan Michael, and Kevin Morey Jeschke

This book is dedicated to all who have suffered loss,
and is written in loving memory of

*Jean Myers Jeschke, Molly Wooddell, Jean Alley, Deanna Freiling,
Marianne Miller, Joanie Duncan, and Hannah Melanie White*

Beloved wives, mothers, daughters, sisters, friends,
and all those dear ones who have left this earthly sphere,
whom, by faith, we expect to embrace again
in our heavenly Home.

Anglo-Oxford/American Glossary

bird: slang term for a young woman, as in the American term "chick"

Bird and Baby: nickname for the Eagle and Child, the pub frequented by C.S. Lewis and the Inklings

biscuit: cookie

Blackwell's: the largest bookshop in Oxford, located on Broad Street

bloke: a guy

Blue: award of colors for representing the University in a sport. Oxford Blues are a dark blue; Cambridge Blues are light blue.

boater: hard, flat-topped straw hat worn in summer, especially when boating and during "Eights"

the Bod, or Bodleian: main library at Oxford University; receives a copy of every book published in England

boot: car trunk

Carfax: the center of the city of Oxford where Cornmarket, The High Street, St. Aldate's, and Queen Street meet. The tower there affords a great view.

ceilidh: (kay-lee) informal evening of song and fun

cheerio: goodbye

the Cherwell (pronounced "charwell"): one of two rivers in Oxford (see Isis)

chips: French fries

Christ Church: the largest and perhaps richest and most prestigious college at Oxford (nicknamed: "The House"). The college chapel is Oxford's cathedral.

coach: long-distance bus

college: one of about forty institutions that make up the University of Oxford

come up: to arrive as a student at Oxford, as in, "Has he come up yet?"

crack or *craic***:** (Irish) talk, conversation, gossip, chat; a tale, a good story or joke

cuppa: cup of tea

daft: crazy

dear: expensive

dinner: lunch or dinner

dinner jacket, or DJ : tuxedo or dark suit with black bow tie and fancy shirt worn for formal dinners and college balls

don: college tutor, from the Latin *"dominus,"* or lord

the Eagle and Child: pub on St. Giles Street that was the meeting place for the Inklings

eight: rowing boat with eight oarsman and a coxswain to steer

Eights Week: intercollegiate rowing regatta held in Fifth Week of the Trinity, or summer term

Exam Schools, or Examination Schools: building on the High Street where exams and some lectures are held

Fellow: member of the governing board of a college. Many of the college tutors are Fellows.

first floor: second floor

flat: apartment

football: soccer

fortnight: two weeks

fresher: first-year student

Fresher's Fair: stalls for all the University clubs and societies held at the beginning of each academic year in the Exam Schools

go down: leave as a student at Oxford either temporarily or permanently

ground floor: first floor

Hall: communal eating place in (a) college. One eats "in Hall" and lives "in college."

Head of the River: winning crew or college in Eights Week. Also the name of the pub near the finishing line at Folly Bridge.

Hilary Term: Oxford's spring term. Americans would call it a winter term, as the eight-week term lasts from mid-January to mid-March.

holiday: vacation

The House: another name for Christ Church

The Inklings: perhaps the most important literary club of the twentieth century, which met informally for more than thirty years on Thursday evenings in C.S. Lewis's Magdalen rooms and Tuesday mornings in the Eagle and Child pub. When Lewis commuted from Cambridge on weekends, they continued to meet on Monday mornings at the Lamb and Flag until Lewis's death in 1963. One had to be invited, normally by C.S. ("Jack") Lewis; members included his brother, Major Warren ("Warnie") Lewis; J.R.R. Tolkien; Charles Williams; Owen Barfield; Hugo Dyson; Dr. Robert (Humphrey) Havard; and Nevill Coghill. The friends read aloud their works in progress (including Tolkien's *The Lord* *of the Rings* and Lewis's The Chronicles of Narnia) for the others to critique and discuss, but the meetings often had no agenda other than good conversation and rich fellowship.

interval: intermission

Isis: a tributary of the Thames River in Oxford

Jack: the name with which C.S. Lewis christened himself when he was four

JCR, or Junior Common Room: club and lounge for Oxford undergraduates

the King's Arms, or the KA: possibly the pub most frequented by Oxford students, at the corner of Parks Road and Holywell Street

let: rent

lift: elevator

loo: toilet, or bathroom

mackintosh, or mac: raincoat

Magdalen College (pronounced "maudlin"): the college in Oxford where C.S. Lewis was a Fellow from 1925 to 1954. When Lewis took a Chair in Medieval and Renaissance literature at Cambridge in 1955, his rooms there were in **Magdalene College** (also pronounced "maudlin").

mate: friend (male or female)

May Morning: May 1. A carol is sung at sunrise from the top of Magdalen Tower and students welcome May with all manner of frivolity.

MCR, or Middle Common Room: club and lounge for Oxford graduate students

Merton College: where J.R.R. Tolkien was Merton Professor of English

Michaelmas: the eight-week autumn term, October–December

nappies: diapers

nought: zero. Nought Week is the week before the term officially begins.

the other place: Cambridge. At Cambridge, "the other place" is Oxford.

Oxbridge: Oxford and Cambridge Universities

paralytic: drunk

porter: guard at the front gate of each college. The porters serve as concierges, confidants, and bulldogs (policemen).

Porters' Lodge: building for the porters by the front gate that also serves as the mailroom for students

the pond: the Atlantic Ocean. The "other side of the pond" is the U.S.A.

pitch: playing field

punt: flat-bottomed boat

quad: short for **quadrangle,** a rectangular courtyard inside a college. Only dons are allowed to walk on the grass. Called "courts" at "the other place."

queue: line

queue up: line up

Radcliffe Camera, or Rad Cam: distinctive domed library in Oxford

ring up: call, telephone

St. Hilda's College: a women's college in Oxford, located along the Cherwell River. Home of the Jacqueline du Pré Music Building.

scout: person who cleans college rooms, more like a servant in Lewis's times

SCR, or Senior Common Room: club for Oxford Fellows

sent down: expelled

the Sheldonian: the Sheldonian Theatre, where matriculation and degree ceremonies, as well as concerts, are held

solicitor: lawyer

Somerville College: formerly a women's college (now coed) at Oxford; college of Margaret Thatcher and unofficial Inkling Dorothy L. Sayers

sporting the oak: in college rooms with two doors, if the outer door is open the occupant is receiving visitors. If the outer door is closed, the occupant does not wish to be disturbed and is "sporting the oak."

stalls: Orchestra section of a theatre

toff: someone with money or from the upper class

Trinity Term: eight-week "summer" term, from April to June

tube: subway

tutor: college teacher. In term time, a student meets with his tutor at least once a week for a tutorial, or "tut," to read aloud and discuss an eight-page essay on the subject he is "reading," or studying.

underground: subway

Wellingtons, wellies: boots

Compiled with assistance from Rick Steve's *Great Britain and Ireland 2001,* Emeryville, California; Avalon Travel Publishing by John Muir Publications; and the University of Oxford website's "Glossary of Terms" (Jonathan.Bowen @comlab.ox.ac.uk., 1994).

French/English Glossary of Phrases

Au revoir: goodbye, until we meet again

Arrondissement: district. In Paris they are numbered. Passy is in the sixteenth arrondissement.

Bâteaux-Mouches: guided touring boats along the Seine River in Paris

bébé: baby

"Belle mademoiselle! Comment ca va?": "Beautiful young lady, how are you?" or "Hey, pretty girl, how's it going?"

bon appétit: good eating

Bonjour: hello, good day

Bonne nuit: goodnight

Bonsoir: hello, good evening

certainment: certainly

croque-monsieur: a grilled sandwich with ham and melted cheese

formidable: marvelous, awesome

incroyable: unbelievable

la joie de vivre: enjoyment of life

limonade: lemonade or a fizzy citrus drink

Je t'aime beaucoup, mon amour: I love you very much, my love.

Je t'aime beaucoup aussi: I love you very much too.

merci: thank you

Metro: Parisian underground transport

pommes frites: French fries or chips (British)

s'il vous plâit: please

très bon: very good

Map of Oxford

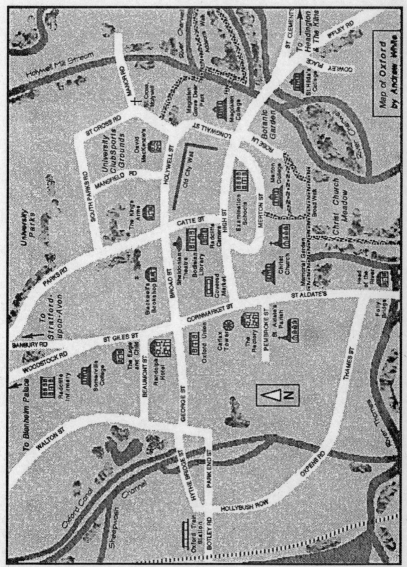

ANDREW WHITE

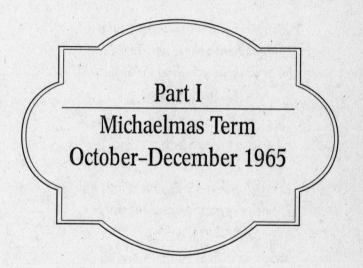

Part I

Michaelmas Term

October–December 1965

We know that in everything God works
for good with those who love him,
who are called according to his purpose.

—ROMANS 8:28

Every day in a life fills the whole life
with expectation and memory.

—C.S. LEWIS
from *Out of the Silent Planet*, chapter 12

1

First Week
Oxford

*N*ewlywed Kate MacKenzie felt ill.

I'm so nauseous, she thought miserably. *No, not nauseous.* She could hear David's proper British accent gently correcting her. "*You mean nauseated, darling. You feel nauseated.*" Kate trudged along the High Street oblivious to the beauty of the bright blue October sky serving as a brilliant backdrop to the gleaming spires of Oxford. She kept her head looking down toward the dull pavement as she contemplated the news she had just received from the physician at the Radcliffe Infirmary.

Pregnant! How is it possible? And married little more than three months! But what a wonderful three months, she mused. In her heart, her Oxford wedding to David MacKenzie in July had been storybook perfect. The lovely service with David's father officiating at St. Aldate's, the small reception in the rectory garden with only their family and close friends, the honeymoon night in a converted castle, their first week together in the MacKenzie cottage overlooking the sea near St. Andrew's, Scotland, and then their leisurely summer tour throughout

Europe had all been a fairy-tale dream come true. After a splendid summer, her father had booked a stateroom on the Queen Mary for their passage to the States. She and David had savored the September transatlantic crossing with dining and dancing and moonlit walks on the decks. They had marveled together at the immense blanket of stars wrapping around them and their great ship—which had suddenly seemed a mere speck in the dark cosmos.

That relative sense of insignificance vanished after arriving in Richmond, Virginia, where Kate was feted and gushed over by her family and friends with a whirl of showers, coffees, and parties. David good-naturedly endured it all, and she was proud, so very proud, to show off her handsome British husband. *Homecoming Queen of Douglas Freeman High School and Pledge Queen of William and Mary marries Oxford professor* boasted the society columns in the Virginia papers, complete with photos of the beautiful, smiling couple.

They had planned only to renew their vows in America, but in typical fashion Kate's mother had staged a full-scale wedding ceremony at St. Giles Presbyterian Church, with hundreds of guests attending the dinner-dance reception at the Country Club of Virginia. Still, it had all been magical. And then the quiet and peaceful conclusion of their honeymoon took them to David's grandparents' farm near Charlottesville, where they could visit his American mother's family and truly rest before returning to Oxford for the new school term—as Mr. and Mrs. David MacKenzie.

But pregnant! What will my friends think of me now? I may be married to an Oxford don, but I'm still a student with a year of college to complete. Kate dashed tears from her eyes. *I wanted to enjoy this year—not be pregnant and feel lousy and get fat!*

Oh, I do want a family sometime, but I'm not ready yet. I want to enjoy my husband and have fun and...

Kate considered how she had insisted on using birth control for these very reasons. David had preferred to leave the family planning in God's hands, but in regard for her strong feelings on the subject, he had acquiesced. *How could I be pregnant?* Kate thought angrily. *I can't believe it! I was so careful.*

Then she suddenly remembered a night in Tuscany—the sparkling wine, the languid summer air, the heavy scent of roses, and a violin's poignant strains drifting over the deserted garden of the villa. They had been drunk with love...and she had not been so very careful. Even though she was a married woman now, Kate blushed at the memory, and looked up guiltily to see if anyone had read her thoughts. Seeing only the sign for the Eastgate Hotel, where she was to meet David and Austen and Yvette for tea, she pushed open the door and sank onto the nearest sofa to wait.

☙

David MacKenzie quickly scanned the contents of the letter and let out a whoop that startled the staid, middle-aged scout who was straightening David's study in Magdalen College.

"Good news, Mr. MacKenzie?" asked Watson with his usual deference to the much younger don.

"Splendid, Watson." David beamed as he slipped the letter in the breast pocket of his warm-up jacket. "I will let you in on it tomorrow after I show it to my wife. Cheers!"

"Right, sir. Cheerio." Watson suppressed a smile, but his pale blue eyes crinkled with amusement at David's evident satisfaction in turning his new phrase, "my wife," as often as possible. Watson allowed himself a chuckle as his master bounded down the staircase of the New Buildings and jogged across the lawn of the college quad toward Addison's Walk.

David embraced the brisk autumn air as he embraced all of life—with boundless enthusiasm. He relished a late afternoon run along the quiet river bank before heading to the Eastgate Hotel for tea with his wife and friends. Golden leaves swirled around him in a frolicking dance that was in harmony with his own happiness.

Thank You, Lord, for this wonderful news. I can't wait to tell Kate. And thank You for her, for answering my heart's desire. Thank You for my job, for my students, for my family, and friends. Thank You for all the opportunities You have given me to serve You and do what I love. I am so very, very blessed. Thank You for this gorgeous day and for all Your blessings to me. How wonderful You are, Lord! Help me to be just as grateful for Your loving-kindness when I go through tough times again. But, Lord, I am very grateful for what I have now and the richness of my life. Thank You! Thank You!

David's heart nearly burst with gratitude as he sped from the grounds of Magdalen to the Eastgate Hotel, eager to share his good news.

Yvette Goodman walked briskly to her appointment at the Eastgate. She loved this season of the year. The crisp air, the vibrant colors, the promise of new beginnings all invigorated her. Her birthday was in October. For as long as she could remember, she loved this month of possibility. She felt special and ready for some great destiny.

Then she thought of the coming chill, the gloomy rain, and the stacks of mediocre essays to be marked. She decided she really hated this season of the year. After all, her birthday was this month and she would be twenty-nine.

Twenty-nine! Almost thirty. And what do I have to show for it? Well, I am the only woman—no, the only person—in my family to graduate from a university. Not only graduate, but earn a master's degree and then be elected as a Fellow at the University of Oxford. Not bad for the daughter of a working-class Anglo-Irish woman and a West Indian taxicab driver in London. I've worked really hard and achieved goals unthinkable to my family. But...

Yvette impatiently kicked aside some leaves. *But, I've hoped that by the time I turn thirty I would be married and have children. I love my job, but what I really want is a family and a home of my own.*

Yvette had accomplished vocationally what had seemed impossible, and yet she was a realist. She knew the odds were against her finding a husband—at least a good one. She was attractive, but not particularly pretty. She was a mulatto woman in a bastion of white male elitism. And she was too well-educated for men—those outside the dreaming spires, at any rate—not to feel intimidated by her. Besides all of that, she was uncompromising. She wanted an intelligent, considerate man who shared her Christian beliefs and her reverence for marriage. Simply put, like Flannery O'Connor she knew "a good man is hard to find." And she was growing tired of waiting.

✑

Austen Holmes, another young Oxford don, glanced at his watch as he hurried toward the Eastgate Hotel. He liked to be punctual for all his appointments, but today he had taken a detour. The deep blue October sky had beckoned him outdoors, drawing him irresistibly to the Holywell Cemetery at St. Cross. He often stopped there, opening the creaking iron gate and stepping past the Celtic crosses leaning at crazy angles in the tall grass, to pause at a well-tended plot not far from the graves of the Inklings Charles Williams and Hugo Dyson. He had chosen this spot because its proximity to Merton College allowed him to frequent it, and he thought with satisfaction that here *she* would rest in good company. Sometimes he felt solace among the dead and their living companions— woodland creatures who had crept in to share the overgrown grasses. But sometimes the rows of forlorn stone crosses overwhelmed him with a sense of desolation.

Autumn was a particularly difficult season for Austen. It was in autumn that he had met Marianne. And it was in autumn that he had lost her.

2

First Week, Monday Afternoon

A seventeenth-century inn, the Eastgate Hotel crouched on the corner of the High and Merton Streets next to its imposing neighbor, Merton College. Only a small swinging sign distinguished its yellow stone walls and mullioned windows from the surrounding colleges. C.S. Lewis and J.R.R. Tolkien, the two most prominent members of the Oxford Christian writers known as the "Inklings," frequented the Eastgate. It also served as the site of the first fateful meeting between Lewis and his wife, Joy Davidman Gresham, in September 1952.

David and Austen decided to meet at the Eastgate for the same reasons the original Inklings likely did. Its proximity to their respective colleges and its quiet and genteel ambience provided a more gracious gathering place than their favorite pubs—particularly preferable now that two women had joined their ranks.

David impatiently watched the front door for Austen's arrival. He could barely contain himself from spilling out the contents of the letter he felt burning in his breast pocket while Kate and Yvette sipped their tea and cordially chatted. But when at last Austen blew in with the brisk autumn wind, David's ready rebuke died on his lips.

Austen smoothed back his tousled blond hair and slowly unwound his scarf as he settled onto the sofa next to Yvette.

"So sorry I'm late," he said contritely. He paused, uncertain whether or not an excuse was required. He glanced at David. "I stopped by St. Cross."

David pressed his lips into a grim smile and nodded with sympathy.

Austen sighed heavily. "I still miss her so much."

The silence that inevitably occurs when someone speaks of a departed loved one hung awkwardly among them. The women knew Austen's bride had died several years earlier of cancer, but Austen seldom spoke of her. They felt the compassion women always feel for a widower—particularly a young one. And Yvette's compassion was not unmixed with a vague expectation of possibility. She had always found her two handsome colleagues attractive, but since David's heart had been claimed by Kate, Yvette nurtured the faint hope that her friendship with Austen might blossom into something more. Austen's remark revealed starkly that his heart still remained claimed as well. The usually loquacious Yvette could think of nothing to say.

David reached over and clasped Austen's arm. "I miss her too." He spoke more cheerfully to the women. "Marianne was such a wonderful girl. She was always a frail little thing, but she had an indomitable spirit like Melanie in *Gone with the Wind*. And like Melanie, she was one of the kindest and most generous creatures I've ever known. She was one of whom the world was not worthy…she was much too good for any of us."

Austen smiled sadly. "Yes, she was. It's nice to hear her spoken of sometimes. Makes her seem closer somehow…" He collected himself. "Thanks, old boy. Well now, what have I missed?"

David's eyes gleamed with excitement as he withdrew the letter from his pocket. "Nothing yet. I've been waiting to show you all this."

Kate looked at him in surprise.

David grinned mischievously. "I didn't want to create any false hopes in you, my darling, so I've been rather circumspect about some solicitations I've been receiving from the dean at the American College in Paris. This is their formal offer for a visiting professorship for their spring semester. And get this— just lectures. No tutorials or papers to mark! I'll have a graduate assistant for the dirty work. And in addition to a stipend, they will provide a generous housing allowance. I've already written to the landlady in Passy where my family lived when my dad was on sabbatical. She has a flat available in January." He put his arm around Kate. "Just think, darling. We'll be able to see the top of the Eiffel Tower from our bedroom balcony and kitchen window."

Kate sat in stunned silence. This was all too overwhelming. Her own news lay heavily on her heart. What if her pregnancy prevented them from accepting this offer?

"You lucky dog, MacKenzie!" Austen exclaimed. "And you've been cooking this all up behind our backs. What are you going to teach?"

"Shakespeare and Renaissance poetry. I've also contracted to give a Shakespeare lecture once a week at the Sorbonne. But it gets better: The American College has asked me to teach a class on old C.S.L. himself."

"A class on Lewis? That's marvelous! What an incredible opportunity." Austen chuckled with genuine pleasure. "Well, Yvette, I guess we'll have to let him go. I suppose we can handle the Inklings Society without him for a while. But I suspect without our 'next Charles Williams' that we'll lose the crowd of fawning young women who follow him around."

"Pshaw!" David scoffed. "I'm a married man now. We'll lose them anyway."

"Right," said Yvette, casting Austen a knowing, skeptical glance. "But tell me about this American College, David. Do they have a branch in Switzerland? I've always wanted to go to Switzerland and bet they could use a good visiting Oxford tutor like me there."

"Sorry. No school in Switzerland. They do have one in Beirut, though."

"I'll pass on that."

"Beirut is a lovely city—very cosmopolitan and right on the Mediterranean with beautiful beaches."

"No, thanks. If I can't go to Switzerland, I'll stick to Oxford."

Their banter swirled around Kate along with the cigarette smoke and the strong odor of beer from the bar. Her stomach heaved.

"Excuse me," she whispered, rising suddenly from the couch. She ran toward the ladies' room, her hand clasped over her mouth.

When she emerged, shaken and pale, she found David anxiously pacing in the hallway. He took her in his arms.

"Are you all right?"

"I threw up," she confessed, resting her head on his chest like a small child.

"Oh, darling, I'm so sorry," he said, stroking her hair. "Let me get you home. Should I fetch the car or do you want me to hail a taxi?"

"No, no. I'm fine to walk. It's not far."

After making their apologies to Austen and Yvette, David encircled Kate with his arm and guided her across the High Street. They took a shortcut through Queen's Lane, a narrow street winding along the high stone walls of St. Edmund's Hall and Queen's College. Then they slipped through an even narrower alley, skirting by the yard of the Turf Tavern and the ancient medieval wall of the old city to Bath Place and its easily missed entrance onto Holywell Street.

"Have you caught a bug from someone or do you think you've eaten something bad?" David asked.

"Neither," Kate replied flatly. "I'm—pregnant."

David continued walking until her announcement registered with him. He suddenly stopped short. "You're pregnant?"

Her eyes welled with tears as she nodded.

"You're quite sure?"

"Yes. I just saw the doctor."

"But...how?" he asked incredulously. "I thought you were using birth control."

"Tuscany," she whispered.

Realization swept away the puzzled expression on his face, replacing it with joy. He laughed. "Tuscany! That night in the garden. You naughty girl, you were unprepared, weren't you? Pregnant? Kate, that's wonderful!" He lifted her in his arms and twirled her around in the middle of the street.

"David, please! Remember, I'm sick."

He put her down gently. "Right, I'm so sorry." Holding her tightly, he nestled his face in her hair. "Oh, my darling Kate, I didn't think that it could be possible to be any happier than I've been today. But now you've done it."

Kate pushed away from him and walked toward their flat. "Yes, now I've done it. I've spoiled your chance to go to Paris."

"What are you talking about?" David asked as he quickly caught up to her, unlocked the front door to a yellow row house, and opened their apartment door for her. "How does this change anything?"

Kate flung herself down on their sofa. "I can't have a baby in Paris!"

Shutting the door, he said, "Kate, you're not making any sense. It's not like Paris is barbaric or something. I'm quite sure that pregnant women live in Paris and have babies every day without any difficulty."

"But what about doctors? I don't want to go to some French doctor. My French isn't that good."

"There's an American hospital in Paris. You can go there. Besides, when are you due?"

"Sometime in May."

"Don't fret. We'll either make arrangements there or we'll whisk you back here to deliver the baby."

She bit her lip. "You're really happy about this? You're not just pretending—to make me feel better?"

David put his arms around her.

"My love, I meant it when I said I couldn't be happier. A baby is God's greatest gift to us—other than His own Son. I'm thrilled. Truly. And I can't wait to tell my parents."

"My parents!" Kate groaned. "My mother will hate being a grandmother!"

"She will no such thing. She'll just rue letting you come over here because she'll be so far from her grandchild. Grandchild!

That does sound strange, doesn't it? My mum looks much too young to be mistaken for a grandma. And here Hannah is only four years old, and she'll be an aunt! And Ginny and Natalie too. And the boys—uncles!" He chuckled and kissed her. "This is wonderful!"

"Well, I'm glad you're happy." Kate sighed. "But, David, would you mind going to dine in Hall tonight? I can't face making dinner."

"Oh, darling, I'm sorry. I forgot you're not feeling well. Can I get you anything?"

"David, you can't cook!"

He grinned. "I can make a splendid cuppa tea."

She smiled in return. "No, thank you. I don't want anything now except a nap. Maybe later I'll make some soup. But right now I just don't want to smell food—would you please go eat at the college?"

"Yes, all right. Mum used to say that she could always tell when she was pregnant because her sense of smell was quite acute."

"Bad smells, anyway," Kate agreed.

"I hate to leave you, sweetheart, even for dinner."

"Coming from you, I know that's love. I'll be fine. Just stop at Tuck's shop on your way home and get some crackers for me, please."

"Will do." David gathered her up in his arms and carried her into their bedroom. "You take your nap while I take a bath and dress for dinner." Gently laying her on the bed, he kissed her forehead.

Kate smiled at him as he tucked the coverlet around her. Her smile faded as he closed the door to the bathroom. She could hear his lusty baritone above the racket of faucets shutting on and off. *He sounds really happy. How can I ever explain to him my misgivings and fears? He couldn't understand and I will not ruin this for him. I won't be selfish and spoil his joy.* She buried her face into her pillow and resisted the impulse to cry. *I'll just have to make the best of things.*

3

Second Week, Wednesday

*S*tuart Devereux casually perused a collection of second-edition Dickens in the used bookstore on Turl Street near the Covered Market. He looked up as the tinkling sound of the shop bell announced the arrival of a new customer. At first glance he thought the pretty young brunette was Kate Hughes—he still had difficulty thinking of her as Kate MacKenzie—with her long hair cut to shoulder length. He was about to speak when he realized his error. The resemblance was sufficiently strong that the girl certainly could have been mistaken for Kate's sister. But he recognized that she was, in fact, her sister-in-law.

Stuart hurried toward the door and intentionally bumped lightly into her.

"Oh, so sorry. How clumsy of me!" he exclaimed. "Why, you're Miss Natalie MacKenzie, aren't you? I met you at your brother's wedding."

Natalie's annoyance faded as she regarded the solicitous green eyes of the tall, classically handsome student. "Yes, I remember. Lord Devereux."

"Call me Stuart, please. It's wonderful to run into you like this, pardon the pun. And how are the newlyweds?"

"Quite well, thank you. In fact, they just told us that Kate is expecting a baby."

This revelation surprised the usually unflappable Viscount Devereux. "Really? My word, that was fast work! I presume they are happy with this news?"

"Of course," Natalie answered shortly. Then she added, "David is ecstatic. Poor Kate has not been feeling well, though."

"I'm very sorry to hear that. Please extend to them my best wishes."

"I will. Now, if you will excuse me, I need to look for a book." Natalie tried to squeeze past him in the narrow aisle.

Stuart was not so easily dismissed. "I say, Natalie, what brings you to Oxford in the middle of the school week? Aren't you at the University of London?"

"I was. But I was accepted at St. Catherine's and decided to transfer."

"Then you didn't like London?"

"It's all right. At first I was desperate to get out of Oxford and away from my family, but I really prefer Oxford to the big city, and I missed my family and our church. I wanted to try being on my own, but one year was enough for me. So here I am, back home."

"Lucky us." Stuart smiled broadly. "Are you rooming at St. Cats?"

"No, it's cheaper to live at home in the rectory. And with my sister Ginny still in London, I have a room to myself, which works out fine."

"Hmm." Stuart would have preferred that Natalie not be under the watchful eyes of her parents, but he was undaunted. Ever since he had met Kate, he had developed a strong preference for petite brunettes. "Perhaps I can help you find that book," he offered cheerfully.

"You're not working here, are you, Lord Devereux?"

"Stuart. No, just looking myself. But always happy to be of service."

"Thanks, but I'll ask the shopkeeper." Natalie managed to slip past.

"Would you care to join me for tea?"

"No, thank you. I need to get to my tutorial."

Stuart persisted. "Now that you are here in Oxford, Natalie, I would like to see you again. There's a dance this Friday at the Oxford Student Union. Would you care to go with me?"

"I'm sorry, but I already have plans."

"Well, what about Saturday? Would you like to see *The Importance of Being Earnest* at the Oxford Playhouse?"

"I'd love to see *The Importance of Being Earnest*, but…"

"Excellent!" Stuart interrupted. "It's a date, then?"

"But," Natalie resumed, "not with you."

Stuart laughed. "You're a clever one, aren't you? Then you must be clever enough to know I'm a man who is accustomed to getting what I want. And I want to see you again."

Natalie shrugged. "If you mean by 'seeing me again' that you would like to take me on a date, then I'm sorry, but you will just have to be disappointed. If you mean 'look at me,' then the only place you can 'see' me is in church at St. Aldate's every Sunday and on Wednesday evenings at our college dinner and Bible study."

Stuart had been truthful in stating he was accustomed to getting whatever he desired—with the notable exception of Katherine Hughes MacKenzie. But rather than being perturbed by this girl's indifference to his charms, he was intrigued.

He smiled. "You drive a hard bargain, Miss MacKenzie."

"I do indeed, Lord Devereux. Now, good day."

After returning from Reading, where he had coached the Oxford University soccer team in an evening varsity match, David eagerly opened the door to his flat. He found Kate asleep on the sofa and sighed.

Poor little one. You've had a rough go of it, haven't you?

Putting his arms around her to carry her to bed, he could not resist brushing his lips across her warm cheek.

Kate opened her eyes and smiled sleepily. "Hi, honey. I missed you."

"I missed you too, darling. I'm sorry I woke you, but it's hard to resist kissing a sleeping princess. Let me put you in bed."

"No, not yet. I was just taking a little nap. I've been so tired." She yawned and patted the couch. "Sit down and talk to me. How was the game? Who won?"

David joined her. "We did. One–nil."

"That's great! Did y'all play well?"

"Adequately. It was not a particularly brilliant match. We had plenty of opportunities, but the lads didn't finish properly. Coach wants me to work with the strikers tomorrow on shooting." He smoothed back a loose strand of her hair. "I don't want to bore you with football. How was your day? How are you feeling?"

"Okay. I went to St. Aldate's tonight for the Bible study."

"Good! Did you get some supper?"

"I was going to, but the smells from the Hall kitchen were awful, so I sneaked into the rectory to see what your mom was making. She gave me a baked potato, which was perfect."

"You need to eat more than a baked potato," he chided, placing his hand on her still-flat stomach.

She covered his hand with her own. "I will when I feel better. Anyway, I did go back in for the Bible study, and you'll never guess who was there."

"Natalie?"

"Of course Natalie. But who else?"

"I don't know. Nigel?"

"Yes. But no. I mean Stuart Devereux."

"Devereux? What the deuce was he doing there? Hasn't he given up on you yet?"

"Maybe he wants to learn more about God."

"Right. Like he did when he was pursuing you."

"I think he may be interested in Natalie now. He seemed to be watching her a lot."

David groaned. "Brilliant! Why can't we get rid of this chap? He's always lurking about."

"He admires you, David. Remember, if it wasn't for Stuart, we might still have Charlotte lurking about too. Anyway, I think he really is searching and that he's genuinely attracted to the Christ in you MacKenzies."

"I think he's more attracted to pretty girls like you and Nat. Hopefully she will be a little wiser than you were. I am grateful for what Stuart did for us, but if he thinks about laying one hand on my sister..."

"Take it easy, David. He just showed up at the Bible study. And Natalie didn't even talk to him."

"Listen, I had an idea about Natalie since she doesn't know many University people yet. Magdalen is sponsoring the Blenheim Ball again in a fortnight. Why don't we ask her to come along with us for fun and have Austen be her quasi chaperone–escort?"

"David, she's not going to want to go with us!"

"Why? Don't you want her to?"

"Of course I'd like her to come. It would be fun for me to have Nat along. But why would she want to go with her brother and his friend—who in her opinion are ancient of days?"

"Do you think I'm ancient of days?"

"I did at first. But you're younger than Austen, anyway."

"Austen's only twenty-seven. Besides, I'm not thinking of it as a date. In any case, he'll probably want to come along as a chaperone like he did last year. As much as he misses Marianne, he still enjoys being around the young ladies."

"But what about Yvette? Won't she feel left out?"

"Yvette can come as a chaperone with some of the St. Hilda's Fellows, if she likes."

"David, I really think Natalie would prefer getting her own date. I'm sure lots of boys would ask her."

"Well, that's what I want to avoid. I know these blokes, and I don't trust any of them."

"Do you trust yourself?"

"Of course not. That's why I married the most gorgeous girl in the world and this year she is going to be my date to the Blenheim Ball."

Kate smiled. "Is that an invitation?"

"Yes, Mrs. MacKenzie. Would you please accompany me to the ball?"

"I'd be delighted." She laced her hands around his neck and kissed him. He leaned over and kissed her again, slowly and gently. She sat up suddenly. "What will I wear? I chose my wedding gown because I could wear it again to formal dances. But what if I'm too fat for it?" she fretted.

David placed his hand on her stomach again. "Kate darling, you've lost weight since you've been pregnant and you're not very far along. I don't think you need to worry about being too fat. Let's not think about that now." He drew her to him and kissed her again with increasing urgency. Her concerns about dresses faded away.

"Mrs. MacKenzie," he said huskily. "I believe it's time I took you to bed."

4

End of Fourth Week
The Blenheim Ball

The chilling mist that shrouded Blenheim Palace did little to dampen the festivities within her walls. Resplendently dressed students reflected the warmth of cheerfully blazing fires, good wine, and energetic dancing. The Palace had thrown open her arms to countless balls over her long years and little—except for the eager faces and the musical beat—had changed in the rituals of courtship that she embraced.

Among the beauties at the ball, few could rival Kate MacKenzie. Although she felt poured into her white strapless gown and inwardly complained of appearing too fat, the truth was that pregnancy became her. The snugness of the gown enhanced her full figure and her delicate features glowed with maternal health. David basked in virile pride that this beautiful woman was his and that she carried his child. Each time he looked at her, he felt a rush of wonder and an irrepressible sense of vitality and well-being.

One of Kate's competitors was Natalie MacKenzie, and David tried to keep her fawning young suitors at bay by dancing frequently with his sister himself. Not one to be casily deterred, however, Stuart Devereux boldly cut in during a quiet, slow song.

"May I?" he asked with a winning and assured smile.

David shot him a look as if to say, "Watch it, mate!" but stepped aside with a slight bow and then sought out his wife.

Natalie teasingly chided her new partner. "You really don't want to antagonize my big brother, Lord Devereux."

Memories of his confrontation with David at the previous ball flashed through Stuart's mind. "No, Miss MacKenzie, I don't. You can take my word on that. But all I've asked for is this dance, and I promise to behave myself. Are you here with anyone?"

Natalie shook her head. "Not unless you count David and Kate and Austen Holmes."

"A sort of group chaperone?" Stuart smiled. "Don't they trust you?"

"Oh, they trust me. It's the gentlemen like you they don't trust."

"I see, ha! But you trust me, Natalie, don't you?"

Natalie peered at him askance. "Why should I trust you, Lord Devereux?"

"Stuart," he corrected. "Because I've proven to be a good friend to your brother and sister-in-law by helping them out of a real pickle. Besides, I've been faithfully attending your church since that time you invited me at the bookstore. And by the way, you did invite me, you know, but whenever I've come you've been most unwelcoming. I mean, quite honestly, you hardly acknowledge I'm there. You're not much encouragement to your guests, Natalie."

"You're supposed to be coming to church to worship God, not to talk to me."

Stuart adopted a puppy dog look. "At least I am coming, Natalie. I did fulfill your request. Now, why don't you fulfill mine by going out with me? Please?"

"Look, Lord Devereux, I am sorry to have to be quite so blunt, but your persistence requires it. I'm really not interested in dating you."

"My dear girl, why ever not? You ask Kate. Whatever disparaging things she may have said about me, she'll tell you the truth: She really liked me and I'm a lot of fun."

Natalie repressed a smile and tried to appear stern. "I'm sure you are, but I'm not Kate. I will not be so easily swept off my feet by someone just because he's rich and handsome."

"Don't forget charming," he added.

Natalie laughed.

"Besides," he said with some genuine humility, "I didn't sweep Kate off her feet. I was merely a detour from her true love." He glanced ruefully toward Kate and David, who were dancing nearby.

David was holding Kate tightly. "Darling," he murmured, "do you remember last year's ball? You were dazzling. And I was completely smitten and ecstatic when I stole that dance with you." He drew her even closer. "I can't believe it was just a year ago. Then I scarcely dared hope we'd be together."

"Oh, David," she said, sighing. "I wish I could still dazzle you. But now that we're married, I'm afraid I'm just getting matronly and fat."

"Kate, don't be silly. You're not at all fat. You're not even showing yet, and you're more beautiful than ever. Besides, don't you know that many men find pregnant women very sexy?"

Kate could not hide her skepticism. "Do you?"

"Yes…I mean…" He laughed. "That's a trick question! I find *you* very alluring, Mrs. MacKenzie. In fact," he nuzzled her neck as he whispered, "I desperately want to make love to you. Let's go home."

Smiling, she gently pushed him away. "Your behavior is shocking, Mr. MacKenzie! What will your students think? And besides, we brought your sister along, remember?"

"Oh, right!" He scanned the room until he saw Natalie dancing with Stuart. "Good grief, she's still with Stuart Devereux. Maybe we should take her home."

"Now you're the one being silly."

David craned his neck, glancing about. "Where is Austen, anyway? Not chaperoning very well, is he?"

"He's over there talking to Yvette." Kate nodded toward an alcove near the dance floor of the vast library-*cum*-ballroom.

"Let's get him to cut in on Stuart."

"David, no! If Austen is going to dance, he should ask Yvette. She looks as though she would love to dance."

Indeed, she did. Yvette's head was nodding to the beat of the music. David noted that she cut a striking appearance in an aqua satin gown that accentuated her statuesque figure. But Austen seemed as oblivious to her charms as he was to her desire for a partner.

"Yvette may want to dance, but I don't think Austen is interested."

"Why not? If he can dance with Natalie, why can't he dance with Yvette?"

"Oh, Kate, come on. Natalie's my little sister and Yvette is just a friend."

"Isn't that practically the same thing?"

"Well, perhaps. But dancing with a peer could border too near to romance."

"What if it does? Aren't you the one who told me that the best thing for Austen would be to find a good woman?"

"But Yvette?" David asked incredulously. "Yvette and Austen? Kate, they are just good friends."

"I suspect Yvette would like it to be more."

"Nope." David was emphatic. "Never will happen."

"Why? Since when are you the official matchmaker? What makes you say that?"

"My dear, I've known Austen for many years. We are closer than brothers. First of all, there's the ever-present memory of Marianne to contend with—a woman who was about as close to a saint as you can get. And Yvette couldn't be more unlike her. Not that she's not saintly, mind you. But they are quite different in appearance, class, personality, everything!"

"But maybe that's why Yvette could be right for Austen now," Kate persisted.

"No, darling. Give it up. It won't happen. And if you think Yvette has any such notions, maybe I should disabuse her of them." The dance ended and David began to lead Kate toward his friends.

Kate tugged on his arm. "David, don't you dare!"

He laughed. "Don't worry. I don't mean now."

"Not ever," she corrected. "You leave her alone and let nature take its course."

"Very well. I will, and you will see that I am right." He read the disagreement in her eyes. "Look, darling, I know you would like our friends to be as happy as we are, but that doesn't mean their course lies together. Now you quit playing matchmaker and let's get Natalie away from Stuart Devereux so we can go home."

As they approached the alcove, David greeted Austen and Yvette. "Hullo, you two. What are you discussing that's so fascinating that you'd neglect to chaperone my sister?"

"Why, David, don't you know everything I discuss is fascinating?" Yvette teased. "Actually, I was just telling Austen I'm reading *The Lord of the Rings*."

"For the first time?"

"That's right. I know I'm not in vogue with everyone else, but I'm so engrossed in the Victorian era that I really didn't expect to enjoy a fantasy about creatures with big hairy feet."

This amused David. "Well, has your expectation been verified or have you been 'surprised by joy'?"

"I've been delightfully surprised. It started off in a similar vein to *The Hobbit*, almost like a continuation of a children's story. But now I'm about halfway through the second book, and as I was telling Austen, I'm astounded by the breadth of Tolkien's myth and the beauty of the language. In many places the elevated speech is reminiscent of *Beowulf* or other Anglo-Saxon epic poems. I still have a lot to read, but thus far I think it's a remarkable piece of literature and I'm beginning to understand what all the brouhaha is about."

"Speaking of brouhaha," David interjected, "we really should get Mr. Tolkien back to speak to our Inklings meeting. Do you think you can line something up, Austen?"

"I'm working on it. I'm supposed to have tea with the Tolkiens next week. I'll try to pin him down then."

"Tea with the Tolkiens?" Yvette repeated. "Boy, I'm envious. I would love to have the opportunity to talk to him."

"Didn't you meet him when he spoke last term?"

"Yes, I met him—along with several scores of students. But to meet him one-on-one—now that would be another matter altogether."

Kate chimed in. "Why don't you take Yvette with you, Austen?"

"No, no. I wasn't hankering for an invitation," Yvette quickly replied.

"Oh, come on, Austen! Why don't you invite her to go along?" Kate coaxed.

David shot her a look, but she smiled sweetly at him.

"Would you want to?" Austen asked Yvette.

"Of course, but only if it's not a burden to them or to you."

"Not at all. I'll ask them. I doubt they would mind."

Kate smirked triumphantly at her husband.

As the music resumed, he said, "Austen, old boy, would you mind finding my sister and getting her away from Stuart Devereux? I'm hoping to clear out of here soon."

"Right. Excuse me, ladies." Austen seemed reluctant to leave, and the disappointment that crossed Yvette's face did not escape David's notice. He felt a stab of guilt.

"Yvette, would you like to dance?"

"Oh, yes!" she replied eagerly and then turned to Kate. "You don't mind, do you?"

"No, I'm really tired," she answered honestly. "Please go on."

David leaned over his wife and murmured, "I get the next slow dance with you and then we'll go home. But stop playing cupid, will you?"

Kate gave him a coy smile. "I'm just helping nature take its course. But you make sure you're not getting in the way, okay?"

David returned her smile with a laugh. "Okay."

5

Fifth Week, Wednesday
Tea with the Tolkiens

Austen and Yvette rode the bus from Oxford up the great hill of the London road to Headington. They disembarked in front of a row of old houses with swinging signs advertising Bed-and-Breakfast and walked back to turn down Sandfield Road at the Pickwick Inn. They wrapped their coats around more tightly and braced themselves against the sharp jabs of the wind as they pushed down the long straight street. Yvette was beginning to wonder if they should have driven when at last they came near the end of the lane to Number 76, a white-stucco detached home much like all the others with one major distinction: This unassuming and modest suburban house belonged to the famous creator of Middle Earth.

"Here we are," Austen said as he opened the gate. He then followed Yvette up the short walkway bordered by rose bushes and rang the front doorbell. After a time the door opened, and there stood Professor John Ronald Reuel Tolkien. He eyed

Yvette suspiciously, but when he recognized Austen, his face broke into a warm smile.

"Ah, Austen, my boy! Good to see you. Do come in. And is this young lady with you?"

"Yes, sir. This is my colleague Miss Yvette Goodman. Remember I rang you about bringing her?"

"Yes, yes, of course. Hello, Miss Goodman. So sorry. These days we get quite a few unexpected visitors—total strangers, really—just showing up on our doorstep. Most inconvenient. Do come in."

He ushered them into a narrow foyer and then to a parlor, where he introduced them to a small elderly woman with warm brown eyes and white hair pulled tightly into a bun. "Edith, my love," Tolkien said, "here is Austen and his colleague Miss Yvette Goodman."

Edith stayed seated but extended her hand to welcome her guests. "Nice to meet you, Yvette. Lovely to see you again, Austen. How are you, my dear?"

"Very well, thank you," he answered with a smile. "And you?"

"Oh, can't complain. But the arthritis is acting up again. Forgive me for not standing now, but these old knees of mine are quite sore. Anyway, have a seat and tell us the news."

"Edith," Tolkien interrupted, "let me steal Austen away for a few minutes to the garage while the water boils. I want to ask his opinion on something."

"All right, dear. Just don't get lost out there and not remember to come back. Yvette—" she patted the cushion next to her on the sofa.

The men excused themselves. Edith smiled at Yvette. "He's not asking Austen's opinion on a car. We haven't owned one since the war. The garage is where my husband has his study. Most of his books are out there." This statement surprised Yvette, who could not see much of the room where they sat for the numerous floor-to-ceiling bookshelves groaning under the weight of countless tomes. "Tell me about yourself. How did you come to know Austen?"

"I joined the English Faculty this year when I was elected a Junior Fellow at St. Hilda's. I met Austen and David MacKenzie at some of the Faculty meetings and they invited me to help them with their Inklings Society."

"Excellent. And where are you from originally?"

"London. I grew up there and studied at the University of London." Yvette knew Edith was curious about more than her home. Her café au lait skin did not reflect a typical Anglo-Saxon heritage. She added, "My mother is Irish and my father is from the West Indies."

"Oh, right. Well, they must be very proud of you."

"Yes, I think they are." Yvette spied a piano tucked into the corner of the room. "Mrs. Tolkien, do you play?"

"Yes, I do, although it's more difficult these days with my arthritis. You'd scarcely believe it now, but there was a time when I was considered capable of being a concert pianist. How about you? Do you play?"

"I do," Yvette answered honestly. "But I'm more of a singer."

"Excellent. Perhaps we should try a duet together. Do you know something? At one time Ronald's family, the Tolkiens, were known for the pianos they crafted. Of course, that was before our day, but I always thought it interesting that a pianist would marry the descendant of piano manufacturers. One of those threads of destiny that God weaves together in our lives. We've always shared a love for music."

As if on cue, a high-pitched note blasted merrily from the kitchen. "Oh, kettle's boiling! Yvette, would you mind switching off the burner and filling the teapot?"

"No, not at all." She rose quickly.

"The kitchen is down the hallway and the tea tray is all set out. And then be a dear and go out the back door and around to the garage to get the men. Ronald will carry the tray in for you."

Yvette excused herself and followed the shrill whistle of the kettle to the kitchen, where she left the tea to brew before stepping outside to the short walk to the garage. Through the windowpanes of the garage door, she could see a room cluttered with piles of books, papers, and ink pots. Having just passed through a hallway lined with books, she was reminded of a description she had heard of C.S. Lewis's home, the Kilns: "A house of books held together by cobwebs." Edith Tolkien kept things clean and tidy, so perhaps this home was more aptly described as a house of books held together by love. In either case, since Yvette, like her colleagues, was a true bibliophile, it was a house in which she felt perfectly at home.

She tapped her knuckles lightly against the window. The two men glanced up from the hand-drawn map of Middle Earth over which they had been huddled. Yvette noted that Austen stood much taller than Professor Tolkien, who was a slightly built man of average height, a little stooped now with advancing years, but who still cut quite a distinguished and handsome figure. His long, almost elvish face was framed by gray hair and bushy gray eyebrows, and he dressed in the typical flannel and tweed garb of an Oxford don, with the exception of his bright red-and-gold vest. A cloud of smoke hovered over them as they both puffed away on their pipes. Yvette had often seen Austen chewing on the stem of his pipe, but it seldom held tobacco. She liked the heavy scent that greeted her when she opened the door. It reminded her of her father and of home.

"Tea's ready," she announced.

"Oh, I had quite forgotten! Austen and I were just discussing the geography of Gondor. So sorry. I mustn't keep Edith waiting." Tolkien moved quickly and agilely for a man in his mid-seventies. Yvette remembered Austen telling her that his professor had been a rugby player and that he still relished watching a good football match.

When they rejoined Edith in the parlor, she had moved to the piano and was playing a Bach two-part invention. She finished with a flourish and they rewarded her with applause.

"Yvette," she called. "Come sing something for us."

"No, really. Your playing was beautiful. You don't need me to sing."

"Come," Edith insisted. "Just one short number. It's fun for me to accompany someone." She tapped a large music book. "Why not some Gilbert and Sullivan while Ronald pours the tea?"

"Well, all right." Yvette leafed through the book. "How about 'Poor Wandering One!' from the *Pirates of Penzance*?"

Edith nodded. "Excellent." Propping the book on the music stand, she expertly played the introduction. Yvette's warm contralto had a wide range, and she effortlessly soared up to the higher notes. The men arrested the rattling of their teacups to listen. Austen had heard Yvette sing at David and Kate's wedding, but something special on this day caught his attention. For a moment an unaccountable and poignant yearning welled up in him.

At the song's conclusion and the men's applause, the women flushed with shared pleasure. A new friendship had been forged.

Yvette helped Edith back to the sofa, and they both took their tea. The Tolkiens chatted a while about their children and grandchildren as well as Edith's health and their frustrations with trying to get out. Edith had always enjoyed the Headington shops, but she could no longer negotiate the long walk up the street and now had to rely on taxi service to go anywhere. Mr. Tolkien seemed wistful when he asked about the University and the English Faculty and eagerly seized on another opportunity to speak to the Inklings Society. For a while he launched into an esoteric discussion with Austen about his ongoing effort to complete his history and mythology of Middle Earth in *The Silmarillion*. Occasionally he would pause briefly to ask Austen's opinion before he would be off again into his own ideas. It struck Yvette that he spoke as if he were discussing real kingdoms and peoples and history, not imaginary realms. And yet it occurred to her that perhaps this detailed attention to his complex creation—in developing languages, alphabets, legends—and his passion for conveying it in a consistent and accurate manner were the very reasons his creation had resonated so strongly with so many people around the world.

At times his discourse was difficult to follow. He spoke in a rapid mutter common to many of his countrymen and consequently maddening to Americans, who felt they needed a translator to understand their mother tongue. His articulation was further tortured by the ubiquitous pipe, which left his mouth only when he swallowed his tea. Every time his inflection indicated a question, Yvette feared it was directed to her. But to her relief, Austen apparently understood the tenor of the conversation better than she did and would make some astute reply.

Finally she summoned up the courage to ask a query of her own. "Mr. Tolkien, it seems to me that although there aren't any overt references to Christianity in the *The Lord of the Rings*, there are many scenes which allude to biblical stories and the overall theme is Christian. Would you agree with that?"

He peered at her quizzically for a moment as if he had almost forgotten she was present, and then he responded. "Now, I think you know I am a Christian and a Catholic and *The Lord of the Rings* is, of course, a fundamentally religious and Catholic work. The religious element is absorbed into the story and the symbolism. But don't make the mistake of taking it as allegory. Austen knows I despise allegory in all its forms. I don't like hitting the reader over the head with my ideas. Anyway, I didn't set out to write specifically Christian books. *The Hobbit*, after all, began as a bedtime story I concocted to entertain my own children, particularly Christopher, who was bedridden with a heart ailment. Many people have read my books with no concept that they have any Christian overtones, and yet I hope that something in them will point them in that direction. Jack Lewis once said that 'all manner of theology can be smuggled into people's mind under the guise of romance.' That's the subtle approach I've tried to take. Jack was not always quite so subtle in my estimation. I still think *The Lion, the Witch, and the Wardrobe* borders too closely on allegory. Of course, Jack hotly contested my opinion."

"You miss Mr. Lewis, don't you?" Austen asked suddenly.

"Of course I miss him. He was one of the finest friends a man could have—even though we did drift apart a bit in the last years after he married that American woman."

"Oh, Ronald," interjected Edith. "I liked Joy."

"Yes, well, once Jack got married, he became appropriately more occupied with his wife, so we didn't see each other as much. Still, he was the best of friends and an unparalleled colleague. Without him I feel quite like an ancient Ent who's had someone take a hatchet to my roots. Of course, I do have Edith here and my family, and for that I'm very grateful. But you must know how I feel, Austen. Even though you are quite young, you've lost your dear wife. I am glad we have the comfort of looking forward to seeing our loved ones and friends again in eternity. By the way, thank you, my boy, for coming to visit us today. It's a pleasure to have some company from the University."

"Our pleasure," Austen replied, rising. "But we'd best be going. Thanks very much for having us."

"Yes, thank you." Yvette rose also. "It was so lovely to meet you both."

"Lovely to meet you as well. Please come again," said Edith.

"We'd be delighted. And Mrs. T," Austen added, "if you need a ride anyplace and I'm available, I'd be happy to pick you up. I'd be glad to take you to the store or church or even out to dinner sometime to one of the inns you like."

"That would be wonderful, Austen." Edith beamed.

Yvette gathered her coat and handbag, but she hesitated with one more question as she took a second look at a distinctive china clock on the mantle piece. "Mrs. Tolkien, I've been admiring your clock since we got here. I've been searching for something like that for my mother for Christmas. Forgive me for being presumptuous, but would you mind telling me where you found your clock? It's exquisite."

"Why thank you. It is, isn't it? We actually acquired our clock from Austen! His family owns a little antique shop in a small village in the Cotswolds."

"Really?" Yvette looked at Austen. This quiet man was full of surprises.

"Yes," answered Edith. "Austen, you really should take Yvette with you the next time you go home. Help her find a clock for her mother. How is your mother, by the way?"

"Fine. Thank you for asking. She has her good days and her bad. But I don't think she'll ever fully recover from the damage caused by the polio."

"Poor thing. I really don't have cause to complain about my arthritis. I should think of and pray for your mother more often. Now, Austen, do take Yvette with you the next time you go."

They said their thank-yous and goodbyes. As soon as Austen and Yvette had closed the garden gate and were striding back up the street to the bus stop, she plunged in. "Austen, I wasn't hinting for a trip to the Cotswolds, so please don't feel obligated to follow Mrs. Tolkien's suggestion."

"Does that mean you don't want to go or that you're concerned you would be imposing on me?"

"Honestly, the latter. I really do want to find a clock for my mother and I love the Cotswolds, but I don't want to horn in on you or your family time."

"It just so happens I am due for a visit and wouldn't mind the company. I could ring up my brother-in-law and ask him to keep an eye out for a clock like the Tolkiens'. Don't worry. I'll make sure he gives you a good deal."

Yvette smiled at him. "That is really nice of you."

"Of course it is." Austen returned the smile. "Don't listen to David's disparaging comments about me. I'm really a very nice bloke. Well then, would you like to go? Saturday, week?"

"Sure, that would be great! I'd love to find something before the Christmas shopping rush. What village are you from, anyway?"

"A little place called Castle Combe."

6

Sixth Week, Monday

*D*avid wrote a detailed comment on a student essay and tossed it into the basket of graded papers on his desk. He glanced at his watch and saw that he had time to mark one more before dinner. Sighing heavily, he reached for another, thinking how glad he would be when his term in Paris began. There he would have a graduate assistant do the grunt work for him. His conscience countered, *Stop complaining! Even illustrious dons like Jack Lewis and Professor Tolkien had to mark essays. And Tolkien took on judging exams to bring in needed income for his wife and four children.* Musing, he tapped his pencil. *Still they hated it too, and a break from it all will be most welcome.*

His thoughts and work were interrupted by a knock on his door. He stifled his impatience.

"Yes?" he called out.

"It's Stuart Devereux, sir. May I come in?"

David grimaced. *Oh bother! Probably wants to talk about Natalie.*

"Yes, come in, Stuart."

Stuart opened the door and stood awkwardly on the threshold. One glimpse of his face quenched David's annoyance and reminded him not to prejudge people. With his face pale and his eyes red, Stuart's usual arrogance and confidence were decidedly absent.

"Come in, Stuart," David repeated gently, "and have a seat."

Stuart sank into the closest chair. "Do you mind if I smoke?" His hands were trembling.

David answered by handing him an ashtray. Stuart sucked on the lit cigarette as if it supplied desperately needed oxygen. After a few puffs, he relaxed slightly.

"I'm sorry to barge in on you unannounced like this," he began. "I've had some dreadful news, and my first thought was to head to the pub. But on my way I thought better of it and decided to come over here instead. Thanks for seeing me."

"No problem."

Stuart took a few more drags. "It's my mother," he finally croaked.

"I'm sorry. Is she ill?"

"She's…she's dead."

David was genuinely shocked. He knew Lady Devereux could only be in her mid-forties. "I'm so sorry, Stuart. Has she been ill or was it an accident?"

Stuart rubbed his forehead. "Both maybe. I don't know if Kate told you, but my mother has a drinking problem and she also takes pills for her nerves. Apparently, last night she took too many and never woke up. Fanny, her maid, found her this morning." He snuffed out his cigarette and promptly lit another. "They're calling it an accident, but I guess we'll never know, will we?"

"Stuart, this really is dreadful news. I am so very sorry."

Stuart thoughtfully drew on his cigarette. "Such a bloody waste of a life," he said bitterly. "My mother was a lovely woman really and she got such a bloody raw deal. Her money for my father's blasted title. And that's all he gave her, unless you count my sister and me, but you really can't count me because I've been a lousy son. Oh, I'm polite and dutiful and all, but I've been so ashamed of her for as long as I can remember." He jabbed this cigarette out as well. "You know, I've seen how you are with your mother; how all you MacKenzies are. I've seen your respect and love for each other and I've never known that. At least, I know I never showed that kind of love to my mother." He hid his face in his hands. "Maybe if I had been a better son she would have had a reason to live. I failed her. I really failed her. If only I had…" He choked on a sob and then utterly broke down.

While Stuart wept, David prayed silently. He had seldom seen a man so racked with grief, but he recollected his own distress when he thought Kate had died after she had been hit by a car. Then he recalled Austen's grief when he had lost Marianne. After a time, he sympathetically placed his hand on Stuart's shaking shoulder.

When his outburst of grief was finally spent, Stuart sheepishly wiped his eyes and nose with his handkerchief. "I'm sorry—I shouldn't have burdened you with my problems."

"Not at all. I only wish there were something more I could do for you."

"No, no. You've done enough just listening. Sorry for the ridiculous display of emotion."

"Please, don't apologize. That stiff upper lip bit is all rubbish. There is a time to mourn. I'm just so sorry it's yours. But how else can I help? Have any arrangements been made yet? Will you be going down soon?"

Stuart collected himself. "Yes. The funeral is Saturday in Essex. A small affair at Clifton Manor."

"Then if it's private, I suppose it's by invitation only?"

Stuart looked up quickly. "Would you come? You and Kate?"

"If you would like us to—if we would not be imposing."

Stuart's face clouded with emotion. "I would appreciate it very much."

David clasped Stuart's shoulder again. "All right, then. Do you know the time?"

"Two o'clock. Tea—or more likely cocktails—to follow back at the house." Stuart stood to leave. "Apparently, she requested in her will to be buried in the parish churchyard rather than the family chapel, so the service will be there. If you are able to come, it would be most splendid of you. But please don't put yourselves out. I heard that Kate hasn't been feeling well, and I wouldn't want to cause her any discomfort."

"That's thoughtful of you, Stuart. We'll see how she's feeling, and if she's under the weather, I'll come alone. But we'll do our best to be there. I'm sure Kate will want to offer her condolences to you as well. And we'll be praying for you and your family. May I let my father and St. Aldate's know?"

"Yes." Then shame crept over Stuart's face. "But not the details."

"Of course not," David assured him. "You have my word."

Stuart clasped David's proffered hand. "Thank you."

7

Sixth Week, Saturday
Clifton Manor, Essex

*D*avid switched off the ignition and turned to Kate with a chagrined sigh. "Here we are, but this rain is beastly. Why don't you stay in the car and I'll go up to the graveside to represent us?"

"No, I would like to be there too. I'll be fine."

David frowned with protective tenderness. "I don't want you getting chilled."

She placed her hand on his arm. "I'll be fine," she repeated. "The umbrella is in the back. Besides, aren't you the one who told me that the weather here can switch in a moment?"

David relented, quickly stepped out of the car, and reached behind the seat for the umbrella. By the time he had put it up, opened Kate's door, and given her his hand, the rain had indeed stopped. They both regarded the lych-gate where the funeral cortège gathered under the covered archway. David had seen hundreds of such roofed churchyard gates, which derived the name "lych" or "lich" from the Old English word for "corpse," as this was the momentary resting place of the bier before entering the cemetery. But he preferred the more euphemistic name of "resurrection gate." A crown of vines draped over the simple carved oak gate, and suddenly streams of sunlight burst through the rain clouds and lit the leaves in a brilliant halo of gold. In an instant, "resurrection gate" became not just a euphemism, and David sensed a quickening in his spirit as if this were a sign that God had welcomed His weary daughter home.

Kate squeezed his arm and whispered, "Look!" So she had seen it too. They both noticed Stuart gazing up at the golden gate. The MacKenzies had prayed that he would receive a supernatural sign of comfort. Perhaps this unexpected display of nature was the answer to their prayer.

The small cortège marched up an avenue of plane trees to the open grave close to the church walls. Kate and David stood a discreet distance back from the family huddled by the graveside as the Anglican cleric earnestly intoned the funeral liturgy. David had wondered about Lady Devereux's request to be buried here rather than in the family chapel. Perhaps it was due to her estrangement from her wandering husband. Then he spied the tiny headstone lying next to the coffin:

Charles Spencer Devereux
Infant son of
Charles Stuart Spencer, Lord Devereux, Earl of Essex
And
Elaine, Lady Devereux, Countess of Essex
January 12, 1940–January 14, 1940

Their son would be about my age, David thought sadly. *Poor Lady Devereux—she lost her husband to dalliance and a child to death. Well, she is with her boy now and at peace.*

The family filed by the coffin. The Lord Devereux, Earl of Essex, bowed his head respectfully. Stuart and a tall young woman—whom David guessed to be his sister—each gently laid a white rose on the casket lid as they passed by. Before walking back down the avenue of plane trees to their waiting limousine, the Devereuxes stopped and graciously greeted their friends. Stuart spied Kate and David and hastened over to them. He kissed Kate on both cheeks with polite affection and clasped David's hand warmly.

"We're so sorry, Stuart," they both murmured.

"Thank you for coming. You will stop by the house now for some refreshments, won't you?" His tone was solicitous, almost plaintive. They nodded in assent. "Excellent. Well, Kate, you can finally meet the old man and my sister. Just follow the Rolls."

David waited for the other mourners to file behind the Devereux limousine and then smoothly shifted his hunter green MG Midget to the rear of the procession—but not without some self-consciousness of its less than mint condition. As much as he loved his little sports coupe, he knew it was the worse for wear, especially in a funeral procession led by a gleaming Rolls-Royce. His discomfort intensified as they passed the dry stone wall that surrounded the park of Clifton Manor. The long winding drive through fields and meadows suddenly opened onto a striking vista of a stone bridge arching over a meandering stream with the honey-colored manor house rising grandly beyond. The view engendered the desired effect of aesthetic delight mingled with awe.

It immediately evoked a more familiar approach in David's mind: that of Blenheim Palace. He gave an appreciative whistle. "Impressive, isn't it? Do you think it was designed by

Capability Brown?" He was referring to the celebrated eigh-teenth-century landscape artist of Blenheim and many estate parks throughout England.

Kate responded quietly. "Yes, it was."

David quickly glanced at her, but her expression revealed nothing. As they drew closer to the great house, David had to admire the ornate stone tracery along the roofline and the eight turrets capped by cupolas. The profusion of mullioned windows confirmed to him the architecture as Jacobean, or concurrent with the reign of King James I and the publication of the authorized English translation of the Bible, which bore the King's name. But David's thoughts did not rest long on King James or his Bible. He glanced again at his wife, who was regarding the house without comment.

"And do you know when the house was built?" he asked. "It looks Jacobean."

"Yes, I think the front court was built in the time of James, although I remember Stuart saying the house was originally a hunting lodge in Elizabethan times. And then an additional wing where the family lives now was built during the reign of Queen Anne."

Kate's wistful tone caught David's attention. *What is she thinking? That she could have been mistress of all this? Does she regret it now? Is she sorry she chose me?*

"Isn't it sad?" Kate's question seemed to echo his thoughts.

"What?" He hoped she wouldn't hear the insecurity he cer-tainly felt.

"That Lady Devereux had this beautiful park and house—all this, yet she was still so unhappy."

David felt a twinge of guilt at his relief. "Yes, it is quite sad," he agreed solemnly.

They parked in the long circular driveway and entered the front portico. A tuxedoed doorman welcomed them, took their coats and umbrella, and directed them to follow the long Tudor gallery to the "new" wing, the eighteenth-century addition where the family resided and waited to receive their guests in the drawing room. David noted the hammer-beamed ceiling of the entrance hall and then the carved oak paneling of the long gallery. They walked past centuries-old portraits and furnishings that David scrutinized with fascination. He knew how much Kate loved historical properties and how having been a houseguest on this palatial estate must have been a highlight of her first autumn in England. He began to understand the allurement this must have been for Kate and how much she had sacrificed by rejecting Stuart's advances, as untoward as they had been. Like the Queen of Sheba, whose heart grew faint at the sight of all of Solomon's riches, David felt overwhelmed with humility.

He suddenly stopped. "Kate, all this could have been yours. You could have been a viscountess. Why in the world did you marry me?"

She peered at him quizzically, and then perceiving the earnestness of his question, she gave him a sober response. "Honestly, I didn't want to end up like Lady Devereux. I met her here, you know, and I saw how unhappy she was. And I don't really know if Stuart was serious about marrying me or was just using that as a line to have his way. Anyway, don't you remember our sonnet?"

"What sonnet?"

"The one you quoted to me at the Bird and Baby last December:

Thy love is better than high birth to me,
Richer than wealth, prouder than garments' costs,
Of more delight than hawks or horses be;
And having thee, of all men's pride I boast...

You know those lines speak for me as well as for you. Besides," her eyes sparkled mischievously, "you're a lot cuter than he is."

David laughed at this decidedly American compliment. "Cuter?"

She smiled and gently brushed back an errant curl from his forehead, happy to know that she had set him at ease again. "Much cuter." She stood on tiptoe to give him a little kiss and he caught her up in his arms.

"I do love you beyond reason," he murmured and then kissed her hungrily.

A valet coughed politely to warn them they were not alone. Surprised, they looked over. "Sorry, old chap." David smiled winningly. "My wife is hard to resist."

The servant tried unsuccessfully to repress his own smile. "The Lord Devereux and his family are receiving in the west drawing room. Just follow the corridor at the end of the gallery, sir."

"Right. Thank you." David gave the young man a parting wink and then offered his arm to Kate. They found the small assemblage in the drawing room, and Stuart quickly made certain they were served tea and made comfortable.

"Thanks again for coming," he said. "I do hope it didn't put too much of a burden on you. Kate, I hear congratulations are in order. How are you feeling? Natalie told me you were having a bit of a rough go."

"Yes, well, I have been feeling queasy, but it shouldn't last much longer."

"I hope not. You look as gorgeous as ever. Ah, here is Clemmie."

The tall young woman whom David had correctly surmised to be Stuart's sister joined them. It struck David that she was the mirror image of Stuart; only a widow's peak of blond hair rather than brown framed the familiar handsome aristocratic features and green eyes. The pair seemed to him to be a photo negative not only of one another, but also of the memorable siblings Sebastian and Julia Flyte of Evelyn Waugh's *Brideshead Revisited*.

"Stu," she was saying, "do introduce me to your friends."

"Clemmie, may I present Mr. and Mrs. David MacKenzie? Kate and David—my sister, Clementine, the Lady Fitzwilliam."

David bowed his head politely. "It's a pleasure, my lady."

"The pleasure is mine." Clementine rested her hand familiarly on Kate's arm. "Stuart has told me all about you, Kate. He was beside himself when you threw him over, but now that I've met your husband, I can see my little brother never had a chance." She smiled warmly at David.

"Clemmie!" Stuart protested.

"Sorry, dear, I must be honest. Now run along and find some more refreshments for your guests. I want them all to myself for a minute."

Stuart grudgingly complied, and as soon as he was out of earshot, Clementine discarded her lighthearted demeanor and drew the couple closer to her, speaking in a hurried whisper. "Listen, I'm honestly quite concerned about Stuart. He's taking Mother's death very badly and blaming himself and Father. He's drinking much more than he should, and I'm really, really worried this could get out of hand or has already. I'm just not around him enough to keep an eye on him, and there isn't anyone else. I'm assuming you wouldn't be here if you didn't care about Stu, and he's talked so much about you and how much he admires you that I wondered if you would look out for him for me. Would you do that, please, and contact me if necessary? With Mummy gone and Father seldom around, he's the only family I have left, and I'd hate to see him turning into a sad sort of character like Sebastian Flyte or someone even worse. It would be simply ghastly."

Funny she would make that Brideshead connection too, David thought, but then he answered, "Of course we'll look out for him."

Clementine's eyes welled with tears. "Thank you. May I keep in touch with you? I have my calling cards out in the Hall. If you would pick one up…"

"Certainly." David pulled out his wallet and handed her one of his own. "And here's mine, if you want to contact me or Kate."

"Thank you," she repeated and dabbed at her eyes with a handkerchief. "Sorry."

"No, we're sorry," Kate said. "This must be a very difficult time for you both, and we'd be glad to help in any way we can."

"You're so kind. It's a comfort to know Stuart has some really good friends."

"What are you saying about me behind my back?" Stuart rejoined their little group as a waiter exchanged the MacKenzies' empty teacups with fresh ones.

"Just telling them what a naughty little brother you are."

"Be glad you have younger sisters who look up to you, David," Stuart said wryly. "My big sister tormented me all my life, and when I was finally old enough to give her a good wallop in return, I was told gentlemen never hit ladies. Didn't seem very cricket of her to change the rules mid-match." The siblings grimaced affectionately at one another.

Their clowning abruptly ended when their father approached. The Lord Devereux was the quintessential English nobleman: elegant in bearing and manner; his attire, impeccable; his silver hair, perfectly coiffed. He spoke with a slightly nasal aristocratic drawl. "Stuart, my boy. Introduce me to your delightful friends."

"Father, may I present Mr. and Mrs. David MacKenzie? Kate and David—the Lord Devereux, Earl of Essex."

David bowed his head, but the Lord Devereux took no notice. He was lifting Kate's hand to his lips. "Charmed." His demeanor bordered on lascivious. She withdrew her hand and steadied her teacup.

David replied, "Honored to make your acquaintance, my lord. My *wife* and I would like to express our condolences."

Lord Devereux reluctantly turned to David. "Thank you. Are you from Oxford then? Christ Church?"

"No, my lord, I'm at Magdalen."

"I'm a Cambridge man, myself. Trinity."

"I'm a Cambridge man too. Magdalene as well."

Lord Devereux appeared puzzled and Stuart hastened to explain. "Mr. MacKenzie took his degree from Cambridge, but he's a Fellow at Oxford, Father."

"A Fellow? I thought you were a student. By Jove, you dons are young these days!" He stared at Kate. "And your wives exceedingly pretty. Please join us for dinner. I'll look forward to getting to know you better." He smiled at her and then excused himself. Kate couldn't help but feel that for all his elegance, the Lord Devereux seemed not polished, but oily.

"Stuart." David hastened to speak when the earl was out of earshot. "We appreciate the invitation to dinner, but I had already made arrangements to meet a friend in Cambridge. In fact, we should probably be leaving soon."

"Don't worry. I shouldn't want Kate to get anywhere near him, either. You just slip out and I'll make excuses for you." He shook David's hand. "Thanks again for coming, old chap. And Kate, I hope it hasn't been too hard on you." He bussed her cheek.

"Not at all. Nice to meet you too, Clemmie."

Clementine offered her hand to them. "And you. It was very good of you to come." She leaned closer to David and murmured, "Don't forget my card when you pick up your coat. You will look out for him?"

David nodded. "Of course. You can count on it."

8

*O*n the same November Saturday that David and Kate traveled east to Essex to attend Lady Devereux's funeral, Austen and Yvette headed west to the small southern Cotswolds village of Castle Combe.

"Oh, I know of Castle Combe!" Yvette exclaimed as they drove past a road sign. "The way you were pronouncing it, I thought it was spelled *C-o-o-m*."

"Well, it is sometimes spelled *C-o-o-m-b-e*," replied Austen.

"Wasn't it voted prettiest village in England by some magazine a few years ago?"

"That's right. The Americans rediscovered us when a travel company organized a competition for England's most beautiful village and they chose us. But the upshot was that we're no longer a quiet little backwater town. During the summer months, loads of tourists descend on us. And yet we really can't complain because the tourists bring plenty of business. Our property values have gone way up, and it's certainly been a boon for Andrew's antique shop."

"Is Andrew your brother?"

"Brother-in-law. He's married to my twin sister, Dianna." He hesitated and then added, "We're twice related really. His sister was my wife, Marianne."

"Oh." Yvette wasn't sure how to respond. Did he want to talk about this or not? She decided to try. "Did you grow up together?"

"For the most part. After the war, the lord of the Manor put the whole village up for auction. Then all our quaint little medieval weaving cottages were sold for as low as seventy-five pounds apiece. That's when both my family and the McAdams moved to Castle Combe. That was in 1947, when I was nine years old. Marianne was only five."

Yvette quickly did the math in her head and calculated to her chagrin that she was two years older than Austen.

"My mother bought a cottage by the town bridge on the Bybrook," Austen continued. "We had been living out on our sheep farm in the country, but my dad died in the war, and it got to be too much for her to handle, what with two little ones. Consequently, she bought the house in town and hired tenants to run the farm. Andrew and Marianne's family came from London. Mr. McAdams bought the big house next door to ours to expand his antique business, and they liked the village so well they decided to move here to raise their family. And then Andrew and I both ended up literally marrying the girls next door."

"That's really lovely. I grew up in London—Bayswater, not Bybrook—and we hardly know our neighbors. But you said it was Andrew's antique shop. Are his parents still alive?"

"Yes, but retired now. After Marianne died, they found it hard to stay in the village. Mrs. McAdams wanted to live by the sea, so they bought a bungalow in Lyme Regis."

"Oh, I've always wanted to go to Lyme! Ever since I read *Persuasion*. I'd love to see the Cobb, the seawall where Louisa fell."

"It's quite picturesque and an excellent spot for a holiday. The Tolkiens have been there a number of times as well."

"I'm sorry to say I can't remember ever taking a proper holiday with my family. Never could afford to. I've always had a bit of wanderlust but not the means to satisfy it. In fact, the little day trips we've taken with David and Kate are the most I've seen of this realm. I'm rather like the proverbial farmer, who after walking three miles down the road to the next village he's never been to before, says, 'I've always wanted to travel.' That's one reason I'm so grateful you asked me along. I haven't had a chance to see much of the Cotswolds. It really is beautiful. Thanks for inviting me."

"Not a problem. But there's not much to *do* except see them. I just hope we'll be able to find a clock suitable for your mother."

By this time they had entered the environs of the village. Austen drove his Morris Minor carefully over the ancient arched bridge and pulled up to some stone cottages overlooking the stream.

"Here we are. Now don't mind Mother. She's of the old school and can be rather prickly," Austen cautioned as he hopped out and opened Yvette's door.

Before she could question this comment, a loud shout rang out and two little boys burst out of the cottage door and into Austen's arms. The chubby blond boys wriggled like puppies and shouted with joy, "Unca Autty! Unca Autty!"

Austen laughed as he embraced the squirming children. "Hullo, lads! How are my favorite nephews?" He reached into his coat jacket and pulled out two lollipops. "Now don't run with these in your mouth and don't tell your mother they're from me."

"I heard that, Austen Holmes," reproached a young blond woman standing in a charming cottage porch thatched with hedgerow timber. She held a fat-cheeked infant on one hip and her hand on the other. Her voice sounded stern, but her blue eyes were laughing. "What do you say, lads, to your Uncle Autty?"

"Thank you! Thank you!" The older boy shouted as he jumped up and down with excitement.

"Tank you! Tank you!" chorused the younger.

"You are both welcome," replied Austen. "Now, I'd like you to meet Miss Goodman. Yvette, this is Robby, Jack, baby Michael, and my sister, Dianna."

Yvette thought the elder boy, Rob, looked about four years old and Jack, two. They both stared at her with open curiosity. Clearly, in this Anglo-Saxon town, they were not accustomed to seeing people with brown skin. She tried to smile reassuringly when she spoke. "Hello, Rob and Jack. Hello, Dianna. Nice to meet you." The boys smiled shyly back.

"Welcome to Castle Combe!" Dianna called out. "Everyone, please come in and get out of the cold." She stepped aside to let the little ones run past her into the house. "You've come for a clock, haven't you?" she asked Yvette. "Well, my husband has a few for you to look at, but first we'll have some dinner." She allowed Austen to wrap her and the baby in a warm embrace. "It's about time you came home," she chided. "We've missed you."

"I know, I know. I'm sorry. How's Mother?"

"About the same, thankfully." She lowered her voice. "But always complaining she doesn't see you enough. Come in. She's waiting for you in the parlor. I'm going to see to the soup."

"May I help you?" asked Yvette. "Or take the baby for you?"

"Certainly," Dianna readily agreed. "If you would take Michael, it would be a big help."

The cherubic Michael easily exchanged his mother's arms for Yvette's. She buried her nose in his silken curls. She loved the fresh smell of baby shampoo, and yet that innocent scent awakened all her maternal yearnings and filled her with sadness.

Austen let Yvette pass and then out of long habit ducked his head under the low oak-beamed lintel and followed her into the tidy front room of the cottage. The oak-plank floors gleamed with polish brightened by the autumn sun streaming through the casement window. The lath-and-plaster walls and ceiling shone with whitewash intersected by fourteenth-century dark oak beams. A fire burned cheerfully in the stone hearth. The room was at once quaint but comfortable, and it conjured up that effect most cherished by the British: coziness.

Austen's mother, Elinor Holmes, sat in a chair by the fire with a cane resting on her knees. Her blond hair, threaded with white, was twisted into a neat bun, and her eyes like Austen's were the elusive color of the sea—shifting from blue to gray to green. She bore a strong familial resemblance to her two children with their Anglo-Saxon features and coloring and a hint of the Nordic in their high cheekbones. Dianna's face and figure were full from childbearing and Austen's hair was wavier, but otherwise the siblings looked like the twins they were.

Elinor held open her arms as if to a small child. "Austen! I'm so glad you've come!"

He knelt to accept her embrace. "Hello, Mother. How are you?"

"Much better with you here. Why have you stayed away so long?"

Austen did not reply but arose and turned to Yvette. "Mother, I'd like you to meet a colleague of mine. This is Yvette Goodman."

"Hello, Mrs. Holmes," Yvette said. "It's nice to meet you. Thank you for allowing me to intrude on your family like this."

"Not at all. We're happy for any excuse to get Austen to come home. Where are you from, Miss Goodman? If you don't mind my saying so, you don't look like an Oxford don."

Yvette did mind her saying so but refrained from expressing her umbrage. She fervently wished that an explanation of her origins was not always necessary, "I'm from London, Mrs. Holmes. My mother is Irish, but my father is from the West Indies. He came over to play football and is now a U.K. citizen." *There. Is that enough information?*

"I see. But how did you come to be a colleague of Austen's?"

Apparently not. Yvette took a breath to explain further when Austen jumped in.

"Mother, Yvette is a Fellow at St. Hilda's College and a member of the English Faculty. That's how David and I made her acquaintance."

"Oh. How is David doing, dear?"

"Excellently. He and Kate are expecting a baby."

"Already? Well, how nice."

Yvette was relieved that the focus of the conversation had turned from her while they chatted about the MacKenzies. The tolling of the church bell interrupted them.

"Noon," Dianna announced as she carried in a soup tureen and placed it on the table by the front window. "Andrew will be over in a minute. Austen, would you please get the high chair for Michael and help Mother to the table? Yvette, I'll take the baby. Thank you very much. Won't you sit here?"

The family was bustling about getting things ready when a darkly handsome young man walked in and planted a kiss on Dianna's cheek and then clasped Austen's hand in greeting. "Hello, old chap. Good to see you! Hello, Mother. Hello, lads."

"Hi, Daddy!"

"And you must be Miss…"

"Goodman," supplied Austen. "Yvette Goodman."

"Well, Miss Goodman, Austen tells me you're looking for an antique clock for your mother. Happily, we have a few to choose from. But first let's eat. Austen, will you say grace, please?"

"Certainly." The family all bowed their heads as Austen uttered the blessing. "We thank Thee, Lord, for our daily bread, both for body and soul. And do Thou keep us ever mindful of Thy good providence. Through Jesus Christ our Lord, amen."

"Amen," everyone echoed.

"Well, Austen," sniffed Elinor Holmes. "You still say our old Protestant grace, even though you've gone and turned Catholic on us?"

Austen sighed.

"Now, Mum," remonstrated Dianna as she filled a bowl of soup for her mother. "You know we're all Christians and one grace is as fine as another to the good Lord."

"It may be to the good Lord, but it didn't seem to be for Austen or he wouldn't have turned away from the Church of England, now would he?"

"Mother, you needn't talk of me in the third person as if I weren't here," Austen said. Then glancing at Yvette, he mastered his irritation at this oft-fought family battle and changed the subject. "So, Andrew, how's business?"

"Slow now that we're in the off season. But it may pick up a bit closer to Christmas. I say, Austen, has Dianna told you about the film they're going to make here next year?"

"Film? Do you mean for the cinema?"

"Right! Some Hollywood film scouts came over and decided that since we're the 'prettiest village' in England, we'll make the perfect setting for *Dr. Dolittle!*"

"*Dr. Dolittle*? You're kidding. They're going to film it here?"

"Yes!" Dianna's eyes glowed with excitement as she carried in a platter of meat and potatoes. She served her mother first and then the others. "And Rex Harrison is the star. They're going to build a jetty along the Bybrook right out in front of our house to make the town look like a seaport. Our house in a film! I think it's so exciting!"

"I think it's a bunch of hooey," groused Elinor. "They picked our village because it's picturesque and then they want to go and change it into a seaport. They even want us to take down our telly aerials. With all those film folk about, we'll have no peace and quiet for weeks."

"Well, I think it's exciting," Dianna insisted. "Nothing much happens around here except the Circuit races at the track down the road. Now all we'll have to do is walk out our front door and we'll be on a real live movie set."

They continued to chat about the film while they ate their dinner.

"It will be good for business," Andrew concluded. "Plus they're paying the townspeople to be extras and have promised to provide clothing, meals, and even drinks."

"And fifty shillings a day," added Dianna.

"Are you going to be an extra?" Austen asked with a laugh.

"Why not? I've always fancied being in a film."

"You're pretty enough to be," Andrew said as he drew her over and kissed her cheek.

Dianna blushed. "Oh, pshaw, Andrew. They probably wouldn't want me anyway, what with the boys and all."

"I don't know, Di," Austen reassured her. "You're probably just what they do want: a rosy-cheeked village girl with a rosy-cheeked baby on her hip. They might even pay you fifty shillings for each boy."

Little Robby had followed the conversation with interest. "Fifty for me?"

They laughed.

"Yeah, Rob," Austen teased. "They're going to sell you to the gypsies for fifty shillings."

"Na-uh. I gonna be in *Dr. Do.*"

"You're gonna be in bed, little man," said Dianna. "Time for naps."

"Oh, Mummy," groaned Rob.

"Come on. You too, Jack." Dianna wiped their faces and hands and helped them down from the table. "Andrew, will you get Michael while I put them down?"

"May I?" asked Yvette.

"That'd be fine, if you don't mind. I'll be back in a minute."

Yvette cleaned up the baby and lifted him into her arms. She clasped him tightly for a brief moment while that poignant yearning washed over her again. Then as the men settled Mrs. Holmes in her chair and began clearing the table, Yvette carried the baby over to his grandmother.

"You have a beautiful grandson, Mrs. Holmes. In fact, three beautiful grandsons. You are very blessed."

"Yes, I suppose I am. But it's hard to feel blessed sometimes when I've been so crippled by polio. I'd like to be more help to Dianna, and I'm just someone else for her to take care of now. Here, let me hold the baby. That's one thing I can still do."

Overcoming her reluctance to relinquish the infant, Yvette nestled him in his grandmother's arms, where he promptly fell asleep.

"You go next door with Andrew and Austen, Miss Goodman, and see if you can find that clock you're looking for. Then you and Austen can visit with the baby and me. We're not going anywhere."

"Very well," Yvette agreed. "We'll be back soon."

9

Sixth Week, Saturday Afternoon
Castle Combe

Come, Yvette," Austen said. "Andrew will have reopened the shop and you can see if there is anything to suit you."

Even though they had only to step outside and walk next door, Austen brought their coats. He thought she might like to have a look around the village.

"Andrew and Dianna moved into our house to tend to Mother," he said as he opened the shop door. "It's allowed the business to expand, but I've wondered if they won't have to swap back, what with their family growing."

Although more spacious and open, the ground floor of the shop was not unlike the house next door with its dark oak-beamed ceiling and the wood-planked floor shining with polish. Antiques filled the rooms without cluttering them. The glassware was artfully arranged to catch the sunbeams streaming through the mullioned windows and cast rainbows of fractured light onto the white plaster walls.

Andrew greeted them and led them to a mahogany Empire desk on which he had displayed several porcelain clocks. "I don't know if we have what you're looking for, but if not, I'd be willing to try to find it for you."

Yvette's eyes immediately fell on a mantle clock of the distinctive soft blue and white of Wedgwood's jasperware. She easily could envision it gracing their dining room fireplace mantle. "I love this one," she said as she gingerly picked it up. "It would go perfectly with my mum's good dishes. How much is it?"

Andrew seemed pained as if he were embarrassed to have to charge her anything. "Um…I'm afraid it's a bit dear. Could you manage twenty quid?"

"Twenty pounds? Is that all? Surely it costs more than that."

"No, twenty would be plenty. Really. That is, if it's not too much."

"Not at all." Yvette pulled a crisp twenty-pound note out of her purse and handed it to him. "This is perfect. My mum will adore it." She looked up at the men and smiled broadly. "Thank you ever so much!"

"You're welcome!" They smiled back, happy at her pleasure.

"Well, that was easy enough," Andrew said. "Let me wrap it up for you."

"May I poke around while you do?"

"Certainly. Please make yourself at home, and let me know if there is anything else I can help you with."

Andrew carefully wrapped the clock in layers of brown paper to prevent breakage while he and Austen fell into the easy conversation common to long familial acquaintance and affection. Yvette walked about the store, admiring the many pieces evidently chosen with an eye for beauty and fine craftsmanship. Picking up and handling things that had belonged to others in far away times and places filled her with an unexpected sense of heritage and even awe. It was a sensation not unlike that which she had experienced as a young girl when her mother had allowed her to touch her great-grandmother's good Wedgwood china—a material and tangible link with people who had left this temporal world. Although not a materialistic person, she was happy to be able to add to that family link with the china clock. She knew it was something her mother would never indulge herself in buying, but that, nevertheless, would bring not only beauty into her life but would also serve as a daily reminder of her daughter's love. Yes, Yvette was quite happy with her purchase.

"All set," said Andrew as he handed her the well-packaged clock. "I hope your mother will enjoy it."

"I am certain she will," Yvette assured him. "Thank you very much!"

"Right. Are you staying for tea, then?" Andrew addressed this question to Austen.

"Yes, but I thought first I'd show Yvette about the village. That is," he looked at her, "if you'd like to see it."

"That would be splendid!"

"Good. Then we'll just put this parcel in the car and take a walk about. Thanks, Andrew. We'll see you at teatime."

"Right. But Austen, don't avoid your mother for too long. Despite her trying to rile you on the Catholic issue, she really misses you."

"Don't worry. I'll give her my proper attention." Austen opened the door for Yvette. "Cheers."

Austen placed the clock on the backseat of his sedan before walking with Yvette toward the center of the village. There were only two major streets in Castle Combe, and they intersected at the fourteenth-century Market Cross and the old water pump. Austen and Yvette passed a modest but attractive memorial to the townsmen lost in World War I. Yvette quickly counted eight names under the inscription "Lest we forget…" For a village of only fifty cottages, the cost was high. Every village in England had such a memorial, as did every college in Oxford University. It always pained Yvette to see the long lists of young men lost in both the great wars. So many bright and brave boys had been struck down. She often thought of the line from Shakespeare's *Henry V: "Here was a royal fellowship of death."* She was grateful for the freedom their sacrifice had bought, and also that professors Tolkien and Lewis had survived the horrible trenches of the First War and that her own father had served his adopted country and returned safely from the Second War. Then she remembered with another pang that Austen's father had not.

"Let's go see the church," Austen suggested, and they walked through the lych-gate into the little churchyard. "We're quite proud of St. Andrew's. It's lovely and dates back to Norman times."

The church was indeed lovely with its stone arches, white plaster walls, and dark oak hammer-beamed roof. In the nave a large glass case held an enormous mechanism. Yvette read the placard indicating that it was the fifteenth-century clock formerly used to ring the hours from the tower.

"Now that's a clock that would be hard to take home to your mother," Austen joked. "Come look at our crusader." Along the left aisle by the chancel lay the finely carved tomb of a knight in full chain armor with a dog resting at his feet.

Yvette read the date on the tomb: 1270. "My word, this is ancient and so well preserved. Why are his legs crossed?"

"That's to indicate he went on two Crusades. He's Walter de Dunstaville, a Norman and one of the first Lords of the Manor. His family owned the castle, but he wanted to be buried in the church. Medieval people believed that the closer you were buried to the chancel, the better your chances of getting into heaven. In fact, such a great number of wealthy people were buried under the flagstones that the churches started to smell. That's where we get the expression 'stinking rich.'"

Yvette laughed. "Are you serious?"

"Absolutely."

"Can we see the castle? After all, this is Castle Combe."

"Well, ironically the castle is long gone. But there is the Manor House. It was sold with the rest of the village in the forties and is now a posh hotel. We can see it, if you like."

"Sure, if it's not far and you don't mind."

"Nothing is far here and I never mind walking."

They left the church and passed the market square down a lane of quaint row houses in the now-familiar, honey-colored Cotswold stone. One, known as the Archway Cottage, stretched over the roadway like a "Bridge of Sighs."

"These are pretty!" exclaimed Yvette.

"Yes. They are more of the weavers' cottages. This was a booming weaving center in the fifteenth century. We even had our own signature red-and-white cloth known as 'Castle-combe.' But then centuries went by and we dropped into obscurity until that travel agency rediscovered us."

"It's a little like *Brigadoon*, isn't it?"

"A little, I suppose. But we're still here muddling through, not just waking up once a century. These cottages are now owned by the hotel and let out as private suites. That's kind of ironic, isn't it, when poor tradesmen lived in them for centuries?

The Manor House seems more fitting for a posh hotel since it was built for a lord—fourteenth-century ambience with twentieth-century luxury. Ah, well here is the back gate to the Manor grounds. You can get a peek."

Yvette peered through the wrought iron gate at a perfectly manicured lawn gently sloping to a sprawling and imposing stone Hall.

"It's absolutely gorgeous! Do you ever go up there?"

"Sometimes. There's a fine golf course, and since David's dad is a keen golfer, I've brought them out here on occasion." He hesitated. "This is where Marianne and I had our wedding reception."

Yvette regarded him with warm sympathy. "Really? It must have been quite delightful. Were you married here?"

"Yes, in the village church."

Yvette summoned up the courage to ask what had been plaguing her since the lunchtime exchange. "Austen, if you don't mind my asking, how is it that you're from an Anglican family, were married in an Anglican church, and yet you are a professed Roman Catholic?"

He smiled sadly. "Ah, you didn't miss my mother's dig. Well, it's really not like I had a big doctrinal break with the Church of England. She's taken my confirmation in the Catholic Church as some sort of repudiation of my family's faith, as though I've become a Muslim or Buddhist or something. The irony is that our little village church of St. Andrews was originally a Catholic church. When it was built, there was no such thing as the Church of England; not, of course, until three hundred years later under Henry VIII. Anyway, my mother blames Mr. Tolkien for my conversion and thinks he led me astray."

"Did he influence you?"

"I guess you could say that. But actually, when Marianne died, it just became too painful for me to go back to our church. Everything reminded me of her. So the Tolkiens kindly invited me to go with them, and I've found great comfort in the mass. It could be strong identification with Christ's sufferings, but I guess I'm really at heart a Pre-Raphaelite. There's something in the pageantry and ritual—the romantic mystery of the Eucharist—that appeals to me. So I converted. But I'm first and foremost a Christian. I just decided that the church where I felt most at home was the Catholic Church. That doesn't imply—like my mother fears—that I believe everyone who is not baptized as a Catholic is going to hell. I still believe it's by faith we're saved and not because of good works or the church we belong to. Frankly, I don't think God cares much about denominations. He cares what we believe about His Son. Do you know what I mean?"

"Sure, and I completely agree. You know, the funny thing is that I'm not C of E, either. My mother's Irish-Catholic. She wasn't practicing when she married my father, who has never been much of a churchgoer. But she wanted all of us to be christened and confirmed in the Catholic Church, and that was fine with him."

"I didn't realize you were baptized a Catholic," Austen said in surprise. "I thought you went to St. Aldate's and attended chapel at St. Hilda's."

"Well, I do. When I went off to university, I just followed the crowd to the Anglican services because it was easier and I found I enjoyed them. But I still attend mass too. And I agree with you—the important thing is that we have a common bond of faith, that we are 'mere Christians,' as C.S. Lewis put it. I like his analogy that 'mere Christianity' is like a large hall with doors to different rooms where we can find fellowship. It doesn't matter so much what room we choose—the Methodist room, the Anglican room, or the Catholic room—as long as we settle in one where we can minister to others and be ministered to. But the important thing is to be connected to the central hall of the Christian faith."

"Right! I like his analogy too. My problem is that my mother thinks that the hall is for Anglicans only."

They were drawing close to the Bybrook Bridge.

"Is that why you come home so seldom?"

Austen's handsome brow furrowed. "That's one reason." He kicked at some loose stones. "But more than that. It's the memories. They haunt me here. Everywhere I go, I see *her*. Everything reminds me of Marianne. Even being with Andrew. He looks like her, for goodness' sake. It's just too painful."

Yvette placed her hand lightly on his arm. "Austen, I didn't know. I'm so sorry. I wouldn't have asked to come."

"No. I should come more often. I should spend more time with them, especially Mother. And besides…" He smiled at her and her heart leapt. "Showing you about actually took my mind off Marianne. I was able to see this village through different eyes. Now don't be sorry. Let's go in and face the tigress, shall we?"

"All right. You go talk to your mother and I'll see if I can help Dianna with the tea."

"You're not afraid of her, are you?"

Yvette laughed. "No! I just think she would like to have a tête-à-tête with you. You're not afraid of her, are you?"

He smiled. "Not of her, but perhaps I am a bit afraid of a tempest brewing. I admit—I don't much enjoy conflict."

"Oh, don't fret. Most likely the only thing brewing is the tea."

"I hope you're right."

10

Sixth Week, Saturday Afternoon
Castle Combe

After Austen and Yvette entered the cottage, he helped her out of her coat and hung it on a peg behind the front door. Then he went into the parlor to talk to his mother, while Yvette headed down the hallway to the kitchen, where she found Dianna bustling about with a fussing baby on her hip. The two small boys sat at a breakfast table and were busily stuffing their chubby cheeks with scones and jelly.

"Hello there," Yvette said, announcing her arrival. "May I help you or take the baby for you?"

Dianna pushed back a stray lock of blond hair from her face with her free hand. "Oh, that would be brilliant! Here, take Michael for me. You can give him his bottle, if you don't mind. He's always hungry. Guess he takes after me." She smiled as she passed the baby to Yvette. The two young women were on eye level with one another. Yvette smiled back. They shared an immediate rapport, both sensing that given time, they could become very good friends. Dianna took the bottle from the warming pan on the stove and watched as Yvette settled easily into feeding the baby. "You're quite a natural with little ones," Dianna said approvingly.

"I have two younger brothers, so I've had some experience with babysitting."

"Are you the oldest, then?"

"No, I have two older brothers as well. I'm smack in the middle and the only girl." Yvette smiled broadly at Rob and Jack, who had jelly smeared over their faces. "I'm used to being around boys."

"Well, you're a godsend. You've been really kind about helping and you're quite welcome to come back anytime you can talk Austen into it. It's nice to have another young woman around. I'm surrounded by boys all the time. Of course, before Marianne died it was different. She and Austen came home often to see us then."

"You all must miss her very much."

"Yes, we do." Dianna paused a moment from her preparations. "Austen hasn't told you much about her, has he? Well, he's not one for talking a lot anyway. We're twins, but obviously not identical. Now, I'm a big talker. I'll bet you'd like to know more about her, wouldn't you?"

Yvette nodded.

"'Course you would. Well, Marianne was the sweetest thing on God's green earth. She was gentle and kind and never had a bad word for anyone, and she never, ever complained. Can you imagine going to hospital and having all those terrible treatments and never complaining? I can't. I complain all the time, and I have nothing to complain about! And she was very brave, leastways I thought so, even though she didn't claim to be brave. The thing was, when she took sick, she wasn't afraid of dying. She had such grace and faith. She knew for certain she would be with Jesus, and she didn't cling to this life. Except for our sakes. She knew it would be hard on all of us who loved her so—especially Austen, of course. She was sad for him and worried he would be lonely, but she wasn't sad for herself—only for us."

"It is sad," Yvette said softly, "for someone to die so young. It doesn't seem fair somehow, especially such a lovely person."

"Well, that's it. I can't help asking God 'Why?' sometimes. Why Marianne? Why not the village bum who's never done a lick of work his whole life and beats his wife? But then I think maybe the Good Lord is giving that man more time to repent and maybe He spared Marianne some worse trials or hardships on this earth. There are verses in Isaiah 57 that I've found comfort in and I think Austen has too. They say: 'Devout men are taken away, while no one understands. For the righteous man is taken away from calamity, he enters into peace.' If you could have seen the peace on her face as she left us—I'm not saying that the fight in her body wasn't a hard one—but when she let go, or maybe when *we* let *her* go…there was such peace there. It really does pass understanding."

"Still, it must be quite difficult for you, losing her like that."

"Aye, for sure. We all miss her so. And yet…" Dianna stacked scones and sandwiches on a plate as she talked. "Sometimes, when I'm missing my loved ones…Marianne, my dad, or my little baby girl whom I miscarried…and I want to get angry at God for taking them from me, I remind myself that I'm being selfish wanting them back with me. If they were given a choice to come back here with all of life's sufferings and heartache or stay enjoying all the glories of heaven, they wouldn't want to come back. And I remember what King

David said when his baby died: 'I shall go to him, but he will not return to me.' The important thing to remember is that this life is not the end, and we have eternity together to look forward to. At least, that's what I believe and it brings me comfort."

"I believe it too, although it's good to be reminded," Yvette said as she gently placed the baby on her shoulder to burp him.

"Here, let me take him now." Dianna lifted her son from Yvette's arms. "If you would take the tray in, I'd be much obliged. I'll wager Austen and Mother are ready to take their tea."

"Be glad to." Yvette began to carry the tray out.

"There's a picture of Marianne and Austen on their wedding day, if you'd like to see what she looked like. It's on the left-hand side of the hall."

"All right. Thanks."

Yvette stopped midway down the hall to view the family portrait gallery. There were several stern-faced Victorian-era family portraits and one of a young man in uniform, bearing a remarkable resemblance to Austen, who undoubtedly was Captain Holmes going off to war. There were Andrew and Dianna, handsome and happy on their wedding day, and then one of Austen and his bride. David had described Marianne like Melanie Hamilton in *Gone with the Wind*. Gazing at the photo, Yvette thought that was an apt comparison—not to the glowing-with-health beauty of Olivia de Haviland in the film, but the fragile, dark-haired, dark-eyed saint depicted by Margaret Mitchell in her book. The young couple in the photo seemed so blissfully unaware of the tragic days ahead that it pierced Yvette's heart.

She had to confess her feelings for Austen had begun to grow beyond friendship to a stronger attraction, and this day's glimpse into his family and home life had merely served to increase her affection and esteem for him. She looked again at the wedding portrait in perplexity. *How can I ever hope to compete with such a beautiful memory?*

As she paused in the hallway, she gradually became aware of Austen's and his mother's voices coming from the front parlor. She did not want to eavesdrop or interrupt and therefore hesitated indecisively.

"Now, Austen," Elinor Homes said in a lecturing tone, "it's about time you found yourself a nice young lady and got married again. It can't be good for you to live like an old bachelor when you're still so young."

"Mother…"

"I know you're going to say you haven't found anyone yet, but you really haven't given the girls in the village a chance. There's Mary Thorpe—she's a pretty girl. As is her cousin Kitty. And what about Julia Gardiner from Chippenham? She's even gone to university. And…"

"Mother, please! I don't want to talk about this."

"Austen, it's been three years. It's time you allowed someone to take Marianne's place in your life."

"Mother, no one will ever take Marianne's place." His tone was unwavering in its conviction.

Yvette felt her heart sink. *How can I compete with a memory?* She asked herself again. *I can't. Forget it, old girl. Just forget it. This man is off-limits. You keep on being his friend and don't you ever let yourself think of anything more. Not for one second. You treat him simply as a brother in Christ. That's the best thing for you and for him.*

The tea tray grew suddenly leaden and Yvette inadvertently rattled the dishes. As the voices hushed, she began walking toward the parlor. She willed a cheerful smile to spread across her face, revealing the charming gap between her teeth.

"Tea, anyone?" she asked pleasantly.

11

Seventh Week, Tuesday Evening
Oxford

*I*n a front alcove of the Eagle and Child pub, David, Austen, and Yvette feasted on fish, chips, and mushy peas while discussing their agenda for that night's meeting of The Inklings Society. Unable to stomach the grease and smell of traditional pub grub, Kate picked at her jacket potato. She knew that to keep nausea at bay she needed something in her stomach, and salty items seemed to help.

I hate feeling nauseated all the time. I wonder if I'll ever feel good again. I thought I would in the second trimester, like the books say. Her skirt felt snug and she unbuttoned the waistband under her large pullover sweater. Every evening her belly swelled uncomfortably, but the few maternity clothes she had purchased seemed to engulf her. She almost wished she could wear a sign that read, "I'm not fat; I'm pregnant." But she did love putting on David's big T-shirts over her unsnapped jeans. Somehow, wearing something of his always made her feel deliciously close to him. Subconsciously sensing her thoughts of him, David placed his hand on her knee and rubbed it gently. She dropped her hand over his and squeezed it. All the while he continued to talk as if their discreet exchanges of affection were unobserved, which, indeed, they were.

"Well then, how was your weekend?" Austen asked. "Did you make it to Cambridge?"

"We did. We stayed in a very nice B-and-B and had dinner with my friend Kevin Ryan. The Inklings Society at Cambridge is going quite well. Very exciting. Oh, you won't believe this, Austen." David leaned forward. "Kevin told me he's been writing to Ginny. And he's been seeing her when he goes up to London."

"Why wouldn't I believe that?"

"Kevin? With my sister?"

"I could see that coming a long time ago. Didn't you notice how much they were together at your wedding?"

"No. But I guess I was rather preoccupied with my bride." He patted Kate's knee. "But still—Kevin and Ginny?"

"Why not? Kevin's always loved your family. They're both believers; they're both in medicine. What could be more perfect than a doctor and nurse?"

"Well, right. And Kevin may do an internship at a teaching hospital in London. I guess I just hadn't pictured a friend of mine with one of my sisters."

"You know, David, you are rather clueless."

"I am?"

"In fact, I'd say you're a pathetic matchmaker."

Kate pushed her knee against David's and smiled knowingly at him.

"Anyway," Austen said, changing the subject, "how was the funeral? How is our Lord Devereux holding up?"

"Hmm…To be honest, I think he's having a difficult time. We invited him to come tonight, as a matter of fact. His sister asked us to look out for him. She was a very nice sort. Ironic, isn't it? I'm asked to be my rival's keeper."

"He's not your rival anymore," Kate reassured him.

"I hope he knows that. No, to be fair, I think he does. He actually tried to protect Kate from his father. Now, the old earl is a piece of work. It's no wonder Stuart has his struggles. Anyway, despite all the words we've had in the past, I can't help liking him. But you should see the guy's estate. Gorgeous grounds by Capability Brown and a huge Jacobean house—really almost a palace. A bit like the Manor House at Castle Combe but on a much grander scale. By the way, Austen, did you go home this weekend?"

"Yes, on Saturday. Yvette went with me."

Kate poked David's knee again.

"Really? Well, how did you like Castle Combe, Yvette?"

"It was charming. And Austen's brother-in-law had just the clock I've been searching for for my mother's Christmas gift. It's Wedgwood and absolutely perfect."

"That's excellent. And Austen, how's your family?"

"Good. The boys are brilliant. As are Dianna and Andrew. And Mother seems about the same."

"Did everyone get on?"

"Yes. Yvette and Di hit it off rather well. Mother was pleasant enough but had to take her usual digs at me."

"What? The Catholic controversy again or the not visiting her often enough scenario?"

"Both. And she keeps nagging me about finding a new wife. She wants me to go out with some of the local girls. Thinks they'll help me forget Marianne or something."

"Well?"

"Well, what? It's absurd! I'll never find another girl like Marianne."

This time David's knee poked Kate's, but he noted Yvette was keeping her eyes fixed on her empty plate and this tempered his triumph. "Of course not, old chap. Still, I'm glad it was a good visit all in all and that Yvette had a successful shopping trip. Speaking of trips, I thought since Kate was reading Dickens with you this term, Yvette, we should try to go to a production of *A Christmas Carol*. There's one in Stratford in a fortnight. Would you be up for it?"

"Oh, that would be delightful!" exclaimed Yvette.

"Austen?"

"Sounds brilliant."

"Good. Then you can drive. My car won't hold everyone."

"I see how it is," Austen said, chuckling. "You're only inviting me for my reliable Morris Minor."

David grinned. "Just trying to make you feel useful for something, old boy."

Since the students were beginning to arrive for the meeting, they collected their belongings and adjourned to the snug paneled room of the pub where the original Inklings met. David gave his sister Natalie an affectionate hug before seating her with Kate. As he and Austen chatted with some students, he watched Stuart come in with Nigel Elliot. Stuart nodded his greetings and headed to the bar to pick up a pint before insinuating himself at Kate and Natalie's little round table.

"Hello, ladies. May I join you?" His usual dapper appearance was marred by deep rings under his eyes.

"Sure," Kate answered. "I'm glad you made it tonight, Stuart. How are you doing?"

"All right, I suppose. I say, Kate, that was quite nice of you and David to come to the funeral. That meant a lot to me."

"We were glad to be able to."

"I hope it wasn't too difficult for you—in your condition, I mean."

Kate blushed. "I was fine."

"Did you make it to Cambridge?"

"Yes, and we had a good visit with David's college roommate."

"Excellent." This last remark of Stuart's was whispered as David and Austen had called for the meeting to begin. Their discussion that evening was on *The Screwtape Letters,* and although Stuart did not contribute anything, he appeared to listen closely. When the meeting drew to a close, he turned to Natalie.

"I must confess that I haven't read *Screwtape* yet. But it sounds rather interesting and now I'm inspired to give it a go. Miss MacKenzie, may I walk you home? Since St. Aldate's is across from Christ Church, we're practically next-door neighbors, you know."

Natalie hesitated.

"Don't worry. I won't bite. Look, I've only had one pint, and I promise I'll be quite well-behaved. Besides, Nigel will walk with us."

Natalie relented. "All right." They said their goodbyes. Touching her fingers to her lips, Natalie waved to David, who, although engrossed in conversation with one of the students, acknowledged her with a smile and a nod.

They stepped out into the chilled night air and walked towards Cornmarket Street. Natalie wrapped her coat more tightly around her as she braced against the wind.

"Nigel," she asked. "Are you and Kate's friend Connie still together?"

Nigel flashed a toothy smile. "Indeed we are, although it's a bit challenging keeping up a correspondence across the pond. Still, if your brother and Kate could do it, I suppose we can."

"Did you get over to the States this summer?"

"I did. I stayed with Connie's family in Bethesda for a fortnight—you know, in Maryland, right outside Washington, D.C.—so I was able to do quite a bit of sightseeing. And then we headed down south to Richmond for the Hughes–MacKenzie nuptial celebrations. It was quite fun, actually. But it may be next spring or summer before either of us can make the trip again."

"That's a long time to wait."

"It is, but I think it will be a good indication whether or not we can go the distance." They had reached the intersection with Broad Street. "Look, I'm so sorry, but I need to cut out here. I've got to get over to the Bod before closing time. I'll see you later, Stu. Natalie, cheers."

"Cheers." Natalie and Stuart called after Nigel.

As they crossed the street and headed down Cornmarket, Stuart smiled sheepishly. "Sorry. I really thought he was going all the way back with us. Hope you don't mind. I'll be on my best behavior. Well, Natalie, how have you been enjoying your first term at Oxford?"

"I've really liked it. It's definitely more demanding than London, but thus far I think I'm handling it all right. I have good tutors."

"What are you reading?"

"Psychology. I enjoy children and figure that I can either teach or work in counseling. That is, before I have children of my own."

"Then you'll psychoanalyze them?"

She laughed. "Right." She grew more sober. "Stuart, I'm really sorry about your mother."

"Thanks." He shrugged. "It was awfully nice of your brother and Kate to come to the funeral. That meant a lot to me."

"Well, I know it sounds like a cliché—but if we can do anything to help, we'd be happy to. I can't imagine what it would be like to lose my mum. It would be horrible."

"Hmm. Quite. I must confess, though, I was never close to my mother the way you are to yours. My parents followed the typical upper-class pattern of giving us a nanny and sending us off to boarding school as soon as we could talk—handing us blithely over to some sadistic schoolmaster. It's all rather ghastly." He sighed deeply. "Sometimes I wonder why we English do that to our children."

"Because we've always…"

"…done it this way." Stuart said, finishing the sentence with her. "Anyway, you're lucky to have such a lovely American mother. And your father seems great too…" He grinned. "For a Scotsman. Really, Natalie, I do envy you MacKenzies and your family. I have the highest respect for your brother, even though he's tried to set me to rights a few times. By the way, have you heard him lecture yet?"

"No, I haven't."

"You're not serious? You really should go sometime. He's probably one of the finest in the University. I had to change from English to econ, but I still love to attend his lectures. He's absolutely outstanding."

"Really? It's hard to think of my own brother like that. I mean, I look up to him and all—but as my big brother, not as a don. I will try to go; I'm sure it would please him." They had reached the rectory. "Well, goodnight then, Stuart. And thanks for the escort."

"Natalie, would you like to do something with me on Thursday night?"

"This Thursday?" She grimaced. "Um—sorry, but Thursday is Thanksgiving."

"Thanksgiving?"

"Oh, right. We celebrate the American Thanksgiving. Every year my mum makes a big feast for all the American students."

"Right. I remember Kate talking about that last year. Then, how about Friday or Saturday?"

"No, I'm sorry, but we make the whole weekend a family holiday. My sister Ginny is coming home, and David and Kate will even stay over."

"That sounds nice. So when may I see you again?" His tone was polite but persistent.

Natalie smiled sweetly. "How about at church?"

He laughed. "All right. You win. I'll see you Sunday."

12

Eighth Week, Friday

"Do you think they'll get there in time for Christmas?" Kate anxiously asked the shopkeeper as she wrote gift cards for her family and matched them to the merchandise piled on the store counter.

"Don't you worry, miss." The gentleman's bright blue eyes smiled kindly at her. "We'll wrap these up for you and post them tomorrow. They'll get there, all right, and I'm sure your family will be pleased as punch, seeing as you can't be there yourself."

"Yes, I hope so. This will be my first Christmas away from home, Mr. Kay." Kate checked the pile again. A pretty Shetland wool cardigan for her mother; a Magdalen College jacket for her father; Oxford sweatshirts and hats for her siblings Debbie, Scott, and Tim. And then some added surprises for Timmy: a little coin bank in the shape of a bright red double-decker bus and a set of tin soldiers clad like the Queen's Guard with their tall fur helmets. Timmy had Down's syndrome, and of all her family, she would miss him the most. His joy at Christmas was infectious, especially in his eagerness to pass out gifts to others. Kate wished she could be there when he opened his presents. She could just picture his round face spread with innocent joy and see the delight in his almond-shaped eyes.

"Aye, it's a hard thing to be away from your loved ones at Christmas. But you are lucky to have such a wonderful new family here in Oxford," Mr. Kay said as he rang up the sale.

"You're right. I am. And just last week I celebrated Thanksgiving with them. Mrs. MacKenzie is American, you know, and each year she has a big turkey dinner for all the American students. It helps all of us with our homesickness, I think."

"Aye, to be sure." Mr. Kay smiled. "Will there be anything else, miss?"

"No, thank you. That will be all. No, wait!" Kate snatched a Cadbury chocolate bar from a box by the register. "I'll take this too." She paid for her purchases, and stepping out onto Broad Street called, "Goodnight, Mr. Kay! Thanks!"

In truth, it was just after four-thirty, but the December sky had already darkened into early evening. Kate had found these premature winter nights in England depressing. She now understood why the Brits took tea at this hour. Dusk brought thoughts of dinner. She unwrapped the candy bar and bit off a wedge, letting the dark chocolate sit on the edge of her tongue where she could savor it. She felt much like a smoker, desperate for a cigarette, as the chocolate flavor comforted her. With all the queasiness she had experienced, she hadn't needed to worry about gaining too much weight, and chocolate was an indulgence she could allow herself.

Although the nausea and fatigue served as a constant reminder, she was still unused to the thought that she could actually be expecting a baby. In the deepest corner of her heart, she did not want to be. But she would never admit it to anyone, especially David. A part of her resented the pregnancy; simultaneously, she was horrified at her resentment and vulnerable to waves of guilt. Surely the baby didn't merit this vexation. *It's not the baby's fault. But sometimes I can't even fathom that there really is a baby.* Her reproachful thoughts, her homesickness for her family, and her dread of the early sunsets all threatened at times to overwhelm her with depression.

As she let the chocolate melt on her tongue, she glanced up. Near the circle marking where the Protestant martyrs Latimer, Ridley, and Cranmer had been burned at the stake towered a magnificent evergreen strung with brightly colored lights. The festive tree, like the chocolate, buoyed her spirits, just as the Christmas lights festooned along Cornmarket and the High Street did whenever she passed them. She enjoyed another piece of chocolate as she hurried toward Turl Street and Exeter College, where she was to meet David.

He was waiting for her at the Porters' Lodge, and she watched his eyes brighten with pleased recognition. He hugged her tightly. "Hello there, my darling. Did you get your shopping done?"

"Yes. And Mr. Kay is going to wrap everything and mail it for me tomorrow."

"Excellent! You must be feeling good about having that behind you. And your essays are all in. Now you can relax a bit and enjoy the holidays."

"I hope so. How about you?"

"Still a lot of work left, but I'm doing all right. Let's go in and get a seat. Austen and Yvette are already here. How are you feeling? Can you make it until dinner?"

She held up the half-eaten candy bar and nodded. He smiled. "Chocolate always works."

They passed through the entrance gate of Exeter College into the front quad and then to the Chapel, where the college choir was giving a special carol service. Austen and Yvette greeted them. Because they had arrived early, they were instructed to sit in the rows of chairs lining the chancel. All four friends were grateful for a few moments of reflection and prayer to the accompaniment of a quiet organ prelude.

Kate especially liked the splendid Chapel at Exeter. By design it reflected that perfect architectural gem, Sainte-Chapelle in Paris. Although not as breathtaking or grand, Exeter's Chapel was nevertheless quite beautiful, and there was something almost quintessentially British in its cozy size. She bowed her head and offered thanks for completing all her schoolwork and prayed for David to be given strength and time to finish his. She also prayed for the baby and that God would grant her the grace to accept this pregnancy with joy as a gift from Him.

Then the choristers filed in, lit their candles, and stood to sing. What glorious music poured forth! Traditional English carols and intricate Renaissance madrigals mingled with the Scripture readings, proclaiming the joyful news of God's Love coming to earth as a little babe. The songs stirred their hearts and sent them soaring heavenward. When the choirmaster invited the congregation to join them with, "O Come, All Ye Faithful," Kate's soprano, Yvette's contralto, Austen's tenor, and David's baritone blended with the happy chorus. As the organ swelled in a rapturous postlude, the four friends followed the throng out of the church. All had been awestruck.

"That was tremendous!" Austen exclaimed.

"Amazing," agreed Yvette. "What a great way to start the Christmas season. What did you think, Kate?"

"It was wonderful! The acoustics in there are incredible, and the conductor did such a great job with the choir. I just love Renaissance music! I didn't hear it much in the States, except when I sang in a madrigals group, so that was a special treat."

They stopped while David introduced them to a young don and his wife. The tutor held a chubby-cheeked infant, dressed head to foot in a jaunty St. Nicholas outfit.

"May I hold him?" David asked and then held out his hands. The baby took one look at him and dove straight into his arms. David lifted him high and then swooped him around until he chuckled with glee.

"You're a natural, MacKenzie," the young father complimented. "You should have children of your own."

David beamed. "I will. Kate here is due in May."

"Congratulations, old boy!" He clapped David on the back. "I'll bet you're thrilled."

"I am. I love kids and can't wait to have them. Your own wee laddie is a real charmer." He reluctantly handed him back. "Cheers."

Kate smiled at David's evident delight in the baby. The jolly little Santa was undeniably cute with his fat ruddy cheeks and dimples. She wondered if their baby would be as adorable.

"Right," David said, turning back to his friends. "Anyone hungry?"

"Famished," answered Austen. "Where do you want to eat?"

"How about the Mitre? It's right up the street and the end of term deserves a little celebratory splurge."

"Sounds good to me. Yvette?"

"Let's go," she agreed.

They quickly settled in the elegant paneled dining room of the inn and perused the menu.

"Everybody heading home for the holidays?" David asked.

"I'll stick around here for a bit to finish up some work and then go stay with my sister for a few days over Christmas," Austen replied.

"Ditto," added Yvette. "Except I'll be in London for Christmas. What about you two?"

"I've got some work to finish up as well and a book signing at Blackwell's tomorrow. Although I don't know how many people will want to buy a literary criticism of Herbert and Donne for a holiday gift."

"It's a student's guide, isn't it?" Yvette asked. "Good thing you're having the signing tomorrow before they all leave for the holidays."

"I'll come round and buy a copy for my mum," Austen said. "She likes poetry and she'll be thrilled to have a signed book." He laughed. "Thanks, David. I was really scratching my head about a gift for her. Especially since Yvette went all out for her mother with that clock."

"She's going to love it," Yvette enthused. "I can't wait to give it to her." She turned to Kate. "Have you started packing for Paris yet? I'll bet you're getting excited."

"Honestly, I haven't had much time to think about it— what with not feeling too great and having to get all my essays done. But once we get through the holidays, we'll start packing and—"

Some raucous laughter and shouts from the bar interrupted Kate's train of conversation and the refined quietude of the restaurant. David and Austen exchanged glances. Austen nodded and the two young men rose.

"Excuse us, ladies, for a moment," David said. "Sounds like some lads are overly zealous in their celebrations. We'll just go check things out."

When they entered the bar area, the crowd of students milling about quieted quickly, but they heard the voice of Stuart Devereux roaring above the buzz. "You can't tell me to leave! Do you know who I am? I have just as much right as anyone to enjoy some holiday cheer."

As Stuart berated a red-faced barkeep, David jostled his way toward him and placed a restraining hand on his arm. "Hello, Stuart," he said calmly. "What seems to be the problem here?"

Through his stupor Stuart smiled at David. "Hullo, Mr. MacKenzie! My old mate! You were such a good chap to come to my mum's funeral. And your gorgeous wife. Dear sweet Katie...Your sister, Natalie, is a lovely girl too. A lovely girl. You know, I missed church on Sunday. Overslept. Pity. She's a lovely girl. Here, come have a drink on me. We'll drink to gorgeous Kate and lovely Natalie."

"No thanks, Stuart." David nodded reassuringly to the exasperated barkeep, who had vainly been trying to maintain some order. "Listen here, old chap. I'm going to walk you home now."

"I don't want to go home," Stuart protested. "Why should I go—just because this little bugger wants me to? Why..."

David put his arm around him. "Stuart," he said quietly, "you need to go home with me now or else the coppers will be taking you home. Do you understand?"

"The coppers? No, we don't want the coppers. Right. You take me home, Mr. MacKenzie."

David spoke above the crowd. "I'm taking Lord Devereux back to the House. If you lads want to stay here, you need to pipe down a bit and not disturb the other patrons. Otherwise, you'll need to be moving along. Understood?"

The students grunted their assent.

"Right, then." David coaxed Stuart toward the door and spoke to Austen. "I'll just take him down the road. Should be back in a jiffy."

"Shall I come with you?" Austen asked.

"No, no. We'll be fine. Just let Kate know and go ahead and order lamb for me. I'll jog back and be here before the food is served."

"In two shakes of a lamb's tail, eh?" Austen grinned.

"Ha, ha. That's right. I'll see you in a few minutes. Come on, Stuart." David firmly led the inebriated Lord Devereux out to the High Street, got him safely across, and took him down the narrow lanes of Alfred and Blue Boar Streets and along the walls of Christ Church.

"Oh, are we going to the Blue Boar, then?" Stuart asked.

"No. We're not stopping at the Blue Boar. You've had enough celebrating tonight. You are going back to your room and I am going back to the Mitre for my dinner."

"I'm drunk, aren't I?"

"Yes, Stuart, you are quite drunk. Are you going home tomorrow?"

"Home?"

"Right. Are you going home for the holidays?"

Stuart snorted. "Home? No, no. Can't face it."

"Where are you spending Christmas? You're not staying here, are you?"

"Christmas? Oh, right. Christmas. I'm going to Clemmie's. Christmas at Clemmie's. Has a nice ring to it, eh? Christmas at Clemmie's. Clemmie's for Christmas." Stuart stumbled and David caught his arm to steady him.

"Easy, old boy. We're almost there. Is the back gate open?"

"No. No, all locked up. Have to go to Old Tom."

"Right. Come on, then. Stuart, I'd like to come by to see you tomorrow before you leave for Clemmie's. Will that be all right?"

"Come see me?"

"Yes. Look, I'll be at Blackwell's in the morning, but tomorrow afternoon after you've slept this off, I'll come by your rooms. All right? I'd like to talk to you."

"Uh-oh. Stuart's been a naughty boy, hasn't he, Mr. MacKenzie. You aren't going to have me sent down, are you?"

"No, Stuart, nothing like that. I'd just like to talk to you. Now, here we are." They walked through the imposing stone portico of Tom Tower with its coats of arms emblazoned on the bosses above. David helped Stuart up the steps into the Porters' Lodge and read the name badge of the porter on duty.

"Good evening, George. I'm Mr. MacKenzie, a Fellow of Magdalen. I ran into Lord Devereux up at the Mitre and thought it best to bring him back here before things got out of hand. Would you please see to it that he gets to his room?"

"Right you are, Mr. MacKenzie." The porter stepped around the wooden counter and took Stuart's arm. "Come along, my lord. I'll see you put to rights."

"And George," David added, "would you have someone check up on him around noon tomorrow and remind him he has an appointment with Mr. MacKenzie here at two o'clock? I'll leave a note at the desk for you as a reminder."

"No problem, Mr. Mackenzie. I'll make sure he's up and remembers."

Stuart looked sheepishly at David. "Thanks for seeing me back. If you wouldn't mention this little episode to Natalie, I'd be grateful. I'll do my best to see you tomorrow. Cheers."

"Goodnight, Stuart," David answered. "Try to get some sleep."

13

Eighth Week, Saturday

Nigel Elliot smiled broadly as he examined the slim hardback volume of David's first scholarly publication. "Congratulations, Mr. MacKenzie. This looks excellent."

David, sitting with Kate at a small table in Blackwell's, smiled in return. "Thank you, Nigel."

"How's business been?"

"Better since you arrived. No, really, not nearly as bad as I expected. I asked Kate to come so if no one bought any books, I'd at least have my pretty bride to keep me company."

"He's done great," Kate said, rushing to his defense. "A lot of his students have come in, and some I think are buying them as gifts for their parents too."

"Well, I'll add to your quota," said Nigel, amiably. "I'd like for you to sign one for me and one for Connie. I'll post it to her for Christmas."

Kate was pleased. "Oh, Nigel, that's really nice of you. She'll like that."

"You can tell her it's a contribution to our baby fund." David opened a volume to the title page and wrote a message to Kate's friend.

"David!" Kate blushed.

"It's true." David insisted proudly.

"*Further Up, Further In: Everyman's Guide to Donne and Herbert*," Nigel read the title aloud. "Isn't 'further up, further in' taken from The Chronicles of Narnia?"

"Right you are," David praised his student. "It's from *The Last Battle.* I wanted to give Lewis some credit since he taught me everything I know about Donne and Herbert." David signed the second book and handed them both to Nigel. "Thank you, Nigel. I hope you'll enjoy it."

"Well, I'm hoping this will give me an edge since I'm reading Renaissance poets next term—wish it were with you, though."

David laughed. "Still, it shouldn't hurt." His face suddenly sobered with thought and he spoke quietly. "I say, Nigel, did you know that Stuart got rather tanked last night at the Mitre and I had to take him back to the House?"

"No, sir. I didn't. I haven't seen Stuart this morning. But it wouldn't surprise me. He's probably sleeping it off now."

"Right," David replied. "I'm really rather concerned about Stuart and his drinking. I thought I'd try to talk to him about it this afternoon before he goes off on holiday."

Nigel sighed. "You know, I'm concerned too, Mr. MacKenzie, but whenever I've tried to broach the subject, he…well…he hasn't taken it very kindly."

"Would you be willing to come with me to give it another go? I've been thinking that if perhaps the charge came from more than one source, he wouldn't be able to dismiss it quite so easily. And you know that Jesus sent the disciples out two by two."

"What about Kate? She knows about Stuart's little problem."

David placed his hand protectively over Kate's. "No. I don't want her involved in this. She's suffered enough from his excesses."

"Right. I'm sorry to have suggested it. But, Mr. MacKenzie, you aren't thinking of having him sent down, are you?"

"No, but I do want to give him a warning. If he doesn't straighten up, he could be sent down. Anyway, I think he needs help, and he won't get it without a little pressure."

"So what's your plan, sir?" Nigel glanced back at several students who were queuing up behind him.

"I left a message that I'd like an interview with Stuart at two o'clock. Could you meet me at the Porters' Lodge a few minutes before the hour?"

"I'll be there, Mr. MacKenzie," Nigel pledged solemnly. "And Kate, you'd best be praying."

⚬

Just as Old Tom tolled the hour of two, David and Nigel rapped lightly on the outer door of Stuart's set of rooms. After a few moments, Stuart appeared, disheveled and haggard.

"Mr...David...and Nigel...what the...?" Stuart squinted in the bright light. "Sorry," he mumbled. "Come in."

They followed him into his darkened rooms. "Sit down. Please," Stuart said as he lowered himself carefully into a wing chair. "Sorry. Things are a bit of a mess. I overslept. Would you like some tea?"

"I'll make tea," Nigel volunteered, anxious for any occupation.

"Thanks, Nigel. Well, Mr...er...David..." Stuart made an effort to sit up straight. "If this is about last night...I'm sorry…I got a bit carried away I guess. But…uh…thank you for…uh…seeing me back."

"So, Stuart," David's voice was gentle. "You do remember what happened last night?"

"Oh, certainly! I got a little rowdy at the Mitre and you walked me home. That was all, wasn't it? I was just having some fun." A look of fear crossed Stuart's face. "You haven't reported me, have you, sir?"

David ignored the question. "Stuart, you know this isn't the first time I've had to intervene when you've had too much to drink."

"Right. I know, sir. The Blenheim Ball last year. I haven't forgotten."

"And Eights at the Head of the River."

"Ah—right. Both celebrations, though. I love to celebrate," Stuart said, laughing lamely.

"And my wife had another unfortunate run-in with you at your house party last year after term," David persisted with steel in his voice.

Stuart sighed. "Right again. I am so sorry. I've said so on numerous occasions."

"I'm not asking for apologies here. I'm just pointing out a pattern of your drinking to excess and getting into trouble or hurting other people. These are just instances that have involved me or Kate. I'm sure other people can attest to more."

David glanced at Nigel, who handed them each a cup of tea.

"That's right, old boy." Nigel spoke up. "You know I've mentioned this to you before."

Stuart set his cup down. "Nigel!"

Nigel shrugged apologetically. "Sorry, Stu. But it's true. I've been worried about your drinking and have told you so."

Stuart mustered up some of his cavalier charm. "I say, chaps, you're taking this much too seriously. Yes, I knock down a few once in a while and I may get a bit rowdy, but it's nothing to get your knickers in a twist about."

"It's where this could lead, Stuart, that has us really concerned." David spoke softly but firmly. "You said yourself that your mother had a problem."

Stuart clenched his fists and stood. "You leave my mother out of this!"

"Stuart," David replied calmly, "I'm not criticizing your mother. I just want to remind you of what you already know. Her dependence on alcohol led either directly or indirectly to her untimely death. We're worried that you're heading down the same path, which could be quite detrimental to your health and well-being—not to mention the well-being of others who care about you."

Stuart edged toward the door as if he were contemplating an escape, but David had strategically placed his chair to block such an easy exit. "Oh," Stuart accused them, "you two are just after me because you're Christians and don't approve of drinking."

"Stuart, we have no quarrel with enjoying the fruit of the vine in moderation. The issue we're concerned about is that of excess—specifically, your excesses."

"I say, fellows, I know I get carried away now and then, but I'm just having a bit of fun. I wouldn't call it 'excess.' I have it all under control."

"Stuart," Nigel spoke nervously but with conviction, "you know that's not true. Besides the episodes Mr. MacKenzie is aware of, I've had to get you home from pubs numerous times because you could hardly walk, and sometimes you've just missed getting picked up by the coppers when you were out clubbing. And then there were the times you barely got your essays done because you came home in the small hours nearly paralytic. You know Colin and I've talked to you before because we were worried you might get sent down."

Stuart turned on his friend. "Nigel, why don't you just shut up?"

Nigel held his tongue, but David spoke next. "Stuart, it's not just your friends who are worried. Your sister is too."

"Clemmie?" Stuart laughed his short, barking laugh. "How the devil would you have any idea what Clemmie thinks?"

"Because she talked to me at the funeral and told me so. She asked me to look out for you. And here..." David took a letter from his jacket pocket. "She wrote this to me and I think you should read it."

Stuart reluctantly took the stationery he recognized as his sister's and unfolded it slowly as if in a state of shock. For a few moments, only the ticking of a clock could be heard in the room.

Suddenly a sob from Stuart rent the stillness.

"Oh no," he moaned, putting his head in his hands. "Clemmie! What can I do?"

David knew not to hesitate and lose this advantage. "This problem is really not something you can overcome on your own. There are other people with similar struggles who meet for help and support. As a matter of fact, right across the street at St. Aldate's we have a group that meets several times a week."

Stuart looked up suddenly. "Are you talking about that group called 'AA'?"

"Yes. We call it an 'Overcomers' meeting, but essentially the group follows the AA twelve-step program for recovery from any number of addictions."

"Do you think for one minute, that *I*—Lord Stuart Devereux, a viscount and the son and heir of the Earl of Essex—could show my face in such a meeting?" Stuart's voice had risen. "It would disgrace my family!"

David kept his tone calm. "If you continue on your present course, you will most certainly disgrace them. Besides, Stuart, no one would know who you are. You don't give your full name and rank. Your station and name are kept entirely confidential and anonymous. That's why it's called 'AA'—Alcoholics *Anonymous*."

He shook his head. "No. I won't do it. I won't go to such a meeting. I'll just stop drinking on my own, that's all."

"Stuart, believe me. This is not something you can conquer by yourself. And if you don't get help, then I will be forced to make sure you do."

"What do you mean by that?"

David leaned forward. "So far I've kept this just among ourselves. However, if you don't promise to attend AA meetings and stick to that promise, then I will have no choice but to talk to your Dean and have you gated. And if that restriction doesn't rein you in, then you will be looking at being sent down."

Stuart glared at David. "Why do you hate me? Is it because of Kate?"

"I don't hate you." David replied intensely. "And it's partly because of Kate that I even care about you. She had the grace to forgive you and now I have too. I just want you to get the help you need before something worse happens. I think you know me well enough to trust that I mean what I say. If you persist in refusing to get help and continue this abuse of alcohol, I will bring the college down on your head."

Stuart collapsed with resignation into a chair. "You don't give me a choice." When David did not reply, Stuart reached for a packet of cigarettes and lit one with trembling hands. "When are these meetings you want me to go to?"

David visibly relaxed. "We have several ongoing at different times during the day or evening. You can pick up a list tomorrow if you come to church."

The mention of church brought Stuart up short. "You're not going to tell Natalie about this, are you?"

"No," David answered mildly. "Remember, the meetings are anonymous. Natalie won't know anything unless you tell her yourself. But it would be helpful if you could attend some meetings before you go on holiday. How much longer are you going to be in town?"

"I'm not sure. I thought I'd stick around another week or so."

"Good. Then you can come to church and attend some meetings as well." David glanced at Nigel, who had been following this exchange closely.

"That's right, Stu," Nigel said. "I'm planning to go to the morning service tomorrow, and you can come with me and stay for the student luncheon after. How does that sound?"

"Fine." Stuart sighed. "I'm sorry—both of you—for the things I said."

"Don't mention it, old boy." Nigel smiled kindly. "You've had a rough go of it lately. But I'm glad you're willing to try to set things right."

David stood up. "Well, Stuart, thanks for hearing us out. I'll see you tomorrow, then?"

Stuart did not rise with his companions, but he nodded his acquiescence.

14

Tenth Week, Monday
December 13

Stuart Devereux honored his word by beginning to attend St. Aldate's anonymous recovery meetings and faithfully appearing at Sunday services. In truth, he was mortified by the thought that David would follow through on his disciplinary threats. He also felt ashamed to face his sister Clementine before he could give her some assurances that he had taken steps to amend his ways. But there was even more to it than that. With many of his friends off on holiday and his own family torn apart by tragedy, he longed for sympathetic fellowship. In short, Lord Stuart, Viscount Devereux, was lonely. And for that reason, after he left the small company in the Oak Room at St. Aldate's and had stepped out into the dark December night alone, he wandered down the narrow way of Pembroke Street to the brightly lit rectory home of the MacKenzie family.

❧

"That was fabulous, Mum," David said, leaning back contentedly from the table. "Thanks so much."

His mother smiled. "I'm glad you enjoyed it, honey." Because lavish gifts were out of the question in this frugal household, Annie celebrated her children's birthdays with their favorite meals.

The rest of the MacKenzie clan concurred. David's twenty-fifth birthday dinner of roast beef with all the trimmings had left them all satisfied. And they were a large group to keep happy: three girls, four boys. As the oldest, David was undeniably idolized by his younger siblings.

Sixteen-year-old William cleared his throat to venture a question. "I say, David, do you think that since you're twenty-five and married now I might be able to have your old room in the garret?"

David laughed. "I see how it is. So you think I'm too old to climb the stairs?"

"No, no. It's just that at Thanksgiving you stayed with Kate in the guest bedroom, and I thought perhaps—if you don't mind, that is—I could move upstairs and then Richard and Mark could each have their own rooms."

"Of course, old boy! I was just jesting with you. I'm sorry I didn't think of it before. But you're right. I shan't want to be up there alone anymore. You can just box up my trophies and it's all yours."

Richard and Mark nudged each other while William beamed. "Thanks! But I should like to keep the trophies out, if I may."

"Sure you may—as long as you dust them now and then so that Mum doesn't have to go up there. Say, Ginny, you're not planning to move out permanently to give Natalie her own room, are you?"

His slender fair-haired sister looked askance at him. "Why would I go and do that? Besides, Nat has it all to herself most of the time anyway."

"I heard rumors that you are being courted by a bandy-legged Irishman," David teased, "and I was just checking that things aren't more serious than I supposed."

A flush of crimson crept up Ginny's neck into her cheeks.

"What Irishman?" the boys asked, eager to have a new source of torment for their older sister.

Natalie smiled. "I know."

"Nat!" Ginny protested.

"Who? Who?" the boys chorused.

"I know!" Little Hannah, all of four years old, announced to everyone's amazement. "It's Uncle Kevin!"

"How did you know that, Hannah?" Ginny asked in surprise.

"Ha!" Mark crowed. "You've admitted it! It's David's mate Kevin Ryan."

Ginny blushed again. "How could she know that? We're just writing to each other."

This time their father, the Reverend Eric MacKenzie, spoke up rather sheepishly. "Sorry, Ginny. She must have overheard your mother and me talking about it. Kevin wrote us to ask permission to court you—which we really appreciated him doing, by the way. Very cricket of him."

Hannah slipped out of her seat at the table and clambered up into her oldest brother's lap. "Can I help blow out your candles, David?"

"Sure you may, pumpkin." Smoothing out her tousled blond curls, David planted a kiss on her chubby cheek. "I'm getting so old, I'll need your help. A quarter of a century!"

Annie stood up, "I guess that means I should get the cake ready."

"Would you like a hand?" Kate volunteered.

"No, thanks, Kate. You stay put and keep that birthday boy of yours happy."

"Mum," David said, "don't forget I've invited Austen and Yvette to come by for cake. Perhaps we should wait until they get here."

"Oh, no!" groaned Mark. "That'll mean there won't be enough cake."

"Now, don't be selfish, Mark," Annie chided. "It's David's birthday and he can invite whom he likes. Anyway, I made two cakes, so there'll be enough for everyone. Girls, why don't you clear the table while I make some coffee and we wait for Austen and Yvette?"

Natalie and Ginny quickly complied while the boys talked of football. The doorbell interrupted their conversation.

"That's Austen and Yvette now." David tried unsuccessfully to dislodge Hannah from his lap.

"I'll get it," Richard volunteered. A few moments later, he returned alone to the dining room. "Um…David, it's Lord Stuart Devereux. Shall I show him in?"

David shot a questioning glance to Natalie, who was stacking plates. She shook her head and shrugged. "I'll go," David answered. He carried Hannah with him to the foyer, where he gently put her down before extending his hand to Stuart.

"Hello, Stuart. How are you? You're just in time to help me celebrate my birthday. Come on in."

Stuart shifted uncomfortably. "I'm so sorry to barge in on you like this. I was just over at the church for a meeting and found myself here, but I don't want to interrupt anything. I really shouldn't stay."

"Nonsense. I'm glad you made it to the meeting, and now that you're here, you should be rewarded with a bit of cake. Let me take your coat."

Hesitating, Stuart gazed down at the angelic vision of Hannah, who smiled coyly at him and bent her plump legs into a curtsey.

"Hello, little lady," he said with a slight bow.

"Hello, my lord," Hannah chirped. "Would you like some cake?"

"Well, I believe I would, thank you."

The doorbell rang again. This time it was the expected guests. Welcoming his friends, David brought all the company into the dining room, where he presented them to his family. William and Richard carried in extra chairs, and soon everyone was chatting around the large mahogany table.

A boisterous chorus of "Happy Birthday" broke out when Annie carried in a cake bristling with lighted candles. Puffing out her cheeks, Hannah blew with David and clapped her hands excitedly as the last flame faded to smoke.

"Oh my goodness!" Kate exclaimed clutching her stomach and suddenly silencing the clamor at the table. "I think the baby just kicked...it did...there it is again!" Taking David's hand in her own, Kate placed it on her slightly rounded belly. Everyone watched her expectantly. "There! Did you feel it?"

A grin spread over David's face. "Yes! I did!" He waited another minute. "He must have gone back to sleep. He just wanted to say 'happy birthday' to his old man." David leaned over the top of Hannah's head and tenderly kissed Kate's flushed cheek. "Thank you. That was the best birthday present ever."

Kate squeezed his hand and smiled. "I'm glad today was the first time we could feel the baby move. But you said 'he,' and the baby might be a 'she,' you know."

"Even better then," David replied happily giving Kate another kiss and Hannah one as well. "I've always been partial to girls."

As Annie busily sliced and served the cake to the noisy gathering, David's father slipped his arm around her waist and placed his cheek next to hers. "Look at this lot, Annie," he whispered. "Can you believe it? It seems like yesterday David was a wee bairn and now he's twenty-five and expecting his own wee one. Who would have thought we'd be so blessed with all these beautiful children? Thank you so much, my love."

Annie stopped serving, closed her eyes, and nestled contentedly into the arms of her husband, who then pressed his lips against her cheek.

"Ooh, Mummy and Daddy are getting all mushy!" cried Mark to general laughter.

"Pshaw," Eric rejoined amiably. "You're just jealous. You eat up your cake and there'll be plenty of kisses for you from Mummy at bedtime."

Mark spoke not in jealousy but in juvenile jest. However, jealousy was not absent from others at the gathering who had observed the affectionate exchanges between husbands and wives. Austen felt keenly the absence of Marianne. Yvette yearned to be surrounded by her own loving husband and children. Stuart ached with the awareness that this was the happy home he had always longed for. But all were quickly caught up again in the hilarity of the festivities. The poignant moment passed—but its memory lingered long in their hearts over the Christmas holidays.

Map of Paris

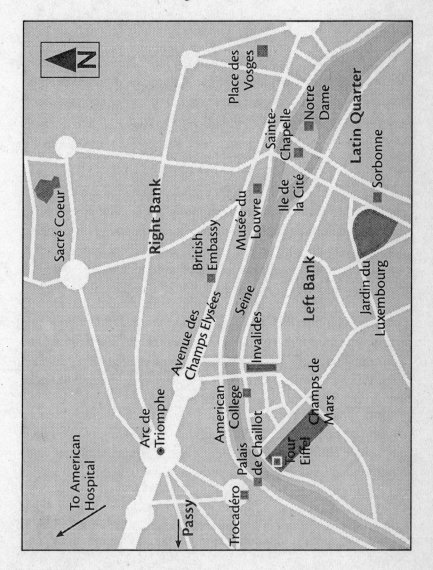

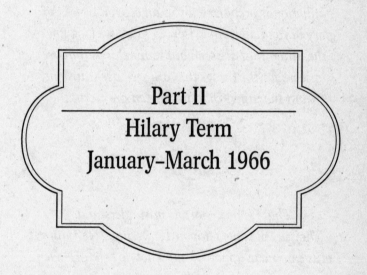

Part II
Hilary Term
January–March 1966

So we do not lose heart...For this slight momentary affliction is preparing for us an eternal weight of glory beyond all comparison, because we look not to the things that are seen but to the things that are unseen; for the things that are seen are transient, but the things that are unseen are eternal.

—2 CORINTHIANS 4:16-18

That is what mortals misunderstand. They say of some temporal suffering, "No future bliss can make up for it," not knowing that Heaven, once attained, will work backward and turn even that agony into a glory.

—C.S. LEWIS

from *The Great Divorce*, chapter 9

15

Nought Week
Oxford

The gentle hum of conversation accented by the occasional clink of a glass or teacup wove a comforting melody of communal camaraderie around Austen. He was sitting in a plush Wedgwood blue wing chair surrounded by the warm, elegantly carved oak-paneled walls of the Senior Common Room of Merton College. Austen had chosen to read among his colleagues on this preterm winter day because he could not endure the crushing loneliness of his empty college rooms. Although he appeared absorbed in his book, in reality his mind dwelt on the Christmas holidays and their ambivalent memories. The happy times with his family juxtaposed sharply with his aching sense of loss and his yearning for companionship. Missing the comradeship of his friend David and—had he dared to admit it—Yvette, Austen had returned to Oxford after the holidays as quickly as he could without distressing his mother.

A nudge on his shoe interrupted his reverie. He glanced up to see David grinning broadly.

"Hey, old chap, can't you get your nose out of a book long enough to say goodbye to an old friend?"

Austen stood smiling. "Well, you're off to Paris. Tomorrow, isn't it?"

"Right. We just finished packing and I thought you might want to join us for dinner at the Eastgate. Kate's holding a table for us now. I tried ringing your rooms, and then decided to just come over here and ferret you out. Want to join us for one last gathering of the Fellowship?"

"Love to. Thanks." Austen hesitated. "What about Yvette? Shouldn't we ask her?"

"I tried ringing her as well, but she was out."

"Pity. Thanks for thinking of me, David," Austen said as the two young men walked out of the SCR and down the stone staircase to the Fellows' Quad. "I don't know if it's this dreary weather or just that there aren't many students around yet, but I've been rather down lately."

"You can't bear the thought of me leaving you for three months," David quipped.

"Honestly, I do think that's part of it," Austen answered soberly. "But the holidays have been really difficult for me. I see you and Kate so happy together and Andrew and Dianna and...there's nobody around for me to talk to."

With hands in pockets and coats wrapped tightly against the cold, they scurried across the flagstones of Merton's Front Quad and through the gate by the Porters' Lodge.

"You know, David, when I was home, my mother harped continually on my finding a new wife. Even Dianna and Andrew encouraged me to think about pursuing a serious relationship with someone. What do you think?"

David glanced at Austen's face. "What do *you* think?"

"I've thought about it a lot over the break. I've said I couldn't replace Marianne, and that's true. But I don't think

I'm meant to dwell alone for the rest of my life, either. Frankly, I'm not wired to be celibate…and I'm lonely. You've been a great friend, but—no offense—you're no substitute for a wife and, of course, now that you have Kate, things have changed. It's even worse that you're going away."

David placed his hand on his friend's shoulder. "Austen, sounds to me like you're ready. Do you need permission?"

"Perhaps."

"Look, you just said Marianne's brother is encouraging you to move on. Marianne herself told me she didn't want you to be alone. She wanted you to be happy and thought you should marry again."

"I know. She told me that too. But I feel guilty somehow. As though I'm betraying her memory or something."

"It speaks well of your marriage that you would want to remarry. It's often the people who were unhappily wed that are the most reluctant to try again."

"But…I know this may sound strange…" Austen stared at the pavement, "I'm worried that if I don't remember her and think of her all the time that I'll…I'll lose her forever."

David clasped his arm. "You won't forget her, Austen. None of us will. But she doesn't live just in our memories. Remember, you have the promise of being with her for all eternity."

"Of course you're right." Austen sighed. "So you think I should be open to finding someone else?"

"Absolutely, old boy. But remember what you used to tell me: Don't go pursuing love in the wrong places. If you continue to serve at your post and stay involved with the church and our Inklings group, I believe God will bring the right girl along at the right time. Kate and I will be praying for that."

"Right. Thanks, David." They had reached the side door to the Eastgate along Merton Street. "Well, let's not keep your beautiful bride waiting."

❧

Yvette hesitated outside the High Street entrance to the Eastgate. One of her colleagues at St. Hilda's had set up a blind date for her. At the time Yvette had been feeling desperate enough to grab the chance. Ever since her twenty-ninth birthday, she had sensed a rising tide of panic—that she would soon be too old to marry and start a family—that she had found difficult to quell. Her friend had assured her that this man, a fellow don from India—charming, cultured, and cosmopolitan—had the potential to be "the one." She had quipped, "East Indian meets West Indian, a perfect match." But now that Yvette stood in front of the Eastgate, she wasn't quite so certain, and she began to regret her reckless acceptance of this invitation. Nevertheless, she took a deep breath and walked into the pub.

Yvette spied the only other brown-skinned person present as he stood to greet her. His smile revealed gleaming white teeth in a handsome, well-proportioned face. Perhaps this wasn't a mistake after all.

"You must be Miss Goodman," he said, extending his hand. "I'm Deepak."

"Yvette," she answered with a firm handshake. "Pleased to meet you."

"I've reserved a table for us in the restaurant. Shall we?"

Yvette nodded and they moved around the tables and couches to the narrow passage leading to the hotel restaurant.

Deepak slipped his arm around her waist with a familiarity that filled her with uneasiness. Keeping his hand against the small of her back, he led her to their table and seated her.

Yvette made a few attempts at small talk while scanning the menu. After placing her order, she glanced about the room and spied Austen, David, and Kate engrossed in conversation. Her heart sank. Unaware of her discomfort, Deepak kept up a steady monologue as he poured her wine and their dinner was served. She tried to concentrate. He talked voluminously about his Cambridge education, his honors, his accomplishments, and his research publications. Yvette ventured to add a comment now and then, but it soon became apparent that this man was not particularly interested in her at all. He was either extremely arrogant and self-absorbed or he was trying much too hard to impress her. In either case she was quickly coming to the conclusion that this blind date had been a terrible mistake. When he began to talk about his Hindu beliefs and the young woman his family had chosen as his bride, Yvette resigned herself to a long evening.

Across the room, Yvette's friends finished up their dinner.

"Austen, old boy, why don't you come over to Paris for the Easter break?" David asked as they stood to leave. "You'd have free digs and an unparalleled tour guide."

"Maybe I'll take you up on that—that is, if Kate doesn't mind having company."

"Not at all," Kate hastened to reassure him. "We'd love to have you. You could even invite Yvette to come along to keep me company."

Austen shifted his weight uncomfortably. He had been watching Yvette and her escort since they had entered the restaurant. "She's sitting right over there, if you'd like to say goodbye to her."

"Yvette's here?" David asked, looking about. "Why didn't you say so?"

"She seems rather…occupied. I wonder who that man is."

"Probably just another don."

"I think he's more than just another don," Austen muttered in undisguised exasperation. "He had his arm around her."

"Really?" Not missing his tone, David studied his friend with surprise. "Well, let's find out who he is. We're not going to leave without saying goodbye to Yvette."

The group walked over to her table and introduced themselves. Yvette felt the blood rush to her face. She hoped her light brown complexion covered any evidence of her embarrassment. After a few awkward pleasantries and the MacKenzies' warm farewells, her friends left.

Yvette suffered through another hour of her date's self-congratulatory monologue. To her chagrin, he insisted on seeing her all the way back to St. Hilda's.

"Thanks very much for dinner, Deepak," she said as she unlocked the gate.

He bent to kiss her, but she turned her head so that his lips met her cheek. "May I see you again, Yvette?" he asked eagerly.

She hesitated. Sometimes honesty was the best policy. "Deepak, I really appreciate the lovely dinner and the evening out. But since you have a bride waiting for you in India, I think it's best we don't spend a lot of time together. I'm sure we'll see each other around. Thanks again. Goodnight."

Before he could protest, she slipped inside the college gate and closed it behind her. Although it was a cold night, she wandered down the front lawn to the river's edge and stared into the shimmering water as she prayed.

Oh, God, I give up! You know how desperately I want to be married and to have a family, but even I have reached my limit. I can't go on like this anymore. No more blind dates; no more searching for Mr. Right. I yield my life completely to You. Either bring the right man into my life or give me purpose and contentment in being single. Please help me to rest in You and Your plan. Help me to keep You as my first love. Help me to seek first the kingdom of God in every aspect of my life. Help me to be content in Your love.

Tears of frustration and grief for her lost dreams streamed down Yvette's cheeks. But as she prayed and wept, an unexplainable peace enfolded her—and she was comforted. Gazing up at the brilliant stars, sparkling like gems fastened on the velvet mantle of the midnight blue sky, she whispered, "Thank You, Lord." She brushed the tears from her cheeks and walked contentedly back to the Hall.

16

Nought Week
France

Wrapping his arms around Kate, David held her close to protect her from the brisk February wind. The ferry's horn belched in a short farewell salute. With the decks vibrating and the sea churning beneath them, they slowly pulled away from shore and their last glimpse for several months of the white chalk cliffs of their island home.

"You know what's strange?" Kate leaned back into David's embrace. "I've just begun to feel at home in England, and now we're pulling up our stakes and leaving. It makes me kind of sad."

"Well, you know the old saying 'Home is where the heart is,'" he replied, hugging her more tightly. "As long as we're together we'll be at home. It'll be a grand sight, though, to see the Dover cliffs again, especially when we've been away for a time."

"Remember when we sailed into New York on the Queen Mary and watched the sun rise over the Statue of Liberty? After being gone so long, it was amazing to be welcomed back to the States by such an incredible sight."

"It was thrilling," agreed David. "It made me proud to be half-American."

"It still strikes me as funny that you're part American. I always think of you as pure English."

"And I'm not English at all!" David exclaimed, laughing. "I'm half-Scot, half-American."

Kate smiled. "You're *hawf* and *haff*. You *sound* and act English—or British at least, anyway. Just think, the baby will be born in England but will really be one-quarter Scottish and three-quarters American. I wonder if he'll be hopelessly confused."

David drew her closer and placed his hand on her now obviously pregnant belly. "This wee one is already a world traveler and will feel at home anywhere. He'll probably learn French while we're in Paris."

As if enjoying the joke, the baby jabbed David's hand with a tiny foot. "Whoa! Did you feel that?" David asked excitedly. "What a strong little bloke." They stood close together on the deck for a few more minutes, enjoying the sensation of completely belonging to one another and to the small one growing within. A sharp wind suddenly stung their faces with salt water.

"You must be cold, darling. Let's go inside with the other passengers," he suggested.

"I'm afraid if I don't stay out in the fresh air I'll be sick," she replied. "Can't we just huddle under some blankets?"

"Are you feeling ill now?' he asked with concern.

"I'm a little queasy," she honestly answered. "You know I'm not a very good sailor."

David quickly found a stack of blankets and two deck chairs in a sheltered spot where they nestled for the remainder of the

Channel crossing. Buried under the pile of covers, Kate dozed in the faint winter sun while David held her hand and read beside her. Another blast of the ship's horn abruptly signaled the end of their journey. The MacKenzies had arrived in France.

Having missed Normandy on their honeymoon, David had decided to take a detour. He wanted to extend their holiday as long as possible before the second semester began at the American College of Paris. Since the bulk of their clothing, books, and necessities had been previously shipped over in trunks, he drove their tightly packed MG straight from Calais to the small town of Bayeux. They settled at the Lion d'Or, a charming inn whose acclaimed restaurant and wine cellar had hosted wartime guests such as Winston Churchill, King George VI, Generals Eisenhower and de Gaulle, Field Marshal Montgomery, and even Field Marshal Rommel during the German occupation. There David and Kate enjoyed their first superb French dinner of coq au vin accompanied by Norman cider and hospitality.

The next morning Kate awoke to the smell of café au lait and freshly baked croissants. She yawned and stretched, reluctant to relinquish the warmth of their bed, whose satiny duvet covered her like a dollop of meringue.

"Good morning, sleepyhead," David sang out cheerfully. "Time for breakfast."

Kate yawned again. "Do I have to get up? It's so comfy here. I love this pouffy coverlet."

Sitting beside her on the bed, David kissed her gently. "We have a lot to see today. And I'll wager the inn on Mont

Saint-Michel has a 'pouffy' duvet too. Besides, if you don't get up, I'll have to make love to you again."

Kate laughed. "Is that a threat or a promise?"

"Do you want to try me?" he asked, grinning.

Kate answered with a kiss. "I do." She sighed. "But the coffee's getting cold and you're right, we have a lot to see today. So I'll take you up on your promise tonight."

After breakfast they walked around the block to view the Bayeux Tapestry, the crudely embroidered eleventh-century chronicle of the Norman invasion of 1066. They admired the magnificent thirteenth-century Norman Gothic cathedral dominating the medieval town center, where David bought a bouquet of flowers from a bent, black-clad French widow.

Then they packed up the car and drove up to the D-day beaches. As they stood on the bluffs overlooking the spectacular vista of sand and sea, David recounted for Kate the events of those fateful and dreadful days. Twenty years before machine gun fire and men's cries had ripped the air, while on this day only the cry of gulls and the crash of waves broke the silence. Barbed wire kept them from descending to the beaches where active land mines still lay buried. Instead, they slogged through mud to climb up to the remains of a German bunker blackened by fire and eerily quiet. Kate shivered at the thought of the young men who had lost their lives there.

Subdued, David drove above the dunes of Omaha beach to the American cemetery at St. Laurent-sur-Mer. After taking a map from the war memorial, he led Kate down row after row after row of white marble crosses spreading as far as the eye could see over a vast expanse of grass, ending only in the horizon of the ocean beyond. Nearly 10,000 American servicemen rested peacefully after falling in the bloody fury of battle. The enormity of their sacrifice overwhelmed Kate, and as she followed David, her eyes clouded with tears.

Checking the map again, he turned to head down a row of graves. He suddenly stopped and knelt, laying the bouquet of flowers reverently before a cross.

"Here he is: Jeffrey Lawrence Little. My Uncle Jeff."

Kate slipped her hand into David's, squeezing it gently. They bowed their heads and prayed in silence.

Finally, he spoke quietly. "You know, he was my grandparents' only son. Mum had two older sisters, but since she was the youngest, she was always closest to Jeff. Losing him really devastated her. But look at all these graves. So many loved ones lost…so many gave so much…so many," he repeated sadly.

Kate wiped the tears that coursed down her cheeks. "I had no idea," she whispered. "It's overwhelming how many brave young men never made it home—and very, very sad. My dad was one of the fortunate ones. If he hadn't been wounded in the Italian campaign and sent back to the States, I wouldn't have been born."

They stood for a few minutes more contemplating the sea of graves; then hand in hand they walked silently through the cemetery.

❧

As David and Kate drove along the winding roads of Normandy, they passed numerous villages still scarred from battle. Short, stout women clothed in mourning from their kerchiefs to their shoes scuttled about like black beetles. Twenty years had passed since the occupation, yet all remained so bleak and deserted that Kate could easily envision Nazi storm troopers marching past the scorched stone walls.

Later that afternoon on their arrival at the island of Mont Saint-Michel, visions of medieval monks replaced those of modern soldiers. David and Kate hiked up the twisting lanes to the impressive Gothic abbey and fortress rising like a colossus from the bay. Since first seeing the island depicted on travel posters in her high school French class, Kate had longed to experience in person this amazing marvel of medieval ingenuity. She was not disappointed.

After exploring the cloisters, church, and Knight's Hall, they wandered about the town unhindered by the crowds of tourists who normally jammed the streets during the hot summer months. The numerous shops and narrow alleys tucked into the medieval walls evoked past ages when pilgrims and warriors jostled one another on their climb up to the rocky summit of the abbey. Arms entwined, David and Kate walked leisurely back down to the main gate to the renowned La Mère Poulard Restaurant, where they savored a supper of fluffy omelets.

Their moods and thoughts had been somber since visiting the cemetery, and Kate could not get the image of the thousands of crosses from her mind.

"I wish more Parisians would come up here and walk through that cemetery," she reflected to David over their meal. "Maybe they wouldn't hate us so much."

"They don't hate us. And haven't you noticed how friendly the Normans have been?"

"Well, yes. And I guess that's why I'd like other Frenchmen to come here. I'd like them to see for themselves the sacrifices the Americans and Brits made to end the German occupation. I think they'd be nicer to foreigners if they thought about it."

"I'm sure many of them do understand, but perhaps some are ashamed and even resentful. Gallic pride runs deep."

"They do seem very proud, even arrogant," Kate agreed. "Anyway, on a different note, I've been thinking a lot about your Uncle Jeff today. I know your mom will be glad we came here to visit his grave, but—I'd like to do something more to remember him than just leaving flowers."

David glanced up from his meal. "What did you have in mind?"

"Well…what would you think of naming the baby for him—if it's a boy, that is."

A smile spread across David's face. "I think that's a splendid idea, darling. I like the name Jeff, even with the Americanized spelling. And it would really please Mum and my grandparents. But what if it's a girl? Have you thought of a girl's name?"

"No, not specifically. Have you?"

"Actually, I've been thinking along the same lines. I've thought for a long while that if I were to have a little girl, I would like to call her 'Marianne' after Austen's wife."

"Would he like that?"

David nodded. "I think he would like that very much. Especially since he and Marianne didn't have any children of their own."

Kate took his hand in hers. "Then I would like that too. Marianne is a pretty name, and from what you've told me, Austen's wife was a wonderful person. I think it would be very special to have either another Marianne or Jeffrey in the family."

"Kate, I'm glad you're thinking about names for the baby. I'd hoped you were feeling better."

"Well, sure, I feel better. I got a little nauseated on the ferry, though."

"No, darling, I wasn't referring to feeling better physically."

"What do you mean, then?"

"Honestly, Kate, I know this has been hard for you. You didn't want to start a family right away, and it must be difficult for you to be a student and newlywed, and then have a pregnancy thrust upon you—especially before you've finished school. It's not what you had bargained for at all."

Kate's eyes brimmed with tears. "But how did you know? I didn't say anything."

"No, you didn't." He squeezed her hand. "My love, you were very brave not to dampen my joy, and I am grateful to you for that. And though I had my suspicions as to your true feelings, I also thought it best not to discuss them until things changed. I didn't want you to say anything that might have given you cause for regret later. So then, am I right? Are you feeling more positive about the baby now?"

She sighed wistfully. "Yes. I guess I'm getting used to the idea. There've been little things that have helped. Like seeing that baby dressed as Santa at the carol service—how cute he was—and how his parents and you—well, everyone really—doted on him. And now that I can feel the baby kicking and swimming around all the time, it all seems much more real to me. So yes…" she squeezed his hand back. "I'm looking forward to having the baby now. Thank you for understanding and not being disappointed in me. I felt really terrible and very guilty."

David turned her hand over and pressed his lips to her palm. "Please don't feel guilty. I'm very proud of you, and you will be a wonderful mother to our child. I do love you so, Kate," he whispered. "*Je t'aime beaucoup, mon amour.*"

She smiled happily. "*Je t'aime beaucoup aussi.*"

Madame Denise, the dark-haired, dark-eyed concierge of their Parisian apartment house, looked like a plump little wren as she welcomed David with pecks on both his cheeks. She rattled on in rapid French, obviously pleased to see him again. Kate picked out a few words here and there and thought the gist of the conversation was of the "My, how you've grown!" tenor. As Madame Denise gestured broadly and smiled knowingly at Kate's pregnant belly, Kate caught the word *bébé* and returned her smile. Perhaps the Parisians were not as arrogant as she had thought.

David responded with a fluent volley of French, and after more smiles and nods, he took the key from Madame Denise and carried their luggage to an ornate brass elevator no larger than a broom closet.

"We're up on the sixth floor and this lift is as slow as the dickens. I'll send you up with a suitcase and then carry the other up," he said. "Thankfully, our trunks arrived and Madame's husband, Monsieur Sebastian, already took them up to our flat."

"David, just stuff the suitcases in here," Kate pleaded. "I want you to come up with me. It will be more fun to see it together."

"All right," he agreed amiably, squeezing beside her. He pulled across a metal accordion safety gate as the glass doors slid shut and the lift lurched upward at a crawl. "It's rather nice to be trapped in close quarters with you. Let's take advantage of the slow ride," he said, bending to kiss her. Kate's mouth yielded eagerly to his until the elevator jolted to a stop on the top landing, and they reluctantly parted. "Hmm…" he sighed. "Not slow enough."

Each floor had only two apartments; David unlocked the one on the left. Putting down the bags and swinging open the door, he suddenly swept Kate up into his arms and carried her laughing over the threshold. He gently set her down in a bright sunny suite of rooms with French doors opening to balconies overlooking the street. The hardwood floors, marble fireplaces, and ornate gold-and-white faux Louis XVI furnishings all delighted Kate. Only later did she appreciate the two incongruous but comfortable reading chairs David had ordered hauled up from a local flea market.

"How do you like it?" he asked her as he carried in the luggage.

"It's so pretty! I love it."

"Come here," he drew her by the hand. "Wait till you see the kitchen."

The galley kitchen had a linoleum floor and, unlike their tight quarters in Oxford, room for a breakfast table. Kate glanced around happily and then spied what David had wanted her to see. From the window above the table she could gaze on the top of the Eiffel Tower thrust above the city skyline. "Oh my goodness," she cried, "La Tour Eiffel! Can we walk to it?"

"Well, yes, but it's across the river on the Left Bank. Right up the street though, we have that fabulous view with all the fountains from the Palais de Chaillot. We'll walk up there after I show you around Passy. But first come see the rest of the flat."

They followed a long, narrow corridor to the bathroom, which contained only a large claw-footed bathtub. Across the hall was the WC. *Funny how the French call it a "water closet" and the Brits call it a "toilet," like the French word "toilette,"* Kate thought. She noticed that a white porcelain bidet squatted next to the toilet. This fixture so familiar to the French tended to puzzle an American like Kate, who preferred taking frequent showers for hygiene. Continuing down the corridor, she entered their nicely appointed bedroom, comprised of a double bed, a massive wooden armoire, a washbasin, and a wide window opening to the back courtyards of several apartment buildings—the pinnacle of the Eiffel Tower looming overhead. Next door was a slightly smaller bedroom, which would double as a guest room and David's study.

"This is great," Kate assured David. "*Formidable!*"

"I'm glad you like it. It's a lot bigger than our Oxford flat, isn't it? This will be like a second honeymoon for us, compliments of the American College. *Formidable, certainment!* Now, come here…let's finish what we started on the lift." He gathered her in his arms and began ardently kissing her again.

17

First Through Fourth Weeks
Paris

After becoming acclimated to their new home, David set out to acquaint Kate with the chic sixteenth arrondissement of Passy. He showed her numerous little stores and kiosks selling everything from stamps and magazines at the corner *tabac* to fat sausages and whole chickens hanging upside down by their skinny claws at the butcher's. They shopped for a few sacks of food and essentials at Prisunic, a small grocery store which bore the closest resemblance to a traditional American supermarket. Kate had never seen so many patisseries or bakeries in the space of just a few blocks; David stopped at one, buying two chocolate éclairs.

"Nobody can make éclairs like the French," he declared. "What I like best is that they have chocolate custard. Try this." Handing one to Kate, he pulled out a chair for her at a little round table. They savored the chocolate custard filling and delicate pastry as they watched the Parisians rush by along the street outside.

"Hmm, this is so yummy," Kate agreed. "How can the Parisians keep from getting fat?" She had just observed several slender girls fashionably dressed in tight miniskirts and leather boots.

"Obviously, they're not all skinny. Take Madame Denise, for example," David said. "But I don't suppose the younger women allow themselves too many visits to the patisseries, and everyone walks a lot. Still, you needn't worry. You could even stand to gain some weight. You're barely showing."

"Ha!" Kate disagreed as she looked down at her rounded abdomen. She thoughtfully chewed her pastry for a few minutes and then asked, "David, why is our street called 'Rue Vineuse'? I've only seen a couple of wine shops as opposed to a slew of bakeries."

"This whole section used to be a vineyard outside the city walls. There was a monastery where the Palais de Chaillot is now. The brotherhood produced red wine until the Revolution. So that's where the name originates. I say, let's drop this food off at our flat and walk up Chaillot Hill to Trocadéro. I want to show you where the other Metro stop is."

Kate knew he also wanted to show her again the spectacular view they had enjoyed on their honeymoon. After putting away their groceries, they walked hand in hand up Rue Vineuse and past a statue of Benjamin Franklin, a former resident of Passy. Kate was warmed by the sight of his familiar and kind American face. Hurrying around the huge spoke of the Trocadéro traffic circle with its impressive bronze equestrian statue of Marshal Foch, they came to the broad terrace connecting the massive marble wings of Chaillot Palace, which housed maritime and natural history museums as well as the city's largest cinema. There, highlighted against the backdrop of brilliantly lit, powerfully jetting fountains, stood what appeared to be a delicately spun filigree latticework tower. It rose triumphantly as one the most famous and awe-inspiring man-made landmarks in the world: La Tour Eiffel. They had arrived at dusk, just as the lights shot up the tower and through the streams of fountains. It was a breathtaking sight.

"I never tire of this view," David said.

"It is amazing," Kate agreed with a happy sigh.

"And just think—we have it all to ourselves whenever we like and with nary a tourist—at least 'til spring, that is."

"Yes," said Kate, snuggling closer to him. "Just us—and those Parisians like us who are crazy enough to brave the cold."

David put his arm around her and held her tightly. "Are you cold, love? You'll have to depend on me to keep you warm—even indoors. They turn the heat off in the entire apartment building at night and during the day through work hours."

Kate groaned. "You're kidding! Why?"

"Conserving energy and money. What did our dear old neighbor Ben say about a penny saved? Anyway, I'll be happy to keep you warm at night, and you've got your little portable stove." He caressed her belly. "If the baby and I are not enough to keep you cozy, I'll buy an electric fire for you."

David was right about the heat switching off promptly at eleven o'clock every night. It came on briefly in the morning and was off again until about five o'clock in the afternoon. Kate welcomed cuddling with David at night, and she placed her slippers strategically by the bed to avoid having to step on the cold floor. Nevertheless, she found it difficult on frosty February mornings to leave the warm bedclothes and face the frigid tiled bathroom. Kate mused that the French may have much to teach Americans about fashion, art, cuisine, and *la joie de vivre,* but she wished that their cultural snobbery did not extend to American conveniences like good central heating.

After warming up with breakfast and hot mocha, David rode the bus with Kate from Trocadéro across the Pont d'Alma to the seventh arrondisement on the Rive Gauche or Left Bank where the American College held their classes in a collection of buildings that included the American Church of Paris. Before they parted—he to his Shakespeare lecture, she to her twentieth-century American literature class—David gave her a map with directions to the college cafeteria, where they would meet for lunch.

Kate found it easily enough, although it was several blocks away and down a narrow alley. She was surprised to find that the little cafeteria appeared much like an ordinary Parisian café with a few round tables and chairs, although a primarily American and Lebanese crowd packed the close quarters. As she stood in the checkout line, a young man turned to her and tried to strike up a conversation. After a few innocuous exchanges about classes, the weather, and their hometowns, he startled her by asking, "Hey, would you like to go to a movie with me tonight? They're showing *Casablanca* at the Palais de Chaillot."

Kate was bewildered. "No, thank you. My husband and I have plans."

The young man nearly choked. "I'm sorry. I didn't know you were married."

His companion hit him in the back and whispered furiously, "Idiot! She's pregnant!"

"I didn't notice!"

Suppressing a smile, Kate turned to pay for her lunch. It soothed her ego to know she could still turn some heads—

even six months pregnant. She glanced about for an empty table and found one close by a group of coeds. She smiled at the girls as she passed, but they merely stared at her. Self-consciously, Kate sat down and put her books on an empty chair to reserve it for David, taking one out to read while she waited. She wished he would come quickly. Eating alone made her feel conspicuous and awkward.

She overheard another bout of whispering—this time from the table of girls behind her.

"Who is she?"

"I don't know, but she's so pretty it makes me sick."

"She looks pregnant."

"That's what being pretty got her—knocked up." The girls giggled.

"Shh! She'll hear you."

Kate blushed deeply. *Do people really think that about me? David, please get here!* Kate decided to open her yogurt carton and begin eating. The girls were no longer whispering and Kate could easily hear their conversation.

"Oh my gosh, have you seen the visiting English professor? What a dreamboat!"

"Who? What does he teach?"

"Mr. MacKenzie. He's from Oxford and teaches Shakespeare and poetry."

"Maybe I should try to add his class."

"Good luck. There was a line of girls trying to add in this morning. He is *so* cute. Oh my gosh! You guys—that's him! He just walked in!"

"Wow, he *is* cute!"

Kate looked up at this and her heart leapt. *He is cute,* she thought, *and he's mine.* She welcomed David with a warm smile. "Hi, honey!"

He leaned over her chair and she caught the fragrance of his Old Spice aftershave as he kissed her.

"Hello, Mrs. MacKenzie," he said. "I'll be right with you, darling. Let me get something to eat; I'm starved. What are you having? Yogurt? I need more than that. I hope they serve croque-monsieurs here. I'll be right back." He straightened up and saw the table full of girls gaping at him. Flashing them a winsome smile, he slipped into the cafeteria line. Kate heard the whispering resume behind her.

"Oh my gosh! She's his wife!"

"Are you sure?"

"Yes! Didn't you hear him call her 'Mrs. MacKenzie'?"

"Guess *he* knocked her up." More giggling; then wistfully, "He is such a hunk. I wish he weren't married."

"How has your morning gone, darling?" David asked Kate as he returned with a tray full of food.

"Good," she said, moving her books aside so he could sit down. "Except," she lowered her voice, "I don't know how easily I'll be able to make friends here."

"Why? Most of the kids are Americans."

"Well, since nobody knows me—I don't think they know what to make of a pregnant student."

David peered at her quizzically.

"I overheard those girls saying I had been 'knocked up.'"

"What?"

Kate nodded. "Anyway, I'm glad you're here and that you called me 'Mrs. MacKenzie.' Now they know we're married.

They were disappointed you're taken though. They think you're cute."

David laughed. "*Cute?* There's that American word again."

"Well, this is the American College, isn't it?"

Smiling, David shook his head and delved into his sandwich.

"One of the guys asked me out to the movies tonight," Kate confessed. "He didn't notice I was pregnant or wearing a ring."

"I'm not surprised. Blinded by your beauty, no doubt. Can't blame him. Just stay away from the French men. They won't be deterred by marriage *or* pregnancy. So, how was your class?"

"Good. I think it will be neat to be reading Hemingway and Fitzgerald while we're right near where all the expatriate writers hung out together in the twenties. How was your lecture?"

"It went well, I think. I wish you could sit in on it to tell me what you think. It was quite crowded and more people are trying to add in."

"Girls, you mean."

"Sorry?"

"More girls trying to add in—not people."

David thought for a minute and then shrugged. "I hadn't thought about it, but I suppose you're right. How did you know that?"

"Just call it woman's intuition..." Kate smiled. "Or overhearing lunchroom gossip." She licked her spoon and held up the yogurt container. "You know, I really like this stuff—dairy, protein, and fruit all in one little package. I've never had it before."

"Really?"

"I don't think we have any in the States—at least not in Virginia. Someone could make a fortune selling it over there."

"You're right. Well, I'm glad you like it as it's got to be good for the baby. But probably before too long you'll be craving peanut butter and jelly. By the way, one of the secretaries' husbands is military and can get us some peanut butter—or whatever other American food your heart desires—from the commissary. So you can make out your list."

"That'll be nice. But we just got here, and right now I'm still enjoying the French food."

"Me too!" David leaned back after devouring his croque-monsieur. "I have to admit, English food can be rather ghastly and I'm going to enjoy this. You know how I love to eat. Just think, we can meet for lunch every day and try a different café each time." He took her hand in his and pressed it to his lips. "We are going to have such a wonderful experience together."

And they did, settling easily into a routine of attending their classes and meeting for lunch. Some mornings David had to leave earlier than Kate; on other days she would go with him to hear his afternoon lectures at the Sorbonne. They would usually linger afterwards in the Latin Quarter, browsing in the American bookstore known as Shakespeare and Company, and mingling with the new generation of black writers such as Chester Himes, William Gardner Smith, and James Baldwin. They found the intellectual atmosphere in Paris more politically provocative than in Oxford, but also less spiritually inquisitive.

David showed Kate the way to a Middle Eastern pastry shop where they watched through the window as dough was spun into donut shapes, fried, and swirled in sugar. Never before had Kate tasted such divine donuts, which melted on her tongue with sweet warmth, and she begged David to buy a sack for their next day's breakfast. With evening closing in quickly, they sometimes dined in the Latin Quarter and then caught a film at the Odéon Theatre. More often, they shopped for fresh ingredients at the local shops in Passy, and Kate cooked an intimate dinner for two in their flat.

On weekends they explored the city's monuments, parks, museums, palaces, and churches. Finding the American Cathedral's worship service beautiful but too "high" Episcopalian for Kate's comfort, they decided to attend regularly the American Church with many of the college students and faculty. On cold winter Sunday afternoons, they took advantage of the Louvre's free admission or the organ recitals in Notre Dame. With ballet, theatre, opera, and art galleries, the cultural offerings of the French rivaled their culinary delights, and David and Kate determined to indulge in as much as they could afford. All in all, they expected to have a wonderful sojourn in this magical city of light and love.

18

Fifth Week
St. Valentine's Day

In the late afternoon David and Kate rode the elevator up to the second platform of the Eiffel Tower to watch the sun set in a blaze of color as the lights of Paris slowly illuminated the spreading skirt of the city below. The River Seine shimmered beneath them like a ribbon of taffeta—subtle, silent, and soft. Kate stood leaning back against David, who held her tightly to keep her warm.

She sighed contentedly. "This must be one of the most romantic spots in the world."

"Hmm," he murmured as he nestled his face in her hair and then kissed the nape of her neck. "If you're with someone you love."

Turning in his arms to face him, Kate smiled. "Well, I am."

"So am I." David gave her a lingering kiss and then pressed her to his chest as they enjoyed the view for a few more quiet moments. "You know," he finally said, "last year on St. Valentine's Day we were an ocean apart. You were back in Virginia and I was in Oxford with no assurance that we'd end up together. I remember being absolutely miserable and missing you so much."

"I missed you too. I remember staying home that night and watching TV with my family, thinking that it'd better be the last Valentine's Day I spent without you. What did you do?"

"Probably nothing. Oh—I think I went to dinner with Austen. The holidays are difficult for him."

"Poor guy, I wonder if he's doing okay while you are away. Maybe he'll ask Yvette out."

David smiled. "Doubtful. Will you quit playing matchmaker?"

"Well, I can't from Paris, anyway. But I can pray for them—that God will bless each of them like He has us."

"Yes," David agreed. "You can pray for them. Now, are you ready for some dinner? I've made reservations at a little café overlooking the Champ de Mars."

"That sounds great to me. I'm starving."

"Off we go then. But one goodbye kiss first."

"Goodbye?"

"Goodbye to the view."

Kate laughed. "After waiting until our wedding day to kiss me, you sure do use any excuse you can think of now."

"You're right, and it's even better now that we're in the City of Love." David grinned. "That's one thing I like about the French. They completely approve of public demonstrations of affection. Come closer." Embracing her, he kissed her again.

After dinner they walked back home across the great Pont d'Iéna to the Palais de Chaillot, up the giant terraced steps, and along the fountains, where David stopped to buy Kate some flowers from a street vendor.

"Here, darling, happy St. Valentine's Day," he said, handing them to her. "A dozen red roses for my sweetheart and a white one for my baby."

Kate smelled the bouquet and pressed them to her cheek. "Thank you so much, David. They're beautiful."

Once they had reached the plaza, they paused to catch their breath and drink in the exquisitely romantic view of the Eiffel Tower framed by the brilliantly lit fountains. Kissing again, they strolled slowly arm in arm back to their flat.

In one of their kitchen cabinets, Kate unearthed a vase for the roses, which she quickly and artfully arranged. But as she picked up the white one, its stem suddenly snapped.

"Oh, rats," she muttered, inserting the flower's fragile head along the rim of the vase.

"Everything all right, love?" David called from the parlor, where he was fiddling with the radio.

"I feel terrible—I broke off a rose by accident," Kate answered, carrying the vase in and placing it on the mantle. "I'm really sorry."

"Not a problem, darling. The flowers still look lovely and so do you. May I have this dance, Mrs. MacKenzie?" he asked, smiling, and then he swept her into his arms.

Austen was alone and lonely.

He too had bought a bouquet of roses for St. Valentine's Day, but his was placed tenderly on his wife's grave. He didn't know if she could see or hear him from the dimension of heaven, but nevertheless it comforted him to talk to her on his visits to the cemetery.

"I love you, Marianne. I miss you so much." He sighed, his eyes welling up. "I still don't understand why you had to leave me, but I know if given the chance you wouldn't want to come back, and I have to let you go. I think of you every day, darling, but it's these blasted holidays that are the worst." He wiped away an errant tear with the back of his hand. "I am so tired of being alone. I am growing in my relationship with God, but after all, He understands it isn't good for man to dwell alone and marriage is His idea. I know you'd want me to move on. I haven't desired to, but I think I'm ready. It would be all right now, wouldn't it?"

As if in answer, a wind whistled through the cemetery, stirring the flowers.

Lord, he began praying, *help me find the right one. Lead me, Lord. Give me wisdom and peace. Help me to carry on and live for You. You suffered the loss of Your Son that we might live forever with You. Thank You for giving us the greatest gift of all in Your Son. Thank You that Marianne is with You and that one day I shall be too. Comfort my mother tonight and all those who are missing loved ones.*

He ran his hand over the gravestone in farewell and then walked slowly back to his rooms in Merton. On his way home he decided to give Yvette a call and invite her to dinner.

Stuart Devereux stood patiently outside the rectory door with a bouquet of red and white carnations in his hand. Hannah opened wide the door and plopped into a curtsey.

"Lord De-ber-ro," she chirped, "please come in."

He smiled and bowed in return. "My lady." A frequent guest at the rectory since David's birthday party, Stuart knew how much she enjoyed this little ritual. "Happy St. Valentine's Day, Miss Hannah."

"For me?" she asked, her blue eyes widening at the sight of the flowers.

He laughed. "Well, they're for all the MacKenzies, but especially for your mum. Is she still here?"

"I'll get her." Hannah clattered down the hallway calling, "Mummy! Mummy! Stuart's here!"

Annie MacKenzie emerged from the kitchen wearing a bibbed apron over her good sapphire blue cocktail dress. "Hello, Stuart. How are you?"

"Happy St. Valentine's Day, Mrs. MacKenzie." He held out the flowers. "These are for you. I wanted to thank you for opening your home to me. You look much too young and pretty to have children as old as I, but I appreciate your letting me adopt you as my mum."

Annie's eyes filled up with tears of sympathy. "Thank you, Stuart." She kissed him gently on the cheek. "Your mother would be very proud of you. The flowers are lovely," she said, taking them. "Thank you. It's very thoughtful of you." Her voice lightened. "Have you had any supper? Natalie's made up a big pot of spaghetti. Come back to the kitchen. I don't think the boys have eaten it all yet."

The MacKenzie boys grunted their greetings to Stuart as they made good headway on the pasta that Natalie was dishing up in copious amounts.

"Hi, Stuart," she said as she filled another plate. "Would you like some?"

"Yes, thank you." Stuart was about to sit down when Eric MacKenzie walked in. "Good evening, Reverend MacKenzie," Stuart said, extending his hand.

"Hello, Stuart," Eric responded warmly. "How are you?"

"Fine, sir." Stuart leaned closer and whispered, "Two months of sobriety, sir."

Eric clasped his hand more tightly. "Well done, lad!"

"Are you and the missus going out tonight?"

"We are indeed. Can you believe it? Someone anonymously made reservations for us at the Cherwell Boathouse, and the even bigger blessing is that they are also picking up the tab!"

"That is a blessing, sir. I hear the Cherwell is very romantic."

"It is. Annie loves to eat there, but we rarely get out."

"Well, you two enjoy yourselves. You certainly deserve it." Stuart caught Natalie's eye and winked.

Yvette usually hated St. Valentine's Day. In previous years it had stood as another painful reminder that she was still single. She hated it so much she traditionally wore black and spent the evening alone feeling sorry for herself. But this year she had adopted a new attitude. It had finally occurred to her that St. Valentine's Day was really about love—not only the love of a man and a woman—but love for family, friends, and above all God's love for mankind.

She had spent the week buying and making valentines and mailing them to all her loved ones. She deliberated a long time about whether or not to send one to Austen. She knew he must be feeling very lonely and especially missing Marianne, and she wanted to cheer him up. But in the end she decided not to. She didn't want him to misinterpret her compassion as flirtation.

This year Yvette was excited about her plans to celebrate St. Valentine's Day, and she dressed in bright red, her favorite color. She had invited all the single women of her acquaintance to high tea at the Randolph Hotel. And she was there—laughing and talking over scones and rich petits fours—when Austen called and didn't find her at home.

"Blast!" Austen cried, hanging up the phone in disgust. *Now, Austen, you idiot, why should you expect her to be waiting for you to ring her up? Why shouldn't she be out with someone on St. Valentine's Day? She's probably with that Deepak bloke. Of course. That's it! You imbecile!*

He thought for a while and then dialed another number. "Hello, Di," he greeted the familiar voice of his sister. "Happy St. Valentine's Day, love."

"Austen, I'm so glad you called!"

"You didn't think I'd forget to call Mother, did you? May I speak to her?"

Dianna hesitated. "No. I'm sorry, but you can't."

"Why not?"

"Austen, Mum's quite ill. The doctor thinks she might have pneumonia. She's having a hard time breathing, and I'm afraid she'll have to go to hospital."

"Oh, no!" he gasped. "I'm so sorry. What can I do? Should I come home?"

"Not yet. Let's see how she gets through the night. I'll ring you if she gets worse. But, Austen, could you maybe come home this weekend? Otherwise, Andrew will have to close the shop. I just can't handle the boys and Mum by myself."

"No, no, of course I'll come. And if you need me sooner, just ring. I can cancel lectures and tutorials if need be. You will ring me if she gets worse, won't you?"

"Yes, I will."

"And, Di, please give her my love and tell her I phoned."

"I will. Are you doing all right, Austen?"

"Yes, love. I'm fine. Just a bit lonely, but it's nothing in the great scheme of things. You take care of Mum and yourself and give my love to everyone. I'll see you this weekend, if not before."

"All right. I love you, Autty."

"Love you too, Di. Bye." He gently replaced the receiver in the cradle and bowed his head to pray.

19

Fifth Week, Tuesday

I think the Inklings meeting went well tonight," Yvette said to Austen as they walked home together from the Eagle and Child. "You did a splendid job facilitating."

"Thank you." The praise meant a lot to Austen. Although considered a good lecturer and tutor, he knew he lacked the dynamism of his friend David. "Seems like the students are still enjoying coming out, even with David gone."

"Of course they are. I know you miss him—we all do—but I think you're doing a great job and it's important to keep the momentum going. Do you think Professor Tolkien will do another reading for us this term?"

"Probably. Before I forget, Mrs. Tolkien asked about you. She really enjoyed accompanying you on her piano and asked me to bring you over for tea again. Says it's been much too long."

"Well, that's nice of her. I like her quite a lot—she's very down to earth—and she plays beautifully. And they are such a lovely couple. They seem so devoted to each other." That thought reminded Yvette of another. "By the way, happy belated St. Valentine's Day."

"Thanks," he grunted in reply. "You too," he added more politely. "Did you have a nice day?"

"Fabulous. I had the best St. Valentine's Day ever! We went to the Randolph for high tea and afterward to a show. It was such fun." She carefully regarded him and misinterpreted his frown. "I thought about you, Austen. The holidays must be quite difficult. Did you spend it with anyone?"

"Not really. I took some flowers to St. Cross." He sighed. "Yeah, the holidays are difficult. But then to top it off, I called home and Dianna said that my mother is not doing well."

"Oh, no! I'm sorry to hear that. Did she say what's wrong?"

"They think it's pneumonia, and if it gets worse, they may have to put her in hospital. I'm going down there this weekend."

"Oh, Austen, I am sorry. If there's anything I can do…" She touched his arm lightly. "Look, I really mean that. If Dianna needs help with the boys or you want me to mark papers for you—anything—just let me know. Will you?"

He gazed at her steadily. "Yes, thanks. I will."

"So, how did your parents enjoy the Cherwell Boathouse last night?" Stuart asked as he walked Natalie home from the Inklings Society meeting.

"They loved it." Natalie answered with a smile. "That was very nice of you, Stuart. They don't get to eat out much. It was a real treat for them."

"Good. They deserve it." He glanced at her sideways. "And how about you, Miss MacKenzie? Do you get to eat out much?"

"Well, more than they do."

"How would you like to go to the Boathouse for dinner?"

"With whom?"

"With me, of course."

Natalie sighed. "Stuart, I'm sorry, but I've already told you that I'm not going to date you. That we can only be friends."

"Can a man and a woman ever really be just friends?" he mused philosophically and then supplied his own answer. "I'm not sure they can. I think one party always wants it to be something more. Through our 'friendship' I'm growing increasingly fond of you, Natalie, and honestly believe I'm in great danger of falling in love with you."

"Stuart," she said, laughing, "it's not me you're falling in love with—it's my family."

He shrugged. "You're right. I am in love with them. I've recognized that in myself. You MacKenzies represent everything I've always wanted in a family—'wanted' in terms of both desire and lack. But I am terribly fond of you too, Natalie. And I do fear I'm falling in love with you." They were standing under a lamppost outside the rectory. "You're quite a beautiful young woman, you know. And it's rather difficult to keep one's feelings to the friendly variety when one wants so very much to kiss one's friend." He leaned closer to her. "May I please have just a little kiss?"

She stepped back. "No, Stuart. And I'm sorry, but if you can't treat me as a friend, then I shan't be able to be friends with you anymore."

"But why not, Natalie? I've done what you've asked. I've been coming to church meetings—several a week, in fact. And I've even given up drinking, which was one of my most favorite pastimes."

"That is all wonderful. And we've been very proud of you. But being a Christian is not all about how many meetings you go to or what things you give up. It's not about rules; it's about a relationship with the Creator of the universe. Frankly, I don't want to date anyone. Not unless I'm convinced that they have a possibility of being someone I would want to marry. And unless that person is someone who loves God the way I do, then he is not for me."

"All right, let's say I become that person…"

"You can't become a Christian just to get a date!" she protested. "There's nothing genuine in that."

"Hold on. Let's just say for the sake of argument that I become that person. What then?"

Natalie considered this. "Then…I don't know. I still can't see it working. Stuart, I'm just a rector's daughter and you'll be an earl someday. Like I said, I don't want to date someone just to go out. I would have to see a future in it. And even if you were to consider a future with me, your family wouldn't stand for it. We're from different classes. Remember that Shakespeare play where a prince asks the heroine if she'll have him and she answers, 'No, you're the prince and I can't afford you for every day' or something like that?"

"You mean Beatrice in *Much Ado About Nothing*. She says, '*Your grace is too costly to wear every day.*' But Natalie, this is the sixties. The class system is on the way out."

"Tell that to your father."

"Don't remind me of my father! He married for money, not for love. I refuse to do that. I will not be like him."

"Well, I hope you won't. But this is all a philosophical argument anyway. First things first. You need time to heal and get your life right with God, and then you can think about finding the right girl to marry."

"In the meantime, may I still see you?" His tone was plaintive. "You won't turn me away now, will you?"

"No. But you need to stick to the family and church parameters."

"All right, I will. Gentleman's honor and all that...Oh, by the way, have you heard anything from David and Kate? How do they like Paris?"

"We just received a St. Valentine's card from them. I think they're doing well. David is loving it. It's a little harder for Kate, I suspect. She's not used to the Parisians and her French isn't as good, but I'm sure it will get better quickly."

"Are you thinking about going to visit them while they're over there?"

"I've thought about going over the spring holidays. It'd be fun to visit for a few days. I do love Paris."

"Perhaps I'll go too."

Natalie looked at him skeptically. "Um...their apartment only has one guest room."

He chuckled. "Don't worry, that's not what I was thinking. The British ambassador's wife is Lady Somerville, one of my Churchill cousins, so I would probably bed down at the embassy. Come to think of it, I should get your brother and Kate an invitation to one of the embassy receptions."

"Kate would love that."

"Maybe they'll have something going on during the holiday and we can all go."

"As friends, you mean?" she asked with a smile.

"Right. Absolutely." He held up his hands in acquiescence. "As friends."

Kate awoke drenched in a cold sweat. *What a terrible dream! I should never let myself roll on my back.* She turned on her side to snuggle with David for comfort and realized his side of the bed was empty. Then she remembered that he had kissed her goodbye early this morning and left for the college, leaving her to fall back into this dreadful slumber. *What was I dreaming?* Then it floated again before her. She remembered seeing David hunched over her sobbing. Then Annie coming to her with tears streaming down her face saying, "I'm so sorry, honey. I understand." *What were they sorry about? And why do I have this terrible feeling of dread? It was just a nightmare.*

Kate sat up, swept her hair off her face, and placed her hands on her belly. *Is everything all right, baby? Please kick and tell me everything is okay.*

Kate quietly waited.

20

Fifth Week, Wednesday Afternoon

*K*ate waited until she knew she would be late for class if she didn't get up and shower. She waited on the bus and she waited while she took notes during her class lecture. She strained to listen or feel any movement, but there was nothing. And as she waited, she began to worry.

"I haven't felt the baby move today." Kate tried to sound casual as she mentioned her concern to David over lunch—too casual perhaps, as he took it even more lightly than she had intended.

"Probably sleeping."

"But I don't remember feeling anything since last night. A lot of thrashing around and then nothing today."

"See. He's tired out after practicing his bicycle kicks."

Kate frowned but was silent. She didn't want to tell David about the dream. Somehow articulating it might make it become real.

He studied her face. "You're worried about this, aren't you?"

She nodded.

"When's your next doctor's appointment?"

"Well, it wasn't until next week, but I called them to see if I could get in today. I just want to know everything's all right."

"Did they give you an appointment?"

"Yes, at 3:30."

"Would you like me to go with you?"

Kate looked at him expectantly. "Could you? I would feel so much better with you along."

"Sure. I've got a meeting, but I can cancel. I'll just stop by the faculty secretary's office and leave a message. And I'll drive you out there so you won't have to hassle with the Metro." David lifted her chin. "Don't worry, love. You drink some orange juice or limonade, and I'll bet the baby will wake up before we get there."

Kate was immeasurably relieved to give herself to his care. But as she settled in the car for the ride out to the hospital, she could not help but concentrate on the apparent lack of activity in her womb. Trying to quell a rising sense of panic, she gently joggled her belly and prayed and thought desperately, *Please move! Come on and wiggle or kick me or give me some sign! Come on, baby, wake up!*

Kate's obstetrician, Dr. Harville, listened soberly to her concerns and then asked her to lie on her back while he held his stethoscope to her abdomen. Slowly, he moved the stethoscope from one spot to the next and to the next and to the next. Kate held her breath. The only sound in the room was the click made by the second hand on the large wall clock.

The doctor cleared his throat. "Just a moment, please," he said, excusing himself.

Standing beside her, David squeezed Kate's hand. She rolled over to her side to take the pressure off her back. The clock kept clicking. Several minutes later the doctor reappeared followed by a colleague. "This is Doctor Steele," he said. "I'd like him to take a listen. Would you please lie back down?"

Kate obeyed and felt the cold metal of the stethoscope searching her belly again. She waited as more minutes past. Dr. Steele scowled while he and Dr. Harville each took another turn—this time with a shorter metal tube that resembled an ear trumpet.

Searching, searching, searching…silence. But for the click, click, click of the wall clock.

Finally David burst out, "Well, do you hear anything? Anything at all?"

Dr. Harville helped Kate sit upright and then he spoke quietly. "I'm very sorry, Mr. and Mrs. MacKenzie, but neither of us can find a heartbeat. What we'd recommend is for you to come back in tomorrow afternoon for a follow-up, and we will reassess the situation then."

"What exactly are you reassessing?" David asked.

"We'll try again to find a heartbeat."

"And if you don't?"

The doctors exchanged glances. They knew David would settle for nothing less than the truth. "We can't be absolutely certain," Dr. Harville said, "but coupled with the absence of movement, we are afraid you may need to prepare yourself for the worst."

Tears welled up in Kate's eyes and then began to spill down her cheeks; her fears were confirmed.

But David was incredulous. "No! That can't be. You can't think that the baby is…Kate felt it kicking just last night. Maybe it's turned the wrong way or there's something wrong with the stethoscope…" His voice trailed off. He knew each doctor had used his own.

"We're very sorry. This must be distressing for you, but only time will tell. I recommend that you take your wife home, keep her comfortable, and wait."

Wait? I've been waiting all day, Kate thought.

"Wait—for what?" David asked anxiously.

"If it's as we fear, then Mrs. MacKenzie will probably go into labor."

"And if the baby hasn't...?" Like the doctor, David could not bring himself to say the word.

"Then you'll feel him move."

"Will you please try listening again?" David pleaded.

The doctors exchanged glances and then complied. After several minutes, they sadly shook their heads.

"Can't Kate stay here at the hospital to...wait?" David choked on his question.

"It could be several days, so that wouldn't be a good idea."

"Days?"

Dr. Harville nodded.

"What's she supposed to do—besides wait?"

"Well, you could try to go about your daily lives—study, read, that sort of thing. You probably should lie low, though, as the onset of labor could be very sudden."

"And if she does go into labor?"

"Um...best to call and come on in to the hospital then."

Kate had been lying very quietly during this exchange, but suddenly she began to tremble. "Can't you just knock me out and do a Caesarean or something now?"

"I'm sorry, Mrs. MacKenzie. I know this prospect must be very distressing to you, but unless you are unable to deliver the child, surgery would be unwarranted and therefore too dangerous. And we don't know anything for certain yet. There is some new sonar equipment being tested that could give us a clearer picture of what is going on, but we don't have anything here with that capability. So we just have to rely on our old-fashioned listening devices. You can plan to come back in over the next few days and we'll keep trying."

Both Kate and David seized on this suggestion as a lifeline. Somehow it gave them a little hope.

"Okay," David said, "we'll do that. We'll come back tomorrow afternoon. All right, Kate?"

She nodded weakly and then burst into tears.

21

Fifth Week, Wednesday Evening

$\mathcal{D}$avid was uncharacteristically silent on their way home from the American Hospital. He was stunned by the doctors' diagnosis—stunned and incredulous. Once he muttered, "I can't believe it. This must be a mistake." But beyond that he kept his misgivings to himself, knowing they would not be helpful to Kate. She likewise sat in silent shock as tears rolled unhindered down her face. Not until they were alone in their apartment and he had drawn her into his arms did he venture to speak to her.

"Kate…I don't know what to expect or what to do. I just want you to know that no matter what happens, I love you and will take care of you." He gently stroked her hair. "All we can do is pray and entrust this little one to His care." David continued to hold Kate as he quietly prayed. After a few minutes, he said, "I think we should ring our parents and tell them so they can at least be praying too. Would you like to phone your parents or would you prefer that I talk to them?"

Kate croaked her reply. "Please don't call them yet. Not until we're sure."

"Mine neither?"

"No, you can call your mom and dad. I just don't want to tell mine yet." She sank into a chair. "I…I…I would like your mom to come. Ask her if she will. I think we'll need her."

Nodding, David went to the kitchen to make the call. Kate rested her head on her arms and sobbed softly.

Annie was bustling about her kitchen preparing dinner when the phone rang. She sighed heavily. The phone never seemed to stop ringing in the pastor's household. Usually, it was one of the myriad friends of the MacKenzie children. But even more often it was a parishioner distressed with some new crisis. One never knew when one picked up the phone what to expect. Consequently, Annie found it difficult not to treat every call with dread.

"Hello, MacKenzie residence," Annie answered, determining to maintain a pleasant tone.

"Mum, this is David."

"David!" She was immensely relieved to hear her son's voice. "How are you?"

"Not so good, Mum," he replied quietly. He didn't want Kate to overhear the conversation.

"Why? What's the matter?"

David took a deep breath and willed his voice to stay steady. "There may be something wrong with the baby. Kate hasn't felt any movement since last night. We went to the doctor today and he couldn't find a heartbeat."

"Oh, no!" Annie gasped. "Oh, honey, I'm so sorry. What did he tell you?"

"To just come home and wait. It's terrible, Mum. The uncertainty. They said we could come back tomorrow and they would try to listen again but not to get our hopes up. They think...they think...the baby...is...." His voice trailed off. He could not say it. "They said Kate will probably go into labor in the next few days. She asked if you would come. Could you do that?"

"Of course, honey, if Kate really wants me to. Natalie can help out here and I'm sure it will be fine with your father. I'll talk to him and we'll figure it out. I'll get there as soon as I can—I could possibly get there by tomorrow afternoon. Would that be all right?"

"Yes, Mum. That would be great. Ring me when you decide what to do and I'll ring you when we know more or if—if the baby decides to wake up and start kicking again."

Annie knew from experience the desire David had to hang on to any slender thread of hope. She therefore did not respond except to say, "How is Kate holding up?"

"She's in shock. I think we both are. This is all very surreal. I hope we'll wake up soon and find it was just a bad dream."

"We'll be praying and put you all on the church prayer list."

"Thanks, Mum."

"David?"

"Yes, Mum?"

"David, I love you. I'm so sorry you have to go through this. I wish I could be there right now. I'll come as soon as I can. But meanwhile, try to hold Kate as much as possible. She really needs you right now."

"All right, Mum. I will. Thanks. I'll see you tomorrow. Bye."

"Bye, honey." Annie hung up the phone, covered her face with her hands, and wept.

Kate made a feeble attempt to prepare some supper for David, but for once even he had little appetite. They tried to talk but could think of little to say. When they attempted to formulate what they would do if the baby didn't move, they fell into disbelieving silence. It was all too terrible to contemplate. David finally said, "You know, the Lord said not to worry about tomorrow, that today's troubles are enough. Let's just think about the next step and not about the possibilities. You need to get your rest and try to get a bit of sleep tonight. Why don't you go take a warm, relaxing bath and then we'll read together for a while."

Kate nodded and was soon sitting forlornly in the tub, rubbing her belly and silently begging God, the baby, her body to show some sign of life. When the water became cold, she pulled herself up and slowly, deliberately dressed for bed.

While she was thus occupied, David paced about the apartment, praying.

God, please, please heal this little one. Please let the doctors be wrong. Please wake the baby up. Oh, God, have mercy on us. Help us! David repeated these petitions over and over as he paced. Then suddenly he stopped and knelt by the couch. *Father, if our baby is already gone from us, please receive him or her into Your kingdom. Welcome our little one with Your arms of love. And in Your mercy, please let Kate deliver quickly and easily. Oh, God, comfort, strengthen, and uphold her. Give us grace to walk through this trial.*

Hearing Kate walking about the bedroom, David picked up a Bible and carried it with him down the hallway. He plumped up the pillows on their bed, sat leaning back against the headboard, and smoothed out a place for Kate. She lay beside him, her head against his chest. Opening to the Psalms, he began reading in a soothing, melodious voice. The song that most resonated with him was Psalm 31, and he read it as a prayer, for it echoed the cries of his own heart.

In thee, O LORD, do I seek refuge;
let me never be put to shame;
in thy righteousness deliver me!
Incline thy ear to me,
rescue me speedily!
Be thou a rock of refuge for me;
a strong fortress to save me!

Yea, thou art my rock and my fortress;
for thy name's sake lead me and guide me,
take me out of the net which is hidden for me,
for thou art my refuge.
Into thy hand I commend my spirit;
thou hast redeemed me, O LORD, faithful God...

Be gracious to me, O LORD, for I am in distress;
my eye is wasted with grief,
my soul and my body also.
For my life is spent with sorrow,
and my years with sighing...

But I trust in thee, O LORD,
I say "Thou art my God."
My times are in thy hand...

Blessed be the LORD,
for he has wondrously shown his steadfast love to me
when I was beset as in a besieged city...
But thou didst hear my supplications,
when I cried to Thee for help...

As David read and stroked Kate's hair, he could feel the tension flowing out of her. Gradually, she fell asleep. He prayed the psalm, mentally substituting her name for the words "I" and "me." Then he gently shifted her to a pillow and crept to his study. He attempted to review his lecture notes but abandoned them eventually, finding it too difficult to concentrate. Desperate for anything to get his mind off the dreadful circumstances, he decided to try reading a novel instead. He skimmed through several chapters of Anthony Trollope's *Barchester Towers* and had dozed off when a sudden sharp cry startled him.

He rushed into the bedroom and flicked on the lights. Kate was sitting up in bed drenched in sweat. "No! No!" she cried.

She had been dreaming. A shadowy figure had been stabbing her. As she felt the hot jab of the knife, she heard someone screaming. She awoke to find that it was she.

"What's wrong?" he asked anxiously.

"A dream…a terrible dream…" she whispered. "I'm sorry… I…" She became aware that the sheets below her were wet and sticky. "Oh, no! I think my water broke! I'm sorry. The bed is soaked." She gasped as another pain squeezed itself like a vise around her abdomen.

"It's okay," David reassured her. "I'll clean it up. Here, let's get you to the bathroom." He hurried out, grabbed some towels, and turned the taps on the bidet. Helping her from the bed to the bathroom, he then raced to the kitchen and placed calls to the doctor and the hospital. When he returned to pull the wet sheets off the bed, he noticed stains of blood and a dark, sticky mucous. He had read enough about childbirth to note that the presence of black meconium in the amniotic fluid was evidence of the baby's distress. David determined not to panic or let his mind sidetrack him from the immediate needs of his wife. Slipping a clean gown over Kate's head and wrapping her in a blanket, he carried her to the elevator and down to the ground floor.

Hearing a commotion, Madame Denise emerged from her flat, followed the distressed couple out, opened doors, and helped settle Kate in the car—all the while bemoaning in rapid French their evident plight. David hastily explained the situation and told her to expect his mother the following afternoon. Then he put the MG in gear and sped around Trocadéro toward the American Hospital.

At this predawn hour, the usually busy streets were almost deserted. The pavement glistened from city lights reflected in the drops of a recently fallen rain. Paris was asleep and achingly beautiful. On any other occasion, the sight would have touched the poet's soul in David. Tonight, he observed it all with a twinge of sad irony. *How can such beauty coexist with this terrible sorrow?* Then he thought of Jesus going to the cross. *How the Father must have sorrowed at His beautiful sacrifice of love. How He must have mourned the death of His beloved Son.*

A moan from Kate drew David's attention.

"Are you having another contraction?" he asked, glancing at his watch. "They're coming really close."

"I feel like the baby is ," she gasped.

"Don't push, Kate! We're almost there. Take deep breaths and blow them out slowly. Come on—breathe in with me. That's it. Now hold it. One...two...three...Now exhale slowly, slowly...that's it. Now take a deep breath..."

He continued to coach her until he pulled up to the emergency room entrance. Switching off the car, he hopped over the hood, and yanked open her door. "All right, darling. Here we are. You're going to be all right."

She put her arms around his neck and clung tightly as he carried her into the hospital.

"David," she whimpered, "don't leave me."

22

Fifth Week, Thursday Morning

Because David had phoned ahead, labor and delivery—and even Dr. Harville, who had been on call—were prepared to meet them on arrival at the American Hospital. As David lowered Kate into a wheelchair, the nurses instructed him to wait in the father's lounge. Kate grabbed his arm as though it were a life preserver.

"I'm going in with her," he insisted.

"The delivery may take a long time, Mr. MacKenzie," the nurse said, attempting to dissuade him. "We may have to anesthetize her and you'd be better off..."

"Listen, her contractions are very strong and close together. She felt like pushing in the car, and I don't think she has much time. Let me in while you examine her and we'll see. You don't need to worry about me. I'm not squeamish—my mother's a nurse. This is hard enough for my wife without asking her to go through it without me."

The nurse looked at the doctor, who nodded his acquiescence. Kate groaned and the staff quickly moved her to a labor room.

"Can you stand up, honey?" A nurse with a soothing southern accent asked. "We'll help you up on the bed."

Kate shook her head. "Here comes another one," she gasped, squeezing David's hand tightly. He waited until the pain had subsided and then lifted her to the gurney.

Dr. Harville gently examined her. "She's crowning! Let's get her down to delivery," he said to the nurses.

Another flurry of activity and Kate was being wheeled down the hallway, through swinging doors, and into a sterile delivery room.

"Okay, honey," the nurse said. "We need you to roll over onto the delivery table."

"I can't!" Kate cried.

"Come on, we'll help you," the nurse coaxed. Lifting the bed sheet, they tipped Kate onto the table and turned her over onto her back. They covered her with sheets and placed her feet in the metal stirrups. David stood by her side, holding her hand as another contraction seized her and yet another.

"No…" Kate was panting. "I can't…do this…It's coming… No!" she wailed.

Then—silence.

David stared in shocked disbelief at the tiny lifeless form lying on the delivery table. No cry of angry protest announced the infant's arrival—only the dreadful silence.

Finally the nurse whispered, "I'm so sorry. She was a beautiful little girl."

Another groan came from Kate as the doctor pushed on her abdomen to hasten the dispelling of the placenta.

"The cord has a knot in it, which prevented oxygen from getting to the baby," Dr. Harville observed sadly, cutting and clamping the umbilical cord. "There wasn't anything anyone could have done."

David could not take his eyes off of his still daughter. Until this moment he had hoped against hope that the doctors were wrong, that they would all be so happy when the baby surprised them all as she squalled with life. Suddenly the enormity of their loss hit him with crushing reality.

He broke.

A horrible sob rent from his chest as he bent over and embraced Kate. They clung to each other and wept together. While the storm of sorrow swept over them, the hospital staff kept a respectful distance, quietly attending to their medical needs. At last the waves of sobs subsided, and the nurse gingerly approached them with the tiny infant wrapped in a blanket.

"Would you like to see her?" she asked David.

He held out his arms in reply. He could cradle the bundle in one of his large hands. "She's so small," he whispered. "She's so perfect." The tears coursed unchecked down his face. "Kate—would you like to hold little Marianne?"

Her reply was barely audible. "Yes. Bring me my baby."

David gently gave her to Kate and then wrapped his arms around them both. "Isn't she beautiful?" he murmured.

"Yes!" Kate tried to stifle a sob. "I'm so sorry! I'm so sorry!"

Overhearing her cries, Dr. Harville intervened. "Mrs. MacKenzie, there was a knot in the baby's cord. It wasn't your fault. It's just one of those things that occurs at times for which nothing can be done. We're very sorry. We're going to wheel you to recovery and then find a bed for you up on the surgical postoperative floor. Would you like us to take her now?"

"No!" Kate clung tightly to her little bundle. "No. Please don't take her yet. I will never get to hold her again. Please don't take her away."

The doctor nodded. "All right, Mrs. MacKenzie. But let your husband have the baby for a moment while we shift you back to the gurney and wheel you to recovery. Then you can hold your daughter again." Dr. Harville turned to the nurses and said in a low voice, "Give them a private room and as much time as they need."

Kate acquiesced and David carefully took the bundle. He followed the solemn procession down the corridor. As they passed another delivery room, the door swung open and the lusty cry of a healthy newborn pierced him with painful reality. David hugged his silent, still child and wept.

23

Annie and Eric MacKenzie had attempted to telephone David early in the morning. Not receiving a reply, they called the concierge, Madame Denise, who gave her dolorous version of David and Kate's predawn departure to the hospital. Realizing that delivery was imminent, David's parents made the decision to book Annie on the earliest available flight from London to Paris. On landing, she headed straight for the American Hospital.

After making inquiries at the reception desk, Annie learned that Kate had been given a room on the postsurgical floor and that there was no record of a live birth. She knew all too well that only one outcome was then possible. Annie had just lost her first grandchild.

As she rode the elevator up to Kate's room, Annie prayed silently but fervently—*Lord, we need You now more than ever. We don't understand why You allow these things to happen. Help us to trust You even when we don't understand. Send us the Comforter, Your Holy Spirit. Supernaturally comfort David and Kate. Use me as an instrument of comfort. Lord, I don't know what to say or do. Please use me, guide me, and give me Your words to share. Help us, O Lord!*

Finding the room, Annie hesitated outside the closed door. She started at the sight of a little paper butterfly taped to the heavy door. Annie knew these butterflies were a signal to alert the hospital staff that the patient had lost a baby. Her knowledge came not from her experience as a nurse, but rather from that of a grieving mother. In this same hospital a decade earlier, Annie had lost a child to miscarriage. The painful reminders would never leave her. *Help me, Lord,* she repeated. Then gathering her courage, she knocked.

She heard David's voice call out, "Come in."

When she stepped into the room, David exclaimed, "Mum!" simultaneously with Kate's "Annie!" In a glance, Annie saw that Kate had transformed overnight from a young bride giddy with love to a woman who had lost her child. Annie's instinct was to head for Kate, who was sitting up in bed and clutching her tiny bundle, but David intercepted his mother first, hugging her tightly.

"Thanks, Mum, for coming. How did you get here so fast?"

Annie held him, murmuring, "I'm so sorry, honey. I came as soon as I could." When he finally released her, Annie turned to Kate.

"The baby's dead!" Kate burst out as if the stillness of the child in her arms begged explanation. "She's dead…" Then sobbing, "Her…name…is…Marianne."

Annie's eyes swam with tears as she rushed to the side of her daughter-in-law. "Oh, my dear, I'm so sorry!"

"No…I'm…sorry…it's…my…fault. My baby…my baby…"

"It wasn't your fault, Kate," David gently contradicted her. "The doctor said it's just one of those things that happens sometimes and nobody can do anything about it."

Annie looked at him questioningly. "A knot in the cord," he answered softly.

Annie nodded and then asked, "May I hold my granddaughter?"

The question reminded Kate that she was not the only one in the room to have suffered loss that day. She responded by placing the infant in Annie's arms.

Annie pressed her lips together and forced back her tears as she held her grandchild for the first and last time. "Marianne. She's beautiful—bless her little heart—a beautiful baby." Annie carefully unwrapped the blanket and regarded the delicate, tiny fingers and toes. "She's so little," she said quietly. "Such a perfect little baby." Sighing deeply, Annie rewrapped the infant and gave her to David, who had stood close by watching. "Thank you," she whispered. "Well, little Marianne is now with your baby sister in heaven."

"And with Austen's Marianne," David added.

"Yes. Does he know yet?"

"No. It all happened quite suddenly, and we weren't assigned a room until just before you came. I haven't even rung Dad yet or Kate's parents. I'm just so glad you're here. I was…"

A nurse's knock and entrance interrupted him. "Mr. and Mrs. MacKenzie? If you're ready now, I'll take the baby."

"No!" Kate cried.

"It would be best, Mrs. MacKenzie."

"I'll bring her down," David said, "and take care of the arrangements with the hospital. Mum, would you stay with

Kate? Here, darling." He carried the child over to his wife. "It's time to say goodbye."

Sobbing, Kate pressed her lips to Marianne's cheek. Annie kissed her grandchild goodbye and then embraced her daughter-in-law as David quietly followed the nurse, his precious bundle pressed closely to his chest.

"I'm so sorry!" Kate said, weeping. "I've never seen David cry before. When the baby was stillborn, he broke down. It was horrible. He wanted her so badly and I didn't. It's all my fault. If I had wanted her more, God wouldn't have taken her. He's punishing me for my selfishness. I deserve this, but David doesn't. Poor David! My poor baby...I'm so sorry...what am I going to do? Ah!" Her lamentations were silenced by the swift onset of a postpartum contraction. Kate clutched her stomach and moaned, "Oh...I feel like I'm in labor again."

Annie pushed the call button and requested a dose of Demerol for Kate. "We'll get you something for the pain so you can rest. You need some sleep."

After submitting to the injection, Kate piteously asked Annie, "Will you brush my hair, please? I know it's a mess, but I'm so exhausted I don't think I can manage."

Annie found a brush and very gently untangled Kate's long, dark locks and plaited them into a thick braid. As she brushed she said soothingly, "You do have such beautiful hair, Kate. David has always admired long hair on a girl; it's no wonder you caught his eye."

Kate relaxed into the luxury of having her hair brushed. "He likes to tease me that he fell in love with my hair before he learned my name. I hope he'll still love me even when I'm old with thinning hair."

"Of course he will," Annie said. "Just as you will him."

"But the baby…"

"Hush now. No more talking. You should rest." Annie fluffed the pillows and leaned Kate back. "There now. Close your eyes and get some sleep." Sitting beside the bed, Annie held Kate's hand and lightly stroked her arm until she was certain the medication had taken effect and Kate was asleep. Then she quietly stole out of the room.

Alone in the hallway, Annie turned toward the wall, covered her face with her hands, and wept. She wept for the baby, for David and Kate, for Eric and herself, and for her own lost little one.

"Mum?" David's soft voice broke in on her grief.

Annie turned around and laid her head on his chest. "I'm so sorry, honey." *My son, my baby. Now you're a father who has lost a child.* "I'm so sorry."

David put his arms around her and patted her back. "This is hard for you too. To come back here. Thank you, Mum, for coming. It'll be all right," he soothed. "It'll be all right."

He's comforting me! Annie wiped her eyes and composed herself. "Kate's asleep. She's had a shot of Demerol that should ease the postpartum pains and make her sleepy for a while. The more she sleeps the better at this point."

"Right. Poor thing has been through an ordeal and must be exhausted."

"You must be exhausted too. When will you get some rest?"

He shrugged. "Later. I have things to take care of."

"The baby?"

"The hospital has helped me contact a funeral service to transport her back to England. I think we'd like to have her buried at St. Cross beside Austen's Marianne, if it's all right with him. I'll give him a ring tonight. And if Dad could do a graveside service, then when we come home this summer, we'll do something proper for her. Do you think that would be all right?"

"Yes, honey. Do you want me to call Dad?"

"I'll ring him and the Hughes tonight as well when I get back from the hospital, but if you want to talk to him before then that would be fine. Have you been by the flat?"

"No, I came straight here. We phoned this morning, and when we didn't get you, we called Madame Denise and she told us what had happened. Your dad drove me to London to catch a plane so I could get here as soon as possible."

"You flew? Good grief! I'll pay for your ticket."

"No, don't even think about it. It's the least we could do. Now, would you like me to stay here with Kate? Do you need to work today?"

"I cancelled my classes. I think it'd be better for me to stay with her. I'd hate for her to wake up and not find me here. Why don't you go on to the flat and get settled in? I'm afraid we left it in rather a mess, though."

"Well, that's why I'm here. To help. I'll just catch a cab."

"Where's your luggage?"

"The receptionist locked it in a cloakroom for me. Don't worry, I'm all set."

"Let me at least call the taxi and help you with the luggage," he insisted.

Annie acquiesced, knowing that action was one of the best therapies for her son. When he had handled all the details and seen her safely off, David returned to his sleeping wife's bedside and his sorrowful vigil.

24

Fifth Week, Thursday Evening

avid was not the only one keeping a vigil that evening. Unbeknownst to him, across the Channel in a small hospital in the Cotswolds, Austen was sitting by his mother's side listening to her labored breathing. When she had been diagnosed with pneumonia and admitted, Austen had also cancelled his lectures and tutorials and had rushed home to Castle Combe to relieve his sister of some of her burdens. His preference would have been to care for Dianna's children rather than to be at the hospital, but he understood the sense of it. No need for Dianna to stay and watch when she had to care for a husband and three young sons. It wasn't the sitting and waiting that Austen minded. He could certainly be content to read or pray quietly for long stretches of time. He just found hospitals incredibly difficult to face. They conjured up too many memories of Marianne's illness. A portion of her lung had been removed, and from that time on she had always seemed breathless, as indeed she was. She could speak only a few words before having to catch her breath again, and her sentences seemed to stick in her throat. And then near the end, her breathing had sounded more like his mother's now—

which brought Austen, in his circuitous thinking and praying, back to his present concern for her. He patted her hand as he prayed.

Dear Lord, heal my mother. She's suffered so much in this life. Please relieve her of her discomfort. Heal her. Help her to recover. Give the doctors wisdom. And Lord, forgive me for all the times I have lacked the courage to come home and give her the respect and love she deserves. Help me to do better—to honor and love her. Help me to become the son You want me to be. Please heal her and give her a long, prosperous life. Please, Lord. Perhaps I'm being selfish in asking this—but I don't know if I can endure another passing just yet. And neither can Dianna and Andrew. This is dreadfully difficult for us. Please give us all strength and wisdom and peace. Grant us Your mercy and comfort.

Austen leaned back in his chair and repeated his prayers as his mother fought for breath.

Stuart had formed a new habit—a good one—of attending the Wednesday evening Bible studies for University students at St. Aldate's. Yet on this particular Wednesday, he was surprised not to find the faithful Natalie in attendance. He decided to use this unexplained absence as a pretext for stopping by the rectory after the meeting, but he really hadn't expected there to be any cause for concern. Consequently, he was rather taken aback when a somber William opened the door.

"Oh, hello, Stuart," he said. "Won't you come in? We're all back in the kitchen." Then he turned and led the way, not offering any further conversation.

Stuart's breezy greeting died on his lips when he entered the kitchen and saw the undisguised grief on the MacKenzie children's faces. Natalie's eyes and face were reddened with weeping.

"What's happened?" Stuart asked anxiously.

"We just got a phone call from David," Natalie explained, pressing her handkerchief to her eyes. "The most dreadful news. Their baby was stillborn. It was a girl. Kate went into labor last night and delivered her early this morning. Dead. A knot in the cord."

Stuart felt as if the wind had been knocked out him. "You don't mean it!" he exclaimed, although it was very clear by her tears that she did. "Oh no! That's awful! I'm so sorry. What a shock this must be. Poor Kate!"

Natalie looked so distressed that Stuart longed to take her in his arms, but he knew that gesture of sympathy would not likely be appreciated. *Perhaps she'll allow me to place my hand on her shoulder.* He hesitated and then did so. He was gratified when she reached up and squeezed his hand.

"Is there anything I can do for you or them?" he asked.

Natalie shook her head.

"Where are your parents? Do they know yet?"

"Yes. Well, sort of. Daddy had to make some hospital visits tonight, so he's not here and hasn't talked to David yet. At least not tonight. David rang last night when they suspected something was wrong. Then Mummy and Daddy tried ringing them this morning, and when they didn't get an answer, they rang their concierge in Paris. She told them that Kate and David had left in the middle of the night for the hospital. Daddy decided to drive Mummy to London and put her on the earliest available flight so that she could get there as quickly as possible. When

David rang, he said Mummy had gone straight to the hospital and arrived in time to hold the baby. He said they named her 'Marianne' for Austen's wife. They had already chosen her name before all this. He said she was simply beautiful…"

"How is David holding up?"

"Okay, I think. I mean, he must be in terrible shock. He wanted this baby so much. He's always wanted kids, and he was so excited when Kate became pregnant. We all were…"

"And Kate? Did he say how she is?"

"I don't know about emotionally, but I can only imagine. He did say that, mercifully, the labor and delivery went very quickly. He said he had prayed so much that the baby wouldn't be dead, but then he prayed if she were, that they wouldn't have to wait long and that the delivery would go easily for Kate. I think it was traumatic for her, but David seemed relieved that it wasn't long or hard."

"Poor Kate," Stuart repeated.

"Can you imagine? Going into labor and all the while thinking your baby is dead…" Natalie shuddered. "Poor Mummy. She lost a baby before Hannah. Right there at the American Hospital in Paris too, the year Daddy was on sabbatical. Mark was only two and I was ten."

"My mother lost a baby too," Stuart said quietly. "My older brother, Charles. He lived only two days. They don't know why he died. He would have been the next earl if he had lived. She's buried with him in the churchyard now. I don't think she ever got over him dying. That's probably when she started drinking…"

"I'm sorry, Stuart," Natalie said sympathetically. "I know it must still be difficult for you to think about your mother. And you don't need to hear about our troubles."

Stuart waved his hand dismissively. "I'm all right. I didn't mean to take your thoughts away from your brother and Kate. They're the ones who need your concern now."

"And our prayers," Richard added soberly.

"Yes," Stuart agreed. "And our prayers. Listen, I'd better be going. I'm sure there are other people you need to inform and much you need to take care of. I am so sorry. Please express my sympathy to your parents and to David—and what hospital did you say Kate was in?"

"American," Natalie replied.

"Right. I'll try to send her something. Meanwhile, if there's anything I can do—I seem to remember you saying that to me not too long ago and that you really meant it. Well, I do too. Remember, I have connections with the British embassy in Paris. I could alert the embassy if there was something the government could do. Arrange transport. Anything."

Stuart lightly touched Natalie's shoulder again. "You will tell me if I can help, won't you? I'm right across the street, you know."

Natalie nodded. "Yes, I know. Thank you, Stuart."

25

Fifth Week, the Weekend
Castle Combe

ello? McAdams' residence."

Recognizing the voice on the phone as that of Dianna, Yvette could picture her standing in the kitchen with the baby on her hip. She took a deep breath. "Hello, Dianna? This is Yvette Goodman. You know, Austen's friend who bought the clock from you?"

"Yvette. Of course. How are you?" The warmth in Dianna's voice immediately put Yvette at ease.

"I'm fine, but I'm trying to pass along a message to Austen from David MacKenzie. I understand from the porter at Merton that your mother is in hospital—I'm so sorry. How is she?"

Dianna sighed. "Not too well, I'm afraid. She does have pneumonia. Austen is there now, as a matter of fact, or I'd put him on to talk to you—Jack!" Her voice grew more muffled. "Please stop that and eat your supper." It grew clearer. "Sorry about that. It never fails that they start acting up whenever I get on the phone."

"I won't keep you then. Sorry to interrupt your supper. I wonder when would be a good time to ring back."

"If you give me your number, I could have Austen ring you when he gets in—if it's not too late. He may decide to spend the night, though. Well, actually, I'm not sure yet what we're doing. I'd like to go over for a while tomorrow, but Andrew has to mind the shop, and I'm not sure Austen can handle all the boys, so…"

"May I be of help?"

"No, no—I wouldn't ask that of you. I was just trying to explain."

"Really, may I help you?" Yvette was most earnest. "I'm used to boys and babies and I'd love to be able to be of use in some way. I could borrow a car from a colleague of mine and drive over tomorrow—that is, if it would be all right with you…if you don't think Austen would mind."

"Mind? Why should he? Do you mean it?" Dianna was clearly relieved and enthusiastic about this new idea. "That would be really nice of you!"

"Right! Then I'll be there. What would be a good time? Eight o'clock?"

"Eight would be perfect. Thank you so much, Yvette! This is really kind—Oh! Do you want me to pass along that message of David's?"

Yvette paused, considering. "No, I think I'd best give it to Austen myself. I'll see you tomorrow, then. And I'll be continuing to pray for your mother."

"Thanks. I appreciate that. Cheers."

"Cheers." Yvette hung up the phone thoughtfully. She was happy to be of service to Austen's family but troubled at having to be the bearer of more bad news.

Austen slept in a chair by his mother's bedside. When morning broke and her breathing had grown less labored, he kissed her gently, whispering he would go home for a bit of breakfast. She patted his hand gratefully and nodded her approval.

As he drove up to the family cottage along the Bybrook Bridge, he noticed a strange car parked along the street. He wearily entered the house and followed the aroma of bacon and eggs and the raucous noise of children's laughter down the narrow hallway to the family kitchen. There he was astounded to see baby Michael giggling in the arms of Yvette while Dianna scurried about the kitchen serving breakfast to Andrew and the boys.

"Yvette!" Austen exclaimed with genuine joy. "What are you doing here?"

"I hope you don't mind," she said hurriedly. "I talked to Dianna last night and since it sounded like she could use a bit of help on the home front, here I am."

"And I'm glad she is!" Dianna added. "Now I can go visit Mum. How is she?"

"Better." Austen answered. "Her breathing seemed easier this morning, so I felt I could come home for breakfast." He pulled out a chair and sat heavily. "My word, this smells good, Di. I'm starved."

"Well, help yourself. There's plenty. Coffee?"

"Yes, please." Austen served himself and then smiled at Yvette. "It's nice to see you. How did you know I was here?"

"You had told me that your mother was ill and might have to go in hospital. I tried ringing you at Merton, and when I couldn't get you, I went by the Porters' Lodge and they told me you had gone home. So I rang Dianna last night." Yvette did not explain why she had been trying to reach him. "Anyway, I didn't have much planned for today and I thought I could help out with the boys so that Andrew could work in the store and Dianna could visit your mum."

"Speaking of which, I have to go open up." Andrew stood, grabbed an extra piece of toast, and kissed his wife. "If you go, Di, be sure to drive my pickup truck. They're forecasting snow and I don't want you getting stuck on some little country road."

"All right, luv. I'll come by and get the key from you so you'll know when I'm leaving."

"Lads?" The boys paused eating long enough to pay attention to their father. "I want you to be good for Uncle Austen and Miss Yvette, do ye hear? I'm right next door, so they'll know where to find me if you give them any trouble. You'll be good lads now, won't ye?"

The little boys nodded solemnly but kept chewing.

"All right, then. I'll see you for lunch." Andrew kissed each of his children and gave Dianna an extra peck for good measure as he slipped out the back door. "Thanks, Yvette. Thanks, Austen. Cheers."

"Cheers." The family turned back to the business of breakfast, and Yvette helped Dianna clean up the kitchen as the brother and sister discussed their current family crisis.

"I think she's making a turn for the better," Austen said as he drank a second cup of coffee. "But with the portions of her lungs that are damaged from the polio, I think she's in for a long recovery once the penicillin really takes effect. Having her remain in hospital in Chippenham seems really difficult on you and Andrew, and I can't stay here longer than Sunday. I'd like to, but I can't skip any more work next week. So, what's to be done?"

"I guess Andrew and I can take turns," Dianna said as she wiped the boys' dirty mouths and helped them down from the table. "But I don't know how we'll manage here if she's still in need of a lot of nursing when she comes home. I'll have a hard time just keeping the boys quiet, let alone taking care of the house and Mum."

"No, it's too much for you," Austen agreed.

"May I make a suggestion?" Yvette asked tentatively.

"Certainly."

"Well, this may not work for you, either, but there's the Acland Nursing Home in North Oxford, and if you had your mother transported there, then Austen could visit her every day and, Dianna, you and Andrew could just get your lives back to normal here until your mother was strong enough to take care of herself and move back home again."

Austen and Dianna exchanged glances. Dianna nodded.

"Could work," Austen agreed. "Let me check into it on Monday. Thanks for the suggestion, Yvette. This could be just the ticket. Now, Di, thanks for breakfast, but don't you want to get on the road? Andrew was right about that forecast for snow. It may be just flurries, but you never know out here."

"I'll just get the boys dressed and in order first," she said. "Yvette has a message for you from David, I believe. Come along, lads, let's go change."

As the ruckus of the boys clambering up the stairs died down, Austen peered inquisitively at Yvette. "A message from David, she said?"

"Yes. He tried to ring you, but since you were here, he couldn't get ahold of you. Then he rang me and tasked me with tracking you down."

Austen looked puzzled. "Well, what is it? I hope it's not bad news."

"I'm afraid it is—and I'm sorry to be the messenger. I don't know any way to say this but to get straight to the matter." Yvette took a deep breath. "Their baby was stillborn."

Austen stared at her in shocked disbelief.

"It's dreadful, I know," she whispered.

He silently shook his head. "Poor David!" he finally said. "He wanted this baby so badly. And Kate…oh, my word. Do they know what happened?"

"A knot in the umbilical cord. The baby was perfectly fine. 'A beautiful girl,' he said." Yvette lightly touched his arm. "Austen, they had planned to call the baby Marianne if it were a girl."

"Ah!" Austen moaned softly.

"They'd still like to call her that since that's what they had decided on. And if it's all right with you, they'd like to have the little one laid to rest with your Marianne at St. Cross."

Austen appeared to be studying his hands. "Yes," he said quietly. "She would have liked that. She's probably even now welcoming her little namesake into heaven, so it's only fitting that their remains be together here as well." He sighed deeply. "Poor David. Poor Kate. I just wish there was something I could do."

Yvette nodded. "I think you have already. And David asked for our prayers, of course. I think Reverend MacKenzie will share about it at St. Aldate's tomorrow, so I hope to go and support the family then."

"Sure. Sure." He looked up at her. "Thank you, Yvette, for coming and telling me in person. This must have been difficult for you, and I appreciate hearing it from you rather than someone in the SCR. Gives me time to think. And it was nice of you to come help Dianna."

"I'd better help her now so that she can get going," Yvette said, rising.

"You know, I'm two cups of coffee down but I'm still exhausted. I guess sleeping in a chair is not the best night's rest. Would you mind terribly if I took a nap while you keep an eye on the boys?"

"No, that would be fine. That's why I came," Yvette replied, cognizant that Austen needed his time alone as well as his sleep. "You go on up and lie down and I'll take over the boys so Dianna can leave."

"Yvette." Austen momentarily stayed her with a hand on her arm. "Thank you again. You're such a good friend."

Yvette smiled wistfully. "No problem."

26

Fifth Week, Saturday Afternoon

*A*usten stretched out on the bed that had been his but now belonged to Rob. He prayed for his mother, David, and Kate, then he fell into the deep slumber of exhaustion. As he slept, Yvette cleaned up the kitchen and then kept the boys occupied by reading stories aloud to them. When Austen awoke and trudged downstairs, he was struck by the sight of his nephews cuddling with Yvette on the couch, while outside the windows the first flurries of snow were beginning to swirl.

"Well," he said as they glanced up from their book. "You all are snug as bugs. And quiet too. Thanks, lads. I had a good nap there."

"Unca Autty? Would you read us a story too?" piped up Robby.

"Looks to me like Miss Yvette is doing a rather good job of it."

"If you take over," she said, "then I can go make something to eat and heat up the baby's bottle."

"Done." Austen held out his arms for Michael and exchanged places with Yvette. "All right, lads, pick out a book for me." They settled into a new story as Yvette found some fixings for soup and sandwiches and quickly prepared their lunch. When Andrew arrived home for the noonday meal and opened the back door, Yvette noticed that the flurries had morphed into a full-blown storm.

"I've closed the shop," he announced, hanging up his coat on a peg behind the door. "Can't believe anyone will be out shopping for antiques in this. Anyway, I put a sign in the window to inquire over here if anyone actually does show up." He rubbed his hands together. "I hope Dianna sees what's going on and feels she can leave the hospital before the roads get really bad. Smells good, Yvette."

"Just soup and such. Hope it will do."

"That'll be great," Andrew answered cheerfully. "Where are the boys?"

"In the parlor listening to their Uncle Austen reading a story."

"Hope it's not *Beowulf*." Andrew chuckled. As he strode into the parlor, Yvette could hear the boys squealing with delight at the sight of their dad. Within minutes they had washed up and were seated around the kitchen table with their heads bowed for the blessing. As they quickly ate their meal, Austen and Andrew chatted while Yvette busied herself with serving and tending to the baby. She had scarcely sat down to eat when the boys were eager to be excused and get dressed to play outside in the snow.

"I'll get them suited up," Andrew volunteered. "It'll take a good half an hour to find their boots and mittens and get them into their kit, and then they'll be back inside in five minutes clamoring for hot chocolate."

"Should I heat some up now?" asked Yvette.

"I was semi-jesting. I think you can at least wait until we're out the door. Austen, would you find the cocoa for her? And then why don't you come out and join us? If the snow is deep enough, I have a mind to build an igloo or something fun."

"I didn't think to bring any snow kit," Austen said as he took the cocoa and sugar down from the cupboard. "It's been ages since we've had a good snow."

"Just rummage around in the back of the wardrobe. I'm sure I have some old gear you can borrow."

Austen looked apologetically at Yvette. "Would you mind staying in with the baby?"

"No, go ahead." Yvette reassured him with a smile. "It'd be good for you to get out and play."

Austen grinned. "Guess I'm getting a little old for this sort of thing."

"No one is ever too old to play in the snow. Go on. Have a bit of fun."

After a mad scramble of sorting out boots, coats, scarves, and gloves, the two young men and two younger boys were finally dressed for the weather and out the door. Yvette put the baby down for a nap, washed up the lunch dishes, and slowly warmed some milk in a pan on top of the stove. She hummed contentedly as she worked, glancing out of the window periodically to check on the progress of the rising igloo in the back garden. Before long, as predicted, two-year-old Jack came to the door crying from the cold. Yvette ladled out a half cup of hot chocolate to cool while she peeled away his icy wet clothes and hung them up in the scullery to dry. She had him settled at the table, sipping his cocoa and munching on a biscuit when the front door opened and Dianna blew in with a gust of wind.

"Mummy!" Jack cried.

"Hello, darling," Dianna sang out as she kissed her son. "Are you having hot chocolate? Did you go out in the snow to play?"

Jack nodded and Dianna smiled at Yvette. "Looks like you have things well under control here. Where are the big boys?"

"Out in the garden." Yvette returned her smile. "They're building an igloo."

"That husband of mine should have been an engineer. He loves to construct things. Is the baby asleep?"

"Yes. I just put him down. How's your mother?"

"She's better, thanks." Dianna pulled off her coat and gloves. "The doctor said she's out of the woods, so I thought I'd best get on home while I could. The snow was coming down quite fast and I didn't want to get stuck in Chippenham. The hospital promised to ring if anything changes."

"I'm glad to hear she's better. How were the roads?"

"Not good. These country lanes can be tricky in any weather, but in snow they're downright treacherous. Thankfully, I had Andrew's truck." Dianna served herself a cup of hot chocolate and sat at the table. Then she noticed the expression of thoughtful concern on Yvette's face. "Oh, dear, I forgot you'd be wanting to get back to Oxford. I wouldn't recommend it, luv. You could stay here tonight. I'm sure they'll have the roads cleared by morning."

"I wouldn't consider imposing on you—not with all you have going on. If you think the roads are truly bad—perhaps there's a B-and-B in town?"

"Nonsense. You'll stay here. Besides…" Dianna smiled. "You're much more help to me than Austen. I say, would you like to have a go in the snow with the boys? I'm ready to take over babysitting duty."

Yvette gazed longingly out the window. Snow rarely adhered to the busy streets of London. "I didn't bring the proper clothes," she said regretfully.

"I've got some Wellies in the hall wardrobe. Why don't you give them a try? You look about the same size as me. Go on," Dianna coaxed. "Help yourself to whatever you like."

Yvette didn't need much encouragement. She foraged around the wardrobe and retrieved the boots. Pulling them on, she was gratified that she and Dianna did wear the same size. When Yvette was well suited up, she ventured outside. The snow had slowed to an occasional flurry but had fallen heavily enough to transform the garden into a dazzling fairyland. The heavy quiet that first greeted her when she stepped from the house was soon pierced by shouts and laughter. A snowball battle had clearly commenced between Austen and Andrew, their combat lines drawn behind the woodpile and the low rise of Andrew's abandoned igloo. Yvette dashed for the wall during a brief lull while the men stockpiled more ammunition.

"Hello there," Andrew called out as she ducked behind his icy barricade.

"Dianna's home," Yvette said breathlessly. "Mrs. Holmes is doing better."

"Excellent!" Andrew tossed another ball over to the woodpile while Rob molded more with his small hands. The snow was sticky but soft. *No hard ice crystals to cause serious damage,* Yvette thought as she quickly added to the heap of snowballs. *This could be fun!*

"May I?" she asked.

"By all means." Andrew grabbed another and lobbed it over. Austen fired one in return that hit Andrew's hat. Yvette took this moment to aim and landed one directly into Austen's chest.

"Ah! '*A touch! A touch!*'" Austen conceded.

"Nice throw, Yvette," Andrew complimented her. "Where did you learn to do that?"

"Hyde Park—playing cricket with my brothers," Yvette said as she tossed another. Chastened by experience, Austen wisely ducked this time. Having grown up in a family of boys, Yvette was quite athletic and known in her childhood circle as something of a tomboy. But her opportunities to showcase her sporty side had become as infrequent as the opportunity to play in newly fallen snow. "Why don't we storm him?" she suggested eagerly.

"A frontal assault?"

"Sure. He can't hit both of us."

"Right." Andrew turned to instruct his son. "Robby, you man the fort while we attack."

"Yes, sir!" The little boy continued to add diligently to his stack of snowballs. Andrew and Yvette hastily grabbed a few and readied for the charge, but Austen precipitated their attack. Whooping and hurling snowballs, he bounded toward them across the no-man's-land of the garden. Andrew fired off his rounds with no effect. Yvette was poised to throw hers when, to her surprise, Austen came crashing over the snow wall, toppled her over, and landed heavily on her.

"Oh, so sorry!" he cried in bewilderment.

Yvette laughed and smashed her fistful of snow in his face. He felt the tingling sensation not of cold but of desire. He had an overwhelming urge to kiss her. In a surreal suspension of time, an unmistakable physical attraction surged between them. The brief moment passed into present reality as young Robby jumped on them both.

"I gotcha!" he yelled gleefully.

Austen rolled over, gently dumping Rob in the snow. They tussled as Andrew fired another volley at his brother-in-law's back.

Laughing, Austen exclaimed, "All right, all right! I surrender!"

*I*n reality—not in play—Austen found it difficult to surrender. Each time he thought he had yielded his life to God, a memory or event would jar him with the realization that he hadn't truly. Perhaps all of life was like this, he mused—a continuous battle of *not my will but Thine be done* fought over and over on the same no-man's-land. Victories followed by setbacks and retreats followed by victories. Grieving was like that, he had found. He would believe he had passed a milestone of grief only to come upon it again and again. What had Lewis written in *A Grief Observed*? That he could not make a map of grief but rather had to chronicle its history. Hadn't he discovered that sorrow was not a state but a process? Austen had read and reread the little book so often that he had almost committed it to memory.

> Grief is like a long valley where any new bend may present a totally new landscape...not every bend does. Sometimes the surprise is the opposite one; you are presented with exactly the same sort of country you thought you had left behind miles ago. That is when you wonder whether the valley isn't a circular trench. But it isn't. There are partial recurrences, but the sequence doesn't repeat.

After prayer and discussion with his family and friends, Austen had decided it was time to move on with his life. Intellectually, he rationalized he was not meant to live alone; emotionally, however, his contemplations of loving any woman other than Marianne led him to profound feelings of guilt. Would he be dishonoring her memory? He had concluded "no" and convinced himself that she would not have wanted him to remain alone. But then he would find himself back at the same bend in the road, paralyzed with doubt and guilt. *Am I allowed to be happy again? Or is this unwanted celibacy my cross to bear for the rest of my earthly life?*

After the brief moment of heightened tension with Yvette in the snow, he had been plagued again with these doubts. It was certainly not the first time since Marianne's death that he had been physically attracted to a woman, but it was the first time he had a powerful urge to express it—an urge he would have had difficulty suppressing without the timely intervention of his nephew. And that urge troubled him even now as he lay awake in his old bed, quite conscious that the young woman who had aroused these feelings was sleeping next door in the nursery.

Austen stared up at the familiar old beams in the ceiling and recalled the rest of their day together. He had given Yvette his hand to help her up out of the snow and then invited her to walk with him about the village to see it decked in its wintry finery. Castle Combe was renowned for its loveliness. Yet even the homeliest place can appear beautiful and clean under a fresh blanket of snow, and on this day his little village sparkled with enchantment. Somehow the familiar landscape had an aura of magical novelty and the bends in the road revealed not painful memories of his past but the prospective possibilities of future joys. And yet he continued to wonder...*Is this allowed? Is this all right?*

He remembered the evening meal and the relaxed manner in which Yvette and Dianna worked together, chatting like old school chums while they cared for the boys and cleaned up the dishes. Austen was pleased that the two women got on together so well, and then he was suddenly seized with resentment. *Has Dianna forgotten Marianne this easily? No. Don't be ridiculous, old boy!* He felt as though his mind was going in circles and that he had passed this marker in the road before as well. Perhaps Lewis was wrong and grief was a circuitous route, not a process. Or perhaps he was right, and the bend was familiar but not quite the same. *I need to think less and pray more...Help me, Lord!* Austen prayed. *And help mother. Heal and comfort her. And oh, God, comfort David and Kate and their families. Have mercy on them. Give them the strength to walk through this valley of the shadow of death. Help Kate to recover quickly.*

While praying for others, Austen felt his emotions quieting, and he drifted off to sleep. His last conscious thought was that he should send David his copy of *A Grief Observed*.

The next morning the McAdams–Holmes household rose early. Sleeping in was seldom an option with little ones about in any case, but Yvette was eager to return to Oxford to attend St. Aldate's and Austen felt he should as well. Though the roads had been cleared overnight, he also wanted to follow Yvette to ensure that she arrived back safely. They made the journey to Oxford without incident and agreed to meet at St. Aldate's after stopping at their respective colleges for a change of clothing.

Austen entered the church first and waited in the vestibule for Yvette. He nodded to a number of students and members of the Inklings Society—including Stuart Devereux and Nigel Elliot—as they scurried past to find seats in the crowded sanctuary. Just before the church bells rang out the hour, Yvette slipped in and they were seated toward the back.

"Sorry. I did try to hurry," she whispered. "Have you been waiting long?"

"Not at all. And you do have farther to come," he answered graciously. "The MacKenzies are all here except for David's mum. I didn't see her."

"I'm fairly certain he said she had gone over to Paris to help."

"Ah, right." The service began and further talk would have to wait. Austen enjoyed the contemporary worship at St. Aldate's and was pleased to see a large crowd of students among the congregation. Even so, he missed the predictable rhythms of the Catholic liturgy and determined to attend the evening mass at St. Aloysius'. Perhaps he should phone the Tolkiens to see if they would like a ride with him.

When Eric MacKenzie mounted the pulpit steps, he looked weary with sorrow. He smiled sadly at the congregation and began. "Many of you know our son David, who is a don here at Oxford. This term he and his lovely bride, Kate, have taken up a temporary post as a visiting professor of English literature at the American College in Paris. Some of you may also have been aware that they were expecting a baby in May." He paused for a moment and then went on. "I am sorry to say that the child was delivered stillborn on Wednesday morning." A collective moan rose from the congregation.

Eric paused again until the crowd had quieted. "Annie has gone over to provide help. I know David and Kate would appreciate your prayers—we all would. I'm sure you can understand how difficult this is for them and for us. I know personally that some of you have walked through similar trials. I've been with you as you've lost loved ones—even babies. There's something especially tragic about the loss of a child— all the lost potential, never being able to enjoy watching the wee one, who was so wanted and anticipated with such joy, grow up and pass all the wonderful milestones of childhood. Somehow it all seems rather unfair. I know something about that. Not just from walking alongside some of you during these trials, but because Annie and I lost a wee bairn to miscarriage before we were blessed with Hannah."

At the mention of her name, Hannah sat up importantly in Natalie's lap. She hadn't been paying much attention to her daddy's sermon, but she pricked up her ears at this. Natalie hugged her tightly and Hannah's mind began to wander as she relaxed again in her big sister's embrace, playing absently with her bracelet.

"But I am not here today to talk to you in particular about the death of our loved ones," Eric continued, "but rather of the death of a vision. Our Gospel reading today is from John, chapter 20. In choosing this Scripture, I took the liberty of diverging a bit from the liturgical calendar. We have here the familiar story of men who are at the point of despair, as their leader, Jesus—the man they had thought was the chosen Messiah—has been crucified and was buried. All their hopes, dreams, aspirations, and ambitions have been buried with

Him. They have locked themselves in an upper room, are hiding from the authorities, and are frightened and uncertain as to their future. But we who are believers read this story and know what they do not. We know that this is not the end of their story. We know that the resurrection is coming!"

Eric went on to cite several biblical examples of men and women who had been given a vision or promise from God, endured its death, and then watched as God supernaturally fulfilled it—Abraham, Joseph, Moses, Hannah, Lazarus.

"As the oldest son of a large family," Eric said, "David has long held a vision for marriage and a family. I believe God put that vision in his heart—as He did in mine. That vision was partially fulfilled by his marriage last July to Kate. Now with the loss of this child, he is experiencing the death of his vision. I don't pretend to know the whys of this tragedy. I don't believe we will ever understand all the whys in this life. I certainly don't know the end of their story—except the ultimate end of eternal life with Him. We are not as those without hope. I do believe that my little granddaughter is now in heaven with the Lord and is experiencing life far more abundantly than we are. I also have faith that on this earth, in God's timing and in God's way—perhaps in a manner we least expect—God will supernaturally bring the vision to fruition.

"In what area of life are you suffering with disappointment, even despair? What vision or promise do you believe God revealed to you only to have it die? Is it for a spouse? A child? A family? A job? A ministry? A healing? Here is my challenge to you: Persevere in faith, even in those bleakest of times when all hope seems gone. Seek first His kingdom and all these things shall be added unto you. Believe God. Trust Him as He fulfills His vision for you. Watch in wonder—the resurrection is coming!"

Eric then asked the congregation to join him in prayer as they examined their hearts, yielding back to God their disappointments and hurts and asking by faith for His grace and comfort. Many people at St. Aldate's that day were moved by the suffering of their rector and his family. They felt challenged to face their own struggles and disappointments with renewed faith and trust. Among them were Austen Holmes, Yvette Goodman, and Lord Stuart Devereux.

28

Sixth Week, Sunday
Paris

*I*n Paris that same Sunday morning, David and Annie attended the worship service at the American Church. David was gratified to find in the prayer section of the bulletin an expression of condolence for their loss. He had manfully tackled the difficult calls to Kate's parents, his family, the church minister, and the college secretary, but he hoped that announcements such as this one would help to spread the word so that he would not have to recount over and over again the details of their sad story to each acquaintance he encountered. He had found these exchanges to be awkward at best and at worst, upsetting. He could not imagine how Kate could endure them. Perhaps they should have a memorial service here in Paris, he thought. That would be one way of ensuring that everyone would hear the news at once, and it could be a positive means of dealing with their grief.

Certainly, Kate was not dealing with it well at all. In the hospital she had been confined to rest and recuperate from her ordeal. Mercifully, she had been well drugged for much of the time, which enabled her to sleep. When awake she did little but weep inconsolably. David was to bring her home from the hospital that afternoon and he was quite concerned.

When he arrived Kate was dressed in the loose shift he had brought previously to the hospital at her request. Since it would be several weeks before her figure would return, she had to suffer the indignity of continuing to look slightly pregnant. But far worse for her, he knew, was the fact that, despite binding, her breasts were still swollen with milk for an infant who would never suckle. Kate clutched a baby blanket to those breasts as if holding her little one. As the attendant wheeled her down to the hospital entrance, David noticed more than one person peering with an expectant smile at the baby blanket, only to avert their eyes when they realized the young mother's arms were empty. Kate kept her own eyes tightly closed. She could not face anyone.

When David took her arm to help her from the wheelchair, she stubbornly resisted. "I can't," she declared.

Misinterpreting her meaning, he coaxed her. "I'll help you."

"No. I can't—leave her. I can't go home without my baby."

"Oh, darling, I'm sorry." His voice broke. "You must."

At his tone she looked at him and grew more docile. "Must I?"

He nodded. "Yes."

"But I don't think I can."

"I'll help you," he repeated, and then he lifted her and placed her gently in the car. They were both quiet on the long ride home. Both were thinking of their last ride together down those avenues.

At least then I still had her inside me, Kate thought. *We weren't separated. We were still together. It's not fair! I have milk and no baby to feed. I will never get to hold her again. I want to hold her. I miss her. I want to be with her. I want to die. If I died I could be with her. It would be so easy. I could just grab the wheel and turn it and then David and I could be with her.* She stared at the wheel, thinking. Then she saw David's strong hands—the hands she loved so much. She looked up at his face—the face she loved so much. *No, I couldn't take David with me. That would be wrong. He has too much to give this world. He could have more children. It's not his fault the baby died. He wanted her. It's all my fault! I'm sorry, God. I want her now. If You brought her back to me, I would love her so. I do want her now...*

Kate began weeping again. David glanced at her and covered her hand with his own. When they arrived at their apartment building, he put his arm around her and nearly carried her to the elevator.

In the foyer they passed a neighbor who, seeing the overnight bag, exclaimed in rapid French, "Bonjour, monsieur and madame. Did you have a false alarm? You must be getting excited! When is your baby due?"

Mercifully, Kate did not attempt a translation. David understood by the woman's comments that she had not heard their news, but he stood dumbstruck with bewilderment. He was rescued by Madame Denise, who emerged from her office at that moment. After bestowing sympathetic kisses on both cheeks of her young guests, she pulled the neighbor aside with furious whispers. David did not wait for her mortified reaction but hustled Kate quickly into the lift.

Annie welcomed her daughter-in-law with a warm embrace. She knew Kate would be exhausted from the physical exertion of dressing and gathering her things to return home. She also knew the emotional exertion of leaving the hospital with empty arms would be even more taxing.

Annie had not been idle during Kate's confinement. When she was not keeping her company in the hospital, she had been thoroughly cleaning the flat, cooking and freezing meals, and doing the laundry—some of which was even now hanging from the drying rack suspended from the kitchen ceiling. When Kate and David arrived, the flat fairly sparkled and the soft strains of Bach floated from the record player in the salon. Bouquets and baskets of flowers—from Kate's parents, the MacKenzies, St. Aldate's, and Stuart Devereux—brightened each room. David gave his mother an appreciative kiss while Kate stood dully by.

"Let's get you settled," Annie said kindly. "You must be worn out." She gently took Kate's arm to lead her down the hallway to the bedroom. Midway down the hall, Kate balked. She envisioned the room the way she had left it. "It's all right," Annie soothed as if anticipating her thoughts. Kate stumbled on, wanting to keep her eyes closed, dreading what she would find. When they entered the room, she blinked in surprise. A new duvet, like the one she had admired in Normandy, was turned back to reveal fresh flannel sheets. The room was lit by aromatic candles and an electric heater was glowing with cheerful warmth.

"I wanted to be sure you weren't cold," David explained. "I hope you don't mind that Mum and I bought some new stuff. Do you like it?"

When she didn't respond, David asked anxiously, "Kate, is it all right?"

She shook herself as if awakening. "Yes. It's very nice. I'm glad it's different." She sighed heavily. "Now, what am I to do?"

"Rest, dear. Get settled and then come have a bit of supper," Annie said. "The doctors want you to get plenty of rest and to take another week off from school to recuperate."

"A week? Here alone?" Kate croaked. "David will have to go back to work, won't he?" She seemed frightened. David and Annie exchanged glances.

"I'll be here," Annie reassured her. "I can stay until the weekend."

"Would you, please?"

"Yes, honey. I'll be happy to."

"I've talked to your professors, Kate," David said, "and you're excused from classes. They'll give me copies of their lecture notes so you needn't get behind."

"Oh, that's right. School. I had forgotten all about it. It doesn't seem to matter now."

"Well, darling, you needn't face it just yet. But when you're ready, I'll bring everything home for you. Why don't you get comfortable, and then we'll have some supper, all right?"

Kate nodded. With the same sense of dread she had felt on entering their bedroom, she forced herself to go into the bathroom. New linens hung there as well. She didn't want to think about what may have happened to the old ones. She was grateful for the change. Slipping out of the shift and into a clean nightgown, she wrapped herself in a bathrobe and made her way down the hall to the kitchen. Even the simplest of activities seemed to take such effort. She dutifully managed to sip some broth and swallow a few bites of baguette, although she had no appetite. David and Annie made a few feeble attempts at conversation, but Kate did not.

"May I be excused?" she asked wearily when dinner seemed at an end.

David hopped up to assist her from her chair. "Excuse us both, Mum. Thanks for supper."

"You're welcome. You two take care of yourselves. I'll wash up now." Annie set about cleaning the kitchen, humming along to Bach as she worked.

Kate completed her toilette and laid her bathrobe across the foot of their bed. David had folded back the duvet and was stretched out on the bed reading. "I'm really ready for bed, I think, David," she said. "I'm so exhausted, but I don't know if I can go to sleep yet or not."

He patted her place on the bed beside him. "Why don't you lie here and I'll read to you for a while?"

"Okay." Retrieving the baby blanket, Kate clutched it tightly and then gingerly climbed into bed.

"Should I read to you from the Bible?" he asked.

This all seemed like déjà vu to Kate. Then she recalled the last night she had spent in this bed. "No!"

Her vehemence took him aback. "All right." He rolled over onto his stomach and searched the stack of books on the floor. "I know. Something light. How about *The Last Battle* from The Chronicles of Narnia?"

"Okay."

He propped his pillow against the headboard and sat up against it. "Come here," he said, putting his arm around her and drawing her close. "I've missed you so. I'm glad you're back home." He kissed the top of her forehead. "Hmm, having you with me again is much better."

Kate leaned her head on his chest, draping one arm across him while cradling the blanket in the other. "Will you stay with me until I fall asleep?" she asked in a childlike whisper.

"My pleasure." David kissed her again and then stroked her hair as he read. He wasn't sure if she was listening to the words, but she must have found the rhythms of his voice soothing because after a few chapters she fell asleep. He gently covered her with the duvet and crept out.

He found Annie reading in the salon. "Everything all right?" she asked.

"Yes. I read her to sleep. I think she's scared to be alone." He sank into the other chair. "But then, I'm scared to leave her alone. I'm worried about her, Mum. She still seems in such a fog, even though she isn't on any drugs now."

"Well, she's been through a tremendous ordeal, and the 'fog' may be a self-protective way of numbing her to the shock. Give her time. We all deal with grief differently."

"I've been thinking about that. Remember in *Hamlet* when Claudius and the Queen tell him that since the beginning of time men have lost their fathers and they ask him why then his grief is so 'particular' to him? Kate and I have lost the same child, and yet her grief is particular to her. You have lost a baby, and yet you can only partially feel and sympathize with Kate's pain. I wish it were otherwise. I wish I could carry more of this burden for her. Jack Lewis once said that the idea of 'one flesh' could only go so far—that we can't really experience someone else's pain or joy, much as we'd like to. In the end, we all have to face death and stand before God *alone*. I wish I knew what to do to help her now."

Annie smiled at him. "Do just what you're doing. Love her, pray for her, be there for her. You can help bear her burden. And remember, you have to work through your own 'particular' grief as well." She studied his face. "How are you doing, honey?"

"I'm all right, Mum." He sighed. "I'm terribly sad, of course, and disappointed. But I've been thinking about the Bible stories of King David. When his infant son died, he put off his weeping and fasting, saying he couldn't bring the child back. He said, 'I shall go to him, but he will not return to me,' and he worshiped the Lord. He had faith for eternal life. I'm trying to keep that eternal perspective. I feel almost like I'm walking in a bubble of God's grace. I wish Kate were too, but she seems more like what you said—in a state of shock or numbness. I'm worried about what she'll do when she snaps out of it."

"You know, it's hard to say, but there are patterns people tend to follow."

"Like what? I never read much psychology, you know."

"People tend to go through phases of denial, anger, bargaining, depression, and finally find some resolution or acceptance. They may skip a phase or repeat them over and over. But when Kate does snap out of this shock, don't be surprised if she becomes irrationally angry—especially at you because you're closest to her."

"Angry? At me?"

"Who knows? She may direct it at me or herself or even God. She could skip over it, but with all those hormones of hers raging around out of whack—just be prepared."

"Thanks for the warning, but gee, I hope you're wrong. And I hope I won't lose my temper—especially with her or you." David had been restlessly jiggling his foot while they talked. "I say, Mum, I am feeling really antsy, though. I'd like to go out for a walk, if you don't mind."

"Okay, honey. That's a good idea. I'll hold the fort here."

"Thanks, Mum." David bent down and kissed her cheek before donning his father's brown leather flight jacket and going out into the brisk February night.

He quickly walked up Rue Vineuse in the direction of Trocadéro. A view of the Eiffel Tower from the Palais would bring him some diversion. The fountains had been turned off, but the steel edifice still rose majestically above the skyline on the opposite bank of the Seine. He thought of St. Valentine's evening when he and Kate had strolled arm and arm across this plaza. *Could it have been only six days ago? It seems like another lifetime. Why does time go so quickly when life is good and hangs so heavily during sorrow?* He recalled buying her the bouquet of roses and then—*What had happened? Kate was bothered that the white one had snapped off. Could that have been a foreshadowing? A forewarning that God would take their little flower home to bloom in His garden?* David mused on this for a while in a state somewhere between prayer and meditation. A poem began to form itself in his mind, and he pulled a little notebook from his pocket to jot down the lines before they vanished. The poem brought him comfort. He hoped it would to Kate as well. Perhaps he would surprise her with it at the memorial service.

29

Seventh Week, Sunday Afternoon

I won't go!" Kate stubbornly refused to budge from her chair in the salon.

"Kate, whatever is wrong with you?" David asked in exasperation. "You agreed to have a memorial service here. You thought it would be a good idea since you weren't able to go to Oxford for the service there. You know my family is even now on their way to St. Cross—that's why we scheduled the one at the American Church this afternoon. It's already been announced."

"I don't care. If I can't be with her at St. Cross, then I don't want to go."

"You're not making any sense. People will be waiting for us."

"Who?"

"Pastor Roberts and probably President Edwards and a few of my colleagues. Maybe some students. I really don't know all who will come, but it was announced both at church and at the college."

"I don't want to see anybody."

"Kate." David's voice was now gentle. "You're supposed to go back to school tomorrow. I understand you don't want to see people, but you're going to have to sooner or later and this should make it easier."

"I can't do it."

"We can do all things through Christ who strengthens us."

"Don't quote Scripture to me!" A fierce look flashed through her eyes. "He didn't help me keep my baby."

David recognized the anger Annie had warned him about. All the previous week he had "muddled through" in typical British fashion, returning to work and the awkward exchanges with his colleagues. Annie had cared for Kate, who had slowly seemed to emerge from her shell-shocked state. She listlessly tried to attend to her studies but had shown little interest in the world outside their flat. Annie had finally coaxed her out for walks in the terraced gardens of Chaillot, but even these limited outings were a cause for pain. Everywhere Kate saw women pushing baby prams and children running and playing. She wept as she told and retold her story to Annie, and each time Annie sympathetically listened as only another woman who had lost a child could. She offered little in the way of advice, sensing Kate was not ready for any. But David and his mother had talked and prayed long into the evenings.

David had also talked at length to his father and Austen, as well as to the pastor at the American Church. They had agreed with Kate's acquiescence that Annie would return Saturday to England with the baby's tiny coffin for a private interment at the Holywell Cemetery at St. Cross. David and Kate would hold a memorial service at the same time Sunday afternoon at the American Church in Paris. He had come to believe quite strongly that postponing the service until their return to Oxford would only prolong their anguish. This would bring them a sense of closure and would also give him an opportunity to share his heart with some of his associates.

But now he was faced with an angry and recalcitrant wife. He tried gentle persuasion once more. "Darling, the arrangements have all been made and we need to be going."

"You can go by yourself. You don't need me to be there."

In truth, David was afraid to leave Kate alone. Some of her comments to him and to Annie during the past week had indicated she had entertained self-destructive thoughts. She had been so irrational of late that he really couldn't leave her by herself. He had lost his daughter. He could not risk losing his wife as well.

"No, I will not go by myself. You are going to come with me."

"I won't go."

Although he hated to pull out the submission card, he was beginning to feel desperate. "Kate, when we married you vowed to love, honor, and obey me. I seldom do this, but today, as your husband, I am asking you to honor this request of mine and come with me to the service."

"No!"

He frowned. "Okay. As your husband I am ordering you to go. Now."

"You can order me to," she challenged him defiantly, "but you can't make me, you know. The only way you can get me to that service is to carry me there."

"I can do that." David stood up to his full height of nearly six feet. "I've carried you all the way out to the car before. I can do it again."

"You wouldn't dare!"

David sighed heavily. "You're right. I'm just trying to make the point that I *could*. Listen, Kate, this service really, really means a lot to me, but I don't want to force you to go. If you won't go, I'll just have to phone and have them hold the service without us." He glanced at his watch, his voice cracking. "They'll be getting to St. Cross soon. Will you at least pray with me here?" David's face clouded with disappointment and sorrow.

Stricken by his grief, Kate reached up and took his hand. "I'm sorry," she whispered. "I'll go."

ᑫᓕᓫᓕᓕ

David and Kate slipped in from the side door with the minister and sat in the front pew. While the pastor read from the Scriptures and the congregation sang "Great Is Thy Faithfulness," Kate sat rigidly beside David. She knew he had selected the hymns and Scriptures, but she was as surprised as the rest when he rose to speak.

David scanned the assembly with his own amazement. He was touched to see the church packed with people—a few he knew only vaguely and others not at all. He breathed a silent prayer for the words to share and the grace to get through it.

"First of all I'd like to thank you for coming today. I am moved that so many of you—some who don't personally know me or my wife—would come to give us your support and sympathy. It is truly a blessing and we are grateful for your presence here and for your kind notes, meals, and most of all your prayers. We'd also be grateful if you would continue to pray for us in the days ahead.

"It may have struck some of you as strange or unusual to hold a memorial service for a baby girl whom we never really had the opportunity to get to know. But we wanted to express our gratitude for her brief time with us as well as our hope for an eternity together. If you listened to the Scriptures Pastor Roberts read this afternoon, you will understand the reason for our hope. We believe these Scriptures are true. Today I'm not going to give a lengthy philosophical or theological discourse on why I believe them—although I'd be happy to at another time. But since we are having this memorial service for our daughter in a church, I hope you will understand that I feel it's my prerogative to speak to you not as a university professor, but without further apology as a Christian and a father.

"Many of you are familiar with the Scripture John 3:16. It reveals the basic tenet of the Christian faith, but it has an even more poignant meaning for me now. 'For God so loved the world that he gave his only Son, that whoever believes in him should not perish but have eternal life.'

"My heavenly Father knows what it means to lose a child. He understands our pain and sorrow. But the amazing thing to me is that He willingly endured that loss and separation so that we may not be eternally separated from Him.

"Verse 17 goes on to say, 'For God sent the Son into the world, not to condemn the world, but that the world might be saved through him.' I believe that. I believe that because Jesus came to this earth as God in the flesh and suffered and died and rose again, that our daughter, Marianne, is with Him now, and that one day her mother and I will be as well. And that faith is our comfort.

"Now, of course, we grieve her loss. We long for her. We are grateful that we could anticipate her arrival, feel her kicking and swimming about, sing songs to her as she grew in her mother's womb. But we have so little to remember her by: a hospital baby blanket, a lock of hair, a couple of pictures, and her hand and footprints." He smiled. "I was blessed to see that little as she was, she had her daddy's long fingers and toes." Then he paused. "I won't deny, though, that it's very hard to think...that we'll never..." David faltered and his voice broke. "That we'll never get to rock her to sleep or watch her first steps or see her grow up." He saw tears spilling down Kate's cheeks and some in the congregation dabbing their eyes. He took a deep breath and looking beyond their heads, continued.

"We profess a faith in a heavenly kingdom where our little Marianne Faith is now dancing and singing with the angels, and that brings us comfort. But we are still parents who have lost a child and we—like anyone in our circumstances would— have asked and will ask the question 'Why?' or 'Why us?' or 'Why her?' or 'Haven't we tried to serve You? Why would You let this happen?'"

Kate glanced up sharply at this. David spoke directly to her.

"I don't think God is troubled by our questions. Many of His servants and prophets in the Bible asked similar questions. From my readings, sometimes God answers such questions and sometimes He doesn't—at least, not in this earthly life or to our way of understanding.

"Now this is difficult for a professor to admit, but I've come to believe that one reason we may not get the answers we're searching for is that it's quite possible that, with our limited intelligence, we couldn't understand the answers even if He revealed them to us. You know, I like to think that as a graduate of Cambridge and Oxford, I'm a relatively bright man. I can read and speak several languages, but there are hundreds, maybe thousands of languages I don't understand at all. As much as I've read and admired translations of Tolstoy, if someone were to read *War and Peace* to me in Russian, I wouldn't understand one word of it. So what would make me think I can comprehend the ways of the Creator of the universe? His intelligence transcends mine like Einstein's to an ant's.

"In Isaiah 55 it is written: 'For my thoughts are not your thoughts, neither are your ways my ways, says the LORD. For as the heavens are higher than the earth, so are my ways higher than your ways and my thoughts than your thoughts.'

"As Job did, I can question God. But I also know that if He revealed Himself in all His glory, I would, like Job, repent in dust and ashes. And despite my circumstances and sorrow, I can proclaim like Job, 'I know that my Redeemer lives.'

"In C.S. Lewis's novel *Till We Have Faces*, the character Orual questions God and writes, 'I ended my first book with the words *no answer*. I know now, Lord, why you utter no answer. You are yourself the answer. Before your face all questions die away. What other answer would suffice?'

"I'm certain many of you have said to yourselves, 'When I get to heaven, I'm going to ask God about thus and so.' I myself have said so many times. And yet I believe like Orual that when I come face-to-face with God, all my questions will die away on my lips. I will have no more questions because *He* is the Answer."

David paused for a moment. "Thank you for coming today and for listening to my comments. They were as much for me as for anyone here. Now I'd like to beg your indulgence for just a few minutes more." He unfolded a piece of paper and smoothed it out. "The other night I was thinking about our little Marianne Faith, and some lines of poetry came to my mind that I'd like to share with you now."

Kate looked up in astonishment while David read.

This Little Flower

This little flower
did not bloom here.

Perhaps she was too fair—
too frail of tendril,
or root—
to share the air,
weather our winters,
or withstand the turbulence
of our storms.

I would rather think
that her Gardener—
our Father—
saw her seedling beauty
and gently freed her
to lift her up
(and all her substance)
to a well-turned bed.

There she will blossom—
flourish under purer rains,
and gentler light.
There she will find
fuller flower
and tender care
in a more glorious
and Kingly garden.

Kate could not control the tears that coursed down her cheeks, and she tightly clung to the baby's blanket. When David finished reading, he mustered up a reassuring smile and asked the congregation to join together in singing "Amazing Grace."

Across the Channel in the country churchyard of St. Cross in the Holywell Cemetery, a small group gathered around a tiny wooden coffin beside a tombstone engraved:

Marianne McAdams Holmes
Beloved Wife, Daughter, Sister, Friend
August 8, 1940–October 23, 1962

Although overcast, there was no biting wind on this February afternoon, only a gentle breeze. When the Reverend Eric MacKenzie finished the burial rites from the *Book of Common Prayer*, Annie tenderly laid on the casket a bouquet of white rosebuds sent from David and Kate. Then taking a deep breath to compose himself, Austen Holmes read aloud a copy of the poem David had written. Annie, Ginny, and Natalie MacKenzie dabbed at their eyes while even Stuart Devereux had to clench his jaw not to give way to emotion.

When Austen had concluded the poem, Eric offered up a final prayer and then said, "David requested that we close the service by singing together 'Amazing Grace.'" Yvette began the first verse in her splendid contralto and the rest joined in:

Amazing Grace! How sweet the sound
That saved a wretch like me!
I once was lost, but now I'm found;
Was blind, but now I see.

'Twas grace that taught my heart to fear,
And grace my fears relieved.
How precious did that grace appear
The hour I first believed.

Through many dangers, toils, and snares,
I have already come;
'Tis grace hath brought me safe thus far,
And grace will lead me home.

When we've been there ten thousand years,
Bright shining as the sun,
We've no less days to sing God's praise
Than when we've first begun.

As Stuart sang John Newton's familiar words, he struggled in vain to keep back tears. But as grieved as he was for his friends, his tears were not of sorrow. They were of surrender. For months now he had watched this family and desired to understand what made them different. He had been drawn by their love and faith, even in the midst of tragedy. But even though he had listened, studied, and even prayed in his determination to remain sober, he had not come to a place of claiming their faith as his own. He hardly knew how it happened, but as he sang the old hymn he suddenly realized that he believed the words he was singing. He could not explain it, but he felt overcome by the mysterious and amazing grace of God. In that crowded churchyard under an overcast February sky, Stuart had his own personal epiphany. Lord Stuart Devereux surrendered his life to his heavenly Father and yielded it by faith in service to the Lord of lords and King of kings.

30

Seventh Week, Sunday Evening

ow are you doing, Mum? Are you comfortable?" Austen kindly asked his mother, who had just settled in her temporary quarters at the Acland Nursing Home in North Oxford.

"Oh, I'm fine, just fine, thank you. Except for all the bother I've been to you and Dianna."

"Nonsense, Mum," Dianna said cheerfully as she plumped up pillows and busied herself with making the room look more cozy. "I wish we could take you home right away, but until you're better, you'll just have to put up with Austen."

"I'm sorry to be such a burden," Elinor Holmes fretted. "Austen, I know your duties at the University keep you occupied, so don't feel that you have to run over here all the time to sit with me. I'll be just fine."

"I know, but you're not a burden. Honestly." Austen hastened to reassure her. "Merton is not far, and I can get over here easily if you need me. I say, Mum," he added breezily, "I've brought a friend to see you this evening, if you feel up to any other visitors."

"Who would that be?"

"Yvette Goodman."

"Who?"

"Yvette Goodman," he repeated, convinced that she knew perfectly well of whom he was speaking. "You remember—my colleague who came to Castle Combe to buy a clock from Andrew?"

His mother paused. "Oh, yes, of course. You mean the half-caste."

Austen winced. "Yes. Well, anyway, she was at the funeral for the MacKenzie baby and I invited her to come by here with me before we get some supper. Would it be all right for me to bring her in to say hello?"

At the mention of the funeral, Elinor Holmes wilted. "That poor David. I am so sorry. Do tell me about the service. Did they go through with the plan to bury the baby beside Marianne?"

"Mother, Miss Goodman is waiting."

"Oh, right. Sorry. Of course, show her in. Then you can tell me all about it."

When Austen excused himself to find Yvette down in the entrance lobby, Dianna turned to her mother. "Mum, please try to be nice to Yvette."

"Nice? Why shouldn't I be? Don't I treat everyone nicely?"

"Well, just don't insult her by saying anything about her being 'half-caste' or asking about her parentage. She was a great help to me when you were in hospital in Chippenham. She watched the boys last Saturday so that I could go to see you and Andrew could work."

"Really?" Elinor ran her long fingers over the blanket that covered her. "Dianna, tell me—do you think she has designs on Austen? Because if she does, it would be quite inappropriate, you know."

"Mum, this is the twentieth century! But anyway, I don't think she has designs on Austen. I think she's just a very nice person and a very good friend." Dianna felt it wiser not to say that she thought perhaps Austen had designs—even if unknowingly—on Yvette. In any case, their talk on this subject was interrupted by Austen and Yvette's entrance.

"Hello, Mrs. Holmes," Yvette said warmly. "It's good to see you out of hospital. How are you feeling?"

"Much better, thank you, although everyone seems to think not well enough to go home yet."

"I'm sure you'll be on the mend soon." Yvette turned to Dianna. "Hello, Dianna! How are you and your boys?"

Dianna smiled. "Well, thank you. They'd like for you to come back to read some more stories to them."

"What about their uncle?" Austen asked, feigning insult.

"Don't worry. You haven't been supplanted. They always clamor for 'Unca Autty.'"

"You see, Austen," Elinor said. "I told you to come home more often. Those little boys need you."

"Yes, Mum." Austen kissed his mother's forehead in a conciliatory fashion, winking at his sister as he did so.

"Now tell me about the funeral today for that poor baby. Were you there?" She directed this question to Yvette.

"Yes, ma'am."

"Yvette sang," Austen interjected. "She has a beautiful voice."

Yvette glanced up in surprise at this unexpected compliment.

"Is that so?" Elinor didn't seem particularly impressed. "Well, who was there and what was said?"

Austen relayed the details to his mother and sister and then took out the copy of David's poem to read to them.

When he finished, Elinor sighed. "That's a lovely poem."

"'Tis, indeed." Dianna said, wiping away an errant tear. "It made me think of my own little one. I hope it brings Kate some comfort."

"Yes. It's a hard thing to lose a baby—or spouse or any loved one, for that matter," Elinor said quietly. "But a child seems the hardest of all…well!" Straightening her covers again, she spoke more briskly. "I am all set here and you have things to do. Dianna, you need to go home and see to those boys of yours, and Austen, I'm sure you have plenty to attend to. Miss Goodman, thank you for coming by."

"May I visit you again, Mrs. Holmes?" Yvette asked. "I'm often in this part of town and would be happy to stop in or bring you anything you need."

"Well, if you like. But I think these children of mine have taken care of everything." Elinor waved her hand in dismissal. "Now you all get going."

"Mum, you ring Austen if you need anything. He's not far. And I'll come when I can," Dianna said as she kissed her mother.

"You will no such thing, Dianna McAdams. It's too far for you to come and you need to take care of your family. I'll be fine. Right, Austen?"

He bent to kiss her. "Right."

"Now, scat! All of you!" Elinor smiled with satisfaction as her solicitous children departed.

After the memorial service, Kate and David returned to their apartment and heated up leftovers for supper. Kate spoke little while David was his usual loquacious self, trying valiantly but unsuccessfully to distract her with stories of his adventures at the Sorbonne and in the Latin Quarter. Occasionally he coaxed a smile from her, but for the most part she was unresponsive. He tried to keep the conversation light while he cleaned up the kitchen. A blaring of horns interrupted him and Kate rushed to the balcony to see the cause of the cacophony. It was merely a double-parked car.

As she leaned over the railing to look, Kate had the thought: *It would be so easy to throw myself off this balcony and end this pain. I don't need to force David to drive off a bridge. He has too much to live for. I could just jump and…*

"Kate?" David's voice was gentle but held a tremor of fear. He stepped through the open glass doors, taking her elbow firmly. "What's going on out here?"

"Nothing. Someone double-parked and everyone is furious."

"Right. Want to come back inside? Or would you like to go for a walk?"

"No. It's too cold. I'll come back in." They stepped over the sill and David firmly shut and latched the French doors.

"I made some tea," he said. "Your cup is by the settee. Just as you like it."

"Thanks."

Settling beside her, David sipped his tea. "Kate," he finally said, "thank you for coming to the memorial service today. It wasn't so terrible, was it? Did you think it went all right? Aren't you glad in the end that you came?" he asked, eager for reassurance that he had done the right thing.

"No...yes...no."

"You aren't glad?"

"I don't know. I hated being there...but it was a nice service, honey. You did a good job. The poem...the poem..."

"Did you like it?"

Kate's large brown eyes welled up with tears. She nodded. "Yes," she breathed. "It was beautiful. When did you write it?"

"I wrote it the night you came home from the hospital. I wanted to surprise you with it. I'm glad you like it. I asked Austen to read it today at the service at St. Cross."

"Oh, yes," she said faintly. "I had almost forgotten."

"They also sang 'Amazing Grace.'"

"I wish we could have been there."

David covered Kate's hand with his own. "I know. Me too." They sat silently for a few moments. Then he said brightly, "I say, remember the time we were in the garden at St. Clare in Cambridge and I read a Shakespearean sonnet to you?"

"Yes."

"And you asked me if I would still read poetry to my wife after we were married or if I would only do so during courtship?"

"You told me you hoped to always court your wife."

"Right. So how about some poetry tonight?"

Kate snatched her hand away. "Why the romance? You know the doctor said we can't make love for at least six weeks or two full cycles."

He looked pained. "Yes, of course I know that. I wasn't thinking about sex. Why would you assume that?"

"That's what you usually want when you get romantic."

"You know that's unfair. I was very romantic with you while we were courting and I never even kissed you." He put his arm around her. "I showed tremendous restraint toward you before and I can do it again—although it's tortuous being so close to you." He nuzzled her neck. "You do smell simply divine."

That made her giggle. "Stop it! You promised."

"Don't worry. I'll behave. But my mum said that the two-cycle caution is really just for the doctor's own convenience in trying to track your due date should you get pregnant again."

Kate stiffened. "I'm not going to get pregnant again."

David misunderstood her. "Darling, the doctor said he didn't see any reason why you couldn't right away. You're perfectly healthy and obviously fertile."

"No! I won't!" Kate clenched her fists. "I don't want to get pregnant again. I don't ever want to go through losing another baby. I can't do that again. I won't!"

David sat in shocked silence. Finally he said, "You know, I don't think we should be talking about this now. We've been through a lot and our emotions are still very raw."

"I mean it, David!"

"I can see that." He stared down at his hands and then slapping his thighs, stood up. "Right! Well then, what would you like me to read tonight? Shakespeare? Donne? Browning?"

"I don't care," she answered dully. "You pick."

"Right." David brought his emotions under control while he perused his books. "How about Donne? No, not his pre-conversion stuff. Don't want too much eroticism, do we?" He picked up a book. "Oh, this is better. Keats. Let's try this. Splendid stuff." Returning to his place next to Kate again, He said, "But there's no reason why we still can't cuddle and be romantic." Encircling her with his arm, he drew her head onto his chest, gently kissed her hair, and began to read.

Part III

Easter Vacation

March–April 1966

For my thoughts are not your thoughts,
neither are your ways my ways, says the LORD.
For as the heavens are higher than the earth,
so are my ways higher than your ways and
my thoughts than your thoughts.

—ISAIAH 55:8-9

I ended my first book with the words no answer.
I know now, Lord, why you utter no answer.
You are yourself the answer.
Before your face questions die away.

—C.S. LEWIS
from *Till We Have Faces: A Myth Retold, Part II,* chapter 4

31

First Week
Oxford

"*H*ow is your mother doing, Austen?" Edith Tolkien's warm brown eyes regarded him with concern. "Is she still at the Acland?"

"Forgive me for not asking sooner," added Professor Tolkien. "We were dreadfully sorry to hear she had been so ill. We do hope she's better."

Austen put down his teacup. "Yes, much better, thank you. In fact, well enough to be discharged yesterday from Acland and back home at Castle Combe."

"I am glad to hear it," said Edith. "But I am sorry we didn't manage to get over to pay her a visit while she was in town. It is hard for us to get about."

"Please don't worry about it. She saw plenty of me, and Yvette was kind enough to visit her as well."

"Oh," Edith said, smiling at Yvette. "How nice of you."

"It was nothing, really." Yvette glanced up from her tea. "I just stopped by a few times when I was in the area and took her some magazines and such."

"I'm sure it meant a lot to her to have visitors. We certainly enjoy having company like you and Austen or other friends from the University."

"It's the people we don't know who just turn up that are bothersome," Mr. Tolkien groused. "I honestly believe we'll have to move somewhere else and keep it very hush-hush to dissuade tourists from popping in."

"I hope you wouldn't leave Oxford," Yvette said.

"We may have to in order to keep our sanity and so that I can have a bit of peace and quiet to finish *The Silmarillion*. I'm still amazed that *The Lord of the Rings* has been so well received, but success has a double-edged sword. At last we can retire without worrying about how to pay the bills, but all these Middle Earth fans are making themselves a real nuisance. People from America ring up in the middle of the night—quite oblivious to the fact that there's a five-hour time zone difference. I think we need an unlisted number and perhaps we will move altogether."

"Where would you go?" asked Austen.

"We always enjoyed taking our holidays at the seaside, and we've rather fancied settling in a coastal resort town—but nothing so raucous as Brighton. We've had some holidays in Bournemouth and Lyme. Isn't Lyme where your in-laws retired?"

"Yes. They really like it. It's quite pretty."

"I'm partial to Bournemouth myself," Edith said quietly.

"Edith made quite a few friends at the Hotel Miramar there," Mr. Tolkien explained. "We'll probably holiday there again this summer and look about. Anyway, Austen, are you going anywhere interesting over the Easter holiday or are you staying in town?"

"Actually, I'm thinking of going over to Paris for a bit."

"Paris!" The professor nearly shuddered. "Why on earth would you want to go there?"

Edith spoke confidingly to Yvette. "Ronald abhors the French. I think it goes back to being over there during the Great War. He never wanted to return."

"I don't abhor the French, Edith." Mr. Tolkien remonstrated. "Just can't see why anyone would want to go there. Terrible food," he muttered. "Frogs legs. Snails. Disgusting. Always preferred good, plain English food."

"Some people would say that's an oxymoron," Edith said, chuckling.

"Well, your food is plain and good. Much better than what the Frogs eat."

Edith smiled. "Why, thank you, Ronald. Anyway, Austen, are you going to Paris to visit with David MacKenzie?"

"Yes, I thought I would."

"We were so sorry to hear they lost their baby. I can't imagine what that's like. But it was lovely that they named her for Marianne."

"Yes, it was."

"Well, Yvette," Edith turned to her. "Are you also going to Paris?"

Yvette flushed slightly. "No, no. I'll likely stay here and get some work done and then go home to London for Easter."

"Have you ever been to Paris?"

"No, I haven't traveled much."

"You should go while you have friends there. I would think David's wife would be happy for some female companionship."

"Actually," Austen interjected, "Kate did tell me she'd like you to come."

"She did?"

"Yes, before they left."

"There, you see?" Edith beamed.

"Why would anyone want to go to Paris?" Tolkien repeated, shaking his head. "Austen, my boy, come out to the garage for a few moments. I want your opinion on something I'm working on for *The Silmarillion*. Would you ladies please excuse us?"

"Yes, yes." Edith poured more tea for herself and Yvette as the men left. "Now, Yvette, tell me. Do you fancy Austen? Because I think he fancies you."

Yvette's jaw dropped. "No…I don't think he does." She tried to cover her shock with a little laugh, but it sounded strained.

"I've been watching him, and there's a definite difference in the way he looks at you and responds to you than the last time you both were here. I mean, before he clearly admired and liked you, but now he seems to really fancy you. I sense some romance, Yvette, but I'd hate to see Austen hurt after all he's gone through. Do you fancy him?"

Yvette hesitated and then, gazing into the eyes of this kind, friendly woman, decided she could only tell the truth. "Yes," she said quietly. "I do. But I think you're wrong about him. We're just friends. I don't think he'll ever want to marry again. I heard him say once that he could never replace Marianne."

"Of course not, but that doesn't mean he won't come to love anyone else."

"But, Mrs. Tolkien, let's be honest. Even if Austen had never been married before, he'd hardly consider me to be a fit wife.

I'm two years older than he, I'm from a working-class London family, and—well, my skin color makes the rest obvious."

"Now, first of all, age has nothing to do with anything—I'm three years older than Ronald. And I don't believe Austen Holmes gives two hoots about your skin color or your class."

"Perhaps not, but his mother certainly does."

Edith thought for a few moments and then spoke again. "Yvette, have you ever heard the story of my courtship with Ronald?"

"No, ma'am. But I'd like to, if you'd like to share it."

"I would. And I'll tell you something I rarely tell anyone. Ronald and I met when we were teenagers staying in the same foster home. We were both orphans. His father died in South Africa when Ronald was only two, leaving his mother widowed with two small sons thousands of miles away in England. For a while her family helped her, but when she converted to Catholicism, they threw her out and had little to do with her and the boys again. Ronald believes the financial and emotional stress led to a breakdown in her health and her subsequent early death at age thirty-four of diabetes. She died when he was only twelve and his brother, Hilary, ten. I think he sees her as a sort of martyr to the faith, which is one reason he is so devoted to the Catholic Church. By the way, my dear, I was brought up in the Church of England and only converted to Catholicism at Ronald's request."

Edith paused to recollect her thoughts. "Anyway, my mother died about the same time as Ronald's. She was also ostracized by the family but for a different reason." She leaned closer to Yvette. "I'm going to ask you to keep this confidential." When Yvette nodded, Edith continued softly, "I never knew my father. But the truth is…the truth is…my mother was never married. So you see, I had the stain of illegitimacy on me, and I was not university educated, and yet Ronald still loved me and asked me to be his wife."

Yvette looked sympathetically at this sensitive woman, who had entrusted her with these painful details.

"I lived in the room below Ronald's, and we would have long, secret window talks or take bike rides and walks together. We were both so young and so eager to be loved and to belong to someone who loved us. One day we were picnicking in the woods, and I danced for him in an enchanting glade. My hair was quite long—it still is—but then, of course, it wasn't white, but dark brown, and that day I let it down and danced for him. I think then I captured his heart. He's written about it in *The Silmarillion*. In the story a mortal man sees an elven princess dancing in a glade and he falls in love with her and she with him and she becomes mortal to marry him."

"Aragorn and Arwen?"

"Well, that's their story too, but it's actually ancestors of theirs: Beren and Lúthien. Sometimes Ronald calls me his 'Lúthien.'" She smiled. "Anyway, the lovely part of the story is that the men and elves are different races—or classes—if you will, and yet love brings them together."

"That is lovely," Yvette agreed. "So did you two fall in love and live happily ever after?"

"Oh, no," Edith said, laughing. "'*The course of true love never did run smooth.*' We made all sorts of pledges to each other—secretly, of course, as we were very young. Well, we became careless and one day were seen together. The spy turned us in to Ronald's guardian, Father Francis, the priest who had tried to help Mrs. Tolkien during her illness and who had taken care of the boys. Father Francis was very upset with us. He had great plans for Ronald to go to Oxford, and he must have thought I was not a suitable match for Ronald—besides the fact that he was quite young. Father Francis had me sent to another town and forbade us even to communicate by letter until Ronald turned twenty-one. It broke our hearts to leave each other, but we had little choice, and Ronald wanted to honor his guardian. And he did. He won a scholarship to Exeter College and we didn't even correspond for three years."

"You waited for each other for three years?" Yvette was filled with admiration.

"Well, he waited, but to be honest, I didn't. I really couldn't believe that a handsome, intelligent man like Ronald wouldn't find another girl off at Oxford. And I wasn't getting any younger. I was worried that a girl with so little prospects would get left behind, so I took up with a very nice young man by the name of George Field and we became engaged."

"What did Mr. Tolkien do about that?"

Edith laughed softly. "He didn't let that last long. As soon as he turned twenty-one, he came to see me in Cheltenham. When I told him I was engaged, he talked me into breaking it off and marrying him instead. And now it's been nearly fifty years. So you see, even with obstacles, true love can conquer all."

"What can true love conquer, my dear?" The professor and Austen returned to the parlor puffing away on their pipes.

"Everything, darling," Edith said, smiling. "I was just telling Yvette our love story. Now, Yvette, before you two go, please indulge me by singing a song while I accompany you on the piano. Would you?"

"Of course." Yvette rose and helped her elderly friend to her feet and over to the piano bench. "What would you like me to sing?"

"How about 'The Flowers That Bloom in the Spring' from *The Mikado*? That seems fitting for this time of year. Did you see all the jonquils blooming up and down the street? I'll bet they're beautiful in the Fellows' gardens." Edith flipped the pages of her music book until she found the right one. "Ready?"

Yvette nodded and Edith played the introduction. Entering on her cue, Yvette sang with skill, zest, and fun. Austen listened raptly and applauded enthusiastically at the song's conclusion. Edith noted his expression. "You see?" she whispered to Yvette. "Beren and Lúthien. I'd say Austen is captivated by your singing."

32

First Week

Stuart switched off the ignition of his black Jaguar and turned to face Natalie. He had driven her to the Dover pier where she was to meet the ferry for the crossing to Calais on her way to Paris for the spring vacation. On the trip down he had entertained her with his usual stream of humorous anecdotes, but now he grew decidedly more serious in his demeanor.

"Natalie, I have something to tell you," he said soberly.

"Okay."

"This is rather awkward for me to explain, so bear with me."

She gave him a quizzical look.

"I've only shared this with Nigel. I was waiting to sort of test it out and make sure it was genuine and not some fluke before I broadcasted it about."

"All right," she said cautiously. "What is it?"

He took a deep breath and then plunged ahead. "A few weeks ago at the funeral service for Kate and David's baby, I had an unusual experience—an epiphany, if you will. While we were singing 'Amazing Grace,' I suddenly and quite inexplicably came to the realization that I actually believed what we were singing. I could see in my mind's eye the wall of intellectual doubt I've put up between myself and God. But as we sang, I saw that wall growing thinner and thinner until it was merely a gossamer curtain. I knew that by an act of my will and by faith I could step through that curtain, and I did. Suddenly, I truly felt that I was no longer lost, but found; no longer blind, but could see. I know one can't judge these things by feelings; nevertheless, I was overcome with the sensation of being flooded with love and peace such as I've never known. And for a few days there I was literally floating around on cloud nine. I realized that God loves me—wretched sinner that I am. He loves *me*, and in the deepest, most profound way that no human being— my parents, my sister, anyone—could ever replicate."

"Oh, Stuart, that's wonderful!" Natalie's eyes shone with joy. "I wish you had shared this with me sooner."

"Well, like I said, I wanted to process it a bit and think about it before I went off half-cocked making grandiose statements that I was 'saved' or 'born again' or whatever the correct terminology is. I've been trying to read the Bible every day— well, the Gospels and Paul's letters. Nigel cautioned me not to start in Genesis. He said I'd never get past Deuteronomy and Numbers, and I suspect he's right. I read somewhere in the Bible—Paul's letters, I think—that if any man is in Christ he is a new creature; old things are passed away and all things are become new. That's the way I feel—like a brand-new, squeaky-clean baby." He chuckled. "I guess maybe I am 'born again' after all."

Natalie smiled at him. "I guess you are. Welcome to the family of God."

He grinned. "Thanks, I like that! Anyway, I wanted to tell you about it before you left, but I also didn't want you to think I was just saying it to get you to date me."

"I appreciate your discretion, but I'm truly happy for you, Stuart. I know David and Kate will be too. I may tell them, right?"

"Of course. I'm eternally grateful to your brother for showing me compassion despite how much of a cad I was, and I'd be glad for him to know his efforts have made some sort of return. And you can tell Kate that I'm no longer a rat in the cookie jar."

"Sorry—a rat?"

"Right. Once I told her I was a Christian because I had been christened and attended church my entire life, and she quoted someone who said that a rat isn't a cookie just because it's in the cookie jar. That struck me as clever at the time, but I realize the truth of it now." He paused for a moment. "Actually, I would like to talk to David. I was considering coming over to Paris for a few days and staying at the embassy. Would you mind if I did that, or do you think he or Kate would mind?"

"No, I think that'd be fine."

"Good. Then I'll see about it. And I'll also see if the ambassador is throwing any parties I can finagle invitations to."

"That would be fun." Natalie smiled again. "You have David's address and phone number, so give us a ring when you've made your plans." She glanced at her watch. "I'd better get going. Don't want to miss the launch."

Stuart reached out and gingerly smoothed back a strand of her dark hair. "I'm going to miss you," he said quietly.

"Stuart, I'll only be gone for a few weeks. Besides, if I sense that I'm no longer a help to them but an imposition, I'll be back even earlier. You'll hardly have time to miss me."

"Still, I shall miss you and think of you every day. Pray for me, will you? I know I'll need it. It's still one day at a time for me."

"I will. And do try to find some AA meetings while you're in London." She caught his hand and squeezed it. "Listen, I should go now."

"Right! Let me get your luggage out of the boot." Stuart hopped out, opened her door, and took her suitcases out of the trunk of his car. "Can you manage?" he asked. "I should have flown you over."

"Don't worry. I'll be fine." She allowed him to carry the suitcases to the boarding ramp. As they walked Natalie sniffed the sea air. "I like the Channel crossing. Nothing like seeing these white cliffs and watching and hearing the gulls. Thanks so much, Stuart, for the ride down here and the help. It was very sweet of you."

"Well," he said awkwardly as he handed over her luggage, "give my best to Kate and your brother. Bon voyage. Cheerio and all that."

"*Au revoir*—until we see each other again. God be with you." Standing on her tiptoes, Natalie gently kissed his cheek and then turned confidently to walk up the ramp.

"How are things *really* going, Di?" Austen asked as he stirred his tea.

Dianna pushed a stray lock of blond hair back off of her forehead and then finished straightening up the kitchen as she talked. "I'm exhausted, of course, but what mother isn't? Mum seems to have made the transition back home well enough and the boys really have been as good as gold. So I can't complain."

They could hear Andrew humming as he made his way blithely down the hallway. "All the children safe in bed," he announced cheerfully. "Your mother?"

Austen nodded. "All quiet on the Western Front. I'll just finish up my tea and head back to Oxford. Give you two a bit of time alone."

"We wouldn't remember what to do with it," Andrew joshed, drawing Dianna close to him and stealing a kiss.

She blushed but laughed. "Ha! That'd be the day. Say, Austen, before you go sneaking off into the night, how is *your* love life?"

Austen looked at her askance. "Nonexistent as always."

It was Dianna's turn to look askance. "What do you mean, 'as always'? It seems to me you have a bit of a flame smoldering for Yvette."

"No," Austen scoffed.

"You mean 'yes.' Austen, we're twins, remember? We had our own secret language growing up. Should I use it now? What, are you embarrassed to say anything in front of Andrew? Don't be. You know he and I both agree with Mum that it's high time you thought about getting married again. We just couldn't help noticing the way you act around Yvette."

"What are you talking about? Yvette and I are just good friends."

"Then are you denying that you ever think about her as more than just a good friend?"

Austen was silent.

"I knew it!" Dianna smiled triumphantly.

"It doesn't matter, anyway," Austen said with resignation. "She doesn't see me that way."

"Why would you say that? She came down here to this little backwater village to help me out and she visited Mum in the nursing home, and you think that was just a demonstration of her friendship?"

"Well…yes. Yvette's a wonderful person. She'd help out anyone."

"I'm certain she would. But I'm also certain she has more regard for you than friendship."

"Look, Di. I…I…I…" Austen stammered. "Honestly, I do like her a lot, but…I think she has a boyfriend."

Dianna shook her head. "No, that can't be right. Why would you think that?"

"I saw her with this Indian bloke—a don from another college. They were out to dinner together at the Eastgate and they looked like a couple, if you know what I mean."

Dianna frowned. "Have you asked her about him?"

"No, of course not. I didn't think it was any of my business."

"Now, why not? Aren't you 'friends'? Don't friends share about their love lives?"

Austen sighed. "Not necessarily. Especially friends of the opposite sex."

"I wonder," Andrew piped in, "if it's ever possible for a man and a woman to be genuine friends without one or the other secretly harboring romantic feelings."

"I'll confess I've wondered that too. At first I suspected Yvette did have such feelings for me. But they were the furthest thing from my mind. Now…" Austen's voice died away. "But," he continued, "now that I've begun feeling differently, I don't think she cares anymore. I may have lost my opportunity with her."

Dianna reached across the table and squeezed her brother's arm. "Autty, you don't know anything for certain, do you? You saw her with someone, but that doesn't mean anything. Remember the times people have seen us together and thought we were a couple rather than siblings?"

"He was not acting like a brother to her!" Austen replied vehemently.

"Still." Dianna was insistent. "Appearances can be deceiving. You won't know until you talk to her. Are you going to see her over the holiday?"

"Yes. There's a big party for the Tolkien's fiftieth wedding anniversary next weekend at Merton. I'm fairly certain she'll be there. And then…David's invited me to visit them in Paris, and before they left Kate suggested I ask Yvette to come as well."

"Have you?"

"Not yet."

"Austen!"

"You think I should?"

"Of course I do. How can it hurt?"

Austen sat quietly for a moment, and when he spoke his voice was low. "The truth is, Di, I must tell you that another reason I hesitate is because of mother. She called Yvette a half-caste. I think she'd go bonkers if she thought I wanted to date a mulatto, let alone marry one. I mean really—be honest with me—doesn't it bother you at all?"

Dianna considered this. "Andrew and I have talked about this, haven't we, luv?" Andrew nodded in reply. "The thing is— we like Yvette. We never even thought about her color five minutes after meeting her. I personally don't have a problem with mixed marriages. I think that sharing the same beliefs is much more important than the color of one's skin, but I also know that society's opinion is a consideration that has to be reckoned with. Probably not as much in the big cities, but certainly here where you rarely see anyone of color. Then again, you're not planning to live here, so what does it matter? I'm sure Oxford has a much broader mix of people than little ol' Castle Combe. But then, to be honest, I can't say how Mum will react. On the other hand, you're a grown man and certainly don't need her permission."

"No, I don't," agreed Austen, "but it would be hard to go against her wishes. And you know how she can be. Still, I think about the fact that she came from humble origins—she was just a lady's maid at the big house, after all, when Father spied her. If she hadn't been so pretty she would likely have never been able to marry up to a landowner. So I have little patience or understanding of her prejudices."

"Sometimes the biggest snobs come from the humblest homes," said Dianna thoughtfully. "I guess it's a way of feeling better about themselves by putting other people down."

"I say," Andrew interjected, "it's one more thing to pray about, Austen. You need to keep seeking God's will for a wife and just trust Him with the rest. You do a little too much thinking, mate."

"Andrew, are you really all right with all this?" Austen asked. "It doesn't bother you that we're talking about this? You know, being Marianne's brother and all?"

Andrew smiled. "Austen, I want you to be happy. And that's what Marianne wanted. She knew how much you desired to have children." His eyes laughed. "And I really don't think you're the kind of bloke who would be content to live as a celibate the rest of his life."

"You're right about that," Austen said with a sheepish grin.

"So then." Dianna was not going to be dissuaded from her goal. "You'll talk to Yvette at this party for the Tolkiens—if not before? You'll invite her to visit David and Kate along with you? You'll at least try?"

"All right." Austen sighed. "I'll give it a go."

33

First and Second Weeks
Paris

*I*n the lobby of his Parisian apartment building, David greeted Natalie with a warm bear hug.

"Natalie! It's wonderful to see you! How was your trip over?"

"Just fine. No problems." She studied his face. "How are you, David?"

He smiled sadly. "I'm all right, Nat. Truly I am. Thanks so much for coming. It's a real treat for us both."

"And how's Kate?"

"Frankly, not very well. She's taken it all quite hard. But I hope you will be able to cheer her up a bit."

"I'll try my best. Here, help me with this stuff." Natalie indicated a large suitcase and a smaller one.

"My word, you packed a lot," David exclaimed. "You know we have a launderette down the street, don't you?"

"The big suitcase is full of Kate's clothes. Mum and I packed them up for her so she could have a few of her regular clothes to wear now."

"Ah, thank you. That was quite thoughtful of you. Here. I'll stick them on the lift and we'll walk up." David hoisted the luggage into the narrow elevator and shut the accordion gate.

Natalie stared up at the skylight at the top of the stairwell and took a deep breath. "Right. I need some exercise."

Brother and sister looked at each other and burst out laughing. "Would you prefer to wait and I'll send the lift back down for you?" he asked.

"No, I'm fit enough. Just don't expect me to talk to you while we climb the Himalayas."

"Come on, then," David said. "Kate's waiting to see you."

In the end they both chatted and laughed as they mounted the six flights of stairs. At the top David summoned the elevator, retrieved the suitcases, and hauled them into the flat.

"Kate!" he called. "Nat's here!"

Kate came to the door and Natalie hugged her, kissing her on both cheeks in the French fashion. "Hello, Kate. How are you? I'm so sorry for all you've been through."

"Thanks." Kate managed a smile. "It's good to see you, Natalie."

"It's good to be here," she replied, studying Kate's face as she had her brother's. It troubled her to see that Kate's beautiful brown eyes had lost their luster; they appeared lifeless and dull—almost dead.

"I'll just carry your bag back to your room." David cheerfully added, "Kate, Nat brought some of your clothes over so you'll have a bigger wardrobe to choose from."

"That was nice. Thank you," Kate said flatly. Then her hostess instincts took over. "Can we get you something to eat or drink, Natalie? You must be exhausted."

"A cuppa would be grand."

Once they were settled in the parlor sipping tea and munching biscuits, Kate asked Natalie to tell them about the graveside service in Oxford. Natalie recounted all the details to Kate's rapt attention.

"I wish I could have been there," she murmured when Natalie had finished.

"Sounds perfect. Well done—just as we would have wished it," David said. "So did just our family and Austen come?"

"Right. All of us and Austen and Yvette. And—well, I hope you don't mind—but Stuart Devereux asked if he might come. He said that since you both had attended his mother's funeral, he wanted to be there."

David seemed surprised but nodded. "That's fine."

"Really, it was a divine appointment for Stuart," Natalie went on. "You won't believe this, but he told me that the service was an epiphany for him."

"What did he mean?" asked David.

"It was one of those supernatural moments when all of a sudden he realized he really believed what we were reading and singing."

"Stuart Devereux?" David was incredulous. "We are talking about the same person, aren't we?"

"Yep. Lord Stuart Devereux."

"Well, I'll be! Who would have thought?" David laughed with delight. Even Kate smiled. "You know," David said, "we have been praying for him for quite some time now, so I shouldn't be so surprised when our prayers are answered. But can you believe it?" Then his face darkened slightly. "Nat, are you certain this is sincere and not just a ruse to win you over?"

"I believe he's absolutely sincere," she replied emphatically. "He didn't even tell me about it until today. He said he was unsure it was real at first and wanted to test it out. So he waited a fortnight to confess his newfound faith to me."

"*Incroyable!*" David laughed again. "This is good news indeed. It is comforting when God can turn around our sorrows and bring some good from them."

"Yes," Natalie agreed. "We'll have to remember to tell Daddy about it too. I'm sure it would encourage him as well. Anyway, I think Stuart is planning to come over during the holiday. He'd like to talk to you. Says the ambassador's wife is a cousin or something and he'll stay with them and try to finagle some party invitations for us if he can."

"Oh blast, I hate parties," David groaned. "I don't mind seeing Stuart, but I find those high society gatherings such a bore."

"Come now, David," Natalie chided him. "Don't you like to have an excuse to show off your pretty wife?"

"And play chaperone to my pretty sister?"

Natalie shrugged. "If it's such a bore, perhaps Kate and I should just go without you."

David smiled at her teasing. "Right. Not a chance of that. But seriously, Nat, are you keeping your head with Lord Devereux?"

"Absolutely, big brother. You need have no fear on my account. I consider him strictly as a friend."

"Does he?"

"Well, to be honest, he's taken a few stabs at trying to alter the course, but he's respected my boundaries. And I think he will even more so now that he professes to be a believer."

"Nat," he asked quietly. "Do you know if he's staying sober?"

"As far as I can tell he is. And going faithfully to the Overcomers meetings."

David leaned back contentedly. "That's excellent. I think I'll write his sister with an update. She'll be glad of it too."

Kate stared down at the Seine from the Pont de l'Alma. She was supposed to meet Natalie and David for lunch at the college café, but when her class released early, she had wandered down to the Quai d'Orsay and walked out along the bridge. Pedestrians scurried by as horns blared from the traffic behind her. The inky Seine flowed rapidly below as she watched a *Bâteau-Mouche* crowded with lunchtime passengers churn past.

She observed the bustle around her but felt absolutely nothing. Hamlet's lament seemed perfectly to reflect her own state of mind: *"O God, God, how weary, stale, flat, and unprofitable seems to me all the uses of this world!"* She thought, *I wish like Hamlet "that the Everlasting had not fixed His canon against self-slaughter." But I think if I were to end it all, God would forgive me. I'm so weary of this world and just want to go to be with Him and my baby. Wouldn't He accept me into His kingdom? I could just climb over this balustrade and jump in. The current moves so quickly. That's what Javert did in* Les Misérables. *Just jumped right into the Seine and ended it. It would hurt David, but he'd get over it. He's strong—so much stronger than I am. And Natalie's here now and she would help him. He would be all right. It would be so easy to do, and it would be quick and not horrible like Anna Karenina throwing herself in front of a train. That would be too terrible. No, I could just climb over and slip away…*

A tooting horn and wolf calls from a car filled with young men interrupted her morbid thoughts.

"Belle mademoiselle! Comment ça va?"

Kate turned her head at the commotion and then stared again at the river. Suddenly, she heard a voice call her name.

She jerked her head around but saw no one. As she looked back at the river, Kate heard the voice speaking in her mind—just as audible as the young men had been.

Kate, I have called you by name. You are Mine. Do not despair, My daughter. Be not as Rachel weeping for her children and refusing to be comforted because her children are no more. Your little one is with Me. I have spoken by the prophet Jeremiah, "Keep your voice from weeping and your eyes from tears, for your work shall be rewarded. There is hope for your future and your children shall come back to their own country." My daughter, do not throw your life away. It is precious to Me. If you would give your life away, My daughter, then give it to Me. This is what I, the Lord, say to you.

A tear trickled down Kate's cheek. But it was not a tear of sorrow; rather, it was a tear of release. God had spoken to her. He had called her by name. He loved her.

"Yes, Lord," she whispered. "Forgive me. I will trust You, even though I don't understand. Thank You for loving me so much. My life is Yours. Use me as You will."

Then Kate resolutely turned away from the river and walked back over the bridge to meet her husband.

In the American College café, Kate found Natalie seated with two young men at a small round table.

"Kate! Over here," Natalie called, waving her over as they pulled up another chair. "Kate, this is Sam and this is Fred. Boys, this is Kate MacKenzie."

Kate nodded. "Hello."

"We are very glad to meet you," sandy-haired Sam said. "Are you two sisters?"

Natalie smiled. "We are."

"Hot dog! This is our lucky day," Fred exclaimed.

"But actually, Kate is my sister-in-law," Natalie went on sweetly. "Her husband is my brother, David MacKenzie. Perhaps you're in one of his classes? He's a visiting English professor from Oxford."

The smiles on the fellows' faces began to fade. "Uh…really? Uh…no…we're not in his class."

"There he is now." Natalie sat forward and waved to David, who had just walked through the doorway. He spied them and hurried over.

"Hello, darling," he murmured, kissing Kate on the cheek. "Hello, Nat. Hello, gents, I'm David MacKenzie." He extended his hand. Sam and Fred made their introductions and then rapidly excused themselves.

"I hope I didn't scare them off," David whispered with a grin.

"I think you did," Natalie said, laughing. "They were trying to make a pass at Kate and you spoiled it."

"They were trying to make a pass at you," Kate corrected.

Natalie shrugged. "Okay, at both of us. They were nice blokes but rather eager. Anyway, no harm done. You came just in time, David. Well then, who wants some lunch? I couldn't wait and already ate."

"I'm starved." David stood. "What can I get for you, Kate?"

"*Un croque-monsieur et des pommes frites, s'il vous plâit.*"

David nodded. "*Trés bon. Un moment, madame.*"

While he got in line at the counter, Natalie turned to Kate. "How are you? I expected you earlier. Did your class get out late?"

"No, it actually let out a little early," Kate answered. "So I decided to walk down to the quay and have a look at the river."

"Oh." Natalie observed her carefully. "Everything all right?"

Kate smiled. "Yes. It's such a beautiful day. Say, Natalie, you wouldn't happen to have a Bible with you, would you?"

"No, but David might in that book satchel of his."

"You're right. I think he does." Kate dragged the satchel into her lap and unbuckled it. She rifled through some lecture notes and books and then pulled out a small Bible. "*Voilà!*" Watching as Kate flipped through it, Natalie noted that her face appeared more animated than she had seen it since she arrived. When Kate's eyes met hers, they were sparkling—gone was the dull, dead look that had caused them such concern.

"I found it!" Kate exclaimed.

"Found what?" David asked as he put down two plates with grilled ham-and-cheese sandwiches and French fries.

"A Scripture that came to my mind while I was out walking by the river," replied Kate. "Would you like to hear it?"

"Absolutely." David nodded. "Fire away."

"It's in Jeremiah 29. It says: ' "For I know the plans I have for you," declares the LORD, "plans to prosper you and not to harm you, plans to give you hope and a future. Then you will call upon me and come and pray to me, and I will listen to you. You will seek me and find me when you seek me with all your heart." ' " Kate smiled and David's heart leapt to see it. "I know I've been hard for you to deal with, David. I haven't been myself. It's just that since the baby died, I've felt so separated from God—like He didn't love me or He wasn't listening or wasn't even there. But today He spoke to me. Almost with an audible voice. He called me by my name. He called me His daughter…" Her face clouded with tears, but still she smiled. "He loves me," she whispered. "I'm His daughter."

David covered her hand with his own. "Darling, of course He loves you. He's always loved you and always will." He gently squeezed her hand. "I love you too, Kate. Let's give thanks. Shall we?"

As they bowed their heads, David expressed aloud their gratitude for the food as well as for the comforting touch Kate had supernaturally experienced. Then he also silently expressed his gratitude for his wife's restoration. *Thank You, God, for speaking to Kate and for comforting her. And thank You so very much for bringing my wife back to me!* When he finished praying, he looked up and beamed happily. *"Bon appétit!"*

34

Second Week
Oxford

The golden wedding anniversary party for Edith and Ronald Tolkien was a grand affair. Merton College did themselves proud by serving a sumptuous luncheon in the New Senior Common Room in honor of their famous professor emeritus and his beloved wife. Family, friends, and colleagues filled the beautifully appointed Wedgwood blue room with warmth, laughter, and love. Tolkien's publisher, Sir Stanley Unwin, sent fifty golden roses, and well-wishes, poems, tributes, and telegrams from all over the world were read to the glowing couple. A highlight of the festivities was the performance of *The Road Goes Ever On*, a song cycle based on Tolkien's works, performed on the piano by the composer himself, Donald Swann, and a singer by the name of William Elven. On hearing his introduction, Professor Tolkien declared boisterously, "Elven—now that's a name of good omen!"

Yvette felt honored to be included in the august occasion and thoroughly enjoyed the afternoon, particularly the music and—she must admit—sitting beside Austen in a merry mood. As the celebration wound down and everyone had been given an opportunity to mingle and offer their regards to the Tolkiens, Austen maneuvered close to Yvette.

"Would you like to see the secret passageway to the Queen's Rooms?" he asked conspiratorially.

Yvette smiled. "Yes, a secret passageway always sounds intriguing. Will you show me?"

"Certainly. You can actually walk from here to the Queen's Rooms without ever stepping outside." Austen took hold of Yvette's elbow and steered her through the guests lingering over coffee across the hallway in the Upper Bursary. They passed through the oak-paneled Old Senior Common Room and downstairs through the servery, and out into the great Hall, where the college kitchen staff was preparing for the evening dinner. As Yvette walked past the long planked tables and benches, she admired the striking oak-beamed roof and the heraldic stained-glass windows.

"Where's the secret passage?" she asked.

"Right there beyond the high table." Austen pointed to the carved paneled wall behind the dais.

Yvette looked up and laughed. "Secret? It has an emergency exit sign over it."

Austen grinned. "Well, it used to be secret. See how cleverly disguised the door is? Without the sign, of course. Come on, I'll show you." They stepped up on the dais and found the door. Austen pushed it open to a narrow wooden staircase leading straight up a short flight to a small, elegant paneled room with a marble fireplace, leaded-glass mullioned windows, and a molded-plaster ceiling.

"Is this the Queen's Room?" asked Yvette. "It's charming."

"Yes, and this one beyond was the dining room," Austen showed her the adjoining room, which was larger and more ornate with a vaulted ceiling and stained glass.

"Which queen stayed here?"

"Several in fact. Any queen visiting Oxford is to be housed by the University in these rooms. Both Katherine of Aragon and Elizabeth I stayed here and dined in the Hall. But the rooms are most closely associated with Queen Henrietta Maria, who stayed here an entire winter in 1643. You remember from your history lessons, don't you, that Charles I made his headquarters in Oxford during the Civil War when Cromwell and parliament had driven him out of London?"

"Oh right, and didn't Charles stay at Christ Church?"

"That's correct. The queen used the 'secret' passageway down through the Hall and then the kitchen to Mob Quad and on to meet her husband, or to the Chapel so she could attend services."

"This is really impressive. It's amazing that we are surrounded by such history." Yvette gazed around appreciatively. "So, where's the proper entrance?"

"Through this door and down this stairway, which will take us back to the front quad." He led her down a richly carved seventeenth-century staircase. "Look up," he said and Yvette took in a splendid vaulted ceiling decorated with gilded roses and trim.

"Beautiful," she affirmed. "I had no idea this monastic establishment held such hidden treasures."

"We're hardly monastic these days," Austen said as he opened the outer door for her to step through.

"Sorry. That wasn't an accurate word choice, was it? Should I say, 'exclusively male'? Anyway, it's a surprise to see rooms for a queen in a men's college. What other surprises do you have?"

"You've seen our medieval library in Mob Quad, haven't you?"

"Yes, it's lovely." Yvette smiled. "And those chained books would be an effective deterrent for any thief."

"Have you ever seen our Fellows' garden?"

"No."

"I can walk you back that way. It would actually be shorter than going back to the High Street. Shall I?"

"That would be very nice of you. I've always wanted to peek over those high walls and see what was inside."

"All right. Come this way. The MCR is up over this arch," Austen said as he led her through the passageway to the next quad. "A few years ago they were repairing the plaster ceiling and discovered an old timber-beamed roof." Although the adjacent quad of St. Alban's had been rebuilt in the twentieth century, its neo-Gothic style mullioned casements were harmonious in architecture to the Queen's Tower. The fourth side of the quad was enclosed by a tall decorative wrought iron gate, which revealed the Fellows' gardens beyond. In the center of the quad, a young gardener was keeping the impeccably cropped carpet of grass well-groomed by dragging a giant broom across it.

"Combing the grass?" Yvette laughed. "Well done."

The lad tipped his hat and grinned.

"This is very pretty," she said.

"The JCR is here," Austen said, pointing to a staircase as they walked through the courtyard. "The rooms used to be those of T.S. Eliot. Now they've been converted to a telly lounge."

"A bit sad, isn't it? From poetry to pulp in one generation," commented Yvette. "Is there a secret entrance through that gate? It appears rather formidable to climb over."

"Never fear," replied Austen. "Just step through this passageway and *voilà!*"

To the left of the passage a gravel pathway hugged an ancient stone wall. Lanterns glowed like fireflies lighting the path in the gathering dusk. To the right spread the garden to the ancient city wall. Austen pointed out the famous mulberry tree dating from the time of King James I as they passed a surprisingly modern-looking early ninteenth-century sundial. They walked past beds bursting with a profusion of spring flowers and jonquils.

" '*When all at once I saw a crowd, a host, of golden daffodils; beside the lake, beneath the trees, fluttering and dancing in the breeze!*' " Yvette quoted Wordsworth enthusiastically. Austen gingerly put his hand under her elbow as they climbed up the steps to the terrace overlooking the grove of lime trees below in the garden and the meadow stretching beyond the wall. "I had no idea you could walk along the top of the wall like this," Yvette said. "What a great view! Is that Deadman's Walk below us?"

"Yes," Austen answered quietly. "In medieval times, the Jews had to bring their dead along it to bury them outside the city walls."

"That's interesting," said Yvette, "the so-called Christians discriminated against the Jews, and yet Jesus, also a Jew, was crucified and buried outside the city walls too. You'd think they would see the cruel irony in that."

"Shows how ignorant and prejudiced people can be. Well, Jesus certainly knew what it was to be despised and rejected of men," added Austen. "Born in a stable and died on a rubbish heap. Now that's a Messiah who can identify with suffering."

"Yes," she said softly. "That's one reason I love Him so. 'Surely he has borne our griefs and carried our sorrows'—isn't it amazing that Isaiah prophesied so accurately about the Messiah two thousand years before Jesus walked the earth? I still get chills thinking about it. And when I consider that He was willing to suffer and die for me, how can I do anything but serve Him?"

"Yes," Austen agreed. He thought for a few moments in silence as they walked on through the garden and then asked, "Yvette, have you suffered much? You don't have to answer, but I wondered if you've experienced some of that rejection because...because..." he hesitated to say it.

"...because I'm a 'half-caste'?" she finished for him.

Austen nodded.

"To be honest, not too much. And nothing compared to what they go through in America," she said reflectively. "Here, I'm blessed. My parents are color-blind, you see, and that's a great gift. I wish more people were. I read a speech of Dr. Martin Luther King Jr. at a civil rights' march in Washington, D.C. He said people should be judged by their character, not their color. That's what my parents brought us up to believe. Sometimes I feel quite special because I have entrée into both white and colored societies. But then, I confess, there are times when I also feel like I don't quite fit in with either. But don't you ever feel like that? I mean at Faculty meetings—don't you ever feel strange, because of your faith, when the majority of the Faculty are utter agnostics and secularists? It can be a very lonely feeling sometimes."

"Yes, I see what you mean."

"I've learned to be confident that no matter how people view me, in God's sight I am His daughter. I am a child of God, a child of the King—and that's the best pedigree a person can have."

"You're right about that. And very wise. I don't suppose we're meant to fit in or feel completely at home on this earth."

"Heaven is our home," Yvette concurred. "But I have to say," she added as they stepped into Rose Lane along the Botanic Garden, "I certainly think Oxford is a little piece of heaven on earth—the dreaming spires and all this—it's really beautiful."

"It is, indeed." Austen hesitated. "I say, Yvette, have you ever been to Paris?"

"No, but I'm sure it's beautiful too."

"It's very beautiful but quite different."

They walked along in silence over Magdalene Bridge until Austen finally mustered up the courage to say, "Yvette, before they left, the MacKenzies asked me to invite you to come along when I go to Paris. Would you like to do that?"

"I'd love to see Paris. They had invited me too. But I wasn't sure if they really meant it or they were just being polite."

"Oh, no. They really meant it."

"But do you think Kate would still want that?"

"Frankly, I'm not sure Kate is in a frame of mind to know what she wants. She's still recovering from her ordeal. But David would be glad for a woman to keep Kate company and provide some diversion. I was planning to stay in a nearby pension, but they have a guest bedroom where you could stay if you like. Natalie has gone over to help out, and I had hoped to go once I had wrapped up my term duties here. Anyway, would you be interested in coming too? I didn't bring it up before because I wasn't sure your friend would like the idea."

"My friend?"

Austen looked down awkwardly. "You know, that Indian don you've been seeing."

"Who?" Yvette thought for a minute, puzzling over whom he could mean. "Oh, you must mean Deepak! Good grief, I'd hardly call him a friend."

"Right." Austen kept his eyes on the pavement. "I should have said—boyfriend."

Yvette nearly laughed. "Boyfriend! Where on earth did you get such an idea? We only went out once. It was a blind date one of my friends at St. Hilda's set up. Not my type at all. He was way too familiar with me. And his family had betrothed him to a Hindu woman back in India. The whole situation was quite awkward."

Austen couldn't help smiling as he absorbed all this information. "Well, I suppose he wouldn't object to your going to Paris."

"He certainly would not—not that I'd care a whit what he thought."

"So then, would you like to go?" he asked with more confidence.

"That would be splendid!" Yvette beamed. "I've always wanted to see Paris, and it would be great to visit with David and Kate. When were you planning to leave?"

"I thought I'd go over on Good Friday. That would give me a bit of time to visit with David before he has to run off to classes on Monday."

"Oh." Her face fell. "I was planning to be in London then, visiting my family for a few days."

"Can't I meet you there? I was going to take the train, anyway. I should like to meet your family—if they wouldn't mind."

"No, that would be brilliant. You can come down on the train—we live in Bayswater, right near Paddington Station—and then have dinner with us and meet my mum and dad. And then Daddy could drive us in his taxi to Waterloo Station to get the train to Dover."

"That would work. But your parents don't have to feed me."

"No problem. My mum loves to cook. I'll ring them tonight, though, and make sure it's all right for them."

Austen smiled. "Sounds like a good plan to me. And I'll ring David and check on things on that end. Why don't we meet as usual at the Eastgate on Tuesday afternoon and compare notes and plan our strategies?"

"Excellent!" Yvette returned his smile as they reached the Porters' Lodge at St. Hilda's. "Thank you, Austen, for walking me home and for this very kind invitation. I guess now I'll have to bone up on my French. *Bonsoir!*"

35

Fourth Week, Good Friday
London

"hat was fabulous, Mrs. Goodman." Austen sincerely praised his hostess' meal. "What do you call it again?"

"Jambalaya," Molly Goodman, Yvette's mother, replied with a wide smile. "It's a Creole dish from the Caribbean that James introduced to me."

"And you cook it up just right, Molly," added her husband, James Goodman.

They were seated in the dining room of the Goodmans' Georgian terraced house. It was a sunny, gracious room decorated simply in soft blue and white. A large cherry hutch, which Yvette's father had painstakingly refinished after hauling it from the flea market on Portabello Road, filled one wall of the room. Wedgwood china plates were displayed tastefully on its open shelves. On the opposite wall, a matching Wedgwood clock, Yvette's Christmas gift, perched prominently on the mantle of a blocked-off fireplace.

"Would you like more, Mr. Holmes?" Molly asked. "You're too slender for such a tall man. They aren't feeding you enough at that University." She passed the bowl of steaming rice, vegetables, and seafood around again.

Austen could sense that Yvette's mother took great enjoyment in watching others savor her cooking. He piled another generous helping on his plate. "They feed us well enough, but nothing so spicy and delicious as this, Mrs. Goodman."

Molly's smile spread even wider across her round, freckled, unmistakably Irish face. Her plumpness indicated she also enjoyed eating her own cooking. Her ginger-colored hair, sprinkled with white, was pulled up in a casual knot on top of her head; and her cornflower blue eyes crinkled from a network of thin laugh lines. Austen liked her tremendously.

"I am sorry Ben and Adam couldn't be here," Yvette said.

"You know they couldn't get the day off," Molly explained again. "Perhaps Austen can meet them on your way back from Paris. At least Gerrard and Jake could be here." She smiled at Yvette's two younger brothers, who were eagerly consuming copious amounts of jambalaya.

"Lucky you were coming through during the Easter holiday. But then again it seems like the University is always on holiday," James Goodman commented wryly.

Austen chuckled. "It does seem like that. The eight-week terms are short, but the students have to pack a lot of work into a very brief amount of time."

"And we instructors don't get all the time off," added Yvette.

"Is this MacKenzie fellow you're going to visit on holiday too?"

"Actually, no," answered Austen. "He's a guest lecturer at the American College in Paris and they're on a semester system. But he gets a few days off for Easter."

Yvette's father grunted. "What's an Oxford don doing in Paris working for the Americans?"

"I suppose for the Americans it's a feather in their cap to have a visiting don. David had lived in Paris with his family a number of years ago and wanted to return," Austen explained. "Also his mother and wife are both Americans."

"You don't say? My, we're a motley lot, aren't we?" With his brown skin, James Goodman appeared to be from a racially mixed background. "What about you, Mr. Holmes? Are you part American or Irish or…West Indian?" James asked with a mischievous grin that revealed a gap in his front teeth similar to his daughter's.

"No, nothing quite so interesting, I regret to say. I'm just a boring Anglo-Saxon."

"And that's what you teach, right? Anglo-Saxon literature. That's *Beowulf*, isn't it? That poetry might as well be in a foreign language for all that it resembles modern English."

Austen smiled affably. "Yes, you could say that. I also tutor some of the more modern literature like Yvette does."

"Now there's a smart girl," James proudly affirmed. "First Goodman to go to university."

"Perhaps Gerrard or Jake will as well," Yvette offered.

"Perhaps." James shrugged. "They're going to try to pass the A levels, but right now Gerrard seems more interested in pursuing football. Isn't that right, son?"

Gerrard, a strong, athletic young man who resembled his father, nodded with a grin. "I'm trying out for Arsenal's youth league."

"Really? Good for you!" Yvette smiled warmly at him. "You should make it."

"Was Arsenal your club, Mr. Goodman?" Austen asked.

"No," James replied. "I played for Chelsea. Had a good run until I injured my knee. Thankfully, I won Molly's heart before my luck turned." He smiled at his wife, who had begun clearing the table.

"You're not unlucky, James Goodman," she chided. "You got to play professional football, you've made a good living for us, and you have five lovely children to boot."

"And a darling wife who adores me," added James with a wink at Yvette.

Molly laughed. "Aye, that too. See, you're the luckiest man in the world!"

"I am," he agreed. "But I do wish I could still play football."

"And I wish I were still young and fair," Molly retorted as she carried a stack of dishes into the kitchen. "But if we live long, we grow old whether we wish it or not."

"Forever wilt thou love and she be fair." Austen thought of the line from Keats' "Ode on a Grecian Urn" as he watched Yvette help clear the table. *Only in art can youth and beauty be immortalized,* he reflected. *Or in eternity or memory. Marianne will always stay young and beautiful in my memory, even as she is now in heaven. But to grow old with someone you love! To share life's journey even as youth fades and to love even still— that is something far greater than temporal beauty.*

"Would you like coffee?" Yvette asked the men, who both nodded affirmatively.

"Yes, please," Austen replied. "May I help?"

Yvette smiled. "No, thanks. You can keep Daddy company while I help Mum."

James glanced at the clock on the mantle. "We need to keep an eye on the time. You don't want to miss your train."

"Right," Yvette agreed as she pushed past the swinging door into the kitchen. "Coffee's already brewing. I'll just be a few minutes."

Molly poked her head back in. "Gerrard, Jake, come help me with the dishes." The boys followed her obediently and the door swung shut, closing off the clattering of the dishes and the chatter of the women. The men sat in silence as if taking each other's measure. James ran his hand back and forth over his bald head. Notwithstanding his nearly crippled leg, he was still a powerfully built man and not easily intimidated. Yet he wasn't quite certain what to make of this tall, serious Anglo-Saxon friend of his daughter's sitting in their dining room. Austen was not unaware of his host's ambivalence. He wondered if they had been left alone by the women's design. He knew they had only a few moments together and if he didn't speak now, he might not have another chance.

But James spoke first. He had been studying Austen's long slender fingers as they toyed with a spoon. Austen's ring finger still held the indentation from the wedding band he had only recently removed. "Are you married, Mr. Holmes?" James asked evenly.

"Austen. Please call me Austen. " If Austen was surprised by the question, he didn't show it. "I'm a widower. My wife died of cancer about three and a half years ago."

"Ah, I'm sorry." James felt rather chagrined at the outlandish conjectures on the missing ring he had been formulating.

"Thank you." Austen decided to plunge ahead. "Mr. Goodman, I've known your daughter for over a year now. We've been working together both for the University and for the Inklings Society, our little literary club. Anyway, I think very highly of Yvette. She's a fine scholar and colleague and has become a good friend. I think it could become more." He hesitated and took a deep breath. "I'll come right to the point, Mr. Goodman. I would like to ask you for your permission to court your daughter."

This time James' face remained impassive, although he was quite taken aback. "Do you smoke?" he asked as he took out his pipe and a pouch of tobacco.

"Yes, I do." Austen removed his own pipe from his jacket pocket.

While they busied their hands with preparing and lighting their pipes, James said, "I must admit I'm a bit flummoxed. I'm not displeased by your request, but I am puzzled. This is 1966 and you're an Oxford man who has been married. Yvette is a grown woman supporting herself. You two clearly don't need my permission to follow your hearts."

"No, but I'd like to have it before I pursue that path," Austen replied quietly.

"Does Yvette know you are asking me this?"

"No. I wanted to hear what you had to say first. If you have reservations, then I would like to keep matters as they stand. We are very good friends, and I don't want to lose that friendship."

James scrutinized Austen as he puffed on his pipe. "What does your family say?"

"My sister and brother-in-law—who is also my wife's brother—are encouraging. My father died in the war. My mother…" he sighed. "I have not spoken of it to my mother. Frankly, I don't know how she'll react and I don't want to stir things up unnecessarily. But nevertheless, as you said, I am a grown man and a widower. If this relationship leads to marriage, I would like my mother's blessing, but I certainly don't need her permission."

James nodded. "Yvette is my only daughter and she's a very special person. If she likes you and wants this, then I have no objection. Obviously, we don't have any racial prejudices in this family. But you must know, even with her light skin, it won't be easy for you. There are people—mostly your own kind—who will be angry to see you together. You could possibly lose those you thought were your friends. Perhaps not quite as much here in London, and certainly not in Paris. Maybe not even in Oxford. But in little towns, like yours, where they seldom set eyes on a colored person—you have no idea how people will react. If you decide to get married, sooner or later you're going to come up against it. So, you'd better truly love my daughter and take good care of her. I don't ever want to see her hurt."

"Neither do I. That's why I wanted to speak to you first. I know Yvette loves you all very much and that she could not bear to suffer your disapprobation. She would not be happy without your blessing, and I will not selfishly jeopardize her happiness."

James grunted in approval. "Well, there's another thing." He leaned forward. "Since you've been married before and this being the age of free love and all, you may think that you can assume certain intimacies with her. But that would be over my dead body and her brothers'. I admit I was a bit wild back in my day, but believe me, things are quite different when they concern your daughter or sister."

"Don't worry, Mr. Goodman. I have no such intentions. The only woman I have ever known intimately was my wife, and even with her our first kiss was saved until our wedding day."

James laid down his pipe and looked at him skeptically. "No—really?"

Austen nodded. "Really. Our friends the MacKenzies also waited, and I intend to follow suit again."

James shook his head. "Well, I'll be!"

The kitchen door swung open and Yvette sailed in bearing a coffee tray. Her mother followed her carrying a plate topped by a fluffy yellow cake layered with strawberry jam and dusted with powdered sugar. The boys came behind with dessert plates and forks.

"Oh, James," Molly chided. "Not your pipe before dessert. You'll spoil the taste of my Victorian teacake."

"Nothing can spoil the taste of your teacake, Molly," her husband assured her, placing his pipe in the ashtray. "Though I hate to eat it in a hurry—but we must if I'm to get these young people to their train on time."

They quickly dispatched the coffee and dessert with the necessary compliments to Molly's cooking. As Austen shook her hand at the door and thanked her profusely for her hospitality, Molly extended yet more. "You must come by on your way back to Oxford, Austen, so that you can have supper with us and meet Yvette's older brothers and their wives. You are welcome to stay the night in one of our guest rooms." She pointed to the "Bed-and-Breakfast" sign posted in the window. "Since the older children are gone, we're running a regular B-and-B. I cook up a good English breakfast, I do. Yvette, you just let us know when you're coming back through and we'll keep a room open for him."

"Thank you, Mrs. Goodman," Austen said graciously. "I may take you up on that. Thanks again for the delicious dinner. It was a pleasure."

"The pleasure was all ours." Molly smiled broadly. "Now have fun and take good care of Yvette for us."

"I will," Austen said as he exchanged knowing looks with Yvette's father.

James Goodman nodded as if to say, *All right, then. See that you do.*

36

Though uneventful, the Channel crossing was nevertheless exciting for Yvette, who had never before traveled beyond the borders of her home island. She was anxious lest she would prove to be a poor sailor, but her years of cruising up and down the Thames River must have given her sturdy sea legs. She and Austen kept up a steady flow of conversation as they traversed land and sea from London's Waterloo Station to Paris' Gare du Nord. This was the longest span of time they had ever spent alone together, and Yvette's concerns that the often-quiet Austen would be awkwardly silent were quickly put to rest. He talked freely and loquaciously about his boyhood, early schooling, friendships, travel, and even his brief marriage to Marianne. She likewise shared about her family, growing up in Bayswater, and her experiences as a young mulatto woman trying to excel as a scholar in a white male-dominated university system. They both felt utterly at ease talking and laughing together, and consequently both were almost disappointed when the travel ended at the Passy apartment of the MacKenzies.

That stab of disappointment was quickly assuaged by the reunion with their friends. Yvette was pleased that Kate greeted her with kisses to both cheeks in the affectionate manner of the French.

David playfully pretended to follow suit when Austen stepped back holding up his hands. "Don't even think about pulling that Frenchy stuff on me, old boy!"

David laughed and pounded Austen on the back instead. "Welcome to Paris, old chap. Welcome, Yvette! It's great to see you both. Come in and have some tea and biscuits before we get you situated. How was the crossing?"

"Not too rough. The weather was fine," Austen answered as he plopped down into one of the reading chairs.

"It was fabulous," Yvette enthused as she settled on the settee next to Kate. "If teaching doesn't work out for me, I'm going to join the Royal Navy."

"You must be a better sailor than I," said Kate. "I get so seasick."

"You will love the trip back even better," David told Yvette. "There's nothing like watching those white cliffs loom up on the horizon."

"Except maybe seeing the Statue of Liberty at sunrise sailing into New York Harbor," amended Kate.

"Except maybe that," David allowed cheerfully.

"Where's Natalie?" asked Austen, glancing around the flat.

"Here I am," she answered as she carried in a generously loaded tea tray. "How is everyone? Anyone like a cuppa?"

They all helped themselves and chatted comfortably. Austen caught David up on University news, and he and Yvette both described the Tolkien's golden wedding anniversary fete at Merton. While he was talking, Austen's eyes rested on his personal copy of *A Grief Observed* lying on the end table next to his chair.

"Oh, I'm glad it made it over to you all right," Austen said, indicating the book. "Did you find it helpful?"

"Yes, I did," David answered. "Thank you for thinking to send it. I hadn't initially planned to use it for my Lewis class, but when things sorted out the way they did, I decided to and it gave me an opportunity to talk about Jack's marriage and Joy's battle with cancer. It segued into a lot of interesting discussion with the students."

"That's good. But personally, was it helpful?"

"I just read it," Kate volunteered quietly. "And it meant a lot to me. I felt as though Lewis were reading my thoughts and writing them down for me—much more eloquently than I could, of course—but I did start keeping a journal like he did. And it's really been a positive way for me to express my feelings."

David regarded her with surprise. "I didn't know that. I'm glad to hear it."

"What I could most relate to was his ranting about how he sometimes didn't feel like God was there," Kate continued. "As though he were banging on the door of an empty house when he prayed. I appreciated his bluntness and honesty. It's scary to admit that. But then as he worked through his grief he realized that maybe God hadn't moved, but he had. That maybe he couldn't hear God because he was banging and yelling too loudly to listen. I felt like that was how I was. When I finally stopped and listened for a minute, I could hear God speaking to me."

"I could relate to that too," Austen said. "I liked the part where he realized that at times we can put our questions to

God and get a special 'no answer.'" Austen picked up the slim volume and turned the well-worn and marked pages. "He writes: 'It is not the locked door. It is more like a silent, certainly not uncompassionate, gaze. As though He shook His head not in refusal but waiving the question. Like, "Peace child; you don't understand."'"

"No answer," Kate repeated. "That's what you shared at the memorial service, David, from *Till We Have Faces*. That we won't always get answers because we may not possibly be able to understand with our finite intellects. I'm finding peace in that. No one is smart enough to figure out all the whys in the universe, and we can either trust God with them or just try to mush on by ourselves."

"You know, I once heard a Dutch woman speak at a church in London," Yvette interjected. "She and her family had been imprisoned by the Nazis for hiding Jews. Her name was Corrie ten Boom. Anyway, her sister and most of her family died in the prison camps, and yet Corrie was one of the most joyful and serene persons I have ever seen. She had some needlework, and she showed us how on the underside it was all knots and tangled thread. She said that's how our lives look to us at times—especially when incomprehensible things happen. But then she turned the cloth over and held up a beautifully stitched design, and she said that's how God sees our lives. He sees the entire tapestry, and He is weaving something of incredible beauty."

"I like that analogy," David said, and the others murmured their agreement. "Now, I'm sure we can talk all night, but you two must be exhausted from your journey. Shall we call it a day?"

"Sounds good to me," Yvette agreed. "Where should I put my things?"

"I'll show you." Natalie hopped up. "You'll be with me."

"Here, let me get your luggage," David said, picking up Yvette's suitcase.

"I hope you don't mind sharing," Yvette said to Natalie as she followed her down the hallway. "I can get a hotel room if you'd like."

"No, no problem at all," Natalie reassured her. "No need to spend the money. I'm quite used to sharing. Ginny was here with me this past week. Actually, I'd feel quite alone if I were by myself."

"Well, it's kind of you all to put me up and to have so many guests coming and going."

"We're glad of it," David said as he put the suitcase down in the guest room. "It's helped us both to have company. I'll leave Natalie to get you settled. Let us know if you need anything. I'm just going to take Austen down the street to the pension. If you're up for it tomorrow, Yvette, we've got a nice day of sightseeing planned for you."

"That sounds great." She smiled broadly. "I can't wait to see Paris. Just the glimpses from the taxi were tantalizing."

"Right. Then I'll just say *bonne nuit*. It's wonderful to have you with us."

"Thanks! *Bonne nuit!*" Yvette turned to the business of unpacking while David accompanied Austen to the guesthouse.

"Kate seems to be doing rather well," Austen said when they had stepped out onto the sidewalk. "I'm glad to see it—especially after the concerns you wrote about to me."

"Right. She is doing much better. Seems to have turned a corner recently."

"And how are you doing, David?"

"I'm all right." After thinking a moment he added, "To be honest, I've felt like I've had to be strong for her sake. Can't have both of us falling apart. I wouldn't say I've had any crisis of faith over this like she has. But I am...well, sad...for lack of a more descriptive word. I'm very disappointed not to have the child. I hope we will have another baby, but if we don't— then perhaps we'll adopt. God has a bigger plan for the tapestry of our lives and I'm fine with that. It's just the sad- ness...the missing her—the baby, I mean. There's an ache there that doesn't ever really go away. And so many things will jolt it back to mind—seeing a mother pushing a pram in the park or nappies hanging from a clothesline or shelves of baby products in the market. Just a walk down the street can be a bit grim. You can't escape the reminders."

"No, you can't." Austen patted David's shoulder. "I am so sorry, old boy."

David smiled. "Thanks. I know you are. I know you under- stand."

"Somewhat. But I've heard it said that the loss of a child is the most difficult loss of all."

"I don't know how it can be worse than losing a spouse," David wondered. "If your spouse—your best friend—dies, then who can share your pain? Who can listen to your grief?"

"No one can fully understand another's pain, even a spouse; you've probably realized that with Kate. But I think what the experts are referring to is that terrible loss of possi- bility when a child dies. The never-ending pain of what you've missed."

"Perhaps that's so," David conceded. "And yet I suppose any loss is difficult for the one going through it." He then changed the subject from his somber reflections. "But what of you, old boy? Have I detected a bit of a gleam in your eye when you're looking at Yvette?"

Austen laughed. "I'm not that obvious, am I?"

"Maybe not to others, but to me you certainly have a different demeanor around her than you've had in the past. Well, what gives? Is there a hint of romance in the air now that you've arrived in the City of Love?"

"I hardly know myself—it's been quite gradual—sneaking up on me, I suppose. So this trip may be the decisive factor. We'll see how things unfold." Austen hesitated as they stood outside the door to the pension. "I talked to her father, though."

"You met her parents?"

"On our way through London. Had dinner with them— lovely people. Her dad was a football player for Chelsea before the war. Did you know that?"

"Yes. Yvette had told me. But I'm an Arsenal man, remember? I can't be too impressed with a Chelsea footballer," David teased. "Anyway, man, what did you say to her father?"

"I asked his permission to court her."

"Really? I'll bet that shocked the old boy."

"No doubt, but I think he appreciated the fact that I asked. Anyway, he gave me a thumbs-up."

"And Yvette? What does she say about it?"

"I haven't had the courage to raise the question yet. We talked the entire trip over here, but not about 'us.' I don't want to queer things by endless discussions on our relationship. I'm worried that once I bring it up, it could skew our friendship. We'll just see how it goes."

"All right, old man." David smiled at his friend. "Go to bed and get some rest. We have a busy week planned for you. And if you've a mind to start courting, I can't think of a better place to do it than in Paris."

37

Fourth Week, Saturday

Yvette was grateful the next morning when she followed David's advice to wear good walking shoes for her first foray into the city. While Natalie and Kate stayed behind to study and rest, the old triumvirate of colleagues set out early to explore. After gazing at the breathtaking view of the Eiffel Tower from the Palais de Chaillot, they boarded a bus that lumbered past the magnificent Arc de Triomphe and down the impressive, wide boulevard of the Champs-Élysées to the Place de la Concorde. When they alighted, David explained that despite the square's name and classical beauty, it had a history of horror, not harmony. Here, near the Egyptian obelisk marking the spot, over a thousand Parisians, including Queen Marie Antoinette and her husband, Louis XVI, met their death by Madame Guillotine's merciless blade during the bloody Revolution.

David, Austen, and Yvette walked through the elegant formal French gardens of the Tuileries to the Louvre. From the petite arch of the Carrousel they paused to look back down the perfectly straight vista they had traveled from the Arc de Triomphe. By the perspective of distance, it now appeared to be equal in size to the miniature replica under which they were standing.

They arrived at the Louvre at opening time, and David signed them up for a guided tour of the museum highlights with an art curator. Yvette had to restrain herself from laughing at the sight of her two tall British friends following behind the diminutive French guide as he scurried about the galleries, officiously ordering people out of the way of the works he wanted to critique. But he gave the dons an excellent, albeit rapid, overview of art history as he led them among superb sculptures such as the *Winged Victory* and Michelangelo's pair of *Slaves*, and renowned paintings like Leonardo da Vinci's *Mona Lisa* and the *Virgin of the Rocks*, Georges de la Tour's *Joseph the Carpenter*, and Theodore Gericault's *The Raft of the Medusa*.

After their tour they crossed over to the Île de la Cité to visit the tiny jewel-like Sainte-Chapelle, built by pious Louis IX, or Saint Louis, to house the reputed Crown of Thorns. Yvette took in her breath sharply when she entered the ground floor servants' gallery.

"This is exquisite," she exclaimed in awe. "And it was for the servants?"

"Wait till you see the nobles' chapel upstairs," David whispered. "This is only the prelude to a great concerto of color."

He was right. She had never before seen any man-made structure of such delicate beauty. Its splendor was only marred by an ill-conceived neighboring building project that blocked the light from streaming through the western wall of glass.

"Every time I come here, I find it hard to forgive the idiot who built next door," David muttered. "But isn't this divine? I believe it's my favorite room in the whole world."

Austen smiled at his friend's enthusiasm. "I thought the fan-vaulted Divinity School Library in Oxford was your favorite."

"All right," David allowed with a grin. "That's my favorite in England and this, in France. Anyway, let's go have a look at Our Lady, the mother of all cathedrals."

They strolled across Place du Parvis, a plaza crowded with parked cars and bicycles, to the great brooding edifice of Notre Dame. Its massive bell towers and ornately sculpted facade stood blackened by centuries of coal fires and soot.

"Someone should give the old girl a good scrubbing," Austen commented wryly as they slipped into an open portal. The interior of the great cathedral left a far different impression.

Despite the crowds of tourists, the three friends were immediately swept up into the awe-inspiring majesty of the soaring pillars and splendid stained-glass windows. They had arrived in time for a noonday mass in one of the many side aisle chapels, and David prayerfully joined his friends as they knelt down. Since the mass was conducted in Latin, they had little difficulty following the service, and the beauty of the setting lifted their hearts heavenward in reverent worship.

Afterward they walked through the bustling markets of Les Halles, where they bought crêpes for lunch from a street vendor, and then they wandered through the picturesque Marais District with its colorful Jewish neighborhood and its stately Renaissance mansions. David led them to the oldest square in Paris, la Place des Vosges, a charming sixteenth-century square almost completely enclosed on all four sides by elegant pink stone townhouses, tied together by an arcade of shops that ran around the ground floor perimeter like gold thread. Yvette was eager to visit Victor Hugo's house in the corner of the square at Numéro 6. As much a devotee of *Les Misérables* as David, she also expressed a desire to visit the Luxembourg Gardens, declaring, "I must see where Marius first laid eyes on Cosette!"

"Well, I'm not sure we can find the exact bench where Cosette was sitting," David joked as they meandered down the gravel pathways of the park.

"At this point any bench will do—we'll just pretend it's this one." Yvette said amiably. "My feet need a rest. I don't want blisters." She sank onto a green metal bench within view of the broad basin where scores of children sailed their paper boats. "Oh, look! That's the pond where Gavroche's abandoned little brothers fought with the swans over a crust of bread while he lay dying in the barricades. So," she declared, "this must be Cosette's bench."

"Must be," Austen agreed, stretching out his legs. "We won't mention that she and Jean Valjean sat along a deserted path near the Rue de l'Ouest."

"Stop it," she said, laughing. "You just did." They relaxed under broad leafy trees and watched as old men hunched over chessboards, young mothers chatted next to their prams, and couples sauntered along arm in arm, stopping occasionally to indulge in a kiss. In a nearby gazebo, a band struck up some cheerful tunes that filtered among the shouts of children frolicking. David bought lemonade from a vendor's cart, and the three colleagues sat contently sipping from their glass bottles as they drank in the charming atmosphere.

"I love Paris!" Yvette declared happily.

"I'm glad. I love it too," David said. "But there's still much more to see."

"A week seems hardly enough," Yvette sighed. "Okay, I'm rested now. Let's get going!"

They spent the remainder of the afternoon wandering about the Latin Quarter and browsing in the bookshops. Yvette was particularly interested in the burgeoning colony of black writers who had migrated to Paris and mingled at Shakespeare and Company Bookstore. The friends had much to discuss as they met Kate and Natalie for dinner at the oldest café and the first literary coffeehouse in Paris, Le Procope. They sat in the narrow red-and-gold ground floor dining room under elegant crystal chandeliers. Yvette was thrilled with the thought that she was dining in the same room as literary greats Voltaire, Balzac, Rousseau, Verlaine, Hugo, and Wilde. She may not have been as enthusiastic to know that revolutionaries Danton, Marat, and Robespierre met there as well.

The friends ate a relaxed and satisfying dinner before walking leisurely to the bustling Place St. Michel to cross back to Île de la Cité and down to the quay by the Pont Neuf to catch the evening *Bâteau-Mouche* ride. David and Natalie knew that, just as in London, one of the best ways to see the city was from the boats that plied the river, and one of the best times to take the tour was at night when all the monuments were spectacularly lit and Paris truly donned her mantle as the City of Light.

No one was disappointed by the impressive display. As the boat headed toward the quay near the Pont d'Iéna across from the brilliantly lit Eiffel Tower, Natalie stood on the deck alone. But she did not feel at all lonely. She perused the cityscape with a heart full of delighted contentment. Nearby, Kate nestled in David's arms while they both basked in a renewed sense of romance and intimacy. Austen stood next to Yvette, who exclaimed with excitement over the passing sights.

After several fits and starts, he finally summoned up the courage to ask her the question that had been plaguing him since the beginning of their trip.

He plunged in. "You know, Yvette, I have something I've been meaning to ask you."

"Sure, fire away," she answered unsuspectingly.

"You know, this is incredibly awkward...and I'm at a complete loss how not to make a blithering idiot of myself, so I'll just mush on." He hesitated again.

"Yes? What is it, Austen?"

"Well...you see...the thing is...the thing is that we've been great friends for over a year now. And what I've been wondering is...I mean, what I'd like to ask you to consider...well, would you consider being more than friends?"

"More than friends?" Yvette repeated.

"Right."

Yvette's forehead furrowed. "Austen, what exactly do you mean?"

"What I mean is..." he sighed. "What I mean is...uh, would you consider a scenario in which we explored being a more special kind of friend? Like a...a girlfriend-boyfriend scenario?"

Yvette's jaw dropped. "Are you serious?"

"Yes. Absolutely. But if you think it's a dreadful idea, that's all right. I'll understand."

"No, not at all, but this—girlfriend—scenario, do you envision it lasting indefinitely? I mean, with no further commitment in mind?"

"There's not much point in that, is there? If a special friendship or courtship, if you will, doesn't have marriage as the end goal, then why not just remain as friends? Right?"

"Right. So this scenario would have the object of exploring the possibility of a lasting commitment?"

Austen swallowed. "Yes. That's right."

"My word," Yvette breathed and then she leaned over the boat railing to think. Several minutes passed during which Austen felt an increasing dread of humiliation. Finally, she turned back to him. "I must admit I'm absolutely stunned. I thought—indeed, I had even heard you say—that you could never replace Marianne."

"Well, I can't," Austen agreed simply. "But I've come to realize that doesn't mean that I cannot or should not ever love anyone else. I know my frame and I am not meant to dwell alone for the rest of my life. I really do want to have a family and children of my own. I've been praying about marrying again and finding a wife—God's choice for me. And you have been such a good friend, and we get on quite well, and have so many shared interests..." Austen floundered. "But really, there's much more to it than that...You know, when I'm not with you, I can't stop thinking about you..." His voice trailed off.

"Oh, Austen," she murmured.

"And I thought perhaps..." He took a deep breath and pressed on. "Look, Yvette, I know there are some inherent difficulties in a mixed-race relationship. I'm color-blind in my heart but not in my head, and I am aware that this could be problematic if we let it. I did, therefore, take the liberty of speaking to your father."

"You talked to my father?" she asked weakly.

"Yes. I hope you don't mind. I thought that if he had any objections, I would not pursue this further. I didn't feel you could be happy with a relationship not blessed by your parents."

"You're right, but I'm sure he was surprised by your asking. What did he say?"

"He said that he doesn't want you to be hurt and also that he doesn't want me taking any physical liberties with you. I assured him that I don't want you to be hurt, either, and that I intend to conduct myself in purity." Austen fidgeted with his watch. "Yvette, I think you already know my convictions about this—that I believe, aside from the biblical injunction, purity enables one to discern God's will more clearly. And if things don't work out, there's a better likelihood a couple will remain friends."

"Right. I agree with that."

"Good." He glanced up hopefully. "Well then, what do you think of this—girlfriend scenario?"

"To be honest, I don't know what to think, Austen," she replied gently. "I'm frankly still stunned. I simply can't give you an answer right away. I know this isn't a proposal or anything, and that you just want to explore the possibility, but you are a very dear friend and I'd hate to lose that." She looked at him with compassion when she saw his crestfallen face. "I know this hasn't been easy for you to broach and I am deeply honored by your asking. I want you to know that I have great affection and admiration for you. When I think of the qualities I would want in a husband, you are definitely the type of man I could see myself married to. But—and this is difficult for me to explain—I'm not quite certain anymore that marriage is God's will for me. I admit I used to be almost desperate for it. But I've come to a place of contentment and peace in who I am as a single woman, and I have accepted that it may be the long-term state God has called me to. In the last few months, I have felt closer to Him than ever."

Now it was Austen's turn to be stunned. Although he had felt awkward in broaching the subject of courtship with Yvette, he had been under the obviously erroneous impression that all single women were anxiously waiting for such a proposal.

"Oh." He could not think of a response.

"Would it be all right if I took a bit of time to think and pray about this?" Yvette asked.

"Of course. Of course." He stared down at the dark river and then back at her. "You will let me know though, won't you? When you have an answer?"

"Yes." She placed her hand lightly on his arm. "And in the meantime, we can still enjoy each other's company, right?"

"Right. I'm sorry, Yvette. I don't want to make this trip awkward for you."

"Not at all. As I said, I am quite honored. But this would be a big step for us both. Remember Friar Lawrence's counsel that you quoted to David?"

"'*Wisely and slow. They stumble that run fast*,'" Austen repeated.

"Right. I wouldn't want either of us to stumble, so let's both take our time."

38

Fifth Week

*E*aster Sunday morning, the little group of expatriates attended the nearby American Cathedral Church of the Holy Trinity. David knew the High Anglican worship service would appeal to Austen in that it closely resembled a Catholic mass, and to Kate and Yvette because it was conducted in English rather than in French. The ceremony and pageantry were as beautiful and awe-inspiring as the soaring nineteenth-century neo-Gothic church.

Kate reflected on Christians celebrating the resurrection in their own unique styles of worship throughout the entire world that morning, and the idea that she was connected with them all in this "communion of the saints" thrilled her. Then she thought of her little Marianne and envisioned her as a lovely, dark-haired child singing along with them in a vast heavenly chorus. She choked back her tears as the congregation sang "Christ the Lord Is Risen Today," and in a moment of "sweet sorrow" was so overcome with emotion that she had to cease singing the verse penned by Charles Wesley:

> *Lives again our glorious King, Alleluia!*
> *Where, O death, is now thy sting? Alleluia!*

Once He died our souls to save, Alleluia!
Where thy victory, O grave? Alleluia!

For Kate the fact of the resurrection and the promise of eternal life was now of utmost importance and tremendous consolation. She felt David slip his arm around her and draw her close to him as he sang out "Alleluia!" in his strong baritone. She glanced up and saw that his eyes also glistened with unshed tears, and she knew that they were truly one in sorrow and in joy.

Standing farther down the pew, Austen was comforted by a similarly strong awareness of worshiping with the unseen heavenly hosts and his Marianne. Yvette and Natalie also found themselves swept up in the sheer wonder of the Easter celebration, although Yvette took a few moments during the service to kneel on her needlepoint prayer cushion and earnestly pray about her dilemma.

After church the friends returned to Passy to change from their Easter outfits to more comfortable clothes for an excursion to Versailles. Kate, Austen, and Yvette toured the opulent Grand Apartments of State, including the famed Hall of Mirrors. Outside in the formal gardens, David and Natalie talked and waited, holding a small hamper packed with wine, cheese, bread, fruit, and chocolates. After the tour they all reconvened in the gardens, where they found a delightful spot to picnic under the shade of broad leafy trees overlooking the Grand Canal. When they had eaten their fill, they playfully took turns tossing their bread scraps to the ducks and a school of large fish stocked in the canal.

It was a glorious Easter Sunday. The afternoon sun shone brilliantly against the bright cerulean spring sky, and the formal gardens were decked in floral finery embellished by stone statuary and the shooting sprays of the fountains. The friends rented bicycles from a stand along the Grand Canal and peddled around the vast park, stopping to gaze at the Grand and Petite Trianon palaces as well as Marie Antoinette's charmingly pretty but foolishly romantic shepherdess' Hamlet. As the sun began to set, they dined out on the terrace of a café where the Grand Canal intersected the Petite Canal in the form of a giant cross. When they walked back to the train station in the spreading twilight, Natalie chatted with Yvette and Austen, who carried the empty hamper between them. David and Kate strolled slightly behind the trio with their arms linked, occasionally stopping to steal a kiss.

The next day Natalie took Austen and Yvette to Montmartre to ride the funicular to the Basilica of Sacré-Coeur and to wander the picturesque streets, watching the artists and colorful crowds and browsing through the shops. After finishing his classes, David rushed home to find Kate.

"Hi, honey, I'm in here!" she called from the kitchen where she was preparing dinner. Dressed in blue jeans and one of his sweatshirts, she stood over the sink rinsing lettuce. Her long dark hair was pulled back into a ponytail, and David could not resist coming up behind her, lifting her hair, and kissing the nape of her neck.

Kate leaned back into his embrace. "How was your day?"

"Just fine. What's for dinner?" he asked, nuzzling her soft skin.

"Lasagna." Kate shut off the faucet and dried her hands. Then turning in his arms, she tilted up her head. His lips eagerly found hers.

"Mmm..." he murmured. "Is this on the menu? I'm starving."

She sighed. "I'm sorry, but you can only have a taste. The doctor wanted me to wait two full cycles, remember?"

"Right." David reluctantly released her. "Any idea how much longer that will be?"

"I don't know. Maybe a couple more weeks?"

"It's a good thing we've had a lot of company," he said. "A lack of privacy is a good deterrent for me. Otherwise, I'd have to bunk in the guest room to keep away from you."

Kate smiled. "So you still find me desirable?"

"Are you kidding? Irresistible." He sat down at the kitchen table and regarded a stack of letters. "What's new? Any interesting mail today?"

"Yes, lots actually," she answered cheerfully. "The invitation from the embassy finally arrived. The party is this Friday night and everyone is invited."

"Austen and Yvette too?"

"Yep. And Natalie and us. It's formal, though. Do you think Austen remembered his tux?"

"He was forewarned. If not, maybe he can borrow one of Stuart's DJs." David observed her as she blithely bustled about the kitchen. "You're really looking forward to this, aren't you, Kate?"

"Yes! What girl doesn't look forward to dressing up and going to a fancy party? And at the British embassy too!"

David smiled at her enthusiasm, his heart full to see her happy again. "Now what else do we have here?" he asked, sifting through the envelopes.

"We got an Easter card from my mom—only one day late, that's pretty good. And look at this..." She opened the card.

"Timmy colored a picture of some Easter eggs. Isn't that sweet?"

"Yes." He put his hands on her narrow waist and drew her onto his lap. "And so are you. What's that perfume you're wearing? You smell divine."

"Stop, silly." Laughing, she playfully pushed him. "Listen, I also got a letter from Connie today."

"Good. What does your old pal say? Is Nigel visiting her on his spring holiday?"

"Yes. And guess what?"

"What?"

"He proposed! Isn't that great?"

"Really? Yes, that's wonderful. Did she accept?"

"Of course! They're going to be married this summer after she graduates from William and Mary. And then she'll be moving to England. Soon I'll have my best friend in Oxford!"

"I thought you already had your best friend in Oxford."

Kate smiled. "You are my best friend, David. But Connie is my best *girl*friend. You know, she asked me to be her matron of honor."

"Ah! That's spendid. Where's the wedding? Not Oxford, I suppose."

"No. In Maryland. You remember, don't you, that Connie is from Bethesda–Chevy Chase? Her family lives right outside D.C." Kate toyed with David's dark curly hair. "Oh, David, I can tell her yes, can't I?"

"Right. Well, of course you should." He frowned. "But I will hate to be apart from you for even one day, let alone a week or however long you'll be over there."

"Why would we have to be apart? You can come with me."

"Kate, I don't see how we can afford it. Paris hasn't been cheap, you know, even with ACP's bounty."

Kate grinned like the Cheshire cat. "I didn't tell you that I also got a note from my dad in Mom's Easter card. He said Connie had called them about the wedding and he was buying plane tickets so that we can both fly over." She threw her arms around his neck and hugged him tightly. "We can go, can't we? I haven't seen my family since our wedding last summer and I do miss them."

"Of course, darling," he said, savoring her closeness and the herbal scent of her hair across his face. "That's very generous of your father. It'll be wonderful."

⌒〇⌒

For the remainder of the week, Natalie took Austen and Yvette on various excursions around Paris, as well as to some of David's lectures both at the American College and the Sorbonne. Yvette found the city's rich culture, architecture, and fashion vibrant and fascinating. When she had a moment for reflection, she prayerfully considered what her response to Austen's question should be. Although she enjoyed his company immensely and knew she could easily love him deeply, she wrestled with understanding God's will for her. On the morning of the embassy party, she excused herself from her friends and walked through the Chaillot gardens, along the Seine, and around the Champ-de-Mars. She knew Austen hoped for an answer soon, and she needed time alone to think and pray.

After returning to the MacKenzies' apartment in the afternoon, Yvette joined Kate and Natalie in preparations for the embassy party. Since she had grown up without sisters, she especially enjoyed the girlish camaraderie as they giggled and chatted while arranging their hair, applying makeup, and dressing in their gowns.

David and Austen prudently decided to absent themselves from the flurry of feminine activity, spending the afternoon at the Musée de l'Armée. By the time they had returned, bathed, and changed into their tuxedos, the women were at last ready. Kate wore the emerald green satin sheath that had turned heads at the Magdalen Fellows' Eights Dinner the night David had proposed to her. Yvette looked resplendent in a sapphire blue column dress of georgette over taffeta, while Natalie floated out in the pale mint chiffon gown she had donned for her brother's wedding.

Stuart had arranged for a limousine to carry them to the British ambassador's residence on the Rue du Faubourg Saint-Honoré, and he was standing sentry by the door of the eighteenth-century neoclassical mansion to greet them. He kissed Kate and Natalie on both cheeks and warmly shook the hands of the dons. "So glad you all could make it. You ladies look ravishing tonight. Come in, come in, and meet the cousins." He led them to the receiving line to be introduced to Lord and Lady Somerville, the British ambassador and his wife, who graciously welcomed them. After politely conversing for a few moments, they followed the flow of the crowd to a glass gallery extending along the back of the house and connecting the two large wings added by Napoleon's sister Pauline that stretched like arms enclosing the garden on three sides. The wing on the left held the dining room, and the one the right, a long ornate ballroom from which a small orchestra could be heard. A row of French doors along the glass gallery opened to the brightly lit garden, creating the effect of entering an enchanting out-door room. The typically English lawn was perfectly rolled like a grass carpet, beckoning the guests in vain to abandon their shoes and stuffiness to run barefoot across it.

"Can't you just imagine playing croquet out there?" Natalie asked as they stood admiring the prospect.

"Or cricket?" added Yvette.

"Football, anyone? I'd love to kick around a soccer ball myself," David said.

Stuart laughed. "It's been used for all of that. And, in fact, after Paris was liberated, it was even open to convalescing ser-vicemen. Lovely, isn't it? Well then, drinks, anyone? Cham-pagne? Wine?" Then he saw the concern that crossed David's face. "Don't worry, David, this is the British embassy, which means we're also stocked up on ginger beer. That's what I'm drinking. Still on the wagon," he added with a hint of pride.

David clapped him on the shoulder. "Good show, old boy. I'll join you with some ginger beer."

As drinks and hors d'oeuvres were being enjoyed by the Oxford group, Stuart's sister, Clementine, spied them and rushed over. She wore a long, formfitting, original Balmain sleeveless black cocktail dress with a deep scoop neck and back. With her fair hair piled up in a bouffant beehive with a rhinestone clasp, Clemmie resembled a regally blond version of Audrey Hepburn in *Breakfast at Tiffany's*.

"Darlings! I'm delighted to see you both," she cried, bussing Kate and David on both cheeks. "Oh, my poor dears, Stuart told me of your dreadful loss. I am so very sorry."

Kate and David murmured their thanks. Then Clementine lowered her voice. "I am very grateful for all you've done for my baby brother. He's truly a changed man. I can't thank you enough."

"Lady Fitzwilliam," David protested, "we did very little. I believe God Himself intervened with your brother. And certainly your concern made a tremendous difference to Stuart."

"Perhaps. But still, if you hadn't had the courage to confront him, I'm not sure any of us would have. Stuart came up to York to see me for a few days at Easter and didn't touch any liquor. He was an absolute darling to me and my boys—they adore their Uncle Stuart now more than ever. Even my husband, Edward, noticed a marked difference in his behavior. And he asked to attend church with us. It's nothing short of a miracle! Now," she said, glancing over at Natalie, "what do you say about Stuart and that pretty little sister of yours? He seems smitten with her."

David cleared his throat uncomfortably. "I really couldn't say, my lady. My sister is still quite young."

Clementine had a melodic laugh. "I don't think you need fear for her. She seems old enough to hold her own." They glanced again over toward Natalie, who was gaily chatting with several young men, including Stuart. "But perhaps I'd best rescue her from all those admirers. My word, she looks like Scarlett O'Hara surrounded by suitors at the barbecue. Excuse me." A moment later she slipped into the circle around Natalie.

David turned to Kate. "It appears that Lady Fitzwilliam has designated herself Natalie's duenna for the evening, so I can relax. Would you care to dance, Mrs. MacKenzie?"

"My pleasure," Kate answered, taking David's arm as he walked toward the ballroom.

That left Austen and Yvette standing alone. After a slightly awkward pause, Austen drew in his breath and stammered,

"You…you look positively smashing this evening, Yvette. May…may I have this dance?"

"Thank you, Austen." Yvette smiled and placed her hand on his arm. "That would be lovely."

Couples swirled around the parquet floor of the ballroom. With a firm hand against her waist, Austen swept Yvette through the throng. As she relaxed into the sensation of following his lead, she caught the dizzying glitter of ornate gold decorative flourishes and the refracted lights of the massive crystal chandeliers.

Nearby, Stuart danced with Natalie after coaxing her from her coterie of young men.

"Has the queen ever used that throne?" she asked as they whirled past a gilded dais dominating the room's entrance.

"It was built for Queen Victoria for the Exhibition Universelle. I don't know if any other monarchs have sat in it. But I must confess," Stuart bent closer to her and whispered, "Clemmie and I have each secretly taken a turn trying it out."

Natalie laughed. "You are so naughty, Stuart Devereux!"

"Not terribly. Well—perhaps a bit." He grinned wryly. "But I promise not to try anything naughty with you. Since this is your last evening here, what do you say if after supper I get the limo to drive everyone to the Eiffel Tower for their final farewell view of the city?"

Natalie smiled as he spun her about the room. "Sounds like a splendid plan to me."

39

Fifth Week, Saturday Evening

After an evening of dancing, socializing, and a late supper at the British embassy, Stuart hired the limousine to take his Oxford party over to the Eiffel Tower. They were not the only foreigners enjoying the view from the second level of the steel tower. The American High School's senior prom was being held in the glass-enclosed restaurant. Handsome teens in tuxedos and pretty girls in flowing gowns flitted about like fireflies, pausing now and then to join others gazing out over Paris, a bejeweled lady herself, glittering with lights.

"She's incredibly beautiful," Natalie sighed. "I think after I take my degree I shall come back here to live. Perhaps I can get a job at the embassy."

"I thought you had missed Oxford too much when you were in school in London," Stuart said as he leaned on the railing. "How could you leave Oxford for Paris?"

"Oh, you're right about that. But I'm talking about a year from now, and anything could happen in a year."

"Yes, anything could," he agreed. "You know, don't you, that I take my degree this summer? Assuming I pass the examinations, that is. I shall hate to leave Oxford myself. I promised my father I would see to his estate, so I'm off to flat, wet Essex for a while. I'm going to try to make a go of opening Clifton Manor to sightseers—at least during the tourist season."

"I had forgotten you would be graduating," Natalie said slowly.

"Will you miss me, Natalie?"

She laughed lightly. "Yes, Stuart, I believe I will."

He wished at that moment that they had been back at the embassy dancing. Then he would be able to take her in his arms without compunction. "I will miss you, Natalie," he responded warmly. "And all the MacKenzie clan. But I hope to devise some sort of excuses to come back to Oxford now and then so that I may see you."

"You don't need an excuse. You'll always be welcome at our house."

"Thank you," he answered humbly. "I appreciate that. And may I hope for more?"

Natalie smiled sweetly. "There's always hope, Stuart."

A few yards away, David and Kate nestled against each other gazing out over the splendid view of the spraying jets of the Chaillot fountains highlighted against the night sky.

"It will be strange having all our company gone," Kate said.

"You haven't minded?"

"No. Natalie has been really helpful—and such a comfort. So were your mom and Ginny. And it's been fun having Yvette and Austen here." She glanced at them standing nearby. "Yvette looks pretty tonight, don't you think? It's almost like…" she hesitated and smiled slyly, "she's blooming. Like a woman who is loved, perhaps?"

David laughed. "Are you fishing for information? Well, you were right after all. Austen confessed he has taken a fancy to her, but you're not to go spilling the beans to her. He's got to handle it in his own time and in his own way."

"He's a bit shy around women, isn't he? Maybe you should give him a few pointers."

"Me? Just because I won the plum prize?" David drew Kate closer. "Austen will manage just fine, I'm sure."

"David, you've enjoyed being with your friends, haven't you?"

"Yes, of course." He bent and kissed her neck, saying hoarsely, "But it will be nice to have a bit of privacy again."

"But, David…" Kate hesitated. She was grateful he was standing behind her and couldn't see her face. "Even when we can…I…I just don't know if I'm ready to try to have another baby. Not yet. I'm scared. I don't feel I could bear to lose another one. I think God may have been punishing me for not wanting the baby more. And until I'm really ready for one, I'm afraid to take the risk of getting pregnant again only to lose it. You might come to despise me…"

"Kate." David said her name softly, turning her around to face him. His eyes searched her face with compassion. "Is that the burden you've been under? That the baby died because of you?" Her lowered eyes confirmed it. "Kate, darling, you must never blame yourself for what happened. It just happened, and we may never know why this side of eternity. Remember Orual's 'no answer'? God is not a cruel, vindictive tyrant punishing you or a mean butcher. He's more like a kind surgeon who has to allow pain sometimes to bring healing. Can't you trust Him to be at work in all things for good?"

"I want to," she whispered. "But I'm still scared. I still don't know if I can face getting pregnant again yet."

"That's all right," he soothed. "We'll wait until you are ready. I want you to be happy."

"But," she protested, "I know you really want to have children and I want you to be happy too."

David smiled wistfully. "I do want children. But I can wait. I waited for you before, remember? I'm good at waiting." Then he kissed her slowly, gently. "And Kate," he whispered, "I love you. If we don't ever have another child, I will always love you." Kate came into his embrace and he held her tightly against his chest as they looked out over the city.

Austen glanced at them and then back at the cityscape. He yearned for that intimacy again, but with Yvette standing by his side and yet apart, he felt very much alone.

"This is such an amazing view," she said in admiration. "No wonder David loves it so much."

"Yes, it is," Austen agreed. "Have you enjoyed your stay in Paris?"

"Very much!" she enthused. "It's a fascinating city. I really have the travel bug now."

"Yvette, if you could go anywhere in the whole wide world, where would it be?"

"Switzerland," she responded without hesitation. "I've always wanted to see Switzerland. I love mountains, and the scenery in the photos is breathtaking. I've heard the entire country looks as perfect as a picture postcard. But what about you? Where would you go?"

"If I could go anywhere? Well, I've seen most of Europe, so I think I'd go someplace new. I think I would go to…" Austen thought a moment. "I know—I should like to go to New Zealand."

"New Zealand? But it's incredibly far away! Why would you want to go there?"

"Because I've heard it's quite beautiful. It's considered the 'Switzerland of the South.'"

She laughed. "Then why not save the time and money and just go to Switzerland?"

"Touché." He smiled. They turned back silently to the view.

After a few moments, Yvette took courage and a deep breath. "Austen?"

"Yes?"

"Why don't you ask me that question again?"

His brow furrowed. "All right. If you could go anywhere in the world, where would it be?"

"No, not that question. The one you asked me on the *Bâteau-Mouche* ride."

Austen squinted at her quizzically, and then his bewilderment turned to pleased recognition. "Oh! You mean the—girlfriend—scenario?"

Yvette nodded.

"Right. Um…" he cleared his throat. "Yvette, would you—would you consider—being more than friends with me? Would you consider exploring the possibility of a more committed relationship?"

She smiled at him. "I would, Austen."

"You would?"

She nodded again. "Yes, I would.

"Right!" He gripped the railing, beaming happily and resisting the temptation to whoop with joy. When he composed himself, he asked. "What led you to reconsider?"

"Psalm 37."

"Psalm 37?" he echoed.

"Yes. On the wall of David and Kate's guest room is a little plaque inscribed with the Scripture Psalm 37:4. *Trouve auprès du Seigneur ton plasir le plus grand et il donnera ce que tu lui demandes.*"

"Find in the Lord your greatest pleasure and He will give what you ask of Him," Austen slowly translated.

"Or as the Revised Standard Version says: 'Take delight in the LORD, and he will give you the desires of your heart.' I've been staring at that Scripture all week. The other night I told you that over the last few months I've felt closer to God than ever before, and I've been content in being single. I've also immensely enjoyed getting to know you and especially spending this last week with you. And I've had some time to think and pray. My dilemma has been to discern what God's best is for me, because I know that I will only find my true fulfillment in the center of His will. I've asked Him to put *His* desires in my heart. Anyway, tonight when the girls and I were dressing, I looked up and there was that plaque again. It suddenly dawned on me that was the answer."

Austen studied her in puzzlement.

Yvette laughed softly. "I've long had a desire to have a more serious relationship with you, Austen. But it's only as I've made the Lord my first love that He's giving me this opportunity to fulfill that desire."

"Ah, right! Excellent!" Austen smiled with pleased understanding. He paused and then said, "Now then, I have another question for you."

"Fire away."

"Well—you'll have to excuse my bumbling. I knew Marianne from grade school, you know, and we sort of grew up together. Consequently, I managed to avoid the whole courtship-dating scene. I'll frankly make a complete dolt of myself—please forgive me in advance for my awkwardness. It's just that this city and this view are really romantic..."

"Yes, they are. But you said you have another question?"

"Right. Would you mind if...if we...may I...hold you for a moment?"

Yvette smiled. "I'd like that very much." She slipped easily into his embrace, and they stood together gazing out over the City of Love.

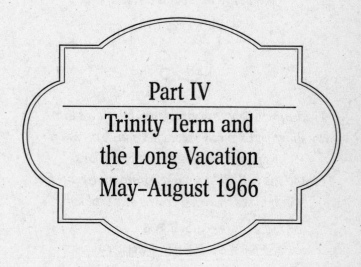

Part IV

Trinity Term and
the Long Vacation
May–August 1966

Hope deferred makes the heart sick;
but a desire fulfilled is a tree of life.

—Proverbs 13:12

Heaven will solve our problems, but not, I think,
by showing us subtle reconciliations between all
our apparently contradictory notions.
The notions will all be knocked from under our feet.
We shall see there never was any problem.

—C.S. Lewis

from *A Grief Observed*, chapter 4

40

May–June

The morning after the embassy party, Natalie, Yvette, and Austen returned together to England via taxi, train, and ferry. Having just arrived in Paris for the weekend, Stuart stayed on and, with Clementine, treated David and Kate to a dinner out at the famed Tour d'Argent restaurant. The waiter raised a conspicuous eyebrow when Lord Devereux declined to look at the wine list, but the little party of expatriates bolstered Stuart's decision to maintain his sobriety by abstaining with him. With his hardened edge noticeably absent, Stuart was as affable and charming as ever, and the foursome passed a pleasant evening of delicious cuisine and delightful conversation.

Stuart then left for his last term at Oxford with the prospect of intense cramming to pass his examinations. Kate and David settled back into the routine they had barely established prior to the crisis and subsequent guests that had disrupted their lives.

The weather turned fine and spring decked the city of Paris in its loveliest garb. As often as possible, the MacKenzies walked or sat outdoors savoring the bright sunshine and the bustling sights. One particularly pleasant May afternoon as David waited for Kate, he sat on a bench under the shadow of the Eiffel Tower's great steel legs straddling the Champ-de-Mars. On a whim, he had ridden over to the Right Bank on the Metro from Passy to the Bir-Hakeim station just so that he could enjoy the prospect of the Seine and the Tower flashing into view as the train emerged from its dark tunnel and crossed the river by the bridge. As he walked briskly to the Champ-de-Mars, a few lines of poetry formed in his head and when he reached the bench he took a notepad out of his book satchel and scribbled them down. He sat engrossed in thought when someone blew softly in his ear.

"Hello, handsome. What's that you're writing?"

Although his heart quickened at the gentle voice and touch, David managed not to turn around but reached for the hand on his shoulder. "You had better be my wife, young lady, or she'll have words with you."

Kate's laughter rippled like music as she slipped onto the bench next to him. "Are you writing poetry again? Is it a love poem?"

He grinned. "Of sorts. It's a poem to a grand lady."

She playfully pouted. "Not me, then?"

"An iron lady." He nodded his head toward the massive steel tower.

"Is it in English or French?"

"English."

"May I read it?"

He shrugged. "I suppose, but I just jotted it down, so it may still be a little rough. It's in free verse."

"I like free verse, as long as it's not too obscure." Kate took the pad from his hands and nestling against him read it aloud quietly.

La Tour Eiffel

Rumble, rumble
The Metro jolts and groans in its
mole-like tunnel and then
is smacked with a burst of sunlight—
And you are there.
I gaze awestruck.

Your silky threads curve upward
swaying slightly in the breeze
yet solid—
threads of steel.
Wisps of clouds caress your metal frame,
never caught in its intricacy.

Surging with hidden strength,
you rule your city.
Yet as a gracious lady—
charming, delicate—
with the Seine's black velvet ribbon
clasped at your throat.

"I like it!" Kate pronounced. "Do you think you'll publish a book of your Parisian poems?"

"I don't know. Half of them are in French. The Oxford Press may not appreciate them." Smiling, he closed the notebook. "Well now, how has your day been?"

"Great! My American lit professor gave me an 'A' on my paper and the girls in my classes have been much friendlier to me—and I have some good news for you."

He put his arm around her. "What's that?"

She took a deep breath. "I've finished my second cycle."

David had not been unaware of the signs, but he had kept his own counsel, waiting for his wife to come to him. "That's good. Now are you feeling more like yourself again?"

"Yes. And I think we should…celebrate. Maybe we could go out to dinner—or something."

David smiled as he drew her closer. "I know just the place."

He had been saving La Colombe or The Dove for just such an occasion. The charming restaurant boasted cooing white doves in the rafters as well as a delicious classic cuisine, and it was quaintly housed in one of the few remaining medieval structures in Paris, a fourteenth-century mansion tucked close to Notre Dame on the Île de la Cité. Since the evening was warm, they sat out on the terrace, soaking up the romantic ambience as a smiling violinist serenaded them with "Lara's Theme" from the film *Dr. Zhivago*.

After dinner they strolled arm in arm along the Seine, stopping to admire the splendor of Notre Dame awash in floodlights and finding the petite Statue of Liberty in the garden behind the cathedral. Back along the quay by the Pont Neuf, they caught the boat to the Quai d'Orsay, watching the lighted palaces and monuments slip past. Then they climbed the broad steps of Chaillot past the fountains—David pausing now and then to kiss Kate among the dancing sprays—and up to the expansive terrace and the glorious view of fountains, lights, river, and tower of which they would never tire. They leaned against the stone balustrade, embracing. Then David took her in his arms and kissed her hungrily and as longing welled up, they turned toward home.

They made love long into that night, gently and tenderly at first, and then in passionate abandon. Joy met Kate as she yielded to her husband's desire and to God's will.

∽

While Natalie took the coach straight back to Oxford on their return trip from Paris, Austen and Yvette detoured to Bayswater to spend an evening with the Goodmans. The entire family, including her older brothers Adam and Ben and their spouses as well as younger brothers Gerrard and Jake, turned out in force to meet their sister's special friend. It pleased Yvette to see that Austen was not only undaunted by the riot of noise and laughter, but that he was also well received by her protective brothers. Adam and Ben gave her a thumbs-up as they kissed her goodnight. Austen and her father remained ensconced in his den for a long discussion to which she was not privy, but afterward, when they emerged smiling and puffing placidly on their pipes, Yvette knew the visit had been a success.

Over the next few weeks of the Trinity term, Austen spent as much time as possible with her. They attended to their ongoing Inklings Society meetings along with their usual duties of lectures, tutorials, marking papers, and keeping abreast of their own studies and research. But whenever their schedules permitted, they would meet for long walks and talks in the Botanic Garden or along Christ Church Meadow; and when they did not, he would ring her for lengthy conversations on the telephone. In the beginning Austen tended to keep their relationship discreet, but as the term unfolded, he began to invite her more frequently to accompany him to public events—concerts, parties, the Eights races and dinner dance—as well as to church or visits to the Tolkiens. It was a heady and happy season for Yvette as she was courted by a man she admired, liked, and—if she would admit it—loved.

One evening in early June, Austen invited her out to dinner at the Cherwell Boathouse. Yvette knew its reputation for fine food and charming ambience, and she was not disappointed. After dinner a waiter brought a wicker hamper to their table.

"Here you go, sir," he said cheerfully. "Fresh strawberries—just as you ordered. And your punt is ready now, sir."

Austen answered Yvette's questioning look with a question of his own. "Would you fancy a punt ride on this fine evening?"

She smiled. "As long as you bring along the strawberries."

Austen carried the hamper easily with one hand and offered his other to Yvette as they walked to the river, where he helped her into the long flat-bottomed boat. When the hamper was safely stowed and Yvette was seated comfortably on a cushion in the bow, Austen slid the long pole into the river and shoved off. Like David, he had earned his pocket money through his undergraduate days by punting tourists along the narrow tributaries and canals of Oxford's Cherwell and Isis Rivers, and he now guided the punt as skillfully as any boatman. To Yvette, gazing up at him standing in the stern with the setting sun shooting its rays around him halo-like, he resembled a Norse god—tall, handsome, golden-haired. She enjoyed the bucolic setting as they serenely slipped past trees and fields. They came to a little inlet where Austen moored the punt and opened the hamper, serving Yvette a bowl of strawberries. Then to her surprise, he lifted out a bottle of champagne and two glasses.

She laughed with delight. "What's the occasion?"

"Can't have strawberries without champagne, can we now?" He poured the bubbly foam into a glass and handed it to her. Then filling his own, he raised it in a toast. "To us!"

"To us!" she echoed, clinking her glass against his.

They sat silently sipping the champagne when Austen asked, "Well, Yvette, what are your plans for the Long Vacation?"

"I don't know really," she answered, contentedly trailing her hand in the river. "To be honest, I've been enjoying this term so much, I haven't given it a great deal of thought. I suppose I should sign on for marking examinations to earn a bit more money. And I'll do the usual extra research and prep for the Michaelmas term. I'll probably spend some time in London and I'd like to go to the seashore for a few days. Maybe this year I'll visit Lyme at last. What about you? Do you have plans?"

He grinned mischievously. "I don't know—I've been thinking about taking a trip on the Continent. Our little jaunt to Paris gave me the itch to travel again. I thought perhaps I should like to go to Switzerland this summer."

"Switzerland?" Yvette felt disappointed at his proposed absence and envious of his destination all at once. "That's a cruel choice."

"How so?"

"I told you I wanted to go there."

He shrugged. "Why don't you?"

"I don't have anyone to go with," she said simply without any hint of suggestion.

"Why don't you come with me?"

"Austen Holmes," she warned. "You are insufferable to tease me like that. I know it's not your intention, but you could almost tempt me to become a dishonest woman."

"You don't have to be a dishonest woman to come with me." He smiled. "Yvette, would you please look in the hamper for a serviette?"

She suppressed her irritation at the odd timing of his request and complied by thrusting her hand down into the hamper and searching by feel for a cloth napkin. *Did he just say what I think he just said?* Her heart quickened as her hand closed around a small box. "Hello—what's this?" she asked as she pulled it out.

"Open it and see."

She did. Inside the box lay a smaller jewelry box. Her heart was pounding. She sprung open the box and there sparkled a simple marquise-cut diamond ring set in platinum. "Oh, my!" she cried and gazed at him with a mixture of expectation and joy.

Austen knelt down on the floor of the punt. "Yvette, my love, would you do me the honor of marrying me?"

Tears sprang to her eyes and then ran down her cheeks. "I will," she whispered.

As he moved closer towards her, the boat began to tip back and forth.

"Be careful," she cautioned with a little laugh. "Don't rock the boat."

"We already have," he said. Then he took her in his arms.

41

June
Castle Combe

Austen and Yvette did rock the boat with the announcement of their engagement. Austen first telephoned the news to Dianna, who was genuinely thrilled for her brother. She was even more pleased when Yvette asked her to stand up with her as an honor attendant. Both women had always longed to have a sister, and now in each other their desire would be fulfilled. Austen asked his brother-in-law, Andrew, along with all of Yvette's brothers, to serve as ushers, while the honor of best man would fall to David. But Austen knew he would need to make a visit himself to Castle Combe to break the news to his mother who, Dianna cautioned, would probably be less than enthusiastic.

Austen entered the house with some apprehension on the first Saturday of June. Dianna had arranged for the boys to be out with her, and Austen found his mother sitting alone reading in the front room.

"Austen!" she cried with pleasure as he came in and kissed her on the cheek.

"Hello, Mother. How are you?"

"I'm fine, but what a surprise! I didn't know you were coming."

"Well, I didn't want to tell you I was coming and then not be able to, so here I am," he said, pulling up a chair.

"Would you like some tea? Or something to eat? I'm sorry; you'll have to get it yourself. Dianna has gone out with the boys. Oh, it's too bad—she'll hate to have missed you. How long can you stay?"

He smiled. "I'm fine, Mum. And I came to see you, not Dianna. Although perhaps she'll be back before I have to go. May I get you anything?"

"No, no, I'm fine. I am so glad to see you. Now what's the news? Have David and his wife returned from Paris yet?"

"Not yet, but they should be back in a fortnight."

"You never told me much about your trip. Did you have a good time in Paris?"

"Paris was wonderful, Mum. We had a fabulous time. One of our students, Lord Stuart Devereux, acquired invitations for us to a party at the British embassy."

"Oh, do tell me about it."

Austen complied, but still avoided speaking of Yvette.

"Did you meet any nice young ladies, Austen? Are there any special girls in your life?"

"Actually, Mum, there is a special girl."

Elinor Holmes gave a little gasp. "I thought so. Who? Do I know her? Please tell me all about her."

"You do know her. You've met her several times. She visited you in hospital, as a matter of fact. It's…Yvette Goodman."

Elinor's face fell. "Oh, Austen, you can't mean it."

"I do mean it." He held his hand up in caution. "Please, Mother, don't say anything you may regret. Over the past several months I've come to realize that I care very deeply for Yvette. I love her—and I have asked her to marry me."

"Oh, no!"

"Yes. And she has accepted. I've already spoken to her father. We plan to marry in August."

"Austen, how could you? What do you see in her?"

"Why, everything. She's kind, generous, intelligent, compassionate, diligent, has a servant's heart, is fun, shares my interests and my faith, loves her family, and, most importantly, loves me. Shall I go on?"

Elinor shook her head. "But she's not that pretty. Surely there are plenty of prettier girls who would love to marry you."

"I find her quite attractive. And besides, you taught me not to judge by appearances—that it's inner beauty that matters. Outer beauty fades."

"But she's beneath you, son."

"In what way? We are both Fellows at Oxford University."

"You know very well what I'm talking about."

"The color of her skin? Can you honestly say that darker skin is inferior to white?" Austen leaned forward and spoke very quietly. "Mother, my father gave his life on the fields of France to silence such lies."

Knowing the truth of this statement, Elinor looked discomforted; still, she stubbornly held her line. "Your father was a gentleman. What is her father? A cabbie, you said?"

"Yes, which is an honorable profession. He has provided well for his family. What's more, when he came to this country he played professional football—for Chelsea."

Elinor sniffed. "And what of the mother?"

"She was a cook for a London hotel. She runs a B-and-B from their home now."

"A cook? Then she was in service?"

Austen stared at his mother incredulously. Surely she, who had been a chambermaid in the Manor House, would not look down on a cook. "Yes. And what of it?"

Elinor started to say something then thought better of it. She sighed instead. "Austen, I am glad you are a man of democratic ideals, but you live in a country that still values class and wealth very highly. It couldn't have been easy for Yvette's parents, football or no, and it won't be easy for you either if you continue down this path. I just don't want to see you hurt or disappointed. Think of your children. Think of us. Think of yourself. You could have the cream of the crop."

"I believe I do," Austen answered softly. "Mother, I have given careful consideration to the things you have mentioned. I'm very well aware that there are prejudices out there." He almost added "*and right here,*" but he restrained himself. "I have talked at length to Yvette's parents and to Yvette herself. I don't expect it to be easy, but frankly, neither is being a widower. I decided you were right. I am not meant to live alone for the rest of my life. I should marry again. And I can think of no other woman I would rather spend the rest of my life with than Yvette. We are going to be married in August, and I would like to ask you for your blessing."

Elinor glowered at him. "Well, son, I don't think I can give it."

Austen bowed his head. "I am very sorry to hear it. I hope you will change your mind."

"And I hope you will change yours."

"That's hardly likely." Austen rose. "Then I hope you will at least come to the wedding. Dianna has been asked to stand up with Yvette as her honor attendant. And I've asked Andrew to be an usher."

Elinor clutched at her heart. "You've told them of this? And they agree with it?"

"Yes. They are quite happy for me."

Her mouth gaped in disbelief. "Well, I am not. I cannot support you in this, Austen. I will think about whether or not to attend the wedding, but it's highly unlikely that I will. I'm sorry. The day you married Marianne was one of the happiest days of my life."

"It was one of the happiest of mine as well," Austen said quietly. "But I know that she wanted me to marry again. I believe she would have liked Yvette very much. I expect that my wedding day to Yvette will be another of the happiest days of my life. But it would be even happier if you would be there, Mum, and would support this marriage. I am not asking you for your permission. I am a man who has supported himself for several years and who has been married before. But I am your son, and as your son, I would like very much for you to bless us." Austen leaned over to kiss her. "Goodbye, Mother. Please pray about this and reconsider. It would mean the world to me to have all of my family represented. Please tell me you'll at least think about it."

But Elinor Holmes just stared into the fireplace and refused to answer.

42

The Long Vacation
June Through August

The first sign Kate noticed that indicated she might be expecting again was her sensitivity to smells. She had always rather liked the acrid smell of hot rubber carried on the warm air of the Metro. It was a familiar and distinctly Parisian odor. But now it smacked her face like a foul wind. The stench from the city trash bins seemed overpowering, and the ubiquitous dog excrement on the sidewalks became more imperative than ever to avoid.

The second sign was the fatigue. Each day it hit her like a brick wall just at teatime, and she struggled to stay awake in class. The third was the queasiness she experienced whenever her stomach was empty. Then, finally, she missed her period and was overwhelmed with a confusing swirl of excitement, anticipation, dread, and terror. Kate decided not to tell David, however, until she had seen a doctor for confirmation.

The suspicion that she was again expecting had helped somewhat in easing her pain in observing baby Marianne's due date in May. With David, she had tearfully looked through the memory book that Annie had made for them with Marianne's little hand and footprints, a lock of her hair, her hospital bracelet, and David's poem. Then they had commemorated the occasion by lighting a candle in their daughter's memory and attending an organ recital at Notre Dame. The glorious music soared to the upper vaults of the vast cathedral, carrying their thoughts heavenward and soothing their broken hearts.

David little suspected that Kate could be expecting even on the ferry ride back to England, when the only way she could control her seasickness was to lie prostrate on the deck. After all, she had never been a good sailor, and he was too preoccupied to pay attention to the signs, what with ending the semester at the American College, packing up their belongings, and saying goodbye to the city he loved.

They both said farewell with a range of mixed emotions. On the one hand, Paris had been magical—a romantic and exhilarating experience. On the other hand, Paris had been the site of their most profound tragedy. And yet Kate thought that if she were indeed pregnant and could carry this child to term, Paris would be the site where their new baby had been conceived.

They arrived back in Oxford in time to see the conferment of degrees on many of David's students and members of the Inklings Society, such as Nigel Elliot and Colin Russell, who earned first-class honours in their respective fields of study. Lord Stuart Devereux had also managed to pass his examinations—even without the ale traditionally allotted on request to all students carrying their swords. Stuart earned a respectable if not stellar second class. The ceremonies were held in the Sheldonian Theatre, which many students entered only on the day of their matriculation and then again on their graduation. As Kate sat in the balcony listening to the Latin orations and watching all the colorfully plumed hats and robes, she vividly recalled attending the Jacqueline du Pré concert there with David and Austen less than two years before. Time had once again passed so quickly. Soon she too would receive her diploma from the College of William and Mary, and she and David had discussed her standing for examinations in December to earn her degree from Oxford as well. She had first sat in this Hall as an excited and naive young student, eager for romance. Now she was happily married to an Oxford don and, she hoped, was once again carrying his child.

Kate and David met proud parents and congratulated jubilant students as they attended a whirl of graduation celebrations. They were pleased to make the acquaintance of Nigel's parents, who expressed their expectation to see them again in a fortnight across the pond at Nigel's wedding to Connie. The Lord Devereux, the Earl of Essex, held an ostentatious graduation dinner for his son and heir, Stuart, in the gardens of Blenheim Palace. Stuart blithely took advantage of his father's benevolence by inviting not only his set from the House but also his new friends among the Inklings—including Austen, Yvette, and the entire MacKenzie family. Even the earl was impressed by the well-behaved MacKenzie children and more than charmed by all the attractive women, including little Hannah, who bestowed on him her prettiest curtsey.

Kate and David quickly settled back into the warm embrace of their natural and church families as well as the familiar mystique of Oxford. Yet Kate still hesitated to share her news with David until she had seen her doctor and could find the appropriate time.

Her opportunity arose on the evening of her twenty-second birthday, when David took her to dinner at the Trout

Inn in Wolvercote, North Oxford. They had planned to meet
Austen and Yvette, who had taken advantage of the fine
summer weather to walk along the Thames towpath and
across the Port Meadow to the Godstow Lock. The Trout, originally built in the twelfth-century days of King Henry II, had
been the birthplace of the *Alice in Wonderland* stories and a
favorite destination of the Inklings, as well as many locals and
tourists. It was easy to understand why. The quaint pub of
warm Cotswold stone was nestled along the river where it cas-
caded over a picturesque weir.

When David helped her out of their MG, she mustered up
the courage to say, "You know, honey, you may have to consider selling this car."

"Whatever for?" he retorted. "You know the Midget is my
baby."

"Well…" Kate said, smiling. "Maybe because it is a midget
and not big enough for a real baby."

David paused long enough to absorb her meaning. "A real
baby?" he repeated softly. "You're…pregnant?"

Kate nodded. David let out a whoop that was decidedly
more American than Brit as he lifted Kate high up in his arms.
"Oh, darling, how are you feeling? When are you due? Are you
all right?"

Kate laughed as he returned her to earth. "I'm feeling pregnant, I'm due the beginning of February, and I'm happy but
scared."

David kissed her on both cheeks. "Thank you, thank you,
thank you! Here it's your birthday and you've given me the
greatest of gifts!" He kissed her again, this time on the mouth.
"You darling girl, I love you so much! May I tell Austen and
Yvette tonight? And my parents? What about your parents?

Oh, no—will you still be able to go to the States for Connie's wedding?"

"Yes. That was the first thing I asked the doctor after I learned that everything's okay. I'll tell my family in person. After all, we're leaving this weekend, so they won't have to wait long. And I think it will be reassuring to my mom when she hears the news to see me and know for certain that I'm all right. But sure, we can tell your family and Austen and Yvette now, if you like."

David led her by the hand through the low-beamed pub out to the stone terrace overlooking the river, where they found their friends seated at a small table, happily throwing crusts of bread to the ducks perched on the wall and the handsome peacocks strutting about the garden.

"Hullo!" Austen called out as he stood to greet them. "Happy birthday, Kate! You picked a fine night to celebrate."

"Thanks!" Kate bussed Yvette on both cheeks before taking a seat.

"Would you ladies like us to fetch your dinners for you?" Austen asked.

"Wait!" David interrupted eagerly. "First, Kate must tell you what she just told me in the car park."

Kate smiled. "You can tell them."

Austen and Yvette curiously regarded David, who didn't hesitate.

"Kate is expecting another baby in February," he said with a barely suppressed note of triumph.

Their friends exclaimed together, "That's wonderful! Congratulations!"

"It is wonderful, isn't it? I'm about to burst." David beamed happily. "But please keep it under wraps for a bit until we can tell our parents." He turned to Kate. "All right, now, darling, what can I get you for dinner?"

The men took their orders and set off to procure supper and beverages while the women discussed wedding plans. When Austen and David returned to the table, the conversation stayed focused on the wedding. Austen expressed his concerns about his mother.

"Thus far the only real obstacle we've run up against is my mum," he said sadly. "Yvette's family and my sister and Andrew—who's Marianne's brother, of course—have been very supportive. But, Mum...well...she's threatened to not even come to the wedding."

"Would it help if I speak to her?" David asked. "Or my dad or the Tolkiens? Surely there's someone she respects who could help her see her way straight."

Austen shook his head. "I don't know. She's quite a stubborn woman. Dianna's tried talking to her several times, but she still won't hear of it. I'm afraid the only recourse we have is prayer. Maybe the Almighty can get through to her. I do feel badly for Yvette, though. It's not right that she should feel rejected by my mother."

Yvette placed her hand over Austen's in commiseration. "It'll be all right, Austen. It will work out in the end. My mother's family practically disowned her for marrying my dad, but when they saw what a hard worker he was and how much he loved her, they came around."

"We'll just have to keep praying," Austen said. "That's all I know to do."

"Right. We know what that feels like," David sympathized. "But sometimes that's the best place to be—completely helpless and totally dependent on God. It's the hardest place to be but the best. Then we can just step aside and let Him do it all. Look what I got by being completely helpless." David put his arm around Kate and smiled broadly. "And a baby on the way too!"

David and Kate flew over to the States the first of July to celebrate their first anniversary and the Fourth of July in the nation's capital city, enjoying the concert on the Mall by the National Symphony Orchestra and the superb display of fireworks over the Washington Monument. They extended their stay in Washington, touring various sights and visiting museums until participating in Connie and Nigel's nuptials in Bethesda, Maryland, the following weekend. Afterward they drove down to Virginia for a long visit with Kate's family in Richmond as well as David's mother's clan in Charlottesville. The young couple was warmly welcomed everywhere and the news of the expected baby was received with great joy. Feeling well rested and well loved, they returned to Oxford for Austen and Yvette's wedding on August 6.

That day dawned with gray skies, but the dark clouds were quickly swept away to reveal a scrubbed summer sky of bright blue with scattered clumps of white puffy clouds like fat wooly sheep. They had chosen to be married in the Merton College Chapel with just under one hundred guests in attendance. The Tolkiens' son John, a Roman Catholic priest, was officiating, with David's father, Eric MacKenzie, giving the homily.

David and Austen readied themselves in Austen's rooms in the Fellow's Quad of Merton while Yvette and Dianna dressed in the Queen's rooms with the assistance of Kate and Yvette's mother, Molly. They would follow Queen Henrietta Maria's path through the secret passage to the Hall and on to the Chapel. Dianna wore an Empire gown of lavender chiffon over taffeta; her blond hair was artfully twisted up and fastened with a matching bow and short net veil. She was brimming with excitement.

"I have the best surprise for Austen!" she exclaimed as they hooked the long row of buttons up the back of Yvette's simple but elegant white satin Empire dress. "Guess who decided to come after all and sit with little Rob?"

Yvette turned her questioning eyes on Dianna.

"Yes—Mum! She's down there in the Chapel now! I just saw Andrew, and he told me Mum decided to come with him after all. I had arranged for the wee ones to be cared for by a friend, and I suppose the thought of sitting stubbornly at home alone missing all this while we were here celebrating together was too much for my mother."

"Saints be praised!" breathed Molly as she fastened Yvette's lace fingertip veil securely, allowing a few brown curls to escape in delicate wisps.

"I hope she won't put a damper on things for you," Dianna said, suddenly uncertain.

"No," Yvette reassured her. "This is wonderful news! It will make Austen very happy." She pressed Dianna's arm. "This makes everything perfect."

"Everybody ready?" Kate asked as she handed the women their bouquets. "It's time."

"You look beautiful, love," Molly declared, kissing her daughter on the cheek. "I'll just go and be seated now. Your dad is waiting in the Hall."

Yvette glowed with joy, a truly radiant bride. Her father echoed her mother's compliment as he offered his arm to escort her across to the Chapel. Kate followed behind carrying her train and then slipped quietly into the back of the Chapel as the organ swelled with Beethoven's "Ode to Joy." The gathering arose as Yvette and her father, Dianna in attendance, passed through the magnificent carved choir screen into the small but splendid thirteenth-century Chapel choir. The Chapel was bright with the rainbows of light refracted through the stained-glass windows gracing the three stone walls. With David by his side, Austen stood tall and handsome, shafts of sunshine highlighting his fair hair. Having already acknowledged his mother's presence with a grateful kiss, Austen smiled expectantly as his beloved bride came to meet him.

Since most of the gathering was not Catholic, Austen and Yvette had privately shared together the sacred Eucharist on the previous evening. Their marriage service was therefore considerably shorter than the traditional Roman Catholic wedding mass, but not any less meaningful. The couple's strong commitment to their Lord and each other was evident in the Scriptures and music chosen, and the Reverend Eric MacKenzie's message of God's eternal love touched many hearts.

The final prayer was read, and then Father John Tolkien presented "Mr. and Mrs. Austen Holmes" to the assembly. As the little chapel erupted in spontaneous applause, Austen bent to take Yvette in his arms and kiss her for the first time. Then the happy couple carried a long-stemmed white rose to each of their mothers. Yvette handed one to Austen's mother and murmured sweetly, "Thank you for coming, Mrs. Holmes. It means so much."

Austen embraced his mother again tightly. "Thank you, Mum. You've made me very happy," he said, his voice thick with emotion. "I love you."

Elinor's eyes filled with tears. "I love you too, son," she whispered.

Turning to Yvette with a joyous smile, Austen tucked her arm into his and proudly recessed to their reception in the Fellows' gardens as the jubilant peal of Merton's bells proclaimed their happy union to all of Oxford.

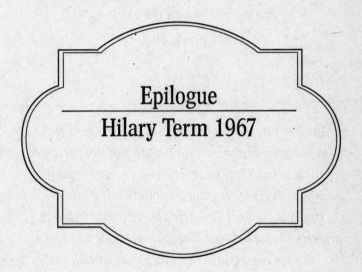

Epilogue

Hilary Term 1967

Weeping may tarry for the night,
but joy comes with the morning.

—PSALM 30:5

You can't develop a false sense of a duty to cling to
sadness if—and when, for nature will not preserve
any psychological state forever—sadness begins to
vanish. There is great good in bearing sorrow
patiently. I don't know that there is any virtue in
sorrow as such. It is a Christian duty, as you know,
for everyone to be as happy as he can.

—C.S. LEWIS
from *A Severe Mercy,* letter to
Sheldon Vanauken, April 6, 1955

43

St. Valentine's Day

Austen and Yvette passed a blissful honeymoon in a Swiss chalet overlooking Mont Blanc along Lac Léman in the picturesque town of Nyon midway between Geneva and Lausanne. They spent leisurely days exploring the surrounding countryside, boating on the lake, and hiking in the Alps. The enormity of the realization of having her heart's desire met by enjoying this beautiful land with the man she loved often brought Yvette to awestruck tears. Austen likewise felt immensely humbled and grateful that he could experience such earthly happiness once again.

They returned to Oxford with a renewed sense of excitement and dedication to serving together in the academic and spiritual circles to which they had been called, and formed an even more formidable team with their friends the MacKenzies as they fostered the Inklings Society. David and Kate, to their landlady Mrs. Bingley's sorrow, moved down the block to the larger quarters of Number 99 Holywell Street, the house formerly occupied by the Tolkiens. Austen and Yvette took up residence in a white three-storied row house directly across the street in Number 4. Newlyweds Nigel and Connie Elliot joined their ranks as sponsors of the Inklings Society as Nigel pursued his graduate degree in English literature under David's tutelage. Kate was thrilled to have her college room-mate living just a few blocks away at Number 10 Ship Street in a quaint narrow medieval row house with a low, bright yellow door.

The emotional and prayer support of her friends and family proved crucial in helping Kate maintain her equilib-rium in the difficult months of awaiting the birth of their baby. Studying for and passing her examinations to earn her degree from Oxford presented a needed distraction and sense of accomplishment. But the most trying time came as she approached the Christmas season and the seven-month mark. Each day she seemed to hold her breath wondering if the unthinkable could happen again. David would console her with gentle reminders not to project into the future, but to live one day at a time as God would always give them grace for the moment, like manna from heaven.

Somehow, day by day, Kate persevered by faith and sud-denly she had not only reached her due date, but passed it. Whereas she had been living for months in constant dread of the onset of premature labor, she then began to wonder if the baby would ever come. A week went by before her labor began in earnest during the Inklings meeting held on the Monday evening before St. Valentine's Day, in consideration of that hol-iday's observance. She sat quietly in the Eagle and Child pub as the students discussed *Till We Have Faces*, glancing every few minutes at her watch to time the contractions.

When the session concluded and they were gathering their things, she drew Connie aside and whispered that she thought the baby would be arriving that night. The word spread quickly and the little band gathered around her to pray for a safe and easy delivery. David drove her back to their house to pick up her overnight case and placed calls to their families to let them know they were on their way to the Radcliffe Infirmary.

Since her previous delivery had evidently prepared her, the labor went more quickly than expected for someone as petite as Kate. Her doctor, well aware of her first traumatic birth, quietly agreed to make an exception and allow David to stay by her side. David thanked him profusely and breathed a prayer of gratitude, as he had strong reservations about Kate's ability to cope if left on her own.

The nurses gave Kate whiffs of nitrous oxide when the contractions grew too frequent and strong for her to tolerate. After a long night of labor, she began to moan at their intensity and then suddenly she was instructed to push.

David held her up in a sitting position, coaching her like an athlete. "Come on, Kate, you can do it, push, push, that's it, push!"

"I can't do it," she gasped after nearly an hour of grunting effort. "I can't. I quit! Oh, no," she groaned. "Here comes another one!"

"Come on, you're almost there, Kate. Keep pushing!"

"We can see the head, Mrs. MacKenzie," the doctor coaxed her. "The baby's crowning. One more time—big push."

With a great cry, Kate bore down. A dreadful moment of silence passed and then the sweetest sound in the universe: the indignant bawling of a vigorous newborn.

"It's a boy!" cried the nurse. "Congratulations!"

Kate's eyes were clenched shut. She daren't open them; she was still too afraid that something could be wrong. "Is he all right? Is everything all right?" she whispered.

David bent over to embrace her. "Yes! He's beautiful. Oh, Kate! Thank you—" Then his voice broke and he sobbed, "Everything is fine. Everything is all right." They clung together, weeping with relief and joy.

"He was born at 7:12 A.M.," the nurse announced as she noted the clock.

David brushed the tears from his eyes. " 'Weeping may tarry for the night, but joy cometh in the morning,' " he murmured, smiling.

"Mrs. MacKenzie, you have a fine, healthy boy: seven pounds, twelve ounces," the nurse said as she weighed the baby and wrapped him in a blanket. "Would you like to hold him?"

"Isn't that something—7.12 at 7:12," David marveled, "and on St. Valentine's Day. What a happy gift of love sent by God! Here, Kate, would you like to hold him? Shall I help you?" The nurse gently laid the baby in Kate's arms as David supported them with his own, nestling his cheek close to his son's downy hair to savor his warmth.

"Is he really all right?" Kate asked timidly, her eyes still squeezed shut.

"Yes. Open your eyes and see," David urged.

"I can't."

"Let's give a prayer of thanks," he said with sudden inspiration, bowing his head as he stood with his arms encircling his wife and child. "Heavenly Father, we are so grateful for this gift. Thank You for blessing us with this son. Thank You for protecting Kate and giving her strength. Help us to be good parents to this precious child. In Jesus' name, amen."

"Amen," Kate repeated and then, from long habit, opened her eyes. "Oh!" she gasped. "He *is* beautiful! He's perfect!" And then the realization of all they had suffered, her grief at losing Marianne, and her joy and consolation at this new healthy little one swept over her once more in its crushing reality, and she began sobbing again. "I can't believe it. He's all right. He's all right!"

"Yes, yes," David soothed as he hugged his family tightly, "He's fine." Simultaneously their son opened his mouth and wailed. Kate and David looked at him in surprise and then broke into delighted laughter.

Later that evening, when Kate had recovered sufficiently to receive visitors, a long parade of family and friends came to offer their congratulations and love. While Annie and Eric MacKenzie spent a few more minutes with the new mother, the others stood before the large plate-glass window of the nursery marveling at all the tiny gifts from heaven.

David nearly burst with pride as he pointed out his healthy son. "There he is. Second bassinet from the right. Look at all that dark hair. And he's a strong little bloke. He can already grip my fingers."

"I wish I were a nurse here," Ginny said wistfully. "Then I could go in there and take care of him myself."

"What's his name again?" Nigel asked as he peered through the window.

"Jeffrey Thomas," David answered. "Jeff for my mum's brother, who died at Normandy, and Thomas for Kate's dad."

"He's so cute!" Connie gushed. "I can't wait to hold him!" She glanced at Nigel, "Oh, honey, wouldn't you like to have a baby like that?"

Nigel laughed good-naturedly. "Ah, sure, Connie. But we've got plenty of time for children."

With his arm around Yvette, Austen cleared his throat for attention. "We have an announcement to make." He paused until the group had quieted down. "Yvette and I are expecting a baby!"

"Well done, old chap!" David clapped his friend on the back. "Congratulations!"

"That's wonderful!" Natalie concurred. "When are you due?"

Yvette smiled contentedly. "In August. Around our first anniversary."

Annie and Eric joined the admiring throng bunched around the nursery window. "Congratulations!" Eric shook Austen's hand. "Children are such a blessing. You won't believe how much joy they bring."

"How are you feeling, Yvette?" Annie asked.

"Rather well, actually," she replied. "I'm more tired than usual, but I haven't had any nausea."

"Good for you." Annie smiled warmly at Yvette and then turned back to admire the baby.

"There he is, Mum, second from the right," David said. "Can you believe you're a grandmother?"

"He's darling," Annie sighed. "I'm so happy for you." She turned to Stuart, who was hanging back a little to allow the others a closer look. "Stuart, the flowers are gorgeous. Thank you very much. That was quite thoughtful of you."

Stuart beamed, evidently pleased at her approval. "Thank you for adopting me into your family, Mrs. MacKenzie. Happy St. Valentine's Day!"

"So, Stu," David said with a wry grin. "You've been busy in the flower department today. The arrangement you sent Kate was lovely too. And I heard rumors that Natalie received a dozen long-stemmed red roses from an admirer today."

Stuart and Natalie both flushed as the group turned their eyes on them. Then Stuart laughed lightly. "It's St. Valentine's Day, and I found a three-for-one special."

"Right!" David laughed. "Well, everyone, I'd better get back to my valentine before she feels neglected. Thanks for coming by and thanks especially for all your prayers." He kissed Annie's cheek. "Happy St. Valentine's Day, Mum."

"You too, honey," she said, hugging him. "And congratulations."

"Thanks." David exuberantly hugged his father too. "Thanks, Dad. Cheers, everyone!"

"Cheers!" they called after him as he headed back down the hall to Kate's room.

"Well, now," Stuart announced. "The MacKenzies and I, and Ginny's friend Kevin Ryan, were planning to dine at the Cherwell Boathouse tonight. Would the Elliots and Holmes care to join us?"

"We'd be pleased to join you," Austen replied. "As a matter of fact, Yvette and I had reservations there ourselves."

"We went there the night Austen proposed to me," Yvette added in explanation.

"Excellent." Stuart looked at Nigel and Connie. "Nigel?"

"Love to," Nigel tucked Connie's hand into the crook of his arm. "We'll see you over there."

"Right. Anyone need a ride? I have my Jag here."

Since everyone was set with their own transportation, they agreed to meet at the restaurant. After making their last admiring observations of the baby, they turned to leave. Stuart lingered to walk with Natalie.

"Well then, Natalie," he said quietly. "It seems our friends' lives are working out quite neatly. Kate and David have a healthy baby boy, Austen and Yvette are married and expecting, Nigel and Connie are happy newlyweds, and Ginny and Kevin are seeing each other. That leaves…just us." He stared down at the floor and then into her face, catching her eyes. "Do you think, perhaps, there may be some hope for us now?"

"Like I've said before, Stuart, there's always hope." Natalie smiled as she slipped her arm through his. "There's always hope."

Author's Note
and Acknowledgments

Although this novel is a work of fiction, as in the first volume of The Oxford Chronicles, *Inklings* (and *Intentions*), I have made every attempt to be as historically accurate as possible, particularly in regard to stories associated with J.R.R. Tolkien, C.S. Lewis, and the Inklings. In this second volume, I write about the Tolkiens as actual characters, but their opinions and stories are based on information gleaned from J.R.R. Tolkien's biographies and letters. I am indebted to Julian Reid and Dr. Julia Walworth of Merton College, Oxford, for finding details regarding the Tolkiens' fiftieth wedding anniversary, and to Kim Cameron for making it possible for me to stay in Merton as well as on Holywell Street. A special thanks to Merton's George Johnston for all of his kind assistance. I am also once again greatly beholden to Dr. Stanley Mattson, the C.S. Lewis Foundation, and the Kilns for their continued encouragement and gracious support.

Having had the privilege of living in Paris as a teenager and even attending a birthday party at the British embassy in the late sixties, I took many of the descriptions of Paris from my girlhood diary and memories. I am grateful to my sister Debbie Holden for sharing her recollections of attending the American College of Paris (now the American University of Paris). Innumerable thanks go to my parents, Earl and Betty Morey, and especially my mother, not only for reminding me of details about Paris, but also for giving me their invaluable corrections and suggestions to the manuscript.

Thank you to Drs. Ellen and Jim Jenkins for their assistance on medical questions, and to Dr. Tessa Hare for explaining childbirth and medical practices in the U.K. of the 1960s, as well as to her daughter Dr. Elizabeth Sheridan and son John Hare for checking the manuscript for errors and correcting my Brit-speak. Thank you also to Karen Walker and Karen Hanna and her father, Ron Borzoni, for their help on British wording and information.

Many thanks to Pastor Derrel Emmerson for permission to use his poem "This Little Flower," written in memory of my precious namesake, Hannah Melanie White, stillborn daughter of Dianna and Andrew White. Thanks also to Andrew for his assistance on the maps. Great appreciation also goes to Diane DeMark, Nancy Freiling, Dianna White, and Julie Woodell White for honestly and openly sharing their stories and lives and for being such powerful witnesses to God's grace in time of need.

So many people have prayed for me and encouraged me as I've embarked on this project. I am grateful to each of you, especially my church family at the King's Chapel in Fairfax, Virginia. Many of you I thanked specifically before in *Inklings*, and I do so again now. Abundant gratitude to Inece Yvette Bryant and Marilyn McAdams White for your ongoing support, suggestions, encouragement, and prayers. Many thanks also to Tom Freiling of Xulon Press for giving me the vision for this series and to Kim Moore, my wonderful editor at Harvest House.

And finally, thank you to the readers who have taken the time to write to me and to all of you who have read this book. I hope that it will be a blessing, comfort, and inspiration to you.

> *Soli Deo Gloria.*
> Melanie Morey Jeschke
> Vienna, Virginia
> December 2004

List of References

Books on or by C.S. Lewis

Carpenter, Humphrey. *The Inklings: C.S. Lewis, J.R.R. Tolkien, Charles Williams, and Their Friends.* London: Allen & Unwin, 1979.

Como, James T., ed. *C.S. Lewis at the Breakfast Table and Other Reminiscences.* New York: MacMillan, 1979. Contains Walter Hooper's exhaustive bibliography.

Dorsett, Lyle. *A Love Observed.* Wheaton, IL: Harold Shaw, 1983.

Duncan, John Ryan. *The Magic Never Ends: The Life and Work of C.S. Lewis.* Nashville, TN: W. Publishing Group, a Division of Thomas Nelson, Inc., 2001.

Duriez, Colin. *The C.S. Lewis Encyclopedia.* Wheaton, IL: Crossway Books, 2000.

Duriez, Colin, and David Porter. *The Inklings Handbook.* St. Louis, MO: Chalice Press, 2001.

Glaspey, Terry. *Not a Tame Lion: The Spiritual Legacy of C.S. Lewis.* Nashville, TN: Cumberland House,1996.

Green, Roger Lancelyn, and Walter Hooper. *C.S. Lewis: A Biography.* London: Collins, 1974; New York: Harcourt Brace Jovanovich, 1974. Revised British Edition: HarperCollins, 2002.

Gresham, Douglas. *Lentenlands.* New York: Macmillan, 1988.

Hooper, Walter. *Through Joy and Beyond: A Pictorial Biography of C.S. Lewis.* New York: Macmillan, 1982.

Lewis, C.S., *A Grief Observed.* London: Faber and Faber Limited, 1961.

———. *The Problem of Pain.* London: Geoffrey Bles, 1940.

———. *Till We Have Faces: A Myth Retold.* London: Geoffrey Bles, 1956.

———. *Surprised by Joy: The Shape of My Early Life.* London: Geoffrey Bles, 1955.

Sayer, George. *Jack: A Life of C.S. Lewis.* Wheaton, IL: Crossway Books, 1994. First edition titled *Jack: C.S. Lewis and His Times,* Harper & Row, 1988.

Sibley, Brian. *C.S. Lewis Through the Shadowlands: The Story of his Life with Joy Davidman.* Grand Rapids, MI: Baker Books, 1994; Spire Books,1999.

Vanauken, Sheldon. *A Severe Mercy.* New York: Harper & Row, 1977. London: Hodder and Stoughton, 1979.

Books on or by J.R.R. Tolkien

Carpenter, Humphrey. *Tolkien: A Biography.* Boston: Houghton Mifflin Company, 1977.

Coren, Michael. J.R.R. Tolkien: *The Man Who Created The Lord of the Rings.* New York: Scholastic, Inc., 2001.

Duriez, Colin. *The J.R.R. Tolkien Handbook.* Grand Rapids, MI: Baker Books, 1992, 2002.

Pearce, Joseph. *Tolkien: Man and Myth.* Harper Collins/Ignatius Press, 1998.

Tolkien, J.R.R. *The Hobbit or There and Back Again.* London: George Allen and Unwin, 1937.

Tolkien, J.R.R. *The Lord of the Rings.* London: George Allen and Unwin, 1954–1956.

Tolkien, J.R.R. *The Silmarillion.* London: George Allen and Unwin, 1977.

Other References

Bott, Alan. *Merton College: A Short History of the Buildings.* Merton College, Oxford, 1993.

Johnson, Vernon E. *I'll Quit Tomorrow: A Practical Guide to Alcoholism Treatment.* San Francisco, CA: Harper & Row Publishers, 1980.

Kaplan, Robbie Miller. *How to Say It When You Don't Know What to Say: The Right Words for Difficult Times.* New York: Prentice Hall Press, 2004.

Yancey, Philip. *Disappointment with God: Three Questions No One Asks Aloud.* Grand Rapids, MI: Zondervan Publishing House, 1988.

The Oxford Chronicles
Inklings
Melanie M. Jeschke

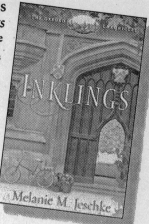

It's 1964 and young American Kate Hughes anticipates finding knowledge—and perhaps love—at Oxford University. She discovers possibilities in David MacKenzie, a young lecturer who carries on the legacy of his friend and mentor, C.S. Lewis. But conflict arises when she also catches the eye of the dashing Lord Stuart Devereux. Sprinkled with allusions to classic English literature, references to C.S. Lewis, and an appearance from Professor J.R.R. Tolkien himself, this wonderful first novel of the Oxford Chronicles unfolds with grace into an endearing story that will delight both devotees of the Inklings and readers of romance. This new Harvest House edition of *Inklings* contains the original novel and an all-new sequel titled *Intentions*.

The English Garden
The Proposal
Lori Wick

Lori Wick's English Garden series opens with *The Proposal*, a captivating tale of one determined man—set in his negative views about God, women, and children—and the woman who has a chance to show him the world in a different light. William Jennings suddenly becomes the guardian of two boys and one girl. Unsure of what to do about this situation, he turns to his sister and her husband for help and becomes acquainted with their neighbor, Marianne. Intelligent in nature and deeply grounded in her faith, Marianne turns Jennings' beliefs about women and God upside down with her gentle reasoning and Christ-honoring lifestyle. Jennings cannot believe he is drawn to this woman—and to the God she so obviously loves.

The Austen Series
Reason and Romance
Debra White Smith

First Impressions revealed the soul of Jane Austen's *Pride and Prejudice*. Now, echoing the themes in Austen's *Sense and Sensibility*, Debra White Smith crafts a delightful, contemporary story about passion and love. When Ted arrives, Elaina assumes he can't be interested in her. But Ted surprises her. Attracted by his charming personality, Elaina dreams about love. But then comes shocking news. Has she made a mistake? The handsome Willis hints at engagement…and Elaina's sister, Anna, is delighted. But when he is called away, he doesn't leave a forwarding address. Brokenhearted, Anna falls into depression. Will she love again? Readers will be enraptured by this story about the joys and follies of infatuation and how faith in God reveals true love.

About the Author

*M*elanie Morey Jeschke is a pastor's wife, homeschooling mother of nine children, and former high school English teacher who writes travel articles and fiction. She graduated with an honors degree in English literature from the University of Virginia, where she also studied European and English history. Melanie has made a number of trips to England and Oxford, where she has attended several conferences on C.S. Lewis. She resides in Northern Virginia with her children and husband, Bill Jeschke, senior pastor of The King's Chapel.